FINDING THE WAY BACK TO LOVE

Lakeside Porches Series Book Three

KATIE O'BOYLE

Katie Boyle

SMP

SOUL MATE PUBLISHING

New York

FINDING THE WAY BACK TO LOVE

Copyright©2015

KATIE O'BOYLE

Cover Design by Niina Cord

Published in the United States of America by
Soul Mate Publishing
P.O. Box 24
Macedon, New York, 14502

ISBN: 978-1-61935-971-0

ebook ISBN: 978-1-61935-700-6

www.SoulMatePublishing.com

The publisher does not have any control over and does not assume any responsibility for author or third-party websites or their content.

To all the Burroughs Girls—

talented, smart, and strong!

Acknowledgements

So many people have contributed to the writing of this book. Kim Gore provided a hard-hitting critique of the opening chapter. Judges of The Sheila Contest (Valley Forge Romance Writers of America) and of the Fool for Love Contest (Virginia Romance Writers of America) gave suggestions that made the book an award winner. Author Elizabeth Kelly provided insightful feedback from a psychological perspective. As always, I am indebted to my Sunday Critters critique group and to the Lilac City Rochester Writers. First, last, and always, warm thanks (and promises of more good books to come!) to my beta readers Anne, Martha, and Kathy.

Chapter 1

Gwen Forrester knew every tricky turn of her private, half-mile road. Just after eleven on a cool August night, she made the drive alone from East Lake Road to her house on Chestnut Lake, with the windows rolled down to the breeze off the lake. As she navigated, turn-by-turn, she rehashed the ridiculous argument with Ned, until an eight-point buck sprang from the trees on her right.

She screamed and slammed on the brake, as the magnificent animal arched across the hood of the car and filled her windshield. Gwen held her breath while he hung there for an endless moment. Then he stomped his rear hoof inches from the windshield and vanished into the woods.

The car skidded on the gravel and a rear wheel dropped toward the ditch. Gwen steered into the skid, pressed the accelerator, and regained control. Shaking, she coaxed the car to a stop and jammed it into 'park.' With both feet on the brake, just to be sure, she folded her arms across her middle and leaned back on the headrest.

"Good job," she said out loud to herself. The scent of evergreens and wildflowers wafted in through the open window. *Thank you, God.* She drew in a deep breath and, with the exhale, told herself, "I am a competent driver." With the next exhale, she asserted, "I am a competent woman." She surprised herself with the next one. "I will stop dating Ned."

Her eyes opened wide. *I need to do that. I feel like a bimbo with him.* Maybe the sex was amazing, but that was the only decent thing she could say about her relationship with Porsche-driving hottie Ned Williams. So what if every woman wanted him? She didn't.

When the shakes subsided, she put the car in gear and rolled forward. "Done," she with a nod of her head as she rounded the final curve to her house. "I'm done with Ned, and with all the others like him. I want a real man, one who appreciates me for who I am and who wants to— Ohmigod!"

The pulsing lights of a Tompkins Falls police car bounced off the front windows of her white frame house and washed the turnaround in red.

Officer Peter Shaughnessy cracked open the door from the office to an enclosed porch in the Forrester home. Moonlight flooded through floor-to-ceiling windows.

Instinct held him in place at the doorway. He probed the porch with his eyes and ears, sure now that the slight movement and soft rustle in the far corner belonged to a person. With his body solidly behind the doorframe, he slid his weapon out of its holster and kicked the door wide. Someone gasped. Whoever hid there sounded more like a frightened child than a hardened criminal.

However, after the bullets he'd taken last summer, he wasn't taking chances. "Walk into the patch of moonlight by the window," he ordered. "Keep your hands where I can see them."

He counted four seconds before the shape detached itself from the shadows. First into the moonlight was a big old T-shirt stretched tight over a rounded belly. The pregnant woman's next step revealed that she was slender, medium height, and very young.

"Stay there."

Tangled brown hair nearly covered her face. She licked her lips and bit the lower one. Her erratic breathing made him worry she might pass out.

"Are you alone?"

"Yes, sir." Her voice quavered.

"What's your name, miss?"

"Haley Ursula Forrester," she squeaked and then cleared her throat.

He thumbed the switch on his walkie-talkie to tell his partner Sam he'd found their trespasser. "And do you live here, Haley?"

"No sir, I'm a student at SUNY Albany. This is my Aunt Gwen's house."

"And does she know you're here?"

"No, sir. I've been calling her since this afternoon when my bus left Albany." Her voice was stronger now. "It's a straight shot west to Tompkins Falls from Albany, on the Thruway, but you probably know that."

"Was your aunt expecting you?"

She looked down at the painted wood floor. "No, sir."

"How did you get here from the city bus terminal?" As he asked the question, he moved through the doorway and scanned the porch. Twenty feet long and ten feet wide. A double door in the middle led out to the yard and the lake. He wondered why Haley hadn't used it as an exit.

"I walked. It's miles, and I had to pee really bad by the time I got here." Her chin came forward. "I know where the key is."

Peter grimaced. *Not the whole truth.* She might have used a key for the door from the garage to the kitchen, but she had demolished the lock on the outside door to the garage, apparently by smashing it with a rock, multiple times. He'd have just broken the window on the door and turned the lock from the inside. *Not a seasoned criminal, just a desperate kid.*

He felt the wall for a light switch. "Haley, do you know you tripped an alarm when you broke into the house?"

"Uh, yeah." The answer dripped with teenage sarcasm. "Everyone on the lake heard it." When he cleared his throat, she squeezed her eyes shut. "I'm sorry, I know it's not funny."

Peter found a dimmer switch on the left. With one press and a turn of the knob, the porch flooded with light.

Haley blinked as she shrugged out of her sweat jacket, gathered her long hair into a ponytail, and held it in place with a rubber band from her wrist. Peter studied a face free of makeup, big dark eyes, a pouty mouth, and cheekbones that belonged on the cover of a fashion magazine.

"How old are you, Haley?"

She gave him a ready smile showing perfect white teeth. "Nineteen."

Housebreaker and heartbreaker.

Gwen huddled in the front seat of her car, phone clutched in her hand, resisting the impulse to spring from the car and fix whatever was wrong. As the 911 operator—Sally, who she knew from Power Yoga—had directed, she sat with the windows up and doors locked, while she waited on the line for some kind of update.

"Gwen?" Sally's voice crackled. "Officer Sam Pinelli is coming out to escort you. They have a suspect who claims to know you."

"A suspect? What's happened in my house, Sally? Is someone hurt?"

"I don't have that information."

Gwen's attention shifted anxiously from the front door to the garage door. Finally, a buff young man emerged through the side door. When he came into the light from her headlights, she saw his face. "Sam is Tony's brother, isn't he?" she asked Sally.

"Sam's the youngest of the three Pinellis. Joined the force a year ago."

"Thanks, Sally, I'm okay now." She closed her phone and slid out of the car. When she tried to stand, though, her knees buckled, still shaky from the adrenaline. She leaned back on the front seat. While Sam made his way to the car, she stretched her legs one at a time and did ankle circles.

"Ms. Forrester? You okay there?"

She laughed at herself. "Still shaking. I nearly hit a big buck on the way in from the highway, and when I turned the last corner, instead of home sweet home, I saw your cruiser."

He reached out a hand to help her stand and stayed close, probably smelling her breath to see if she'd been drinking.

"You're Tony's brother?"

"How do you know Tony?"

"We see each other Friday nights at the Town Hall AA meeting. I celebrated eight years sober a few weeks ago."

Sam just smiled. And sniffed her breath. He pointed to a hoof-shaped dent on the hood. "Your buck left a calling card."

Gwen suppressed a shudder. "What's happening inside, Officer?"

"Housebreaking. My partner found her on the lakeside porch. Says she's your niece Haley. If you'll—"

Shaky legs forgotten, Gwen dashed into the garage, flew up the kitchen steps, raced down the hall and skidded on the turn into her office. She stopped at the porch door with a gasp, her attention arrested by the commanding stance and compelling green gaze of the officer blocking her path. His face and physique could be the work of a Renaissance sculptor, and his black, wavy hair tempted her fingers.

"Gwen Forrester?" Peter asked. At her nod, he stepped aside.

Her startled gaze shifted to Haley and softened with love.

Haley stood like a racehorse straining at the gate, tipping up on her toes, her mouth giving little gasps that suggested a torrent of words, barely held in check.

Gwen's face lit up with delight when she spied the big belly. "Oh!"

The two rushed toward each other, embracing, laughing, crying, talking so low he could make out only a few words— "your mother?" and "boy we met at Christmas" and "when?"

"October, really?" Gwen stepped back. "Just two more months?" She caressed Haley's face. "Have you had anything to eat today?"

"I'm starved." Haley grinned.

"Ma'am?" Peter got no response. He might as well be invisible. "Ms. Forrester?" he said louder.

Gwen turned with a look of pure joy, cheeks flushed, eyes wide. She was a chic, older, ash-blond version of Haley. *Even more beautiful.*

"Yes, Officer?"

Her dreamy gaze made him wonder if she was flirting with him. *Get real, Shaughnessy.* "If you won't be pressing charges, my partner and I will clear out of here, Ms. Forrester."

She held out her hand, tilted her head coquettishly, and told him, "It's Gwen. And you are?"

"Officer Peter Shaughnessy." Her handshake was firm and surprisingly strong for such a slender, feminine woman. He cleared his throat. "You'll need to get those locks fixed right away, ma'am."

"Gwen," she reminded him with a flutter of thick, dark eyelashes.

"Gwen, my partner and I recommend that you put your vehicle in the garage tonight, close and lock the overhead door, deadbolt the kitchen door, and set the alarm. Call a locksmith first thing in the morning."

Her only response was, "Haley and I will be having breakfast around nine. We'd love to have you join us, Officer."

He opened his mouth to repeat the caution but closed it again. His partner had told him Tompkins Falls operated more like a small town than a city. This definitely wasn't going by the Syracuse Police Department procedure book that he still had in his head.

Haley touched his arm and winked. "Come for breakfast, Officer. I need protection from the Inquisition. And Gwen makes a mean omelet."

Are they sucking up, embarrassed at bothering the police with family business?

"Please, Officer Shaughnessy," Gwen added.

He surrendered. Sam was always on him to extend a hand to the community. He'd have time after his shift to shower and stop by the home improvement store. "Okay, I will, and I'll bring a new lock and replace the outside one that Haley damaged."

"Cool, thanks," Haley said. "I'll pay for the lock."

"And, Haley, you heard my instructions about locking up tonight, right? Maybe you can help your aunt with that."

"Absolutely."

"Let me show you out," Gwen offered.

"I'm good." He held up his hands to stop her. "You ladies have a lot to talk about." With a quick salute, he headed back through the house.

Peter navigated the final, treacherous turn of the Forrester Road, signaled a left onto the main road, and headed the cruiser back toward town. He asked his partner, "What's the story with Gwen Forrester? She lives there alone?"

Sam answered with a laugh. "She did until tonight. Nice place, isn't it? She spares no expense. Man, did you see her Range Rover? Latest model. Shame about the hoof print."

"The place is so isolated. I don't get why she lives there by herself." It was pitch black on this stretch of highway. They wouldn't see city lights for a few miles yet.

"The property has been in the Forrester family a few generations. There's a brother somewhere, who I guess would be Haley's father. Good family. Gwen's dad delivered babies in Tompkins Falls for a few decades. His wife did a lot for charity—raised money, ran the thrift shop, started a food pantry, things like that."

Peter loved it when his partner got on a roll like this. It was a quick lesson in local history and a Who's Who in Tompkins Falls rolled into one. As a newcomer he was determined to fit in, and he needed all the information he could get, as fast as he could get it. "The doc and his wife are gone now?"

"They died one after the other, like some couples do. She had a heart condition of some kind, and he died a few weeks after they buried her."

Peter wondered what it was like to have two loving parents.

"I was in high school," Sam continued, "so it was six or seven years ago. Seemed like the whole town was in mourning. Gwen was widowed around the same time."

A widow? "Rough."

"I'm sure it was. Gwen and her husband, Jeb Brewster, had their own place on the lake, down the west side past Cady's Point, but she sold it and moved back to the family home after he died. She moved her practice here, too. You saw the office."

"She's a doctor like her dad?"

"Psychologist. I talked to my brother Tony while I waited for you to finish inside. He knows her well and can't say enough good things about her. She helps a lot of people, especially recovering alcoholics and addicts. Sometimes for free or on a sliding scale. If they want to get well, she's willing to help them."

"That's a recipe for disaster." As they rounded the curve at the north end of the lake, he saw the highway lights on the downtown bypass a couple miles ahead. On the left, a popular lakeside park stretched for two miles. He usually went for a run on the gravel path after his shift.

"What do you mean disaster?" Sam asked.

"Woman alone, miles from town, lives down a long, private road. Sees clients with psychological problems, alone, all day. Sure there's an alarm, which is what brought us out tonight. A lot could happen between the time an alarm is triggered and an emergency vehicle arrives. It took us, what, seven minutes to get out there, from the time the 911 dispatcher called us. You figure there had to be some delay before that while the alarm company phoned the homeowner, got no response and relayed information to the police." He shook his head. "Plus, if one of her patients went off on her during a session, no alarm would summon help."

Peter sensed his partner's gaze on him. He glanced over and saw both Sam's eyebrows raised in amusement.

"Well, I wouldn't want my wife or—or sister or girlfriend in that situation, would you?" Sam's chuckle pushed Peter's buttons. "What?"

Sam shrugged. "Just never thought of it that way. What do you think of her?"

"Gwen Forrester? She's either made of steel or out of her mind."

Sam nudged Peter's arm. He pointed to a sedan that had emerged from the park with no headlights. It weaved ahead of them toward town. "Let's get this guy."

Gwen watched as Haley settled herself on a stool at the kitchen island and gave a loving pat to her big belly.

She loves this baby. Gwen wanted to hear about the boyfriend and their plans, but she knew from experience that Haley would shy away like a high-strung filly if she felt threatened or judged. After putting the teakettle and a pot of water to boil on the stove, she rummaged through the freezer for a pint of her homemade pasta sauce. "Beef or veggie?"

"Beef, please."

Good appetite. "Does your mother know you're here?"

Haley's smile faded to a grim line. Her shoulders slumped and she focused on a broken fingernail.

That went well. "Guess not, huh?"

Haley shook her head and picked at a loose bit of polish.
We need a spa day. Probably some maternity clothes, too. "Tell you what," Gwen said.

Haley looked up at her through thick, dark lashes.

"You open the package of pasta." Gwen handed her the wheat linguini. "I'll call Ursula and leave a message, just in case she's worried about you."

Haley snorted and picked at the end flaps of the box.

"Then my conscience will be clear. And yours, too."

"You're right."

Gwen dialed her ex-sister-in-law's phone number and heard the call switch immediately to voicemail. "It's Gwen. Haley is here with me at the lake. She's safe. I'd appreciate a call back tomorrow." She gave her cell number and broke the connection. "Done."

"I'll call Dad tomorrow, I promise."

"Good thinking." Gwen placed two pasta bowls, two forks, and two big spoons on the island. She smiled when Haley slid off her stool and set their places using two placemats from the linen drawer. *She's already at home here. That helps.* "Thanks, sweetie."

"Welcome."

"There's Italian bread in the box. How about slicing a big hunk for both of us?"

"Sure. Can I make a salad?"

"Great idea."

When the kettle shrilled, Gwen plopped two chamomile teabags in a white teapot, poured in boiling water, and grabbed two white mugs from the cupboard. She started the linguini cooking and went to work microwaving the frozen sauce.

Over their midnight supper, they chatted about Haley's classes at the State University of New York at Albany, her double major in art and botany, and her summer job waitressing in Saratoga Springs.

When she was satisfied Haley had eaten a healthy supper,

Gwen broached a harder topic. "Do you want to talk tonight about the baby and why you're here, or wait until morning?"

Haley licked her lips and studied the veins in the marble counter top. Finally, she met Gwen's gaze and swallowed. "Tomorrow."

Gwen stared.

Haley glared back.

Gwen conceded. "Good enough. The guestroom is all made up. Sleep well, sweetie."

Haley climbed the stairs, but Gwen stayed to perch a while at the island.

She sipped and savored the soothing tea, as her thoughts unfolded. It was no surprise that Ursula opposed Haley's pregnancy, but it troubled Gwen that Haley had sought out the Forrester homestead in the Finger Lakes, now, two weeks before the start of the fall semester and two months before the baby was due. Had Ursula kicked her out? Cut off her funds? *Must be.*

There were so many unanswered questions. Did Haley want to take classes in the fall? Stay here or move back to Albany? From their discussion, Gwen had inferred that Haley still loved school, so she probably wasn't planning to drop out. Did Haley want to have her baby here? And then what? And where was the boyfriend?

Gwen had no answers, so she did what was in front of her—cleaned up from their meal. Once she had the dishwasher chugging, she sponged off the inside of the microwave and the top of the range and cleaned the marble counters. *Good.* She rested her hands on her hips.

Whatever possessed me to invite Peter Shaughnessy to breakfast? A smile spread across her face. *Adonis in uniform, and no wedding ring.* She drew out one more placemat and set the island for three.

When he and Sam arrived back at the station, Peter remarked, "Our shift is off to a wild start." He grabbed an apple for himself and tossed another to Sam.

Sam fielded it with one hand. "You want to handle the report on the Forrester break-in while I book the DWI?"

Since Peter had never lost his disdain for drunks, he gladly went with Sam's plan. "Good deal, and I'll make fresh coffee." He started a new pot, and then hunkered at his desk. Entering data in field after field was part of the job, and it made him glad he'd learned office skills in high school. He'd been ribbed for taking "girly classes," but a few well-placed punches had shut that down. He never let on that meeting girls was half the motivation.

He'd met Cynthia in Keyboarding Lab. They'd married right after high school and had nine good years together before she decided being a cop's wife meant too much stress and too little money. The divorce was official last month, just after his move, and he was waiting for the final bill from his lawyer. He had his eye on a little Cape Cod a few streets from Tompkins College. Soon he'd know if he could swing it or if it was just a nice dream.

Either way, he knew in his heart moving from Syracuse to the Finger Lakes and a smaller city—Tompkins Falls was population twenty thousand plus a thousand or so college students—was right for him. He was only thirty, not too old to find a good woman and start a family.

So Gwen Forrester is a widow? Beautiful, athletic body, just the way he liked a woman be. But is she out of my league?

Her lakefront home must be more than a century old, and in beautiful condition, with wide oak floors that gleamed as though someone had polished them lovingly for decades. The property must be worth a million or more. Situated a good four miles down the east side of the lake, it probably sat south of the cluster of gumdrop islands, giving it a clear view of Chestnut Lake to the west and south.

The lake was one of the lesser-known Finger Lakes, about twenty miles long and a couple miles wide. No one had a name for the tiny islands in the northeast corner of the lake, but everyone knew what he meant when he called them gumdrop islands. They were little mounds covered with evergreens, like spearmint gumdrops coated with dark-green sugar crystals.

With his mind back on the report, he detailed the damage to Gwen Forrester's locks and thought about the young woman who'd done the damage, Haley. He checked his memory for the odd-sounding middle name, Ursula, and shook his head as he entered the full name in the report. Why had her folks picked Ursula? The name didn't fit Haley.

The two Forrester women were so beautiful and charming, most visitors to the lakeside house would probably overlook the not-so-charming details, like the smashed lock. Haley had said her baby was due in October, but he'd say sooner, and her aunt had not known anything about the pregnancy. Why did Haley arrive unannounced and break into her aunt's house, instead of planning a visit?

And walking from the bus terminal, six or seven miles, couldn't have been fun. According to the bus schedule, she'd arrived in town a few minutes after seven, and he'd bet the last few miles of her walk had been in total darkness. Dangerous for anyone, especially a teenage girl, pregnant or not.

Maybe the aunt had her phone turned off while she was out. But, as a psychologist, wouldn't she check messages pretty often? *So, what, Haley just showed up and broke in?*

He was curious if Haley had a record. Even though the homeowner had not pressed charges, he checked the state database. No record. Facebook told him more.

Haley's personal page showed her with her boyfriend Rick, an engineering major at prestigious Rensselaer Polytechnic Institute. The photo gallery told the story of their hiking, cross-country skiing and kayaking.

But Haley's timeline stopped in early May, more than three months ago. Maybe it was the end of the semester. Maybe she broke up with Rick. Maybe she found out she was pregnant. Maybe she dropped out of sight. Maybe all or none of those things.

Haley's artist page on Facebook led him to the website for her online business, H. Forrester, where she sold original, botanical prints to an upscale clientele. He barely recognized the scared, pregnant teen on Gwen's porch as the polished young woman wearing a white lab coat, perched at an easel in a greenhouse, surrounded by flowering plants and miniature fruit trees. Science and reference books formed a tall stack beside her, and a glossy picture book by her feet lay open to the plant she drew. H. Forrester's photo made her seem in her twenties, business-savvy, intelligent, and very talented. And not pregnant.

He sat back and stretched. Was it any of his business? No, except something was off, and he wanted to know what it was. Haley's actions were those of a desperate teen—a lot like his sister, Bree, had been half a dozen years ago. That behavior didn't jive with someone who ran an online business and had the talent and brains Haley obviously did.

And Gwen was putting herself at risk out there on the family estate. Why was Gwen Forrester still alone, years after her husband's death? She was a beautiful, desirable woman.

"Still working on that report?" Sam's voice pulled him out of his musings.

"Almost done."

"I'm heading to Wegmans to pick up pizza. What kind do you want?"

"See if they have a mushroom and sausage for me. Otherwise anything. And a salad, with peppers, if you can find one." He opened his wallet, peeled off a twenty, and held it out to Sam. "Thanks, pal."

Peter read through the report, added details, and corrected his typos. He'd have Sam read it and add his stamp of approval over pizza.

Just because he was already online, he searched on the name of Gwen's husband, Jeb Brewster. An obituary in the archives of the local newspaper featured a photo of him with his Ski Patrol team and told of a skiing accident in Pennsylvania five years ago. A lengthy tribute in a Rochester newspaper cited Jonathan Evans "Jeb" Brewster, Esq., partner with Fitch, Brewster and Allan in Rochester, as a hero who had given his life rescuing two boys trapped in a broken gondola lift. Jeb was survived by his beloved wife, Gwendolyn Forrester, no children. This time the accompanying photo showed Brewster as a blond, blue-eyed, Ivy-League-type attorney. *Shaughnessy, you don't come close to this woman's taste in men.*

Gwen had no presence on the web, except as a psychologist in a regional listing for health services. Peter grabbed the phone book and found an ad for her as 'Gwendolyn C. Forrester, Ph.D., Psychologist, specializing in addictions.' Not how he'd want to spend his time. He remembered what he'd said to Sam, that she was either made of steel or out of her mind. *So why can't I get her and her sleek body out of my mind?*

Chapter 2

Gwen's arrival at the Chestnut Lake Café a few hours later, just after it opened at six-thirty, drew a raised eyebrow from Deirdre Calhoun. At Gwen's nod, Deirdre tucked in a bookmark and closed the cover on Stephen King. Coral fingernails tapped a worried beat on the tabletop.

Gwen dumped her purse on the chair across from her AA sponsor, fished out her wallet, and threaded through the throng of arriving customers to the pastry case.

Lynnie, the proprietor of the Chestnut Lake Café, rested an arm on the case and waited.

Gwen's eyes sparkled as she pointed from one tray to the next. "One of those and one of those and . . ."

Lynnie gave up a hearty laugh. "Not if you want those skinny jeans to fit tomorrow, Gwen."

"Darn." Gwen snapped her fingers in mock frustration. "Reality is a drag. I'll go with a large coffee, no room."

Lynnie winked. "Good choice."

Gwen set down her mug, slid the sturdy chair back from the scarred wooden table, and sat. "Stephen King? I thought you were strictly the whodunit type, Deirdre."

"Needed some chills and thrills. What's new with you?"

"Lots."

"Do tell. Did the Beamer guy propose?"

"Who?" Gwen gave her a puzzled frown.

"The hot shot you've been dating. Ned Somebody, drives the Beamer."

"Porsche. And it's Williams. No. I decided—on my perilous drive home last night—that I needed to stop seeing him."

"Smartest thing I've heard you say in months. So why are you here?"

"Because this is where I can find my sponsor every morning between six-thirty and eight."

"Except in the four years I've been your sponsor, this is only the second time you've taken me up on that offer."

Gwen shrugged and took three sugar packets from the white ceramic container in the middle of the table. She opened each in turn, emptied the contents into her drink, and stirred idly.

"Nod if you're just here for sugar and caffeine." Deirdre shifted in her chair.

"It's serious," Gwen told her. "I may have lost my mind." Gwen picked up her mug and blew across the hot liquid.

"If I want suspense, I'll go back to Stephen King."

Gwen held up a finger while she took a hot sip of strong, sweet coffee. "There. Now I can talk."

"Start with why you're dumping Ned." Deirdre rested her elbows on the table.

"I vowed to stop seeing Ned because the sex was outstanding but, beyond that, there was no relationship. Same with all the others I've been dating the past few months. Eye candy and a hot car might be cool when you're twenty, but I'm thirty-two, Deirdre, and I want a meaningful relationship with a man I admire and respect and who wants to have a family." She ran out of breath.

"It's about time you figured that out." Deirdre's tone was stern, but a smile tugged at the corners of her mouth.

"I got there a lot slower than you wanted, I know. But the guy who's coming to breakfast at nine might be Mr. Right."

"Wait. After you drove home from Eye Candy's house, you met someone else and you're having breakfast with him?"

"At nine o'clock this morning."

"Gwen, do you hear yourself? As a psychologist, you're a thoughtful, intelligent, dedicated professional. But when it comes to men, you're a flake."

"And I want to stop that. Deirdre, I think the universe put this man in my path last night." *Like the deer that forced me to stop and decide to end it with Ned.* "He's the kind of man I want to date. He's strong, he's dependable, and he's making a contribution to the community."

"That's good. And where is this man now? At home in your bed?"

Gwen's face flamed at the criticism. "No." *I deserved that.* "He's a cop, and he's finishing his shift." Gwen turned to see the clock on the wall behind Lynnie.

Deirdre tapped a coral fingernail on the table to reclaim Gwen's attention. "I'll watch the clock. You talk. How did you meet him? Were you speeding?"

Gwen shook her head. "He and his partner, Tony Pinelli's brother Sam, were in my house when I got home, and their cruiser was out front with its lights going. I called 911. Sam came out and informed me it was a break-in and they'd caught my niece Haley."

"Haley, the straight-A student who's operating a responsible business as an artist and halfway through her degree in botany? That Haley broke into your house?"

"Haley has an online business?"

Deirdre waved her hand at the wall beside their table. "You know those fruit and vegetable posters above my kitchen table that you like so much? Haley did those."

"I had no idea. How come you know about her business and I don't?"

"Gwen, I keep telling you, there's a whole world on the Internet that's passing you by. You're only thirty-two, but you're stuck in the last millennium. Maybe Haley can teach you a few things while she's here. How long is she staying?"

"I hope she'll be here until the baby."

"You're planning to have a baby?"

"No. Didn't I tell you Haley's seven months pregnant?"

"Sheesh. Anything else you left out?" Deirdre counted on her fingers. "She's due in October?"

"Yes, but she's really big."

"And she came unannounced. I'll bet she's planning to stay until the baby is born."

"I agree." Gwen sipped her coffee without further comment.

"Tell me what your Mr. Right looks like."

"Why do you always want to know what my dates look like?"

"Humor me."

"He's taller than me by—I don't know—five or six inches." Gwen took another sip.

"Huh."

"Dark hair, kind of curly, a little too long, probably cuts it himself."

"Already you've found something you can fix." Deirdre chuckled.

"Hush. Green eyes, like sea glass, that just scream, 'I'm a good guy.'"

"Now, wait. What does that mean exactly?"

"You know, the eyes are the windows of the soul, and this guy seems like a 'What you see is what you get' kind of guy."

"And you can tell he's a good guy from one interaction?"

"Well, he was kind to Haley." Gwen held her mug with both hands. "And he was concerned about our safety, told us to close and lock the garage door and bolt the kitchen door. And when he accepted our invitation to breakfast, he said he'd bring a new lock to replace the one Haley broke. Haley's going to pay for it. That was her idea."

"I'm going to come back to Haley and the break-in. But right now I have to say this guy doesn't sound anything like Jeb."

"My Jeb? No, of course not. Why should he be anything like my late husband?" Gwen inhaled the intoxicating smell of pastries behind her. Lynnie must have opened the case to fill an order. *I want one.*

"Gwen." Deirdre stretched halfway across the table and tapped her fingernails for attention. "Think about it. Every man you've dated since you decided to 'move on' a few months ago could be Jeb's twin—blond, preppie, athletic, hotshot professional, sharp dresser. If they didn't match up with Jeb as he was five years ago, right before he died, you rejected their profiles."

"I did?" Gwen squinted. The aroma of the cinnamon-pecan rolls beckoned her.

"Yes, and finally you're interested in a guy who's not a Jeb look-alike. Not even a lawyer, he's a cop. But I don't get why you think he's the guy you want to have a baby with."

"I never said that. Haley's the one that's pregnant. I just had a hunch he might be solid and interested in a family and . . ."

"How old is he?"

"He's probably thirty. Do you think I'm out of my mind?"

"I think you're jumping too far ahead, but the fact he's not a Jeb clone is real progress." Deirdre smiled and patted Gwen's arm. "And inviting him to breakfast?" She flipped two thumbs up. "Spontaneous. You have broken out of your dating rut. Maybe he is Mr. Right, maybe he's not, but he's a big step in the right direction. Just take it one step at a time, honey."

Gwen gulped the rest of her coffee. "Listen, do we have time for a quick walk along the lakeshore? I want to talk about Haley, but not here."

Deirdre glanced at the clock. "Forty-five minutes. Let's do it."

"Yo. Bro," Tony Pinelli called across the crowded Bagel Depot. He had just emerged from the Early Riser's AA meeting that congregated every day in the back room of Tompkins Falls' refurbished train depot.

The brothers often ran into each other this time of day, as Sam rolled off his shift and grabbed a bite to eat before heading home to bed. "I got your text. Give me details. Who's this Peter that has his eye on my good friend Gwen?"

Sam pointed to his full mouth and then to his half-eaten bagel smothered with ham, egg, and cheese.

Tony clapped him on the shoulder. "I'll get some coffee. Need a refill?"

Sam nodded and chewed.

Settled at Sam's table with their coffees, Tony pumped his brother for details.

"What can I tell you?" Sam shrugged. "We got the call, like I told you last night. The niece broke in and made a mess of the outside lock. Ms. Forrester—"

"Gwen."

"Whatever. So I tell her it's her niece inside with my partner, and she bolts into the house. One minute she's too shaky to stand up, and the next—"

"Back up. Gwen was too shaky to stand up?"

"She said a buck almost wiped her out as she came down her road. Big hoof print on the hood, maybe four inches from the windshield. I'd be shaking, too." He took another bite of his breakfast sandwich.

"Okay, so she bolts for the house to see if her niece is all right."

Sam nodded and chewed.

Tony tapped his foot impatiently and blew on his coffee.

Sam swallowed and told him, "He was full of questions about Gwen. She's a beautiful woman, you know."

"Well, yeah, if you like the type."

"And we all know your type." Sam guffawed and pantomimed two big breasts in front of his chest. "Now Gwen, she's more the athletic type. And classy. Some men go for that."

"I hear you. What's your partner look like?"

"Tall. Works out. Handsome. Dark hair kind of falls in his face. Women love that stuff."

"So they're both fit and great looking," Tony said. "Probably the only things they've got in common."

"Come on, bro. Maybe they're both ready to start a family. They can make beautiful babies."

"You've already got them married?" Tony laughed.

"I'm just saying, I think he's hot for her." He leaned closer and lowered his voice. "Only thing is, he has a hang-up about drunks. His father was one."

Tony drew back his fist before he realized he was doing it. "What, you told him she's in recovery? Did I tell you she's in recovery?"

"Easy, man. No way would I tell him that. She told me she knows you, and when I asked how, she said she just celebrated eight years sober, or something like that. But the thing is, Peter always lets the other guys book the drunks. We brought one in last night on our way back from the Forrester house. Peter let me handle it, as usual. Says he's the best one to write up reports and chase down details. And he's good at that. Really fast with paperwork, and everyone else hates doing it. But you told me her whole practice is about helping drunks and druggies recover. Right?"

Tony nodded.

"Well, Peter's got very definite ideas about women. Doesn't want them in danger. Doesn't think she should be dealing with psychos."

"They're not psychos. Gwen's not in danger." Tony snorted. "But maybe I'd better meet this dude. Teach him a few things about ex-drunks who are cleaning up their act."

"Sure, come on over some night." Sam sat back. "We shoot baskets outside the police station on break, most mornings around two-thirty. Kids come around. They're just out roaming with no supervision, and they like playing there, where nobody's going to yell at them. They really dig Peter, like he's one of them."

"Two-thirty in the morning? Yeah, that'll happen. Is he any good?"

Sam drained his coffee. "Might want him for the team this fall."

Deirdre's sneakers scuffed the gravel path along the lakeshore. "This is the first you knew about Haley's pregnancy?"

Gwen lifted her face to the cool morning breeze and inhaled the clean smell of lake water. "She hadn't told me, no. She'd been working at a restaurant this summer, in Saratoga Springs, near where she lives with her mom. Lived, that is."

"Her mom is your weird sister-in-law, Olga?"

"Ex. And it's Ursula." Gwen stuffed her hands in the pocket of her hoodie. "I'm guessing she threw Haley out. I'm not sure why Haley came here yesterday, but I know she needs support. She hasn't seen a doctor yet, for starters, and she has no clothes that fit her belly. I got that much out of her."

"She needs a woman's help. And you're the go-to woman in her young life."

"Thank you. I intend to live up to that."

"Has she been engaging in dangerous behavior?"

"Aside from unprotected sex—which, by the way, is not like her—I doubt it. She's not a drinker, as far as I know. In the past she's been dead set against drugs, even pot. My sense is she has taken good care of her health. I think she wants this baby to have every chance. I hope she's willing to give it up for adoption, but as far as I know she hasn't done anything about that yet."

"Does she want you to raise her baby?" Deirdre's tone was direct.

"Wh-What?" Gwen's heart jackhammered.

Deirdre did not back down.

"Surely she's not thinking that?" Gwen willed her heart to settle down. When that didn't work, she let out a laugh.

"Why wouldn't she think that?" Deirdre posed.

"Are you suggesting I should do it?" Gwen asked, shocked.

Deirdre raised an eyebrow. "Let's brainstorm it, Gwen. Because I guarantee you, if it hasn't occurred to Haley before this, it will while she's in your care. So, answer your own question."

"Professionally, I think it's a terrible idea." Gwen walked on, faster than before.

"Slow down. I'm forty-four, not thirty-two. Why is it a terrible idea?"

"Because whose baby is it? Let's say Haley finishes college and finds a nice man. Wouldn't she want her baby with her? Without a commitment to adoption, she's not likely to let go, now or later, is she? If she and Rick marry each other eventually, they would want their baby with them. But would I want to let it go after a few years of cooing and creeping and learning to walk and talk? My heart would break, Deirdre. And even if I could find it in me to do that, what kind of family dynamic does that create?"

"Agreed. But flip it around. You want a baby. Here's a very special one about to be born, and you'll probably be present at the birth. It will be hard for Haley and, I think, for you, too, to give it up. Raising the baby yourself means you get a child you're already in love with. No labor pain. Plus no more messy dating, no interfering husband who's going to leave his underwear on the floor or die on you."

Gwen swallowed hard. Leave it to Deirdre to tack on the one detail that would open up old wounds. She gave her a jab in return. "Vince leaving his underwear around the house again?"

"Nonsense." Deirdre put her arm around Gwen's shoulders and gave a squeeze. "But you see what I mean, don't you?"

Gwen slowed her steps and checked the time. "Let's turn back. Yes, I do see. I'm a respectable widow of childbearing age. No one's going to bat an eye about my raising Haley's baby or even adopting it. But the emotional fallout? Come on, Deirdre. I'd be insane to take that on."

"And frankly, I agree. You came from a loving, two-parent family, where you saw commitment and intimacy. You were raised in a stable, stimulating home environment. I think, deep inside, you want that for yourself and your husband and kids. Taking responsibility for a baby right now would seriously complicate your search for a life partner. Or maybe I'm wrong. Did you and Jeb not want kids?"

"We did want kids, but we were too busy building our careers." She squinted. *Is that really true?* She waved a hand to banish her sudden confusion about the past and simply repeated the well-honed story she'd given to people after Jeb's death. "It was always, 'Maybe next year.' And then the years were up for us."

Deirdre frowned at the lack of emotion or conviction in Gwen's tone, but she didn't stop to question it. "Here's my perspective, as a fellow psychologist and as your friend and sponsor. Haley's arrival jolted you into realizing how much you want a family of your own. I think your head is on a little straighter now than it has been the past few months. Keep it that way."

"Thank you. I will, with a lot of help from my sponsor." She squeezed Deirdre's waist.

"And just in case you had any doubt about where I stand, for you to take responsibility for an unplanned pregnancy—when it's not even your baby—is the wrong thing, for all the reasons we've said."

"So my job with Haley is to keep her moving forward with obstetrical care and with the adoption options." She stopped. "She does have options, doesn't she?"

Peter Shaughnessy's presence in Gwen's kitchen transformed it from gray to full color. Haley's faded-pink sweatshirt next to Peter's unzipped, Syracuse-orange hoodie picked up hues in the paisley placemats.

Gwen watched Peter work through his omelet with an occasional comment for her or smile for Haley. He wasn't methodical about it, the way she would be. He took a few bites from the center—loaded with asparagus, spinach, mushrooms and cheese—then a couple bites from one end, followed by a forkful of home fries.

At a lull in the conversation, he gave Haley an easy smile and asked her, "So what does your young man think about all this?"

The wheat bagel, dripping with peanut butter, stopped halfway to Haley's mouth. She looked left and right.

Peter glanced at Gwen, his eyebrows pinched together in puzzlement.

Gwen shrugged. This was new territory for her, too.

"Rick doesn't know." Haley set her bagel on the plate and licked a dollop of peanut butter from her thumb.

Peter set down his fork and pressed back with an audible exhale. "None of my business, but if I were Rick I would want to know and would want to support you through this and would feel betrayed if you left me out."

Haley did not move a muscle, but tears slipped from her eyes. She choked out, "But I can't."

Peter's shoulders bunched and his hands made fists, but he held his emotion in check when he said to Haley, "I am guessing you and Rick love each other. If so, whatever promise or fear is holding you back can't trump your responsibility to the father of this baby."

"If I saw him, I would not be able to give up the baby." Haley's voice was tremulous. "He would want us to get married, and that would be so unfair to him. He's worked so hard on his engineering degree. I can't take that away from him."

"Haley, if I were Rick I would want the chance to decide that with you."

Haley's forehead creased in pain, and her face turned red. "Excuse me." She slipped off the stool and fled from the kitchen before either of them could reach out.

Gwen held onto the island with both hands to keep from rushing after her. She knew the right thing was to give Haley time alone to wrestle with this new input. Peter was right. Haley and Rick together needed to decide the next steps.

"I apologize," Peter told her. "I had no business saying any of that."

"Don't apologize. She needed to get that out, and she needed to hear what a man thinks. Haley and I both dance around things. It might have taken us days to get to that. And anyway, what do I know about a man's point of view in a situation like this?"

Peter picked up half of his buttered bagel, tapped it on his plate, and let it drop again. "So, she hadn't told you. And when I was online last night, working on the report, I noticed her Facebook page went silent more than three months ago. She's been trying to deal with this by herself too long."

"I could learn a few things from you," Gwen said with admiration in her voice. *Deirdre's right about my being stuck in the last millennium.* "All I know is she was waitressing in Saratoga Springs until last week. I don't know why she quit. Maybe they didn't want her belly in the high-class dining room anymore."

"Or she finally realized she needed help and knew you were the one she could turn to."

Gwen took a nervous sip of almost-cold coffee. "I'm sure her mother was no help. Ursula is completely self-absorbed. She probably threw Haley out on the street." She used a piece of bagel to push the rest of her omelet into the center of the plate and rested the bagel on top. "Haley and I didn't get into the hard questions last night. All I know is she came here by bus with a duffle full of dirty clothes—none of them maternity clothes—and a stash of cash."

"She said last night she walked here from the bus station."

"I didn't even know she was coming." Tears burned Gwen's eyes. "I realized this morning, she had left me about six messages from four o'clock on. I should have been here for her."

"Gwen, you were here for her." Peter's voice was gentle. "Your timing was just off a little. And maybe it's not a bad thing that the police confronted her for breaking in last night. It's a wake-up call that she's making some desperate decisions. Bad ones."

"You're a wise man, Officer Shaughnessy." Gwen dabbed at her eyes with her napkin and gave him a grateful smile.

"I have a sister. She made some bad choices at that age, too."

He drank down his juice and slid off the stool with a fluid motion that rippled the muscles of his torso, under his tight, white T-shirt. A thrill shot through Gwen.

"I need to get that lock changed before I crash. Can you wrap the rest for me, and I'll enjoy it later?"

"Peter, you've been on duty all night. Why don't you finish breakfast and head home? I can call a locksmith."

"Not going to happen." His voice was firm. "I won't rest until I know you two are safe out here. And, listen, if you're not going to finish your omelet, I'd like that, too."

Haley slouched against the frame of the bedroom window. Finger poised over the 'send' button, she searched the lake for courage.

She never imagined growing up was more than getting a college degree and a good-paying job. Why didn't she have a mother who taught her things? One who helped her deal with consequences when she made disastrous mistakes, like this one?

At least she had Gwen. She clung to the thought. Even if Gwen wasn't anyone's mom, she was way smarter than most people about how to deal with horrible messes.

She stood tall and braced herself. Rick's number was lit in the display of her iPhone. *I can't face him.*

Beyond the window, cobalt water sparkled in the late morning sunshine. Close in, by Gwen's sand beach, a lone swan glided on the smooth surface, teasing the watcher into thinking independence was easy and natural and beautiful to behold.

Haley snorted. "As if."

She wanted to be kayaking side by side with Rick right now, weaving through the little, round islands in Gwen's corner of Chestnut Lake. Or hiking along the shoreline, watching for birds and wildflowers—asters and goldenrod and milkweed bursting with silken seed for the wind to carry. She wondered if she and Rick would ever again share hikes like that.

She touched her left forefinger to the windowpane and sketched an invisible swan in the film of dust on the glass. To her eye, the new swan floated next to the lonesome one just beyond the beach.

Peter is right. Rick has to know and decide with me.

She took in a deep, steadying breath then pressed the connect button.

Rick answered the nanosecond her number flashed on the display of his Android. "Are you all right? Where are you?"

Haley's laugh bubbled up like an intoxicant. "Rick? God, it didn't even ring, did it?"

"Haley, tell me where you are. Please. Is the baby okay?"

"How do you . . .?" A sob escaped her.

He softened his voice. "Haley, I know because I've been searching for you for a couple of weeks since I got back from the Gulf. The project wrapped up early. I've been going out of my mind trying to find you."

He knew she was listening because she punctuated each of his sentences with a moan.

"They told me at the restaurant in the Springs that you quit and went to work at a diner. The diner told me you vanished a few days ago. I won't even tell you what your mother said. Where are you?"

Haley choked out her answer. "At my Aunt Gwen's. Rick, I'm so sorry about being pregnant. I didn't want you to know."

He pounded his fist against the lab table. "Why the hell not?" he roared. *You're losing it, Walker.*

He glanced around to see who might have overheard. The tables were empty, but a head appeared at the door to the hall. His major advisor, Professor Singh, stepped into the lab, five minutes early for their session. Rick smacked his forehead and held up his open hand to buy five minutes.

Professor Singh planted both hands on his hips. "Very well, but we will also talk about this complication."

Rick nodded in surrender.

Professor Singh returned to the hall and shut the door behind him.

"Rick?"

"I'm here."

"Do you agree?"

"Someone came in, Haley, and I missed what you said. He's gone now."

"I said I didn't want you to know about the baby because it's my fault and my responsibility."

"God, Haley." He sank onto a hard bench and exhaled two weeks of frustration. "Honey, it's our baby, our responsibility."

She didn't argue.

"Are you healthy, Haley? Is the baby okay?"

"I'm doing okay," she told him. "I need to see a doctor soon, and Gwen will help me find someone around here."

"You mean you haven't seen a doctor yet because you've been feeling well enough? Until now?" Over the two years he'd known her, Rick had developed the patience to translate Haley's rambling answers to fit his need for information. She'd come to accept his endless questions, although in the first few months of their dating, she'd complained he was picking on her.

"Yes. Rick, I'm taking really good care of my health. For the baby. That's why I left the restaurant. I needed my sleep and I needed to get some rest every few hours. The diner was better than working nights at the restaurant, but last week I knew I needed to be with Gwen and see a doctor, too."

"Are you sure it wasn't because I was coming back after four months on a research trip, and you needed to disappear until you delivered?"

"That, too," she admitted.

Anger flared in his chest. "You really weren't going to tell me?"

"I really didn't want you to know how badly I screwed up, and I didn't want to interfere with your plans—your degree and your work. And mostly I needed to see a doctor, to have the baby checked out. And me, too."

His stomach sank. "What changed? Exactly."

"My ankles were really swollen, and I know that can be mean there's a problem. So I told my boss I was sick and needed to go home to see my doctor, and he was cool with that."

"Your fictitious doctor?" Rick forced a chuckle.

Haley's answering laugh was quiet and easy. "Yeah. But I'll find one, for real, today and get an appointment."

"Yes, you will." It came out as an order. "And I need to be there with you. We need to talk. About all of this. About your health and your health care and about the baby."

"Yes and . . ." Another sob.

"Take your time," he said, his voice gentle. "This is hard for me, too." He stole a second to log in to the Rensselaer network and Google 'Gwen Forrester, Psychologist.' The only useful result was the address of a professional office in Tompkins Falls. It was enough for the map app to show him where he needed to be.

Haley's crying eased.

"Haley," Rick implored, his voice soft, "let's do this together. I love you, and it's important that we work this out, figure out the right thing for the baby and for us. Please don't make any decisions until we're together."

Haley snuffled her nose.

"Okay?"

"Yes." Her voice was full of doubt.

"But?" he teased.

"Rick, are you sure you can take the time to come?"

"I have about two weeks before classes start. I'm meeting with my advisor in a few minutes to plan for fall. After work tomorrow morning I'm all yours for two weeks. And I'll be at your side or on call after that, for as long as you need me."

He heard a *whoosh* of relief.

"Listen, will Gwen be okay if I show up there, like, tomorrow?"

"Sure."

Probably Gwen wouldn't rip him apart. She had been pretty calm at Haley's house over Christmas, and she'd made a science project out of managing Haley's weird mother. *Gwen will ask all the right questions.* They needed that. He and Haley had no idea how to deal with this, except what their hearts told them. It bothered him that Haley's heart had told her to keep her distance and keep him in the dark.

"I have a Google map for Gwen Forrester, a psychologist on the East Lake Road outside of Tompkins Falls. Is that her practice or her house?"

"Both. But it's down a killer private road. If you can get here in daylight, it's a lot easier."

"I can be on the road tomorrow around noon. I'll swing by your mom's." He cringed at the thought. "What can I bring with me that you don't have?"

"I know it's hazardous duty, but I'd love to have my paints and stuff from my mother's house. She threw me out in June. She may have thrown out my stuff, too. I don't know."

"I'll see what I can do. And I'll bring along the things you had at my place. Your camera's here."

"I thought I'd lost it." Haley's voice brightened.

"I'll try to get there around five or six tomorrow afternoon. I'll be starved," he hinted.

That made her laugh. "We'll feed you. I love you, Rick."

"I'm counting on it. I love you, too, Haley. See you soon."

"Bye."

The connection went dead.

Professor Singh stood with his hand on the doorknob.

"So your foolproof, logical plan for life has gone phooey?"

Gwen closed the cupboard door on the last of the breakfast dishes. There was still no sign of Haley, but Haley would talk when she was ready.

She tossed the damp dishtowel on the back of the nearest stool, ran her fingers through her hair, pinched some color into her cheeks, and put on a saucy smile.

When she stepped down to the garage, Peter stood beyond the outside door. A scowl marred his face and his left hand wiggled a screwdriver as he contemplated his handiwork.

He'd shed the hoodie. Muscles filled the white T-shirt, and the cotton clung to his sweaty chest and abdomen. Worn jeans hugged his lean hips and defined the bulges at his crotch.

Even better than the uniform.

He teased her, when he saw the direction of her gaze. "What do you think?"

"Uh." Temporarily speechless, she crossed the garage and stepped out into the sunlight. Even a foot away, she sensed his heat, smelled soap and fresh sweat and wood shavings. "How's it going?"

He stretched to his full height. His lean hips settled forward, and his chest and arm muscles rippled. "Take a look." His gaze shifted to the repair job, and probed a hollow above the new deadbolt with his screwdriver. "There's more damage than I can properly fix. I wish Haley had known what she was doing when she broke in."

Gwen stepped closer and saw what he meant.

He moved his screwdriver a few inches down, where splintered wood lay exposed around the main lock. "She smashed the old mechanism with a rock, and there's damage to the wood that needs repair. I can use wood filler for now to make it secure, but you should replace the door. And I recommend a door with no window next time."

"I'll call Tony later and have him put it on his list."

"Tony?" His shoulder stiffened and he gave her a sideways glance.

A little jealous? "Your partner Sam's brother Tony does carpentry on the side. He's a security officer at the college."

Judging by the tightness around his mouth, she hadn't completely satisfied his curiosity.

She smiled and touched his forearm. "I've known the Pinellis since we were kids."

He shifted his hips, as if his jeans had just gotten snug.

"Tony and Sam's sister Maria is a little younger than me, and we were cheerleaders together in high school."

"Cheerleaders?" A slow grin spread over Peter's face as he perused her body.

She skipped away, shook imaginary pompoms in the air, turned with a beaming smile, and swished her hips. "Go, Tigers, go!"

"So Tompkins Falls teams are the Tigers? I'll bet you were at the top of the pyramid."

"Nope. Center, bottom row. I'm strong, even though I'm slender."

"All that canoeing," he guessed. He gestured inside the garage, up toward the rafters.

There sat the old green canoe, straddling two rafters.

"I didn't realize we still had it." *Why have I never looked up there?*

Peter tossed the screwdriver onto his toolkit, came up behind her, and squeezed her shoulders with both hands. "She's a classic. Wooden, right?"

"Yes, I think the gunwales are mahogany. Haley's dad and I spent hours as kids, paddling up and down the shore, exploring the islands. Mom and Dad loved it, too."

His breath tickled the hair by her ear. "Canoeing was my favorite part of Scout camp."

"We should get it out on the water."

"We should." Peter's hands slid down her arms. "You are vibrating."

She laughed and hugged herself. "I loved that boat."

"Feel like bringing it down from the rafters right now?"

"Let's." She turned to face him and saw exhaustion etched into his forehead and around his mouth—lines she hadn't seen before. "Wait, you're just coming off your shift. You've got to be wiped out."

"I'm good for ten minutes." He started into the garage. "That's long enough to haul it down and move it out to the grass."

Gwen studied the situation while Peter wrestled with a rake, hoe, and spade that blocked access to a tall stepladder.

"You're sure about this?" she asked.

"Nothing to it." He set up the ladder directly under the crossbar closest to the stern. Gwen held the ladder steady while he climbed, and he told her his plan. "I'll slide it back, until the bow clears the rafter, then tip it down to you. Can you bring the nose to the floor without hurting yourself?"

"No problem." Gwen eyeballed the clearances as he shifted the canoe back a foot at a time. She could see the plan would work.

She should have known, though, from the bits of dust that slipped off the canoe on its backward path, that she was in for it. As soon as the bow tipped toward her, decades of grime, dust, and bugs pelted her.

Coughing and laughing and shielding her eyes, she reached blindly for the nose of the old canoe.

Peter groaned. "I am so sorry, Gwen."

"I'm okay. Guide my hand." She waved it around.

"Hold steady. Okay, a few inches to your right. And forward two inches."

Gwen touched the metal strip that capped the bow. The old, canvas-covered, wooden boat felt like an old friend in her hand.

As she brushed off her face with her free hand, she flashed back six weeks, to the moment when her friend Gianessa's bridal bouquet had dropped into her hand, just as unexpectedly. The moment the rose petals caressed her palm, Gwen had intuitively taken possession of the bouquet of fresh, fragrant lilies and roses.

Now, with the forgotten, much-loved nose of the canoe pushing against her fingers, she instinctively tugged it with both hands. As it neared the floor, she kept her right hand on the nose, slid her left hand along the gunwale to the first crossbar, and guided the bow until it rested on the concrete floor. "It's down."

"Hold it there, just like that, for a second."

He rested the tip of the stern on the rafter and climbed down. Together they maneuvered the sixty-pound boat to the floor, turned it over, and rested the bottom on the concrete, without damaging its fifty-year-old skin.

"She's a beauty." Peter trailed his fingers along the gunwale as he came to stand beside Gwen. "Do they even make canoes like this any more?"

She did a little dance of excitement and squeezed his waist. He lifted a few oak leaves out of her hair and showed them to her. "How did these get on top of it, all the way up there on the rafters?"

"Must have been a strong wind swirling through the garage one fall." Gwen bent from the waist and shook out her hair, then stood tall and brushed debris from her once-white T-shirt.

"Thanks to me," Peter said with a chuckle, "you need another shower, and it's not even ten o'clock. Let's carry the canoe out to the lawn and call it quits for now. I need to crash."

When the canoe rested on the soft grass behind the garage, Peter moved to her side. His strong hands caressed her shoulders. "One of these days, we'll take it for a paddle."

Gwen gave him a smile that made his tired eyes sparkle. She lifted up onto her toes and planted a kiss on his cheek. "Soon."

Chapter 3

Who knew an old canoe was the key to a woman's heart? Peter shook his head with a grin as he swung his Jeep into the parking lot of his apartment building. At the moment, home was a one-bedroom dungeon a block from Tompkins College.

As he exited the Jeep, he heard music blare from a neighbor's living room. His shoulders tightened. "Shaughnessy," he told himself, "that's what your noise-canceling headphones are made for."

He really needed to get out of this pit, and he wished the letter would arrive from his attorney with the final accounting from the divorce. When he had come home this morning for a quick shower and picked up his mail, he had been so focused on breakfast with Gwen and Haley that he hadn't even sorted through the pile.

Now he tossed his keys in the basket by the front door, set the wrapped-up breakfast from Gwen's in the microwave for a minute, and poured himself a glass of milk. The mail still waited for him where he'd dropped it on the counter. He poked at the pile and saw his attorney's return address peek out at him.

Ripping open the envelope, he found two pages, neatly folded—a terse letter confirming this was the final bill and a one-page accounting of services, with balance due. No check thanking him for overpayment, but he knew all along that was a dream. He inspected the figures from top to bottom. The amount due was eight thousand more than he'd hoped.

With a heavy sigh, he set the pages aside and took the warmed-up breakfast out of the microwave. As he unwrapped the meal, memories wafted up from the home fries and the cheese and veggie omelet. Haley's expressive face. Gwen's take-charge presence in her own kitchen. The ever-changing cadence of their laughter. Haley licking peanut butter from her fingers. The meticulous way Gwen worked from one end of her omelet to the other, always taking a mouthful of something else between each bite of eggs.

They'll be safe now, with the new lock.

He smiled at the thought, a little surprised by it. He liked taking care of his women. Until now that had meant his traitorous wife Cynthia, his mother—may she rest in peace—and his mixed-up sister, Bree. He'd known Gwen and Haley less than a day, but they felt like family somehow.

He drained the glass of milk, washed and dried it, and put it away. To his surprise, the impossible dream of owning a house faded quickly and painlessly. The real significance of the final bill from his attorney was that, as soon as he paid it, he'd be free.

Tears welled up and he blinked them away. *Free to start over.* Find a decent place to live. Settle into his new city, Tompkins Falls. Explore whatever this was between him and Gwen Forrester.

Thank God Gwen was a good sport about the grit and bugs in her face. Besides getting the canoe on the water, he needed to get her out on a proper date, someplace special. How could he get her away from Haley long enough, and where could he take her on his salary? It had to be special, fit for a classy lady like Gwen. Ralphs, his favorite burger joint, would not cut it.

The calendar on the refrigerator caught his eye, and he noticed the star in the square for Sunday. Tomorrow. That fancy dinner-dance for the outgoing chief at the Manse. Classy? Definitely. He had accepted the invitation a month ago and, without thinking, said he'd bring a guest.

He reached for his phone, but a wave of fatigue stopped him. First sleep. Then invite Gwen. Then write the last payment to the attorney, put out feelers for an apartment, get supper, and go to work.

"I called Rick," Haley announced as she came down the stairs.

"I'm proud of you." Gwen poured glasses of iced tea and carried them to the island. "Can he come to Tompkins Falls?" At Haley's nod, she asked, "When will he get here, sweetie?"

"Suppertime tomorrow." Haley's knuckles were white as she gripped the edge of the island. "You're sure it's okay if he comes?"

"I'm very sure it's okay. That leaves us all day today and most of tomorrow to shop for maternity clothes and get our nails done. I'll make an appointment at the Spa at the Manse."

"Like I can afford a mani-pedi and new clothes," Haley said with a flippant laugh.

"It's an aunt's prerogative to pamper her pregnant niece." Gwen pretended to scowl. "If you don't let me do it, I might hate you."

"Don't." Haley rushed in for a quick hug. "But first I need to make a doctor's appointment. Like highest priority. I promised Rick. And myself." She closed her eyes. "Except I have no idea where to start."

"We could start with a pregnant woman I know."

"That's brilliant." Haley's eyes popped open.

Gwen chuckled as she reached for a pad and paper and her cell phone. She speed-dialed and held up one finger for Haley each time she heard a ring.

On three, she exclaimed, "Gianessa, good, I got you."

Gwen motioned Haley closer and scribbled, 'Gianessa Cushman.'

"All is well, thanks. Gianessa, my niece Haley arrived last night. Surprise, she's seven months pregnant. How—? Yes, we're very excited, thanks. Haley will be staying with me through the birth of her baby, right, Haley?" Haley nodded and leaned closer. "We're calling, because she has not yet seen a doctor, and we need to find one to follow her through the birth. How should we proceed?" Gwen listened and doodled something on the pad.

Haley frowned at Gwen's drawing of a duck on a stream, with steam rising from the water.

"Terrific, thanks. Haley's right here. Can I switch to 'speaker,' Gianessa?"

Haley clapped her hands and slid onto a stool at the island while Gwen placed the phone on the marble surface and punched the speaker key.

Haley didn't wait for an introduction. "Hi, Gianessa. I'm Haley, the unmarried niece. Thanks for helping."

A sweet laugh drifted out of the phone. "Hi, Haley. Someday Gwen and I will tell you my story. But right now, let me ask a lot of questions and then we'll come up with a plan."

"Sounds good."

Gianessa pounded Haley with questions about nutrition, sleep, vitamins, weight, activity level, Rick's health, their alcohol and drug use, and any medications she took. Haley answered each question simply.

"Sounds like you're taking very good care of yourself and your baby," Gianessa said. "Dr. Bowes will be really pleased with that."

"Who's Dr. Bowes?"

"She's my obstetrician in Clifton Springs. She also runs a clinic at the hospital for moms-to-be who don't have an established relationship with a doctor."

"She sounds cool."

"She is. And she's no-nonsense, so you have to promise me you'll do everything she says. She hates whiners. I don't want to bring her a whiner."

"That's perfect, because I'm trying to be really grown up about this, even though I'm scared to death."

"You know, Haley, I'm a little scared, too. I'm having twins."

Haley's strangled response made Gwen laugh.

"Maybe you and I can ride over to our appointments together," Gianessa said.

"That's even more perfect because I don't have a car."

"Haley, you and I will get along very well. I'd like you to call the following number at the clinic," she directed.

Haley wrote it down.

"Tell them I have an appointment with Dr. Bowes Monday, the day after tomorrow, at one o'clock. See if you can come around the same time. Tell them you're riding with me. Okay so far?"

"Yes, I'm ready,"

"They might want you to have blood work done ahead. Will you and Gwen take care of that?"

Haley checked with Gwen, who nodded. "Gwen says yes."

"Call me back with details of your appointment as soon as you know. I'll work on my husband Justin to drive the three of us. Gwen can come, too."

"Oh."

"What?"

"Rick, my boyfriend, will be here by then. He needs to go with me."

Gwen spoke up. "And I have clients Monday, but Rick should ride along."

"No problem," Gianessa agreed. "Anything else right now?"

"Gianessa," Gwen said quickly. "Where can we find some maternity clothes for Haley?"

Gianessa gave her the names of several stores she liked at Eastview Mall in nearby Rochester, and they signed off.

That done, Gwen handed the phone to Haley and took a seat at the island. Haley screwed up her courage to call the doctor's office. It was not an easy negotiation and not without a few tears, but once Haley had booked her appointment at Dr. Bowes' clinic for noon on Monday, Gwen felt more optimistic about her role as the go-to woman in Haley's life.

Another quick phone call assured them that Gianessa's husband was on board with driving Haley and Rick, even though it meant leaving an hour earlier. Gianessa asked Haley to make a list of questions and concerns for Dr. Bowes.

While Haley wrote her list, Gwen caught up with her friend. As their conversation wore down, Gwen said, "I never asked if you want to come shopping with us?"

"I would love to, but I'm picking out furniture for the nursery."

A smile spread over Gwen's face. "Have a wonderful time." A little flutter in her belly made her hope she'd be doing that for her own baby in a year or two.

Justin Cushman offered his elbow, with a wink for his very pregnant spouse. "Come for a drive?" he enticed with a twinkle in his eye.

Gianessa had been cautioned several weeks earlier to stop work, curtail vigorous activity, and guard against falls. She resisted anything that resembled fussing, but a little experimentation had shown Justin that "gallant" worked very well.

Gianessa took his arm, with a raised eyebrow.

"It's time to see our new house," he explained.

Her mouth made an O, and she nodded with gusto. "There's a road and everything?"

"A beautiful gravel drive from the highway."

"Does this mean the house is finished?"

"Very close, sweetheart. We're at day four of a ten-day countdown." As he led her carefully down two flights to Lakeside Terrace, he told her, "Until last week it was a gaping skeleton. Now the windows are in and the systems are working, and it's the home we planned. I think you're going to approve."

His Saab was already at the front door, pointing downhill. "You knew I'd come along, didn't you, dude?" Gianessa's laugh was a melody that warmed his heart.

"You couldn't resist." Justin helped her into the passenger seat and they rolled down to the highway. Once on the Cushman grounds, the Saab crested a high hill and glided down through evergreens to a birch grove. "The last time you saw it, we'd just broken ground."

"But Gwen is across the lake. She's been issuing weekly reports. I know it's three stories and lots of glass."

"That's true."

They emerged from the trees, and Gianessa gasped. Words failed her, but she squeezed his thigh and laughed with delight.

Justin reveled in the wonder in her amethyst eyes. Gianessa Dupioni Cushman was the most desirable woman he'd ever known, and, coming from someone who had done business on four continents, that was saying a great deal. Now pregnant with their twins, she had never been more beautiful.

He stopped near the front door and helped her from the car and across a stone terrace. "The entry makes it look like the house is just one level. The other two levels stack below, as the slope falls away. Do you approve?"

"It's inviting." Gianessa squinted at the massive, teak front door. "Will I be able to open this, dude?"

"Formidable, isn't it?" Justin nodded. "Try it."

She pressed the latch, and the door swung open. "Easy."

Once inside, they passed through a large entry into the great room, made for entertaining. Its wall of windows framed the view they both loved.

She pressed her forehead to the glass and gazed at the deep blue water that stretched like a long finger almost twelve miles to the south, where it bent to the right and disappeared behind a steep hillside of rock and forest. "Justin, this is your dream come true."

"Our dream, sweetheart," he corrected gently.

She turned with dancing eyes. "Our home," she said. "Show me. Already, it's grander than I imagined."

"Come see the kitchen."

Her squeal made him chuckle.

"You haven't seen it yet."

"But I know it's going to be our favorite room."

After steering her through a formal dining room, he swept his hand to show off the dark granite counters and cherry cabinets. "Our gourmet kitchen is complete and ready to use. We can make ourselves *doppio con panna* right now, if you like. Decaf, of course."

"Let's."

While he fussed with the new espresso machine, she opened and closed cupboards, exclaiming at the dishes and glassware. A peek at the pantry revealed shelves filled with their favorite staples and treats. The freezer held entrees from their usual restaurants and grocery stores. "You are the best husband in the world."

He chuckled. "At the table by the window, I've put out the artist's rendering for you. Ask me whatever you want."

She studied the drawings while the machine gurgled and hissed. Finally, Justin spooned on whipped topping and joined her.

"You're awfully quiet," he tested.

"Mesmerized. Have you any idea what a thrill this is?"

"I know you've been anxious that we might have to live at 14 Lakeside Terrace with two babes in arms."

"And now I know we'll be right here before they're born. Justin, even if the great room and the kitchen are the only rooms finished, we could camp out and never go hungry."

Justin barked a laugh. "Well, that's not going to happen. We may not have a deck right away, and the guest floor will not be finished until the holidays, at the earliest, but we'll be living here in comfort—nanny and nurse, too—within two weeks."

"I believe you." She pointed to the plans for the lowest level. "Dude, do we really need three guest bedrooms?"

"I don't know what we were thinking. That's why that level is not finished."

"Are the family bedrooms ready?"

"Nearly ready, yes, and the furniture for babies' rooms will arrive tomorrow."

Gianessa squealed again and raised her glass mug. "To our family."

She took a sip and hummed with pleasure.

"Good?"

"*Perfetto*." She licked whipped cream from her upper lip. "Speaking of Gwen, she told me she has a new beau."

"What do we know about him?"

"His name is Peter. Not only is he handsome, he was the officer on duty when Haley broke into Gwen's the other night. Gwen says he handled the situation with professionalism and compassion."

"Haley, the niece who's coming with us to Clifton Springs? Broke into Gwen's?"

"No cause for worry, Justin. And I know one more thing about Gwen's Peter."

"What's that?"

She raised her eyebrows. "He makes her heart flutter."

"Do *I* make *your* heart flutter?"

She winked. "You do, dude."

"You keep rubbing your arm. Are you sore from the blood work?" Gwen walked ahead of Haley to clear a path through the swarm of back-to-school shoppers at the mall.

"A little. Eleven vials." Haley rolled her eyes. "I thought she'd never finish."

"You were in there a long time," Gwen pressed.

"Somebody had fainted earlier, so she made me lie down and eat crackers and drink apple juice." Haley laughed. "What I wanted was a whole bag of Oreos."

"You just made me hungry. It's not suppertime yet, but let's take a break and see what we still need from your list." Neither of them had checked things off as they moved from store to store.

Haley's face lit up. "Chocolate chip super cookie and an iced tea. Lead me to it."

"You're easy. I'm going for iced Americano and a big piece of carrot cake."

Gwen settled her niece at a table beside the Starbucks kiosk and arranged the half-dozen shopping bags around her. "Put your feet up on the empty chair and dig out your list. I'll get the food, and we'll go through everything."

After a few bites of the giant cookie, Haley's pallor gave way to pink cheeks and bright eyes.

Gwen felt her energy soar once the espresso and sugar hit her system. "How shall we do this? Do you want to root through the bags or check off your list?"

"You root. You can bend over easier than me."

Gwen lifted things out one at a time, and exclaimed over the bright tunic tops and smart pants. She noted bras that offered the right support for Haley's active style. "We'll come back to the mall after you deliver in October and get some warm clothes for winter."

Haley sighed. "Seems a shame to wear these for just a couple of months."

"We'll give them to a thrift shop before the holidays, and make some mom-to-be very happy." Gwen had come to the end of their purchases. "That's all we've got. How are we doing?"

Haley reviewed her list and circled the one item without a check mark. "I just need a hoodie."

"And something decent to wear out to dinner," Gwen added with a sly smile.

Haley laughed. "Why would I be going out to dinner?"

"I might arrange for Rick to take you out for a lovely dinner while he's here."

"Gwen, he can't afford . . ." She stopped herself. "Thank you," she said, and kissed Gwen's cheek. "We'll both really like that. But we need a shirt and tie for him if it's that kind of place."

Gwen took one last swallow of espresso. "Good thinking. Do you know his shirt size?"

"I do." Haley wiped up their spills and stuffed napkins and straw wrappers into Gwen's empty cup. "I got him a shirt for Christmas, because he had an interview coming up for a summer research job."

"Did he get the job?"

Haley nodded. "That's where he was from late April until a couple weeks ago. That's why he didn't know about the baby until now."

"You two have a lot to talk about." Gwen pressed Haley's hand.

"I am really scared."

"Why, honey?"

"Like Peter said, I haven't been honest with Rick. Not telling him something this important is the same as not being honest. I never meant to betray Rick."

"Betray might have been too strong a word. Peter may still be smarting from his divorce. Why didn't you tell Rick?"

"Basically, I panicked." Haley's forehead puckered. "I tried to buy myself some time to figure out what I wanted to do." Haley turned her big, dark eyes on Gwen. "Rick and I have always done things together. He helped me set up my business, and he came with me whenever I wanted to hike through the woods and photograph wildflowers for my paintings. So, why wouldn't I ask for his help with this? With the baby."

"You said earlier you were afraid he would give up his degree to get married."

"He's so Catholic sometimes." Haley glanced down. "In the beginning I thought about having an abortion."

"Did you?" That surprised Gwen. Haley seemed so invested in this baby. Maybe that had come with time.

"When Rick got the summer job, I figured he would never know. But I knew this baby was part of us, and I loved my baby. So I decided to go ahead with the pregnancy, and I just focused on keeping us safe and healthy."

Gwen's heart ached that Haley had been dealing with her pregnancy alone for months. "I'm so glad you came to me and that you're sharing this with me. And I'm proud of you for bringing Rick into it now."

Haley closed her eyes. Pain settled on the bones of her face. "I don't know how to talk to him about this."

"If you speak from your heart, you can't say anything wrong."

A few tears slipped from Haley's eyes. She nodded.

Gwen's cell phone rang, and she ignored it. She fished a package of tissues from her purse. She waited while Haley blew her nose and wondered if she would reveal more. The phone rang again.

"You should take that," Haley decided for them. "I'll dump the trash and get a glass of water."

"Okay," Gwen relented. She checked the caller ID. "Hi, Peter," she answered.

Haley's face lit up as she left the table.

"Hi, yourself. Where are you?"

Gwen kicked off her shoes and put her feet up. "At the mall. Haley and I are taking a break from buying maternity clothes. Did you sleep?"

"Like the dead, and way longer than usual," Peter told her. "Listen, I have a thing Sunday evening, and I want you to come as my guest."

Gwen laughed. "'Thing' as in paint ball, wedding reception, stakeout . . ."

"Farewell dinner and dance for the outgoing chief."

"Chief Barker? Very nice."

"It's at the Manse Inn and Spa, cocktails at five, dinner at six, dancing until whenever."

Gwen slid down in her chair like she had as a teenager when her favorite guy called. "Sounds great. And that will get me out of the house so Haley and Rick can be by themselves for a couple of hours."

"He's coming?" Peter's voice was eager.

"Yes, tomorrow. Tomorrow is Sunday, right?"

"Hey, I'm the one that just woke up." He chuckled.

She gave it back to him. "But you haven't been shopping with half the kids and moms of Rochester for the past three hours. And it's good that we're still shopping, because I want a new dress for the dinner dance."

"I'm flattered," Peter said, his voice soft. "So, shall I pick you up at five-thirty, or do you want to start the cocktail hour exactly at five?"

Gwen laughed. "Peter, I don't drink at all. I have no interest in the cocktail hour."

"So, I'll come for you at five-thirty."

"It's a date." Gwen sat up with a sudden thought. "Do you have to work after the party?"

"Yes, unfortunately. Question for you. Do you know someone named Cushman?"

"Yes, why?"

"This whole shindig is privately funded. Scuttlebutt is that Cushman is backing the party to acknowledge the important contribution the chief made to the town for twenty-plus years."

"That would be Joel Cushman. We were in school together. He owns the Manse where it's being held. I suspect Joel is acknowledging Chief Barker as the person who made our town safe for everyone, including women. Barker was an advocate for women's shelters and services for victims of rape and domestic violence."

"Sounds like I'll learn a lot more about Tompkins Falls tomorrow night."

"You will, and I'll introduce you to Joel if he's in attendance. He's recovering from a serious accident, though, and he may not be up to it."

"You two are friends?"

"We go back a long way. And this is cool: he and his bride Manda were married this summer on the grounds of the Manse. If the weather is good, I'll show you the garden the Manse created for the occasion."

Peter whistled. "That takes money."

"Joel's a good man, and he uses his money to benefit the community. I think you'll like him."

Haley nudged Gwen's outstretched feet.

"Gotta go, Peter. Haley's back and ready to shop."

"Tell her hello. See you at five-thirty tomorrow." He added with a chuckle, "No leaves in your hair."

Gwen laughed and ended the call.

"You've got a date with Peter?" Haley slid into her chair and grabbed Gwen's hand.

Gwen nodded.

"You've got a silly smile on your face, and your eyes are all dreamy," Haley teased her. "It's a good look for you, Aunt Gwen."

"None of this 'Aunt Gwen' stuff. You make me feel old."

"How perfect for your date, that you and I are booked at the spa first thing tomorrow morning."

"The universe is on our side. I'll see if we can get our hair done, too. And before we leave the mall, I need to find The Dress."

"Go sexy. Go all out."

"I just might."

Deirdre surveyed Lynnie's Chestnut Lake Café on Sunday morning and saw mostly empty tables at eleven o'clock. "The calm between storms," she said.

"I'm glad for a little privacy," Gwen admitted as she settled across from her sponsor.

Deirdre brought two coffees and two cinnamon buns to the table. "An update on Mr. Right, please." She leaned close. "Tell me everything."

Gwen blushed and fanned her steaming coffee mug. "He dumped decades of leaves and bugs and grime in my hair."

A horselaugh escaped Deirdre. "This guy is so right for you."

"It was the fallout when we brought the canoe down from the rafters. And later, he called and invited me to an event at the Manse tonight."

"I like it." Deirdre put her elbows on the table.

Gwen chuckled. "I do, too. And he used some tough love with Haley at breakfast, made her open up about what her boyfriend, Rick, was thinking. It turned out she'd kept the pregnancy a secret from Rick all this time."

"Yikes." Deirdre took a sip of her coffee.

"'Yikes' is right. But Peter's words had an effect. Haley called Rick, and Rick's coming around suppertime today. Which reminds me, what food can Haley and I fix this afternoon that will keep her mind occupied but be easy to heat up at the last minute?"

"Comfort food. A big pan of lasagna, a salad with good old Italian dressing, and lots of bread and butter."

"Great. I'll swing by the store after this, and Haley and I will make a project of it."

"And we are now done with distraction number one, correct? The subject on the table is your love life, not Haley's." Deirdre's voice was stern.

"You're right. I distracted us."

Lynnie bustled over. "Anything else, ladies?"

Deirdre replied for both of them, "No, thank you, Lynnie."

Gwen opened her mouth to greet Lynnie. Before she could say a word, Deirdre glared at her and mouthed, "Shut up."

Gwen scowled at her sponsor. *What's up with that?*

Lynnie hesitated a second before she said, "Sure, no problem. It will be quiet now until noon."

To Gwen, her voice sounded puzzled and a little hurt. *No wonder*. She offered Lynnie a weak smile, and Lynnie left them to their conversation.

"What was that about?" Gwen whispered.

"If you'd said one word, Lynnie would have talked for an hour." Deirdre raised an eyebrow.

"Maybe, but it felt rude."

"Sorry, I've only got half an hour, and I really need to know what's going on in your head and in your life. Back to breakfast with Peter, please."

Gwen made a mental note that something was off with her sponsor. It didn't happen often, and it usually had something to do with Vince. She continued her breakfast story. "The three of us laughed and had an interesting conversation. Then, as I said, Peter convinced her to contact Rick. After breakfast Peter fixed the lock Haley had broken, and he asked about the old canoe. It had been sitting up on the rafters in the garage for . . . probably decades. I'd never given it a moment's thought. Tired as he was, he helped me get it down and out to the lawn. I can't tell you how excited I am at the thought of paddling that canoe with him, Deirdre." A smile curved her lips.

Deirdre reached across the table and tapped Gwen's fingers. "Nice nails. You've been to the spa. And your hair is gorgeous. I like the upswept wave on one side."

"I do, too. I'm going to tuck in a couple of sparkly bobby pins for the dinner dance."

"What's the occasion?"

"It's to honor Chief Barker as he retires. I have a hunch Joel arranged it all," Gwen told her. She pointed to Deirdre's mug. "More?"

Deirdre shook her head. "It wouldn't surprise me. Joel

was so appreciative of the chief's handling of the situation with Manda and the pervert professor. After that, Joel made a complete turnaround in his relationship with the police. There had been years and years of animosity between the police and Joel's forefathers."

That sounded like an exaggeration to Gwen, and, again, she wondered what was up with Deirdre.

"So what are you wearing for your first date with Mr. Right?" Deirdre asked.

"His name is Peter." Gwen blushed. "The dress is amazing."

"Sexy?"

"All out, Deirdre. Slinky, shot through with silver threads, low-cut, scoop neckline, sequins across the boobs. It makes the most of what I have in the cleavage department, and I love what it does with my shoulders and hips."

"Sounds like you're prepared for Peter to do all-out things with your shoulders and hips?" Deirdre's smile was wicked. "And maybe your boobs, too?"

Gwen shivered in happy anticipation. "Deirdre, I saw him standing by the canoe in those curve-hugging jeans with the sweaty T-shirt clinging to his pecs and biceps and incredible shoulders. And I wanted him. I swear if Haley hadn't been in the house and he hadn't been dead on his feet after working his night shift . . ."

"You've got it bad, Dr. Forrester."

Gwen gave a full, lusty laugh.

"I think Haley arrived at exactly the right time to keep you from going too fast with this man."

"You mean, the universe is doing for me what I can't do for myself?"

"Exactly." Deirdre patted Gwen's hand. "I like it that you're hot for a great-looking guy, Gwen, but I need you to think about what you said when you dumped Ned the night before last."

"It feels like a week ago." Gwen sipped her coffee.

"To my point, do you remember what you told me?" Gwen squinted.

"About what you want in a man?" Deirdre prompted.

Gwen flattened her fingers on the tabletop. She searched the far corner of the room, in vain, then licked her lips and admitted, "No."

"It was something about eye candy and a hot car being okay when you're twenty but not when you're thirty." Deirdre cocked her head.

"I'm thirty-two," Gwen corrected. "Peter drives a cute little Jeep."

"Oh, what color?" she said with sarcasm.

"Dark green. Same as the old canoe."

"And he'd make beautiful babies with you, but back to my point: Is he what you want in a life partner, Gwen?"

Gwen slid her hands off the table and balled up the napkin in her lap. "How can I know after knowing him one day? I'll learn more tonight and, hopefully, have fun with him. Does that work for you?"

"A little huffy, are we?" Deirdre sat back and eyed her sponsee.

Gwen met her gaze evenly. "Deirdre, how's everything with Vince?"

"I think he's got a honey on the side." Deirdre's mouth tightened. "I hadn't meant to say anything."

Gwen eyes flashed as she hissed. "The snake! What are you going to do?"

Deirdre shrugged. "It remains to be seen." Her abrupt statement closed the discussion.

"Okay, but please know I'm here for you if I can help."

"Thank you. I don't have a good track record with picking the right husband, Gwen. Psychologists have their blind spots, just like everyone else."

"And you think I have a similar blind spot?" Gwen probed.

"Let's just say I would hate to see you marry in haste and have beautiful babies, only to raise them all alone, like I did before Vince came into my life. I think, of all the psychologists I know in our area, you're the only one that had a stable upbringing. You have a chance at a stable marriage. Don't blow it, just because this guy rings your chimes."

Deirdre took off her glasses and tucked them into their case.

"That's why I have a sponsor. Thank you, Deirdre. Sometimes I hate your tough love, but it's what I need."

Chapter 4

"Officer Peter Shaughnessy and date," Peter announced to the hostess, whose nametag identified her as Brandi. She jiggled a pen as she scanned the long list of attendees.

Gwen stood proudly at Peter's side, basking in the warmth of his hand on her hip. Their gazes connected, and she read desire in his eyes.

Finally, Brandi favored Peter with a dazzling smile. "Table four. Follow me." She confided to Gwen as they approached the table, "Your dress is stunning, the most beautiful I've seen tonight."

"Thank you," Gwen murmured.

Brandi winked. "You'll outshine the chiefs' wives."

Uh-oh. Maybe she would sit unobtrusively at the table tonight.

Brandi told them, "You're sitting with this evening's hosts, Joel and Manda Cushman, and Officer Sam Pinelli and his date."

What a relief.

"We have our pick of seats." Peter gestured to their round table.

"Almost. I recognize Joel's cane on that chair." She pointed. "And Manda's purse on the next one. If we keep up the girl-boy-girl-boy, I'll sit next to Joel with you on my right. Sound good?"

"Works for me. Can I get you a drink?"

"There should be bottles of sparkling water." She touched Peter's arm, and pointed to a long table with two-dozen, tall, blue bottles. "Saratoga Water. It's Joel and Manda's favorite."

"I'll bring a bottle for the table."

Gwen sat gracefully on a linen-covered chair and admired the white tablecloth and elegant place settings. Light from the chandeliers sparkled in the silverware and danced in the glasses of ice water. She was mesmerized by the play of light until a firm hand touched her shoulder.

"Imagine seeing my friend Gwen here tonight," Joel Cushman greeted her.

"Surprise." She lifted her cheek for his kiss.

"In truth, I had plenty of warning." His gray-green eyes twinkled with good humor. "Tony told me he expected you'd be coming with Sam's partner."

"The Tompkins Falls grapevine is amazing." She laughed. "I just met Sam and Peter Friday night."

"Ah, but wait." Joel held up his hand. "The town grapevine took second place to the Manse grapevine on this one. First, Sara told Manda, who thought she had the scoop. But she waited to tell me until she and Sara got back from their thrift-shop adventure yesterday."

"In that case, Tony beat Manda to it," Gwen said with mock seriousness. "The town grapevine wins, Joel."

"That debate is still being waged, by text, as we speak." At Gwen's laugh, Joel pleaded, "Do not encourage her."

"Or contradict her, I get it."

Peter set down a chilled, dripping bottle in front of them.

"Thanks, man." Joel held out his hand. "Don't crush. I'm still recuperating."

Peter introduced himself and gave Joel a restrained handshake. "I noticed the cane."

"At just eight months, I'm walking without it most mornings. My doctors are astounded. They think Gianessa has magic powers, which she does." He added, for Peter's benefit, "Gianessa is my physical therapist, recently wedded to my uncle Justin."

"Hi, everybody." Manda's excited voice announced her arrival. The hem of her ice-blue silk gown swirled around her ankles as she moved in on Gwen for a hug. She beamed her appreciation as her eyes swept over Gwen's dress.

Peter introduced himself and held Manda's chair. "Allow me."

Manda thanked him and mouthed to Gwen, "He's handsome." Gwen winked.

Peter eased himself onto the chair next to Gwen's. "I know Gwen and Joel grew up in Tompkins Falls," he said to Manda, "but how did *you* meet them?"

"Um," Manda hesitated, "I work for the Manse in the accounting office?"

Gwen jumped in. "And Manda and I are both bike-riders. We've logged some serious miles together in the last year and a half."

"Right. And Sara, who's coming with your partner Sam, works here at the Spa." She leaned across Joel and informed Gwen in a conspiratorial whisper, "They are really, really serious."

"Sam and Sara?"

Manda's sapphire eyes were round with excitement as she nodded. "I think they're great together."

Peter stood at Sam and Sara's arrival. "Just in time," he told his partner. "The ladies were talking about you." He and Sam bumped knuckles.

"Sara, meet my partner, Peter Shaughnessy." Sam's hand lingered on Sara's lower back. "You know everyone else."

Sara held out a dainty hand for Peter's handshake. She blew kisses to Gwen, Joel, and Manda. Her dress was a long, off-white sheath that showed off her slender hips. The only adornment was a bright-pink, faux flower at her waist that matched the shock of pink in her short blond locks. She chose the chair next to Manda's, and Sam sat shoulder-to-shoulder with Peter.

Gwen traded a nod with Manda and whispered, "She's glowing."

After a few minutes of small talk, Joel cautioned, "Dinner is served."

They sat back as the waiter delivered their choice of prime rib or grilled salmon. Sam and Peter tucked into prime rib while the rest of the table went for salmon.

Manda and Sara kept the discussion lively through dinner, interspersing each topic with questions for Peter. "Tell us about your family," "Where did you grow up?" "Do you miss Syracuse?" "Do you like kids?"

Peter handled the interrogation with good humor. Gwen rubbed his back, squeezed his arm, patted his thigh, smiled sideways—whatever she could, to let him know how much she sympathized and appreciated his cooperation as her friends checked him out.

Peter volunteered that he had grown up "pretty poor" in Syracuse. His mother was a nurse who worked multiple jobs, and his dad was an alcoholic who couldn't hold a job or stay sober. He loved his younger sister, Bree, who had survived a few scrapes with the law in her teens. "Glad I could pull some strings for her," he said without making eye contact with anyone at the table.

When no one responded to that, Manda asked him, "And is she in recovery now?"

"Not necessary," Peter told them, his mouth a grim line. "I forbid her to be an alcoholic."

Manda gasped and leaned forward.

Before she could say another word, Joel's hand stroked her arm from shoulder to wrist. She turned to him, and he leaned close. Gwen overheard his quiet, "Let's not argue that in this forum."

Manda nodded, flashed a worried glance at Gwen, and pressed her eyes shut.

Sam, oblivious of the whispered exchange, jabbed his partner with his elbow. "How's that working for you, Peter?" he said with a friendly chuckle.

"Working fine. I haven't heard a word since then about cures for hangovers or drunken parties or crashing all night at Susie's camp on the lake."

Sara piped up, "Gwen, you look amazing tonight."

"Why thank you, master hairstylist."

"Sara," Joel said, "I understand you're planning a new business. I'd love to hear more."

Sara's blush spread up her neck and into her cheeks.

"Please tell us," Gwen urged.

Sam reached an arm along Sara's shoulders. "Don't be nervous."

"It's—it's kind of in the early stages."

"But it's going to be fabulous," Manda told them.

Gwen gave Sara a chance to regroup. "You're graduating soon, aren't you?"

Sara took a sip of water and fanned her face with her hand. "December. I'm getting my MBA from RIT," she said for Peter's benefit.

"Very impressive."

"Sara is my inspiration," Manda said. "Tell them how long it took you."

"Four years, part time. And I commuted from here to Rochester, just like Manda's doing."

"If you can finish, I can finish," Manda asserted. "It's just one more year."

"But you're going for your CPA, too, right?" Gwen pressed.

"Manda, you're in accounting?" Sam shuddered. "I can't do numbers to save myself. Tools, no problem. Legal codes and procedures, piece of cake. Talk a hungry dog off a meat wagon, just watch me."

The table erupted in laughter.

Peter concurred. "It's true. My partner can get a pair of handcuffs on anyone without laying a finger on them."

"Do I need to worry?" Sara eyed Sam.

Sam kissed her temple and whispered something that made her blush again.

"Where did you ever get that expression?" Gwen asked. "Talk a hungry dog off a meat wagon?"

"My Grandma Callahan said it all the time."

"Wait, wait, wait," Joel said. "The Pinellis have an Irish grandmother named Callahan? Why didn't I ever hear this?"

"Yeah, we do. Why?"

"So does Joel," Manda answered. "Bridie O'Donohue."

"Tompkins," Joel finished the name. "I'm surprised you haven't heard the tales about her."

"Like what?" Sam and Peter asked in unison.

"She read tea leaves, for one thing," Joel told them, with a twinkle in his gray-green eyes. "And Manda and I have encountered a little magic in her attic at 14 Lakeside Terrace, that she might have left behind." He stole a glance at his wife, whose face glowed with pleasure. "And Justin had a couple of uncanny experiences when he first moved into my place on the third floor."

"So did Gianessa," Gwen added.

"You mean here at the Manse when she and I threw our bouquets, right?" Manda nodded.

Everyone seemed puzzled.

Manda said to Sara, "You remember. Gianessa and I threw our bouquets side by side after her wedding. We expected Sara and Grace to grab the bouquets, but mine went way off course, to that beautiful woman in the sari."

"Who, by the way, had an engagement party here yesterday," Joel told them.

"Cool."

Sara cleared her throat and finished Manda's story, with a hint of jealousy in her voice. "And the bouquet with my name on it"—she gestured with a flourish—"landed in Gwen's hands."

Peter's turned to Gwen, and a smile broke over his face.

Gwen dropped her gaze to the tablecloth. Her cheeks flamed, and her fingers trembled.

Peter captured her hand and warmed it.

Joel asked how everyone liked the meal, and Gwen gave him a grateful smile. "Delicious," she said.

They had pushed their plates away and sat sipping coffee, when the band launched into its first number, a lively swing. Sam called across the table, "Manda." His arms and shoulders imitated hers as they moved to the music. "You want to dance?"

After a whispered conversation with Joel, she said, "Sure." Sam took her hand, and they threaded among the tables to the dance floor.

"How about you and me, Peter?" Sara asked.

"I don't know," he hedged, with a question in his eyes for Gwen.

Gwen squeezed his thigh under the table. "Go for it. I've never been much of a dancer."

Sara rushed him onto the floor, leaving Joel and Gwen at the table.

"He's a good sport," Joel told her.

Gwen tipped her head with a little smile. "Yeah, he is. I've learned more about him tonight than I have since we met."

"Which was Friday, you said. How did you meet?"

Gwen recounted Haley's break-in and her first encounter with Sam and Peter.

"Two whole days, and he rates the most elegant dress at the dance?"

"That was a mistake, wasn't it? Even Brandi knew that."

"I've got to tell her to keep her judgments to herself. But did you notice the hierarchy?"

"I'm clueless, Joel. Educate me."

He nodded toward the incoming and outgoing chiefs, both dancing with their spouses. "Protocol dictates that their wives are by far the most gussied up. Followed by the spouses of the visiting chiefs—Canandaigua and Geneva, I think." He pointed across the room. "And Seneca Falls and Clifton Springs, I'm pretty sure. The custom applies on down the ranks."

"This is when I need our old friend Lorraine advising me."

Joel burst out with a laugh that got Manda's attention, on the dance floor. He waved at his wife and turned back to Gwen. "Don't go by Lorraine's advice. She'd tell you to ditch Peter and find a millionaire."

"Absolutely, she would." Gwen sipped her Saratoga water. "You've got to admit, though, she does know about things like fashion protocol."

"Have you been in touch with her?" Joel sat back and eyed her.

"We Skype every so often. I'm crazy about her boys, who are growing like weeds." She expected Joel to smile at that. Instead, he squinted, his brow deeply furrowed.

"You know she blocked our every effort to purchase Cady's Point for Manda's holistic wellness center?"

"Seriously? That's unfortunate."

"I suppose there are other properties, but Manda really believes that's the right place to build, since it was used as a sacred healing ground by the Native Americans."

Gwen took a swallow of sparkling water. "I hope Manda won't give up on her idea."

Joel shrugged. "Remains to be seen. She's working hard on her business plan, hoping for a miracle. And Lorraine will find a duke one of these days," Joel predicted, his tone heavy with sarcasm. Lorraine had been his fiancée until he'd dumped her a few years earlier.

"And in her absence, thanks for the fashion lesson," Gwen said lightly.

"*Faux pas* aside, you are stunning tonight. Peter looks at you like you're edible."

"That's the most delicious compliment I've had in a decade." Gwen's eyes sparkled.

Joel's gaze focused on the outgoing chief. "I remember when Chief Barker arrested me after my car slammed into a bowling alley. He knew that, even though I was only fourteen, I was hell-bent on self-destruction. He and my uncle Justin worked their butts off to get me into treatment for substance abuse and into psychotherapy. I hated them for it, but I wouldn't be alive today if they hadn't taken the stand they did. Getting away from Tompkins Falls for prep school, college, and grad school helped me make a new life for myself."

"It must have been hard to come back here, reconnect with people who knew you at your worst. Yet you established a successful business and made a new reputation as a community leader."

Joel acknowledged the praise with a brief nod, but his face was grim. "I don't like the sound of Peter's response to his sister's alcohol abuse."

Gwen recognized a trademark Joel Cushman maneuver, to introduce a difficult subject, like alcoholism, in a personal way, and then slam home an irrefutable, uncomfortable point.

"I agree. This is the first I've heard about his father. There's a lot of bitterness and denial when he tells it, isn't there?"

"Does he know you're in recovery?" Joel asked.

"Well, of course, he does," Gwen said, flustered. "He knows all about my practice."

Joel's eyes were slits.

The swing tune ended, and Gwen's attention went to the dance floor. Sam and Peter traded partners just as an old-fashioned jitterbug started up. Since neither couple knew the moves, they stood back with the others to cheer on the masters.

Chief Barker and one of the visiting chiefs rocked the crowd as they twisted with the beat and twirled their long-time dance partners. The number blared to a finish, followed by whistles and deafening applause.

The elder chief yelled to the bandleader, "How about a couple of slow ones now?" He patted his heart and laughed along with his wife. "We're not getting any younger, you know."

His wife swatted his arm and planted a kiss on his cheek. The band obliged with the opening bars of "Getting Sentimental Over You."

Sam and Sara moved into each other's arms.

Peter and Manda trailed back to the table. Manda stopped at Joel's side, then bent down for a kiss and a whispered exchange.

Peter stood behind Gwen and massaged her shoulders. She sighed blissfully and closed her eyes.

Manda's voice roused her. "Time for us to say goodnight."

Joel leaned heavily on his ebony-headed cane. "Grand meeting you, Peter."

"Same." Peter shook his outstretched hand and waved to Manda. "Fantastic party for a legendary chief."

Joel beamed.

Gwen stood to kiss their hosts.

When they were alone, Peter asked her, "Dance?"

"There's supposed to be a moon tonight." Gwen stroked his arm. "How about a walk down to the garden where Joel and Manda were married a few months ago?"

Peter touched his warm lips to her cool cheek. "Let's."

Haley opened the oven and slid out a ceramic baking dish. The aroma of tomatoes, basil, and oregano swirled around her as she carried it to the island and set it on a trivet.

"Lasagna." Rick's eyes devoured the steaming pasta. "I'm saved from starvation!"

"You always know how to make me happy," Haley told him, and her bubbling laugh filled the kitchen.

"How can I help get the meal on the table?"

"Placemats are in that middle drawer." She pointed.

"Dishes and glasses in the cabinets above. Silverware in the bins on the counter."

Rick set their places, then stood studying the wall of cabinets. "They really knew how to build storage a hundred fifty years ago."

"Gwen said that was part of the pantry. She knocked down the other walls to open the space, put in the island, and made the kitchen her favorite room. I love the marble countertops and gray paint colors. I'm always relaxed in this room."

A wireless router blinked over Rick's head. He spotted a roll-top desk with a padded stool tucked in a nook. "Does she have a laptop in the old desk?"

"She does. Her office—she's a psychologist—is down the hall, but she does her personal business here."

He added blue cloth napkins beside the plates. "She's cool with you being here?"

Haley set the basket of Italian bread next to the salad.

"Haley?" Rick waited a beat before he asked, "You okay?"

She nodded and licked her lips. "We need to talk seriously, but I need to eat first." Tight lines had appeared around her mouth, and her hands shook.

"Agreed. You sit down, and I'll do whatever."

Haley let him pour their iced teas while she made herself comfortable on a stool across from him.

"While we eat," he said with an easy smile, "I'll tell you about my summer, if you'll tell me about yours."

"Deal. You go first." She blew on a forkful of lasagna.

Rick got her laughing about his hot, tedious research job on the beaches and wetlands of the Florida Panhandle, while the carbs and crisp salads restored their energy.

Haley regaled him with the foibles of the wealthy patrons at her summer job in Saratoga.

"Good tippers?"

"Very good tippers. And plenty of opportunity to steer them to my prints and posters in the gift shops around town."

"Your bottom line for May through July was higher than I've ever seen. Are you sure you want a career in botany? You're a fantastic graphic artist, Haley, and you know how to please your clientele."

"Thank you for saying that," Haley said with a proud smile. "I do want to finish my degree in botany, but I don't know where I'm going with it."

When both of them were full, Rick slid off his stool and gathered their dishes. "I'm cleaning up, and I want you to sit still and keep talking."

Haley swiveled so she could watch him at the sink. "You can just put those in the dishwasher, you know."

He flashed a grin back at her. "I could, but I need to do something with my hands while we talk." He scraped the plates and bowls, put leftovers into the refrigerator, and listened to her talk about everything except her pregnancy.

The garbage disposal interrupted her for a minute. When it finished, he reminded her, "You were going to tell me how Gwen feels about you being here."

"Okay, I guess it's time."

He nodded and began drying the plates and bowls with a watchful eye on her.

She opened with, "Did you know that Ursula got pregnant with me when she was eighteen, and her father made my dad marry her?"

Rick's lost his grip on a bowl. Haley gasped. He grabbed it before it hit the floor. He set the bowl and the dishtowel on the counter and walked a few paces toward her. "Have you always known that?"

She shook her head. "My mother told me when she threw me out in June. Dad quit college, and it took years for him to get his degree." She sat tall. "I talked to Dad about it, and he admitted it and told me about slowly becoming an alcoholic, drinking to escape his life with Ursula." She reached behind her for her glass of iced tea and took a big gulp.

He nodded for her to continue, his forehead creased with worry.

"I looked really hard at how I'd gotten pregnant—forgetting my pills and drinking the eggnog, even though I knew I couldn't handle anything spiked. Rick, you probably didn't know I'd had some scary experiences with drinking last fall."

"Evidently, I wasn't with you those times?"

"No. I'd gone out with some of the girls from my art class, and it wasn't good. This summer, when I stopped working at the diner, I had time to think about all of that, and I knew I needed to talk to Gwen. I don't know if I'm crazy like Ursula, besides being pregnant like she was. And I don't know if I'm an alcoholic like Dad, or just a potential one. But I know that I'm afraid about what happened." She licked her lower lip and bit it. "And I'm really scared that you'll . . ."

"That I'll what?"

"You'll feel an obligation to me and the baby that will mess up your hopes and dreams."

Rick walked the remaining distance and stood in front of her. "I have an obligation. I don't know what I'm going to do about it." He pushed a lock of hair away from her eyes. "Yet."

Haley searched his face. "I'm having a really hard time giving up this baby, but I know that's what I need to do."

"So, you don't want to get married and have us raise the baby together?"

Haley's eyes widened with fear. "No!" Tears spilled over. "I love you, Rick, but—"

"Come here," he coaxed.

She slid off the stool and let his arms enfold her. She cried for what seemed like an hour but was probably just a minute.

Rick rested his chin on top of her head and rubbed her back. "Let's take it a little at a time. We'll see your new doctor tomorrow. We'll talk with Gwen. We'll explore the options. And we'll talk about it as we go along."

She nodded against his chest.

"How about a walk right now? The moon should be up."

"What do you think of our host?" Gwen asked Peter.

"Joel? He's elegant, there's no other word for his style. And smart, I think."

"Yes," Gwen confirmed. "Shrewd, but with integrity." She inhaled the warm breeze off the lake and waved an arm in the direction of the garden a hundred yards ahead, nearly to the lakeshore. "That's where we're going, by the way."

"Manda livens him up," Peter said with a chuckle.

"They're good for each other."

"We're good for each other. Don't you think?"

"I do." Gwen stopped on the lush lawn and turned to face him. "The more I know you, the more I think so." She took his elbow, and they continued their stroll.

After a minute, Peter tugged at her hand and pointed to a lustrous bulge on the horizon across the lake. "Is that what I think it is?"

"Ohmigod, it's the moon rising. Can you believe how huge and orange it is?"

"You're sure it's not Otto the Syracuse Orange?"

"Oh, now, that's romantic." Gwen elbowed him playfully.

"A little Syracuse levity. I *can* do romantic."

"I have no doubt. What new truths did Manda and Sara get out of you on the dance floor?"

"They both think I should have my sister, Bree, come for a weekend, and they'll show her around. They'll take her shopping at their favorite thrift shops and show her the best ice-cream places."

"Take them up on it. I'd love to meet her." As they continued their stroll to the garden, the moon lifted above the horizon and softened to gold.

"I want her to move here and live with me for a while." His voice grew more hesitant as he finished the sentence.

"You don't sound sure about that."

"I was just thinking it's hard enough with my schedule for us to spend time together. Tonight is one example, having to cut it short for my shift. Having Bree live with me would make it even harder."

Gwen mused. "That's true, especially if Haley stays with me for a while." She smiled over at him. "It sounds like we've both made a decision to see each other again."

"See each other a lot, I hope?"

Gwen nodded.

With his hand on her waist, he drew her closer to his side and planted a kiss on her neck that sent delicious shivers to her toes.

"So, you think Haley will stay with you?" he asked.

"I'll let you know. I still haven't got out of her why she has sought me out, but I think she needs me for a while."

"You're not thinking she wants to keep the baby and live with you?"

Gwen's mouth opened, and no words came out.

"I can tell that was a shocker." He captured her hand and interlaced his fingers with hers.

"That's a possibility I hadn't considered." Gwen let out her breath in a *whoosh*. "And, no, I wouldn't entertain that."

"Why?"

"Honestly, I'm not sure, but I need to have an answer ready if she brings it up."

"Want to talk about it?"

The moon rolled out a shimmering ribbon of gold across Chestnut Lake. Gwen turned to him. "I'd rather kiss you under the full moon, Officer Shaughnessy." She slid her hands along the shoulders of his jacket.

"Your dress sparkles like silver." He ran his hands down her sides, over her hips and onto her backside.

She brought her lips close to his.

His hungry kiss made her breasts swell and her nipples pop.

When he let her up for air, she whispered, "Pretty hot first kiss."

"Want more?"

She traced his lower lip with one finger. "I do."

The next kiss was deeper, more demanding. Gwen pressed against him, and he wrapped her tight in his arms. Tingles radiated from her core.

"If we weren't so visible here, I'd undress you and kiss every inch of you."

Gwen glanced at the moon, with a throaty chuckle. "We'd want privacy for that. And a warm bed."

"You're not cold?"

"A little. It's what I get for not watching the weather report."

"Then it's lucky I'm still hot from dancing. Let's find a private corner, and I'll share some of my heat with the most beautiful lady at the ball." Peter circled her shoulders with his arm and held her close as they entered the garden.

After a few steps, he pointed to a shadowy nook on the upper terrace. The fragrance of late-summer flowers enveloped them as they passed—heady lilies, sweet syringa, and calming lavender. Gwen inhaled the aromas and exhaled a sigh.

"Happy?"

"Supremely."

Peter touched the planes of her face like a sculptor enchanted with his own creation. He planted little kisses along one cheekbone, down to the tip of her chin and up to the other cheek as she laughed with pleasure.

His mouth was on hers, his tongue teasing her lips.

Raking her fingers through the thick waves of his dark hair, she lost herself in the kiss.

"Beautiful," he whispered as he caressed her hips.

She pressed against his erection and he held her there, tight, and moved just enough to make her exhale with desire.

"I like you breathless." His voice was husky in her ear.

"I do, too," she confessed. Waves of pleasure coursed through her as he nuzzled her neck and nibbled her ear.

"You're killing me, Peter," she whispered.

He studied her face, his eyes dark with desire. A satisfied smile stole across his face.

"We should stop," she whispered.

He stepped back. "I'm going to dream about this my whole shift."

Chapter 5

Gwen dumped the contents of her tiny silver evening bag onto the counter and sorted through it. The cocktail napkin she'd used to blot her lipstick reminded her she'd meant to talk with Peter about his mistaken beliefs about his sister's drinking. *How did I forget that?* She picked up the tube of Plum Passion lipstick, and a smile curved her mouth. *That's how.*

"Hi, Gwen." A deep voice interrupted her musing.

Gwen sucked in a startled breath. A tall, young man slouched against the doorway to her living room. Rick, she thought, but radically different from the cheerful, easy-going boyfriend she'd met at Christmas.

"Sorry, I didn't mean to scare you." He came toward her with a grim smile, his arm outstretched. "I'm Rick Walker. We met at Haley's over the holidays."

"Of course, Rick." Gwen rushed to shake his hand. "I'm still in a daze from my date." Although she knew from his haggard face that it hadn't gone well, she gave him a warm smile and kept her voice light when she asked, "How did it go with you and Haley?"

"That's what I need to talk about. I waited up."

"You know what—" She gazed longingly at the evening bag. *So much for sweet, sexy dreams.* "If you'll make us some tea or coffee, Rick, I'll run upstairs for a quick change. Sequins don't go with problem solving."

That rated a hollow laugh.

"Oh, and get some cookies out of the freezer, too. I can't think on an empty stomach."

She gathered the long skirt of her dress in one hand and flew up the stairs. A quick check of Haley's room showed her sleeping, her face set in a frown. Gwen kissed her cheek, which was still damp with tears.

After changing into sweats and tugging on soft socks, she paused. *God, I'm scared. I'm all these kids have right now*. Just saying it calmed her. She squared her shoulders. As she descended the stairs, she put on her professional face for Rick, detached and nonjudgmental. She softened a little, so he'd know she was in his corner.

"Did you find any chocolate chip cookies?"

"Haley and I finished those on you. Peanut butter okay, and coffee? It's decaf."

"Great." She perched on a stool at the island.

"Cream and sugar?"

"Just sugar."

Rick set two steaming mugs on the marble surface in front of her and brought a plate of cookies with him to sit across from her. "I really lost it after supper tonight." He hunched over his mug and toyed with it, pushing the handle to the left, then right, back and forth.

Gwen wanted to still his hand, but, at the same time, she marveled that his mug made no noise on the hard marble surface. *Focus, Gwen*. "Lost it how, Rick?"

"We went for a walk to your beach. I tried to get her to talk more about the baby and what she wants. At first, she just cried. She feels like a total screw-up, and she's panicked about what to do next. Has she talked to you?"

"Not much. And not about the baby."

He recounted what Haley had told him, that she'd been getting drunk off and on last fall with her girlfriends, and that drugs had become part of their evenings out.

Rick said, "It scared her so much that she stopped drinking and stopped going out with those friends, before the end of the semester. I believe her that she hasn't used any drugs since then. But she forgot to pack her birth-control pills for the holiday break, and she got drunk on some really potent eggnog at a party we went to, and we had hot sex after. That's how she got pregnant.

"Gwen, she never once talked to me about any of that or asked for help or . . ." He shook his head. "I never imagined she was in trouble, in any of those ways. Even thinking back, there was nothing I could have picked up on."

"What you've described sounds like Haley's shadow side coming out after years of having to be perfect for Ursula. Which we know is impossible. I didn't know about the drinking, let alone the drugs. I'll have a tough conversation with her about that. You know her dad is an alcoholic? And I am, too."

Rick gave a brusque nod and continued. "So tonight we took a walk. When we came around the trees to where we could see the beach, the moon was shining on the water. And, unfortunately, a swarm of mosquitoes came out of nowhere and attacked us. I completely lost it." His voice rose in agitation. "I started waving my arms around and screaming at them to stop hurting her. It scared her, and she ran back toward the house and fell and—"

"Is she hurt?" Gwen gripped his arm.

"She says not."

"We can take her to the hospital, if you think we should," Gwen insisted.

"No. Really. She went down on one knee and caught herself with her hands. She said the baby's fine." Rick hung his head and cursed himself. "She cried all the way back to the house, just really upset."

Gwen withdrew her hand. "What scared her, Rick? The mosquitoes?"

He shook his head. "Me, screaming like a madman."

"Do you usually?"

"I've never done anything like that. I'm always this quiet, steady guy."

Gwen reached for another cookie and broke off a piece. *Make it last. Stress eating is not the solution.* "That was my impression when I met you. What got you screaming?"

Rick jumped off the stool and yelled, "Those fucking mosquitoes were biting her, and she couldn't get free of them. I couldn't stand it."

Heart hammering, Gwen listened for any sound that would indicate he might have disturbed Haley's sleep. Quiet reigned upstairs.

Gwen's entire cookie had mysteriously vanished. She touched her mouth. Crumbs on her chin and around her lips told her where that cookie had gone.

Rick's jaw clenched as he paced around the perimeter of the kitchen. "I had to do something, make them stop."

"I'm sure that was frightening for her and infuriating for you." Gwen kept her voice steady.

Rick made another circuit and, as he paced, ran the fingers of one hand through his short blond hair so it stood up in clumps like a mad scientist who'd stuck his finger in a light socket. The comical effect almost made her laugh, and the tension drained out of her.

She replayed what she knew about Rick, through Haley. He came from a poor family and, through dedication and hard work, had gotten a full scholarship to Rensselaer, one of the premier engineering schools in the northeast. All that control failed him tonight. Small wonder. His beautiful girlfriend was in trouble and he didn't know how to help her.

To give Rick a break from his own intensity, she pointed out, "You've been scratching at a few mosquito bites on your neck and the backs of your hands. There's calamine lotion in the hall closet near the bathroom."

He stopped at the sink and scowled across the room at her.

She explained, "Sometimes it helps to identify the pieces of the problem and start with the easy fixes. Mosquito bites can be neutralized with calamine lotion."

"Thank you. I never thought of it."

"Go get some, and then we'll talk some more." She refilled her coffee and did a few stretches until she heard his footsteps in the hallway.

Rick came back to the island wearing polka dots of calamine. "That helps, you're right." He slid onto the stool, picked up a cookie—his first—and took a big bite. "These are good," he mumbled with his mouthful. "All your cookies are good."

"The secret is in the vanilla. Always double what the recipe calls for."

They munched for a minute. Rick placed his palms on the marble and sat tall. The deep wrinkles in his forehead smoothed out. "So you're saying my brain can help with some of this?"

"Yes, actually, with a lot of it."

"How can we help Haley?"

"We'll take it a day at a time." Gwen rubbed the crumbs from her hands. "I'd like the three of us to talk at breakfast, to strategize about the doctor's appointment. I have clients off and on all day, but I can be on call for you, both of you. We'll work together and take things as they come. How does that sound?"

"It sounds good, but I have to tell you I'm scared to death. Mostly for Haley."

"No surprise. Does it help to have my support?"

"Definitely."

She pressed his forearm. "Rick, there are serious decisions you and Haley need to make, pretty quickly. She only has two more months until the baby comes."

"I think her math is off. I think it's sooner."

Gwen swallowed. "Be sure you ask the doctor tomorrow. And I want you to find out all you can about adoption. I'm not sure Haley's able to do that herself right now."

Rick shook crumbs off his hands, brushed them into a pile on the marble, and swept them with his right hand into his left. He emptied them into the sink and came back with a damp paper towel. He looked her in the eye for the first time. "Do you think she's capable of raising this baby on her own?"

Gwen had a queasy feeling in her stomach. "I think Haley can do almost anything she sets her mind to, but I haven't heard her say that's what she wants. Did she tell you that?"

"The only thing I know for sure is, she won't let me quit school and marry her." He sank down on his stool. "I never knew her father married Ursula when she got pregnant with Haley, and he quit college to support them."

Really? She'd do the math another time, but that revelation was probably the truth. She and her brother, Bill, were overdue for a conversation. "Rick, are you saying you want to quit school and marry Haley?" *God, please, no.*

"I know it's the right thing to do." His mouth was a grim line.

"That wasn't my question, though. Is it what you want to do next with your life?"

Rick exhaled hard and pressed his eyelids with his fingers, but not before a few tears escaped. He shook his head.

"Good. You don't want that. Haley doesn't want that. Don't do it." Gwen nudged a box of tissues toward him. "Besides calamine lotion in the closet, I have boxes of tissue all over the house, one in every room. Help yourself anytime."

He croaked a laugh and extracted a few tissues from the box.

"Rick, you're dead on your feet, and I'm not far behind. Go on up to bed while I clean up here. I'll make breakfast at nine, and the three of us will have our strategy session then. If you're up before that, just make yourself at home."

"Thanks, Gwen. I'm sorry you got dragged into this."

"I'm not." Gwen smiled. "I'm just glad Haley finally reached out for help. Like you, I had no idea she was in trouble, and that makes me crazy."

"Tell me about it."

A few days without a bike ride had taken their toll, mentally and physically. Gwen fastened a helmet on her muddled head and hauled her bike out the side door of the garage. A glimpse of the lake through the break in the trees revealed a layer of fog swirling above the charcoal water in the pre-dawn light. Clouds above the western shore blushed as the sun rose; they shifted briefly to reveal the golden full moon as it slipped below the rim of the hills.

Her heart swelled with happiness, not just from the memory of last night's moon and Peter's kisses. Witnessing the transient morning beauty always brought her peace and, with it, a connection to some greater force that was both enriching and enduring.

She pedaled hard up the steep, twisting lower section of her road. The wheels of her bike spit gravel. Her muscles scolded her for the days she'd skipped. When she reached the gentler middle section—a curving tunnel of trees—her mind chattered a chorus of 'shoulds.' She should be fixing breakfast for Haley and Rick. She shouldn't have worn such an elegant dress last night. She should have challenged Peter about his attitude toward his sister's drinking. She should talk with Haley about her drinking.

This is crazy. Why am I so stressed?

The events of the past few days—Haley's break-in and her pregnancy, Peter's arrival in her life that, thankfully, disrupted her go-nowhere dating pattern, their magical moment in the rose garden at the Manse—all were happy and wonderful. *Happy stress is still stress.* She sensed angst underneath it all, and she needed to address that, whatever was causing it.

As she often did on her morning ride, Gwen tuned into her surroundings while putting a gentle focus on her inner landscape: her unexamined feelings, her tangled thought process, her heart, her soul. She dismounted and breathed deeply of the cool morning air.

Thin light filtered through the branches overhead. Her eyes strained to see each tree in her woods. Scattered throughout, shafts of white bark popped out of the gray dawn. Those were the white birches her father had planted, a few at a time, decades ago. *Dad, I wish you could see them now, standing out amid the maples, oaks, ash, and evergreens. Tall and strong.*

"Like you."

Gwen gasped. Had someone spoken those words? Had she?

On her left, a head shot up—a doe caught nibbling the tender undergrowth. Gwen stood still as a statue. The doe's ears twitched. Another head lifted, a faun. With a whicker from the doe, the pair stole into the woods, white flag tails waving goodbye.

A smile spread over Gwen's face. Above her, on the right and left, the branches of the ash trees bobbed and swayed. *I should have them examined for Emerald Ash Borer.* That was one 'should' to act on. Soon. Joel had mentioned last night that the Manse had lost two of its ashes last winter; they were fortunate none of the guests were in the woods at the time.

Eyes closed, she listened to a trickle of water somewhere on the hillside, the rustle of leaves, the rub of branches. She opened her eyes and spotted tiny acorns just forming on the oaks. Her lips parted in wonder.

"Haley's baby is meant for someone else." This time she knew she'd spoken the words herself, giving voice to her deepest belief.

She touched her chest, over her heart. Her tension released, and her breathing eased. She rested her hand on her belly. *In good time.*

A chickadee nosedived into the pin oak on her left with a cheerful, *Dee-dee-dee.* Two more arrived and fluttered onto twiggy perches, one to the left, one below. Gwen informed them, "I'm going to have my own little family, starting with a husband."

A fourth arrived with its own chirpy, *Chick-a-dee-dee.*

"All in good time," Gwen told the new arrival.

On some invisible signal, the little flock lifted from the pin oak and flashed by her into the deep woods.

Chilled from standing still after her sprint up the lower hill, she resumed the uphill trek on foot. After the last turn of the tortuous top section of her private road, she mounted her bike and churned to the highway.

With the bike's headlight switched on and the helmet mirror adjusted, she pedaled hard on the right shoulder for the next four miles. Face to the morning breeze, eyes glancing often at the mirror, she kept her mind on the road. Cars, trucks, and vans sped past her. Finally, she rounded the bend at the head of the lake and slowed for the park entrance. With a careful look ahead and behind, she zipped across both lanes and bumped onto the paved access road to the lakeshore.

Peter slammed into the crash bars of the police station and barreled halfway across the parking lot. For his whole damn shift, instead of dreaming about Gwen in his arms in the moonlight, he'd taken flak from every damn person on duty about "the babe with the shiny dress."

Sam, on his heels, yelled, "I'm telling you, they're jealous. Let it go, Peter."

Peter whipped around so fast Sam bumped into him.

"Jesus H. Christ, you'd think it's a crime for me to date a beautiful woman."

"Seriously? That's not what's going on."

With folded arms, Peter pursed his mouth.

"Come on, man." Sam chuckled. "They're bent out of shape that they can't buy a gown like Gwen's for their wives, and it probably started with their wives snipping at them about it. You know how that whole thing works."

"What thing?" Peter spat back.

"The unwritten rules of bureaucratic organizations, one of which is the chiefs' wives are always the best dressed." At Peter's blank face, he explained, "Around here, when a rookie brings a date to an affair, the date is scrutinized by everyone—officers and spouses—and if anyone is put off by anything, there's hell to pay. You just paid up because Gwen outclassed every woman in the place, except possibly Manda Cushman."

Peter flicked a hand in dismissal. "And I suppose Sara escaped without offending anyone?" They walked side-by-side toward their cars at the far end of the lot.

"With that pink stripe in her hair?" Sam hooted. "They'll be talking about that around the station even after we're married." At Peter's chuckle, he nudged him with his elbow. "Good. Made you laugh."

"Sara's a sweetheart. I'm glad you're going to marry her." He huffed. "And it's nobody's fucking business what either of them wears."

"No, but some people don't see it that way. And by the way, Gwen looked hot and classy. I always knew she was classy, but I never got the 'hot' until last night."

Fists clenched, Peter rounded on him.

Sam stepped back and put up his hands in self-defense. "It was a compliment, bro."

"Shit." Peter spat on the asphalt. "I am fucking never going to fit in here."

"That's just stupid. You're a good cop, and we need you. I've learned a lot from you. But some of these guys and their wives are into everyone else's business, and you've got to accept they're going to be in yours, too."

Peter exhaled eight hours of frustration. "Okay, I get it. Thanks, man. I owe you." He held out his palm.

Sam gave him some skin. "No prob." His tone was casual as he said, "You should show up at the gym Saturday afternoon and meet the team. Four o'clock."

"What team?" Peter's eyes lit up.

"We've got a basketball team that takes on police and security guys from other towns and a couple rival Tompkins Falls teams. My brother Tony is captain, and you'll recognize a few other guys."

"Tony's security at the college, right?" Peter racked his memory. "And a carpenter."

"How'd you know that?" Sam challenged.

"Uh . . . Gwen told me." Peter thought back to their conversation in the garage. "Yeah, she was going to call him about replacing that outside garage door Haley damaged. It needed more than a new lock."

Sam cocked his head and studied his partner. "You're going running this morning, right?"

"You're saying I need to go running?" Peter tested.

"I'm saying." Sam confirmed it with a sharp nod. "Man, you've got a hell of a lot of stress to let go of."

"What? Did I make a complete ass of myself all night?"

"Nah. You were cool. But I know you, and I could see you were bottling it up. And the way you blasted out of there a few minutes ago . . . You can't keep doing that. Being a cop in Tompkins Falls may not be as dangerous as Syracuse, but it's got its own stresses. You've got to learn to roll with them."

"Yeah." Peter flipped his keys. "You're right."

Sam's eyes were serious. "Wouldn't want you to let it loose on Gwen."

"Geez, give me a little credit." Peter's face got warm.

"There's too much of that in jobs like ours, and around here we watch out for each other. Chief Barker's training. Nothing personal."

Peter searched his partner's eyes. "Okay. Appreciated."

"So have a good run."

Peter watched his partner saunter across the lot to his Chevy Cruze. *Family guy already. Sara's smart.* As he opened the door of his Jeep, he asked the crucifix hanging from the mirror, "Are you the one that hooked me up with Sam?"

Gwen flew along the willow path twenty feet behind another cyclist. His wake stirred the willow fronds into a dancing frenzy that made Gwen laugh with joy. When she reached the big parking lot at the halfway point, the other cyclist veered off, and Gwen continued for the final mile.

Why so joyful? Granted, she always loved an early morning ride, but Haley's presence and pregnancy were gifts in her life today. And Peter.

She dismounted at the town end of the path and turned her bike around. After switching off the headlight, she kicked off for the return trip. The sun had risen, bringing with it a stiff headwind. Half a mile past the parking lot, she stopped to rest at a picnic table by the shore.

After guzzling a third of her water, she perched on the table and planted her feet firmly on the bench. Eyes on the lake, she peeled off her gloves, unhooked her helmet and set it beside her with the gloves. A quick comb-through with her fingers told her she'd irreparably smushed the sleek hairstyle Sara had given her for the party last night. *No matter.* Enjoying dawn on Chestnut Lake did not require style. She stretched her arms straight overhead, then kneaded a kink in her neck.

Mallard ducks paddled to greet her. "No handout today, guys," she told them. They milled around, gave a few quacks of reproof, and slowly dispersed. She closed her eyes for a few moments and opened them to a scene that took her breath away. The morning fog gathered itself in swirls of vapor that rose and vanished, revealing pale, blue-gray water. With the fog gone, the morning wind had its way with the water, stirring it into a lively chop. Two sailboats emerged from the marina. Their white sails filled with the wind as they headed south together. *Friends out for an early-morning sail.*

She'd like to get the canoe in the water and take it for a paddle with Peter.

What about Peter? Was it just an infatuation, as lovely and short-lived as the full moon? She laughed. "Otto the Orange? Seriously?" But he'd redeemed himself with every stirring touch, and those hot kisses in the garden.

We are good together. But she had to admit they were an unlikely pair. The cop and the counselor. The scarred-for-life son of a hopeless drunk and the sober alcoholic who devoted her practice to drunks and druggies. The poor boy from the city and the privileged girl from the lakeshore who was sitting on a few million.

Still, they had some things in common, like commitment to the community and a love for canoeing. She pictured their valiant effort to get the canoe down from the rafters, she covered with leaves and bugs and grit. It was a good sign that they could laugh through little disasters like that. But could they negotiate the big incompatibilities?

The party last night had pointed out a couple of mismatches. She really needed to talk with Peter about his sister's substance abuse and the way he was handling it. And, not that she cared much about fashion, but would she ever be comfortable hiding her light, so the women married to higher-ranking officers could shine? Her brow furrowed at the thought of marrying into a bureaucracy.

Feet pounding the path behind her brought her quiet reflection to an end. The runner kept a fast tempo but breathed easily. Gwen turned to watch.

"Peter!"

He slowed, ran in place, scanned the row of willows. Grinning, he came through the trees toward her. "Slacker? Taking a break?" Though his tone was teasing, his eyes sparked with desire.

She blushed but made no move to hug him. *Too*

public, too much daylight. "Just a little reflection. The lake is magical after sunrise."

"Going my way? I'll walk you to the end of the path."

"Deal." She gathered her helmet and gloves and pushed the bike onto the path. "I've had a good night's sleep, but you're coming off a long shift. I'm surprised you can run at this hour."

"It's my usual. Helps me let go of work. Then I sleep until two or so, and I'm ready to go again." He squeezed her shoulder. "Did you dream about me?"

She stroked his back. "I would have, but I came home to a little crisis."

"Sounds familiar," he muttered. "What happened?"

She told him Rick's story, in confidence. "This is tough for me." She exhaled her frustration. "If he were a client I would see him an hour or two a week, and we'd work on anger and grief and problem-solving. But he's in my home and in my heart. He and Haley are a couple of scared, overwhelmed kids living under my roof for a while." She broke the tension with a chuckle. "It's an immersion experience in parenting."

Peter smoothed her hair from her cheek and tucked a stray lock behind her ear. "Any way I can help?"

"I don't know right now, but thanks for offering."

"What's the plan for today?"

"They're going together to Haley's first doctor's appointment, and I want Rick to take the lead with asking about adoption."

"Serious stuff. Why don't I give you a call when I get up, and you tell me then how I can be useful."

Gwen paused on the path and looked up at him through her eyelashes. "What a guy. Thank you."

Peter ran one finger down her cheek and leaned in for a kiss. "It's all going to work out. Take it as it comes."

"I can do that."

With that, he turned back toward town.

Gwen watched him until he hit his stride.

"Sure you're comfortable with having me here?" Rick asked.

Haley confessed, "I'm not comfortable with any of this, but it helps that you're with me."

Rick squeezed her hand and kissed her bare belly. "What are you thinking, Haley?"

"That my whole life might change again, when I see the baby. What are you thinking?"

"I know the best thing is for someone to adopt the baby, but I want us to have some say about who and what kind of environment they provide."

Haley touched his face, then traced the lines in his forehead. "Good thinking. I'm being way too emotional about everything."

"Ready, you two?" Dr. Bowes breezed into the examining room, her gray bob neatly in place, stethoscope over one shoulder. As she checked the instrumentation for the ultrasound, she kept up a steady chatter about the technology, for Rick's benefit.

"Is our little one kicking this morning?" she asked Haley.

"No. Sleeping." A few second's later, Haley's eyes popped open, and she giggled. "Kicking on queue. How did you do that?"

Rick laughed and placed his hand on her belly. His eyes closed against sudden tears. Haley stroked his shoulder, and he nodded.

Dr. Bowes rubbed Haley's belly with "Cool gel" she called it. "It's brave of you to be part of this, Rick, and I'm sure it helps Haley to have you involved." Her voice lifted at the end, as if she wanted Haley to reinforce her message.

"Yes," Haley agreed emphatically.

"Any questions before we proceed?"

"We are talking about adoption, doctor," Rick said, his voice firm, "and we're wondering how we can have some say in the parents and the home environment?"

Dr. Bowes smiled her understanding. "These days you have several options, including arrangements like open adoption and private adoption. While Haley and I talk after this exam, Rick, we'll have you meet with one of our social workers who can tell you about the different avenues. Haley will join the conversation when she and I are finished.

"Right now let's see how things are progressing with your baby's development. This may be a little uncomfortable, Haley, but you should not feel pain. If you have pain, let me know right away. Okay?"

"Okay."

Rick reached for Haley's hand, and she smiled into his eyes.

The doctor helped them make sense of the images on the monitor and assured them the baby was fine. "Normal development, good position. Everything looks good." As the exam concluded, she gave Haley's arm a comforting pat and handed her a towel to clean off her belly.

Once she was upright, Haley reached out for Rick with shaky arms, and he drew her into a warm embrace.

"Do you want to know the sex of your baby?" Dr. Bowes asked them.

Rick replied, "It's a boy, isn't it?"

"Yes, it's a boy."

Haley burst into tears. Rick held her close and kissed her temple. His eyes shut tight, and there was no hiding the anguish written all over his face.

When the two couples arrived back at 14 Lakeside Terrace, where the Cushmans lived, Gianessa insisted that they come up for a cold drink. Haley blotted tears and agreed.

Rick helped Haley up the two flights to the Cushmans' apartment, then excused himself. "Haley will need it cool for the drive home," he explained, "and the air-conditioning in my old car takes forever to get cranking." He headed back down the stairs, wondering if was possible to feel any lower.

After starting the engine and switching on the air, he opened the windows to let the breeze usher out the oven temperature. He'd leave it for five minutes while the compressor got its act together.

Hands in his pockets, he strolled to the top of Lakeside Terrace. At the edge of the bluff, he had a sweeping view of Chestnut Lake. A mile or more straight across was Gwen's property. Shimmering azure water stretched, like a ribbon, to the south, so calm it was almost mystical. He wanted it to be wild, churning with whitecaps, like it had been this morning. That's how he felt inside—tossed around and beat up.

He was no good to Haley this way.

He dug out his phone and scrolled through for Gwen's number.

"Hey, Rick," she answered on the first ring. "Is everything okay?"

"Uh, yeah, mostly. I mean, the baby's healthy and Haley's okay physically, but she really needs you this afternoon. And I need to get my head on straight. I noticed—"

"Whoa, back up a sec. Say more about Haley needing me. What's that about?"

"She did really well through the exam, but it just killed her to know it's a boy."

Gwen gasped.

"Yeah, she really fell apart for a few minutes. And after, when we talked to the social worker about adoption, she had a meltdown. I've never seen her lose it like that."

"Describe the meltdown for me, Rick."

The calm and control in Gwen's voice helped him shift from his hurting heart to his muddled head. With a flash of gratitude for the degrees and experience that stood behind Gwen's steady presence, he told her, "Haley was, like, totally frozen through the first minute with the social worker, and then she just stood up and started yelling at us, saying that she only now found out her baby is a boy and she needs time with that before everyone starts planning how to take him away from her. And by the way, she's due September 20th."

Gwen was silent for ten seconds—he counted—before she said, "Haley actually said 'planning how to take him away from me'?"

"Yeah," Rick said. He replayed it to be sure. "Yeah, that's—those are the words she used."

"That's what I needed to know. Thanks, Rick. I know all this is really hard for you, too."

"The thing with the adoption—I wish we could be sure it's a good home, you know? I want my son to have . . ." A sob stopped him from finishing the sentence.

"I hear you, Rick. We'll find a way. And don't worry about Haley. She and I will do whatever she needs this afternoon. But what about you? What do you need?"

Rick turned away from the water and sat back hard on the guardrail. "Yeah, so I'm going to shoot some baskets. There's a basketball court in the park across from where I'm standing, next to where the Cushmans live. I think I'll get a ball and come back here, after I bring Haley to your place."

"Of course, Rick. You might find an old ball in the garage, and I think there's a pump around, too."

"Thanks, but I'll stop by Wal-Mart and pick one up. I just don't want you to think I'm deserting you and Haley."

"I don't. You need to take care of yourself. Listen, I know a guy who might show up there looking for someone to shoot baskets. His name's Peter."

Rick exhaled a laugh. "Show up, like, accidentally, you mean?"

"Busted. Maybe he can help you talk it out. Is that okay?"

"Sure, thanks, I'll keep an eye out for him. Maybe I could pick up something for all of us for dinner." He stood and faced the calm lake.

"Don't even think about it. I've got it all planned. But I forgot Italian bread, if you're near a bakery or a grocery store. Haley likes it."

"You got it." Behind him, he heard the outside door close. "We're on our way, Gwen." He pocketed the phone and stole one last glance at the calm azure water.

Haley's footsteps were heavy and slow on the last two steps.

He turned and gave her a big smile.

As soon as the apartment door closed behind Haley, Justin reached out a hand to Gianessa.

She joined him at the French door to their lakeside porch. A few moments, simply contemplating the azure finger of Chestnut Lake, calmed her.

"It breaks my heart, Justin, to see them in such agony."

Justin's hand stroked her back as she rested her head on his shoulder.

"I think we can help. Didn't Syd and Danny know someone that wants a baby?" he mused.

"Oh my gosh, you're right."

"We should call them."

Gianessa kissed his cheek. "I'll call Syd, woman-to-woman."

He teased her. "Am I allowed to stay in the room while you have this conversation?"

She laughed. "You'd better. She's your friend, and it's a stronger inquiry coming from both of us." She scrolled through her contacts until she found Syd's number at home in Manhattan.

"When did I give you her number?" Justin wondered aloud.

"You gave me the numbers for each of your wedding invitees so I could call to thank them for the beautiful wedding gifts."

"Didn't we specify, 'No gifts. Only your presence.'?"

"We did, and mostly it didn't work. Syd and Danny gave us a gas grill for our new deck, to be delivered at our request after we move in." With her hand on her round belly, she said, "Which, thank heaven, will be very soon, before the twins are born." She started as the connection went through.

"Syd, it's Gianessa Cushman. I'm so glad we caught you at home."

Sydney gushed in her ear, "My dear! Is everything all right? Did the babies come early?"

"Everything is fine. I'm still eight weeks or so away. Syd, do you have a minute? Justin and I have something important to talk over with you."

"Of course. Do we need Danny?"

"Yes."

"He's watching tennis in the den." Sydney's call to her husband made Gianessa laugh. "Quickly, sweetcakes, it's Gianessa and Justin." She lowered her voice. "He's on his way. What's up? Are you both well?"

"Yes, and you?"

"Always."

Gianessa reached for Justin's hand and he gave hers a squeeze. "Syd, we've just met a wonderful young couple who are dealing with an unplanned pregnancy. The mother is Gwen Forrester's niece, if you remember Gwen from our wedding."

"Of course I do, the one who's putting Justin's head on straight. Is it still?"

"Justin's head is still on straight, yes." Gianessa winked at her husband.

Justin chuckled.

"He's been my rock, but how he puts up with my hormonal craziness is beyond me. I love him more every day."

Sydney hummed her pleasure at the update. "But, Gianessa, my dear, you're not thinking Danny and I want to adopt?"

Gianessa laughed from her belly, and her tension floated away. "No, no, I'm sure you're holding out for grandchildren."

"No prospects yet. Oh! Now I know. You and I talked about our friends Laura and Helmud Hahn who've been trying everything to get pregnant. Danny," she called, louder this time, "come quick. We may have a baby for the Hahns."

"So they haven't gotten pregnant or adopted since we spoke?"

"No, they stopped trying to get pregnant months ago. They've sent out a few feelers through New York area adoption brokers—if that's the right term—but as of a week ago, there'd been no viable candidate. Poor dears would make such wonderful parents. Here's Danny. Can I put you on 'speaker?'"

"Yes, and I'll 'speaker' us, too." Gianessa moved her finger over the smartphone display and found the icon she hoped stood for the speaker. "Can you hear us? Justin, you say something, too."

Justin voiced a hearty, "Hello, Danny and Syd."

"We hear you both just fine," Danny said. "Tell us about this young couple and the pregnancy. Are they serious about giving up the child? Is the baby healthy? When are they due?"

"What Danny means," Sydney interjected, "is we couldn't bear to get the Hahns's hopes up and have the young couple change their minds. Are they married, by the way?"

"Just a second." Gianessa tugged on Justin's hand and motioned him to the sofa. She sat on a straight chair and placed the phone on the coffee table between them. "Can you answer all that for us, dude?"

Justin muted the phone for a moment. "You're all right?"

She waved her hand to cool her face. "Just flustered. I'm so excited and nervous."

"Relax, sweetheart. This will go the way it's supposed to." Justin toggled the mute button and resumed the telling. "They're not married. The baby is due September 20th, a month before us."

"So soon, that's wonderful," Sydney gushed.

"Both parents are bright and sincere; both are going into their junior year in college. He's brilliant, I would say, preparing as an environmental engineer. She's bubbly and smart—a botany major?" He looked to Gianessa for confirmation.

"Yes, and an accomplished artist. She's agreed to do some watercolors for our new home, using photos of flowers that grow near Pop and Ariella's home in Italy."

"Ooh, your honeymoon. Was it wonderful?"

"Grand," Justin assured them. "I'll send pictures as soon as I've picked out the top twenty. Back to the baby's mother, Haley has a website for her online business." He rattled off the easy address, certain Danny would bring it up on his phone while they talked. "She's got spunk. You'd like her."

"And she's beautiful," Gianessa added. "Broken hearted to give up her baby boy, but she's been thinking all along she would go the adoption route. She hadn't initiated anything herself, though. The father, Rick, was away doing research. We were together at the hospital just now, and they seemed overwhelmed about the adoption process."

"You all were at the hospital? Is anything wrong?"

"Not at all. Haley is using my doctor, whose office is at the hospital. We went together for our appointments. She's healthy and has been taking good care throughout the pregnancy. The baby is kicking up a storm. Development is normal. And as I say, the parents are hard-working, smart, talented nineteen-year-olds."

Danny asked, "Have you talked with them about the possibility of a private adoption?"

"We wanted to talk with you first." Justin told him. "No sense getting their hopes up without knowing if it's even a possibility. I do know Rick, the father, is very concerned about placing his son in a stable marriage and a financially-sound home environment that can offer him the best in education, and Haley wants very much for the parents to be supportive of the little boy's interests and talents."

Sydney chimed in, "That's the Hahns to a tee. What do they do, Danny? I know Helmud is in finance."

"He manages mutual funds—very successful, which is saying a lot in this economy. He has integrity and a good nose for value. Serious tennis player, too, with a quick humor.

"Laura is the designer for a major event planning business in Manhattan. She'd give it all up in a heartbeat for a child. And they could afford to have her stay at home with the baby."

"Justin, I think we need to talk with Rick and Haley very quickly."

"Agreed."

Danny said, "And I'll give Laura a call to see how they are and if anything is new. Assuming both parties are interested, we need to get them together. Right away."

Justin cleared his throat. "With legal counsel, I think. These young people are babes in the woods with something like this. Not to say your friends aren't trustworthy."

"Of course," Danny agreed. "Rick and Haley probably have no idea they can be compensated for their baby under the law. They need to think about their needs. Finishing school, for example. Justin, you'll help them find the right attorney?"

"Consider it done, good friends."

Gwen jumped when the car doors squeaked shut. Haley's footsteps were heavy on the stairs from the garage. The moment she saw Gwen, her face puckered and she burst into tears.

"I'm sorry, I was going to be so grown up," Haley choked out.

Gwen folded her in a hug and motioned Rick to pour them some iced tea from the pitcher. "Cookies," she added.

Rick dragged himself to the island. He plunked ice

cubes into three green plastic glasses and poured tea an inch from the rim of each, then stood with his eyes closed for a minute. Gwen thought he would cry, but he just stood with one hand on a cold glass.

When he opened his eyes, he waved to Gwen, stuffed a peanut butter cookie in his mouth, and carried his glass out with him.

The car door squeaked open and shut, the engine caught, and tires crunched on the gravel.

"Haley, honey, let's get comfortable and talk about all of this. I made peanut butter cookies for us."

"Shower first," Haley decided. "I'll be quick."

"The new robe is on your bed."

Gwen listened to her trudge up the stairs. *God, you've got to help us. These kids are in so much pain.*

The phone rang.

Gwen reached for it, hesitated, and gave a curious look toward heaven. It rang a second time. "This is Gwen," she answered.

"And this is Peter. Are they back yet?"

"Yes, just now."

"Can you talk?"

"For a few minutes. Rick just beat it out of here for a basketball court, and Haley's in the shower." She sank down on a stool at the island, and tears spilled over. "They are hurting so bad, Peter." Her voice caught, and she put a hand to her eyes. "So bad."

"It will be okay," his voice soothed. "We'll help them through this."

"Thank you. You're a good man, Peter."

"Since you're on Haley duty, why don't I go after Rick?"

"Yes. It would help him a lot to blow off steam with someone. He's so controlled, and this is overwhelming."

"Wish I had some of your training."

"You don't need it. You've got everything you need for this job."

"How do you figure, counselor?"

"You can shoot baskets."

He chuckled.

"You're tuned into kids this age, way more than I am. Look what you did with Haley that first breakfast."

Silence.

"What? Did I say something wrong?"

"No. And thank you."

Her face softened. "You're amazing."

"Any idea where I can find Rick?"

"Overlook Park, I think. He was at the Cushmans at the top end of Lakeside Terrace when he spotted a basketball court. He planned to pick up a ball at Wal-Mart and head back there. He's tall and thin and—"

"Blond hair, nerdy glasses, got it."

"How do you know that?" She reached for the box of tissues.

"Haley's Facebook page."

Gwen's laugh came all the way from her toes. She blotted her face and dried her runny nose. "See what I mean? You don't need any help from me."

"I'll give you a little lesson one of these days," he said with a sexy undertone. "Facebook lesson, I mean."

She grinned at the phone and rested her elbows on the counter. "I'll take you up on that."

Haley slipped into the kitchen and teased her aunt. "That smile must mean it's Peter, right?"

Gwen nodded. "Cute robe. Have a cookie. I just took them out of the oven."

Haley came behind Gwen and rested her chin on Gwen's shoulder. "Hi, Peter. Are you coming for supper?" Her voice was eager.

Gwen tempted him further, "Lemon chicken, sweet potato fries, fresh peas, and all the cookies you can eat."

Peter interjected, "Yes, tell Haley, yes, I'm coming for supper."

Gwen and Haley chorused, "Perfect!"

Chapter 6

Rick parked his clunker outside the Cushmans with a note propped on the dashboard, just in case someone thought it should be towed to a junkyard. The grass was a thick cushion under his feet as he made his way across the park to the fenced basketball court.

He didn't know how to do this. Getting his head on straight was not something he ever worried about. He was usually focused on getting his degree, preparing for a career, relaxing with Haley, supporting her business. Now he had to think about having a son with her, quitting college, and giving up his career plans, because, deep down, part of him believed that's what he was supposed to do, and that deep-down part had come alive the moment he heard his little boy's heart beating.

His mentor at RPI didn't think he should get married. Haley and Gwen didn't either. But a lot of the world did. His mother and grandmother would have said so. Plus all his teachers growing up. And the priest.

Even more important, it was killing Haley to let go of this baby boy. And how could he abandon his own son? Maybe adoption wasn't the right thing. He flipped the ball as he walked. If they could just know what kind of home and parents the baby would have . . .

Our son will be smart and talented. His chest tightened at the thought. Okay, he and Haley wouldn't have money, but they'd care about his education. They'd want him to explore his talents and his interests. Neither of them had had that kind of caring as children, so they knew how important it was to a child.

But what about Haley's education? What about my own? Neither of them could continue college if they decided to raise the baby. Haley had no support now, since her mother had thrown her out. And he'd have to give up his scholarship and his stipend to get a real job. Even so, how could he possibly support the three of them on what he could earn?

He knew just one thing for sure. He wasn't going to walk away from Haley or the baby.

He came to the gate of the basketball court and stood back to study the structure—as he studied every structure—with a curious engineer's eye. The posts were tall and straight. The black chain link had no cuts or gaps as far as his eye could see. Apparently, the court was never locked; there was no padlock hanging loose and no marks where one would have been.

When he let himself in, the hinges didn't even squeak. That threw him. His plan had been to let loose and play hard and smash a few into the net. Vent. Like Haley did in the social worker's office. But, for that to work, the court was supposed to be as beat up as he felt. Why did it have to be so damn pristine?

Rick stepped to the middle of the court. He spun the new ball on his finger. He flipped it back and forth between his palms until he'd tested the entire surface. He bounced it hard on the pavement. Not bad for fifteen bucks. Clean didn't mean he couldn't beat the heck out of it.

As he dribbled over the perimeter of the court, he noted that the playing surface was in good condition, considering how exposed this place was to the weather. There were no scuffmarks on the court and just the one basket with a backboard free of ball marks. The rim rested perfectly perpendicular to it, and the net was clean.

Had they just built this thing? Didn't anyone use it? Probably families came here for picnics or reunions and got a game or two going. *That's* what he'd really like to be doing— coming here with his kids and his wife for a picnic, taking a turn on the court, maybe an ice cream on the way home.

That's how it was meant to be used. Or for pick-up games or practicing foul shots. Not for an idiot like him that had gotten his girlfriend pregnant and needed to clear his head so he could remap his whole future, starting as a nineteen-year-old father.

Frustration flared. He fired the ball at the fence.

The metal clanged and shuddered. "Asshole," he chided himself, "that solved nothing." The chain link quieted and settled itself. The ball rolled back toward him and came to rest a few feet away.

So play a little ball. See if that helps.

He scooped up the ball and carried it to the base of the backboard, then paced the distance to the foul line. If he'd bought some chalk, he could have marked it for himself.

He dribbled, settled into his stance, and swished one through the net. Twelve shots later, he'd made five.

"Keep practicing," someone called from the sideline.

Rick turned to see a tall, muscled guy standing behind the gate, his fingers laced in the links on either side. "Are you Rick?"

"Yeah. You're Peter? Gwen said you might come by. Want to shoot a few?"

Peter strolled onto the court, tossed his own ball into the corner and held up his hand for Rick's. He'd never seen a cleaner ball. "Had it long?" he asked.

"Like half an hour." Rick laughed.

Peter quirked an eyebrow. "Is this their street ball?"

"Yeah, I planned to smash it around a lot, thought it might hold up better."

"And that's your idea of smashing? Shooting to miss a dozen foul shots?"

Rick's face got red, but he came right back with, "You missed my rocket shot into the fence before that."

"Thought I heard some banging and clanging. Hard to do much smashing if you like things neat and orderly." At Rick's puzzled frown, he added, "Heard you're an engineer."

"Maybe. All of a sudden life's not so neat and orderly."

"Listen, I met Haley when she broke into Gwen's the other night." Peter decided to get the issue out in the open. "I'm the cop that investigated the break-in."

"And I'm the expectant father, still in shock. It's a boy, you know." He choked out, "My son."

Peter felt Rick's pain in his own gut. "You two are in a rough spot."

"Yeah." Rick nodded.

Peter shoved the ball hard at Rick. "Let's give this street ball a workout."

They dribbled and passed the ball back and forth in a warm-up drill for a few minutes. Peter broke away and took the first shot. The ball bounced off the rim. Rick grabbed the rebound and put it in the net.

They alternated shots, missing as many as they made. *The kid's in good shape for a nerd.*

Peter slowly ramped up the action, and Rick stayed with him. Peter got sneaky, stole the ball, and got in an extra shot. His prowess rated a nod from Rick.

He blocked Rick's sure shot and stuffed the ball in the net. Rick spat on the pavement.

The longer and harder they played, the more agitated Rick got. That was the plan. Peter knew he'd be pissed in this guy's situation, and the sooner he let it out, the clearer his head and the better he could deal with it.

After twenty minutes, Rick's face was tight. His nostrils

flared. He bared his teeth at Peter's antics. And his shots swished in more than they missed.

They'd worked up a dripping sweat when Peter made a seemingly casual comment, "I made you for a stoic, Rick, but I can see I'm wrong. You can really score when you're on fire. You'll have me on my ass if I'm not careful."

Rick hurled the ball at Peter's head.

Peter blocked it and yelled, "Simmer down."

"I am not fucking stoic," Rick snarled, "I'm pissed as hell."

Peter calmly scooped up the ball and tossed it back to Rick. As Peter approached the basket, Rick fired the ball into the backboard. Peter dropped back a few inches, half-afraid the board would shatter at the impact. He retrieved the ball and stood flipping it idly next to the fence.

Rick bent forward and braced his hands on his knees. Breathing hard, he said, "Sorry, man. I'm out of my mind."

"So tell me about it."

Rick stood up straight, hands on his hips, and looked Peter in the eye. "I hate it that Haley's hurting so bad." He wiped his forehead with the back of his arm and glared around the macadam as if searching for some hole along the fence where he could escape. "And I cannot abandon my son."

"I hear you, but there's more than one way to handle it."

"But I know the right thing is to marry her." Rick shot daggers at him.

Peter's eyebrows shot up. "Is that the right thing for you?"

Rick's face mapped a war of emotions.

"Who exactly is that right for, Rick? For Haley? For your son?"

He held his ground while Rick bunched his fists.

"You need to use your brain, Rick, not some old Catechism lesson. How about we kick around some other possibilities. What do you say?"

In a few seconds, Rick's breathing steadied. He wiped sweat from his chin on the shoulder of his T-shirt. "Sure, why not?"

Peter dribbled within a few feet of Rick and tucked the ball under his arm. "What started you thinking you need to give up your plans and dreams to get married?"

"The whole adoption thing, the horror stories about foster care. God, I heard his little heartbeat." He glanced at Peter and quickly averted his gaze. "He needs a strong dad, one who loves him. Suppose I'm the best father my son can have?"

"Rick—"

"Maybe I should give up my degree program and—"

"Stop. Don't. Rick, you can't undo the pregnancy, but you've got a choice about what you do now. Don't sell out your dream. Or Haley's." He bounced the ball a couple times to hold Rick's attention. "From where I stand you're a natural for the field you're in. Hell, you measure off the foul line practically every time you shoot."

Rick let out a laugh.

"And you need to keep on with that work. You've got important work to do, and the world needs it. You can't be giving it up because you and your girl made a mistake. The father thing will come at the right time, and now is not the right time."

"Okay, I agree that I'm made for engineering and not ready to be a dad, but isn't that selfish?"

"Sure, some." Peter shrugged. "But it's pretty selfish and egotistical to think you're the best possible father for this little baby right now. And do you think Haley's ready to be a mother? Are you two ready to marry?"

"Shit, no," Rick told him with a wave of his arm. "No to all of that."

Peter bounced the ball to him. "Shoot six from the foul line."

Rick paced the distance from the base of the backboard and drew an imaginary line with the toe of his sneaker.

Peter watched him—so precise, so measured. How had he and Haley gotten into this jam?

Rick's first shot went wide and to the right. He retrieved the ball for himself, paced the distance to the foul line, and got into place. "Do you know how all this happened?" Rick asked Peter.

Peter started. *Did he just read my mind?* He quipped, "In the usual way, I assume."

Rick growled some epithet, too low to make out. He hurled the ball at the backboard just above the net. It caught the rim and dropped through.

Peter picked up the ball and tossed it back to him.

"She left her fucking pills at school when we drove home for the holidays."

"You could have gone back for them."

"Damn straight, we could have. But did she even tell me? No." He aimed and shot. The ball swished through the net without a sound.

Peter tipped it back to him. "Pretty irresponsible of her to have sex under the circumstances."

"No kidding. We went to a party and she had some eggnog that must have been ninety proof. It went straight to her head. Talk about losing all inhibition."

Peter caught a little smile on Rick's face before he ducked his head. *At least they had fun.*

Rick dried one hand on his chinos, then the other. When he lifted his head again, any sign of remembered pleasure was gone. His eyes were determined, focused on the basket. He dribbled hard, the ball pinging the pavement, and fired the ball at the net. It hit the rim, bounced high, and curved away to the right.

Peter retrieved the ball and tossed it to Rick. "You're shooting fouls," he reminded him, "and you're two for four, with two to go." He pointed with his chin to the imaginary foul line. "Then I'm up. I'm going beat your ass, at this rate."

Haley chugged half her iced tea, set down her glass, and reached for a cookie. "Am I spoiling dinner?"

"It's still a couple hours away. How are you feeling?" She patted Haley's knee as they sat side-by-side in the den, just off the kitchen.

Haley circled her index fingers beside her ears. "Crazy. I was okay until . . ." She took a strained breath. A few tears rolled down her cheeks. "Until we found out it's a boy. Rick's son, Gwen. And I lost it."

"Why, sweetie?" Gwen pushed a lock of hair back from her niece's tear-streaked cheek. "Does knowing the sex make it harder for you?"

Haley nodded, scrunched up her face, and turned huge, dark eyes to Gwen. "I love my baby so bad it hurts. And knowing this is Rick's son," she said with her hand on her belly, "I can't just abandon him. But I can't possibly do a good job raising him. I'm just like my mother."

"Sweetie, that's not true. You're nothing like Ursula. For this whole pregnancy, you've been attentive to your baby. You've been responsible with your health. You've always found a safe place to live and put aside money to take care of both of you. You haven't made demands on anyone. But you also had the courage to bring Rick into the hard decisions and to set up a base here with me for the last couple months until the baby comes. You've been a good mom, and you'll continue to be for as long as it makes sense."

"Do you really believe that?" Her scared eyes begged Gwen to say yes.

"I do believe that." Gwen's mouth softened with a smile. "I have the evidence right in front of me."

Haley flashed a tearful smile. "I've got to know where our baby goes and who's taking care of him and if he's okay. Rick needs that, too." She burst into tears, and Gwen drew her into a hug.

"It's okay, Haley. We'll figure this out." Gwen made gentle circles with her hand on Haley's back. When the sobs turned to little hiccoughs, Gwen said brightly, "If you could choose your little boy's home what would it be like?"

"Like this house," Haley told her. "I want you and Peter to be the parents."

Gwen swallowed hard. *Thank god she'd had the conversation with Deirdre, and had quiet moments to think this morning.* She made sure her voice was kind but firm when she answered, "No, Haley. That's not going to happen."

"What?" Haley's eyes narrowed. "Why, Gwen? You're perfect."

"Think it through, sweetie. In a couple of years, you'd finish school and probably find a nice man to marry—maybe Rick, maybe someone else. And you'd have children, and you'd want this little boy to be part of your family."

Haley shook her head in frustration.

"Just as important, Haley, it would break my heart to give up this little boy after raising him for those years."

"I never thought of that." Haley's eyes were lowered. Her painful sigh tugged at Gwen's heart.

With a lighter tone, she said, "I might even resent you and refuse to let him go, and then you'd hate me, and the little boy would be caught in the middle." She continued, her tone serious, "I'm not going to entertain that scenario, Haley."

After a long, silent minute, during which Haley scrutinized every object on the floor-to-ceiling shelves, she puffed out her breath. "You're right. I can see that, Gwen." Her gaze settled on a vase of wildflowers on the hearth, and she leaned toward it. "So, either I raise my baby alone or I give him up for adoption. I'm not going to marry Rick and mess up his plans. His degree is too important."

"Important to you or to Rick?"

"Absolutely to me, and I know how much it means to Rick. He's worked hard his whole life for this chance."

"Okay, I accept that. Do you think you can raise your little boy yourself?" Gwen held her breath.

"No. I don't know how, and I don't have any confidence I can figure it out. Not under stress. My baby would be screwed. We'd both be screwed, and I don't want that."

"So, adoption?"

Haley's eyelids fluttered, and she licked her lips. After a deep sigh, she nodded and said, "Adoption is, and always was, Plan A." She added quickly, "But I can't just let someone take him from me. I can't do it that way. Do you understand, Gwen?"

Gwen pressed her forearm. "I do, sweetie. The good news is, from what I know, there are options."

Haley opened her big eyes. "Like what?" she pleaded.

"Like open adoption, where you make an agreement with the parents to share information."

"So I might be able to know who they are?" Haley sat up straighter. "And how he's doing?"

"Possibly. We'd want a lawyer involved and we'd need him or her to understand what's important to you and to Rick. The lawyer would negotiate on your behalf."

"I can't afford a lawyer, Gwen!" Haley's voice rose in a wail.

"I can." Gwen squeezed Haley's hand. "Haley, I can afford a lawyer, so don't let that be a problem. It's not a problem."

Haley's breathing eased. "This is just so hard. I'm sorry to be hysterical."

"You know what?" Gwen said with a bright smile. "Let's promise not to say 'Sorry' for a while. Everything's okay to say. Everything's okay to feel and to share right now. What do you say?"

Haley gave a solemn nod. "I feel like my heart got ripped out back there in the examining room, and I'm open and raw and hurting. And Rick is, too, and he's angry. I'm afraid he's going to do something stupid like quit school and make me marry him."

"Don't let him," Gwen insisted.

"I mean, I love him, but we're too young and it would screw up our whole lives. And it's not right for the baby. Besides, maybe Rick's not the guy I should marry anyway. How can I even know that?"

Gwen cocked her head. "You might want to practice letting him down easy."

"How's this?" Haley laughed, a little hysterically. "I'll say, 'Thank you, Rick. I love you but I'm not getting married yet, not even to you.'"

"Short and sweet." Gwen nodded her approval.

"So." Haley sucked in a cleansing breath. "How do we find a good mom and dad for our little boy?"

The phone rang. Gwen ignored it. "We can talk with a social worker I know. She can explain the different avenues open to you and Rick."

"I'll bet you've talked to her already," Haley said, her voice teasing.

"A little. I wanted to be sure she wouldn't leave on vacation just when you felt ready to meet her."

When the phone rang a fourth time, they heard the machine click on and bleat Gwen's greeting.

"I can't believe you still have a landline." Haley giggled.

"It's required by the security company."

"How could I forget the security system?" Haley rolled her eyes.

"Hey, Gwen and Haley." Gianessa's voice filled the kitchen. "Justin and I want to talk with you really soon. I know this is presumptuous, but we have a lead on a great couple that wants to adopt, and we wonder—"

Gwen tore into the kitchen and snatched up the receiver. "Don't hang up!"

A few steps behind her, Haley clutched Gwen's arm and pushed her ear close to the phone.

"We'll put it on 'speaker,' okay, Haley?" Gwen

punched the button and rummaged in the top drawer for something to write with.

"Hi, Gianessa." Haley carried the phone to the island and slid onto a stool. "Gwen's getting paper and pencil," she explained.

"Justin's here, too. Is that okay, Haley?"

"Great, yes. I wish Rick was here."

"Go ahead," Gwen told them. "Tell us everything."

Justin ran through what they knew about the Hahns and explained how they'd come by the information. He finished with, "Syd and Danny will check with them today, but only if Haley and Rick are interested."

"Of course we are. I mean, I am, and I think Rick will be, too."

Gwen squeezed Haley's knee. She interjected, "So this would be what's called a private adoption?"

"What does that mean?" Haley asked.

Gianessa told them, "From what I understand, instead of going through an agency, you and the couple would negotiate directly, both of you represented by lawyers. The lawyers would facilitate and insure that all the state laws and regulations are obeyed."

"Typically," Justin added, "the adopting couple would make sure your medical bills are covered and possibly reimburse you for legal fees or other expenses."

"That would be amazing." Haley raised her eyebrows at Gwen, and Gwen smiled her agreement.

"Now remember"—Justin's voice was firm—"nothing's decided until you say so, Haley. Don't feel pressured about this. You and Rick need to talk, we understand that."

Haley turned to Gwen with a question in her big eyes.

"Hold on, Justin," Gwen said and muted the phone. "What, sweetie?"

"I want to tell them to go ahead and contact the parents— the people—to see if they're interested. Would that be all right, do you think? Just that much? Even though Rick's not here?"

"I think so. Justin understands you and Rick need to talk before you take any big steps, so he and Gianessa are not going to go too far."

Haley sat up straight, toggled the mute button and said, "I'd like for your friends to see if the people are really interested, and I'll talk it over with Rick when he gets back, to be sure he's okay with it. And we'll call you after."

Gwen squeezed her eyes against happy tears. Her heart swelled with pride at Haley's sudden strength. Something must be at work in the universe for these two kids to have a possible solution dropped in their laps when they were at their lowest. *Thank you, God.*

"Do you have children?" Rick asked Peter as they crossed Overlook Park toward their cars on Lakeside Terrace.

"No, but I'd like to. I just got divorced, just got the bill. I had hoped to buy a little house over by the college, but that's out. Right now I'll settle for getting out of my crummy apartment. So remarrying and having a family are a ways off for me."

"I think you'll make a good father. What you did over there," Rick said with a jerk of his head back toward the basketball court, "really helped me a lot. You seemed to know where I was coming from and how to get me to open up. Thanks."

"I'm glad I could help. I have a hunch we both came from tough homes. That can make a guy clam up. Soldier on and not feel anything."

"No kidding." Rick snorted. "What were your parents like?"

"My dad was a drunk, and all of us suffered because of it. Thank God he died young."

"He didn't ever get sober?"

Peter shook his head and tossed his basketball high in the air a few times. "My mom worked all the time—two or three jobs. She ate herself into obesity and worked herself into heart trouble. She died young a couple of years ago."

"I'm sorry, man."

Peter nodded. "She and I raised my little sister, who's been in trouble a few times. One reason I want a better place is so I can get Bree up here some weekends, get her away from her friends, maybe get her to live here and go on with her education. What about your family?"

"My folks were poor, and I was the oldest of four kids. Dad was smart but he never went to college. He worked in a factory in Schenectady until he was disabled. Mom went to work as a school secretary. When Dad died I was eight, and we went to live with mom's mother in Watervliet. She had a big house and a huge garden that we devoured every summer. Forget bicycles or summer camp. Or college.

"I don't want it to be like that for Haley and me or my children. I promised myself if I had kids I'd wait until I had the means to support a family." He laughed dryly. "We can see how well that plan worked."

"Tell me how you got to college if your family couldn't afford it."

Rick flipped his ball with his hands as they walked. "I have a full scholarship at Rensselaer. It's a great school. Plus, I work on funded research projects in the Environmental Engineering department, with a couple of professors. That's how I pay rent and food and everything. I was working on a project on the Gulf of Mexico from late April until a couple of weeks ago. It's great money, but it's also why I didn't know Haley was pregnant. I was working all the time, and Haley didn't stay in touch. She was pretty aloof before I left and she wouldn't say why. I thought she was pissed that I'd be away all summer. Or maybe she had another guy. I didn't know."

"Sounds to me like she was trying to keep you at a distance so she could keep the pregnancy secret."

"Yeah, I see that now."

"It also sounds like she was determined to have the baby, not have an abortion."

Rick stopped. The ball stilled in his hands. "Yeah, you're right. And I'm glad about that. But it's been really hard on her. She's been trying to handle this all on her own. I can't believe her mother threw her out. What kind of mother does that?"

Peter laughed. "I wondered the same thing when she told me her middle name is Ursula. What kind of mother—"

"Haley's middle name is Ursula?"

"The things we don't know about our women." Peter clapped him on the shoulder. "Don't get me started. Do you think she'd have decided to keep the baby if she'd had more support?"

"No, I think she always intended to give up the baby, but couldn't take the next step on her own."

"There are millions of couples that want a baby," Peter told him.

"I know, but it's such a crap shoot. I want to have a say in who and where so I know our son has a chance at a good life."

"Rick," a deep voice summoned from Lakeside Terrace.

"Hey, Justin," Rick called back.

"Just the man I want to see," Justin said as he strolled toward them.

"Who is this guy?" Peter whispered.

"Justin Cushman. He and his wife drove Haley and me to the doctor's today. His wife is due after Haley. I think he works at the college and they live on the top floor of that last house." He nodded toward 14 Lakeside Terrace. "Gianessa's thrilled their new house will be finished before the babies come. She must hate those stairs right about now." He turned to welcome Justin.

"Got a minute?" Justin asked.

"Sure. Justin, this is Peter."

"Pleasure, Justin." Peter held out his hand.

"Same."

Peter observed, "You're holding a 'For Rent' sign, sir. I happen to be searching for an apartment."

"Lucky coincidence. I'll show you the place in a minute, if you like." He pointed to the three-story, white house with gingerbread trim, right at the edge of the bluff. "Go on in, up one flight, and let yourself in. I'll be there shortly. I just need a minute with Rick."

Justin walked beside Rick to his beat-up car. "I just spoke with Gwen and Haley about an interesting possibility."

"And what's that, sir?"

"Now, if this hits you the wrong way, you just let me know. Gianessa and I remembered that our good friends in New York know a couple who have been trying for years to have a baby and are now trying to adopt."

Rick's stomach did a dive, and his heart raced. "Wow," he blurted out. "Tell me more. What did Haley say?"

"I won't speak for Haley and Gwen, but they sounded excited. Our mutual friends know the couple very well, and from what we've heard, they would make good parents and provide a stable home and every advantage. Gianessa and I will find out more if you and Haley are interested."

Rick yanked open the door of his car, threw the ball into the backseat, and grabbed Justin's hand. He pumped it with his grimy one and babbled, "I'll talk to Haley. Right now. We'll get back to you, sir. Thanks a million."

Peter leaned on the porch railing, off the living room of the second-floor apartment. *Enjoy the view now, man. This is nothing you can afford.*

The porch had him hooked. He could see the gumdrop islands and the whole eastern shore of Chestnut Lake for miles to the south. He'd never realized it got radically steeper to the south, as though the cliffs rose right from the water, after a certain point. He couldn't make out anything like a cottage on the shore past that point, and he wondered if it was even possible to land. He wanted to take the canoe down there with Gwen and see it up close.

"Do you like the place?" Justin's deep voice roused him.

"Are you kidding?" Peter straightened and faced the older man. "This is every bachelor's dream. Nice place to have friends over, coffee out here in the morning. Plus there's a room for my sister to visit. Wish I could afford it."

"You cook for yourself?" Justin leaned casually against a porch pillar.

"If you could call it that. Meatloaf, stew, eggs, salads, burgers."

"How much are you paying now?"

"Five hundred for a dingy one-bedroom in a basement over by the college."

"Well, this is five seventy-five. Is that out of your range?"

Peter gave him a wide-eyed stare. "You're kidding, right?"

"The only catch is there's renovation below you that won't be done until the middle of September. If you wanted to move in right away you'd have to contend with that from seven in the morning until seven at night for a few weeks."

"Sir, I use ear plugs and noise-canceling headphones where I live now. I can't believe it's any worse than that."

"What do you do for a living, Peter?"

"I joined the Tompkins Falls Police Department earlier this summer. Back in Syracuse I was on the force, too. After I was shot in the line of duty a year ago, I wanted a smaller city."

"Welcome to Tompkins Falls. And to Lakeside Terrace, if you're interested."

"That's a no-brainer." Peter grinned. "When can I move in?"

"Give us the weekend to finish cleaning and painting. Anytime next week will be fine. Tony Pinelli has been handling the cleanup, and he'll have the paperwork with him this weekend. You can stop by Saturday or Sunday to go over the lease with him. Leave a month's rent and a one-month security deposit with him."

"Great. I'll do that. Pinelli. Related to my partner, Sam?"

"I have no idea, but it wouldn't surprise me."

"So you're the landlord?"

"My nephew Joel Cushman owns and manages all of Lakeside Terrace."

"I just met Joel last night, and his wife, Mandy."

"Manda. Don't call her Mandy," Justin cautioned with a chuckle. "So you know Joel's recovering from a serious accident? A few of us are helping out. He'll be moving with his wife into the first floor flat when it's ready."

"If I understood Rick, you and your wife will be moving from the top floor to your own house soon. I'm glad to help any way I can."

"Most kind," Justin said in that formal way he had, with a trace of an accent.

Peter wondered if he'd lived in England for a while.

"We already have an army lined up," Justin finished.

Peter grinned. "And a baby on the way, right?"

"Two. Twins, a boy and a girl."

"Congratulations." *Hope I'm not as old as this guy when I have my first kids.*

"Glad you can move in right away." Justin shook his hand. "The place shouldn't sit empty."

Peter wondered at the twinkle in Justin's eye. Maybe it just went with being happily married and about to have twins.

Chapter 7

Rays of sun touched the cut-glass globe of Gwen's bedside lamp, refracted around the room and teased her awake as they scattered across her eyelids. "Ohmigod, I never set the alarm."

She dragged out of bed and made a quick stop in the bathroom, where she also brushed her teeth and ran a comb through her hair, just in case she encountered Peter on the willow path. Dressed in clean gray sweats and socks, she carried her sneakers through the silent house to the garage. After pedaling hard the full half-mile to the highway, she was winded, waiting for a break in the traffic.

Finally at the park, the empty willow path gave her two uninterrupted miles to reflect on the appearance of the Hahns in Haley and Rick's life. The chain of events started in July when Justin married Gianessa who was then six months pregnant. Justin's friends Syd and Danny came to the wedding, and the two couples' conversation touched on another couple, the Hahns, who had tried everything to have a child. And yesterday, Haley shared a ride with Justin and Gianessa for her first doctor's appointment. Who knew it would add up to the Hahns adopting Gwen's grandnephew? *Why do I anguish when God's got it all covered?*

With that thought, her shoulders relaxed, and the tightness in her neck released. A sudden breeze cooled her face, and she savored its caress on her cheeks as she pedaled on.

In less than a minute, though, little worries surfaced. Haley's drinking. Rick's anger. Haley's interrupted college plans. *Deirdre would say I'm worrying about other people's problems when I should take care of my own business.*

When she reached the town end of the path, she considered stopping at Lynnie's Chestnut Lake Café for coffee and a chat with Deirdre. She hadn't brought money, though, and she'd be seeing Deirdre tonight at the women's meeting. Anyway, a newcomer was probably sitting down with Deirdre this morning, seeking a way out of her addiction, and Gwen wouldn't interfere with that conversation.

As she maneuvered her bike back toward home, a movement by the shore caught her eye. Peter stood from a bench and signaled for her attention. He shrugged into his jacket and slung his running shoes over his shoulder, apparently finished with his run.

"Peter!" she hailed.

He made a megaphone of his hands. "I'll call you around three."

She waved in happy agreement and watched him lope across the grass to his Jeep, strong legs rippling with muscles, sweaty shorts showing off his tight butt. *That is one sexy man.* Gwen fanned the sudden heat on her face and neck.

Once his green Jeep merged into traffic, Gwen started back on the two-mile gravel path. Hundreds of willows lined both sides, their fronds waving lazily in the morning breeze. With nothing to distract her or demand her attention, Gwen's mind lingered on Peter and the rush she'd felt a few minutes earlier.

When she'd first talked to Deirdre about him, she'd acknowledged the intense physical attraction, but she'd felt, even then, it was more. There was something right about them together. Some synergy in the way they handled things with Haley and Rick. Something intuitive about their connection with each other.

She wanted time alone with Peter to explore this relationship. They were so far apart on issues like alcoholism and recovery. They needed time to talk, to argue, to find common ground that would serve them both. But with their crazy schedules, his night shifts, her clients, Haley's fulltime presence, how could they work it out?

A group of six spandex-clothed racers approached, running three abreast. Rather than break their strides, Gwen dismounted and rolled her bike to the water's edge for a minute's rest. A flat rock beckoned. Knees drawn up, chin on her hands, she breathed in the clean, moist air off the lake. It was so different today from yesterday. Small boats, each with one or two fishermen, dotted the water's calm surface. The rising sun flashed on the aluminum hulls and intensified the colors of the fishermen's hats—every shade of green, a few red, one blue. Kayaks scuttled out of the marina, one or two at a time.

Maybe Rick will help me test the canoe this morning.

She grinned at the thought and scrambled off the rock. Once she knew the canoe was solid, she and Peter could go for a paddle, just the two of them. If not today, then soon.

As she reached for a colander of fresh-washed blueberries, her phone jangled and displayed Justin's cell number. She said a quick prayer that the Hahns had not changed their minds.

"Hi, Justin. What's up?"

"Gwen, glad I caught you. Can you talk for a minute?"

She surveyed the counters and range top. Everything would keep for a minute. "I sure can."

"I heard back from the attorney I had in mind to handle the adoption for Rick and Haley. She's available and interested and wants to meet with them soon. She'd like you to call her office today to schedule. Her assistant will have questions for Rick and Haley to work on before the meeting." He gave her the firm's Rochester phone number and the attorney's name.

"Wonderful. And the Hahns?" She held her breath.

"Very excited. They want to meet face-to-face and are willing to come here at everyone's convenience, the sooner the better."

"It's real, isn't it, Justin?" Gwen clutched the phone and let out a sob. "Sorry." She tried and failed to hold back the tears. "These are happy tears, nothing more."

"No call for apology. Gianessa and I shed a few tears ourselves, when Rick and Haley called last night with their go-ahead and again this morning when Syd and Danny reported they'd reached the Hahns."

Gwen collected herself. "Will the attorney need the fee upfront?"

"No, but I intend to handle that myself, Gwen, if you'll allow me to."

"Why?" She backed up to the counter for support. *Is it some outrageous amount?*

Justin cleared his throat. "Because we all know I would not be happily married and on the threshold of fatherhood without your expert therapy a few months ago."

When she'd thought earlier about all the coincidences leading up to the Hahn's decision to adopt Haley and Rick's baby, she had jumped over the part she'd played in making Justin's marriage to Gianessa possible. *That's why I do the work I do.* She wished she could share that with Peter. She wanted him to believe in her work.

"Justin, that's exceedingly generous and completely unnecessary. I do appreciate the offer, but no."

He lowered his voice. "This is not a hardship for you or the young parents?"

Gwen lightened the mood with a laugh. "For them, sure it is. But I have no problem handling it, and I think it's most appropriate for me, as Haley's aunt and stand-in mother, to worry about that detail."

"Of course." Justin's brusque tone signaled his readiness to drop the matter.

"Justin, thank you for all that you and Gianessa are doing for these kids. It means the world to them and to their baby. And to the Hahns. None of us could have made this happen without your compassion and skill. I'm most grateful."

"Now you're embarrassing me." Justin chuckled. "I'm glad to help and glad that things are working out. I know Gianessa feels the same."

"I need to spend some quality time with your wife very soon. She'll be swept up in moving and motherhood in no time."

"She'd be thrilled to have lunch anytime. Even better, perhaps the two of you would like a day at the spa in the next week or so?"

"Justin, you know how to treat a woman."

"Do I smell blueberry pancakes?" Rick croaked as he rubbed sleep from his eyes. "I thought I was dreaming."

"I couldn't wait any longer." Gwen laughed and motioned him to the coffee pot. "I took a twelve-mile bike ride at dawn, and I'm famished."

Haley appeared in the doorway. "I need coffee," she grumbled. She wore the new white waffle robe and slippers they'd found at Eastview in the spa section of a new shop, The Two of You.

"Are you allowed to drink caffeine?"

Haley's eyes opened wide with apprehension.

"Oops," Gwen guessed, "didn't think of that, huh?"

"No, and I've been drinking it all along. A big cup every morning." She stroked her belly. "Sorry, little guy."

Rick handed her a full mug. "If that's the only goof, let's not worry about it."

Haley smiled over the rim of the mug and mouthed, "Thank you."

"We're having blueberry pancakes." He grinned. "Your aunt runs the best inn on Chestnut Lake."

"This inn requires guests to clean up at the end of the meal. Unless they cook the meal, of course. Your choice, guys."

"Use me any way you want," Rick told Gwen.

"You could be in a lot of trouble," Haley stage-whispered as she elbowed him.

Gwen brought the first plate of pancakes to the table and signaled Haley to set three places. *What a change from yesterday.*

"Rick, how would you feel about making a test run with me in the old wooden canoe? It's out behind the garage, and it hasn't been in the water for probably fifteen or twenty years."

"I'm game."

"Water's perfect this morning. We could paddle along the shore to my neighbor Phil's house and see how it holds up."

Haley perked up. "And I could walk to Phil's through the woods and meet you there. It's a cleared path, right? I'd love to see Phil."

"It's a plan. One of us should call Phil after breakfast, see if he's on board with it."

"I'll do it," Haley volunteered. "And I'll take a dozen cookies."

"A dozen is about all that's left," Rick informed them.

"It's supposed to rain all afternoon." Gwen said, "While I see clients, you and Rick can make more cookies to replenish our supply."

"Do you know how to make cookies?" Rick asked.

Haley shrugged. "More or less. We'll pick a simple recipe."

"Healthier than we've been eating," Gwen suggested. "How about oatmeal with dried cherries and pecans?"

"Yum," Haley agreed.

"I'm in."

"You can do all the measuring," Haley told him. "And make sure I do all the steps in the right order."

Rick raised his hands to signal a touchdown. "Score! We've got it covered, Gwen."

"Eat those pancakes while they're hot. Maple syrup—the real thing, from down county—is behind you on the counter."

"How much does it weigh?" Rick wondered as he lugged the back end of the old wooden canoe. "Fifty, sixty pounds?"

"Sixty, I think. When we get it to the cobblestone ramp, we'll set it down and let gravity and buoyancy do most of the work."

"Ah, that's why there are extra wooden strips on the bottom," Rick realized.

"Yes, they protect the canvas whenever you're putting in or out."

"How old were you when you learned to paddle?"

Gwen burst out laughing. "You mean, grabbed a paddle and splashed the water with it?"

"I'll bet they had you in the middle with a life jacket on, from the time you were a baby."

"The earliest I remember is a voyage to that island." She gestured to a round island a hundred yards offshore. "There's a tiny beach hidden around the back, where we put out. We rambled all over the place, the whole family, for an hour or so." She glanced at Rick. "I was really small, maybe four, when I was allowed to try with a kiddie-size paddle." She set the bow of the canoe on the cobbles and coaxed it down the gentle ramp. "I never asked if you know how to do this?"

"I do." Rick's face lit up. "My grandfather and I did a lot of fishing from his canoe when I was a boy. I sat in the bow, and we pretended I knew what I was doing. It wasn't until he passed that I got serious about canoeing. My mom was really good, and she was a patient teacher. I think it relaxed her to get out on the water once in a while."

Gwen stood ankle deep in lake water. "Why don't you sit up front here, and I'll steer us to Phil's?" she proposed.

Once Rick was in place with paddle in hand, Gwen shoved off and hopped neatly into the back. She knelt on a scrap of rug on the ribs of the wooden bottom and hauled her paddle from under the crossbars. "Feels like home to have a paddle in my hand," she told Rick.

"Me, too." He grinned back at her.

Gwen steered the canoe to the right, and they dug in their paddles.

"Phil's place is about a half mile from here, the first house we'll see." She spotted several level spots on the shore and called them to Rick's attention. "If we start to sink, they'll make good landing places."

"It's a plan. Haley must be there already. I don't see her on the path."

"She knows the paths like the back of her hand, and the way to Phil's is broad and level because he and I walk it so often. He's a good friend as well as a good neighbor."

They paddled in silence for a minute. "Everything all right up there?" Gwen asked.

Rick gave a nod, without saying anything.

She guessed he was thinking about fatherhood and the little boy he was giving up. "I think Haley's okay with the decision to let the Hahns adopt," she said, her voice casual.

He gave no response.

"I thought about adopting the baby myself, you know."

He swiveled toward her in surprise, and the canoe rocked. He turned his face away, but not before she saw tears. *So much pain.*

She went on, "But it's not the right time for me to have a baby. It's important to me to have a husband first. And it would get terribly complicated for me to be a mother to Haley's baby."

He cleared his throat. "I think you're right. But you're going to be an awesome mom, Gwen."

"Thank you, Rick. From everything I've seen the past few days, you'll be a great dad. When the time is right." She thought he mumbled, "Thanks."

Blue jays shrilled from the island and chickadees chattered on the right. The only other sound was the rhythmic slicing of the paddles as they glided through the water.

"Any rocks or hazards I should be watching for?"

"None at all. And Phil's beach will be a sandy landing. Any water coming through the seams?"

"We're good up here. You?"

"The old canoe is seaworthy, hooray."

"You and Peter need to get it out for a few adventures."

She chuckled lustily. "That we do."

When Haley carried her bundle up the steps to Phil's big lakeside porch, he teased her through the screen door, "What have you got there, Miss Haley?"

Her laugh bubbled up. "Cookies for Gwen's favorite neighbor."

"Did you make them yourself?"

"Not this batch, but Rick and I are on cookie baking duty this afternoon."

Phil held the door open for her. "It appears you two made something else together." He directed his gaze to her belly.

"We did." Haley planted a kiss on his scratchy cheek. "I got drunk and forgot my pills and"—she sucked in a breath—"eight months later we've decided to give up our baby to a couple that's been trying for years to have a baby of their own." She brushed at the tears on her face.

Phil ushered her into his old-fashioned kitchen and held out a chair for her at the scarred oak farm table. "I'll pour the tea, and you tell me whatever you want to tell me, sweetheart. But promise you won't eat all the cookies before I get a couple."

Haley laughed tearfully as she lifted back the corners of the dishtowel to reveal the last dozen peanut butter cookies. "I hope you like PB."

"PB is my second favorite," Phil told her as he poured iced tea into two tall glasses, "behind molasses-raisin. But you could come here empty handed, and I'd be just as pleased."

Haley clinked her glass against his. "To friendship," she toasted.

"To friendship. So, is your boyfriend coming in the canoe with Gwen?"

"He is. They're testing it to be sure it's seaworthy. Then Gwen wants to take some long, private paddles with her new boyfriend Peter."

"Ah, the handsome young cop who's new in town."

Haley marveled, "How do you know that?"

"The AA grapevine. I have big ears. Did you know men over the age of seventy are invisible?"

Haley broke a cookie in half. "You probably know more secrets than anyone else in Tompkins Falls." She took a bite and hummed with pleasure.

"I probably do," he said, "and I never divulge anything told to me in confidence."

Haley shifted on her chair. "That's my cue, right?"

"Smart girl." Phil chuckled.

"Only when I'm sober," she amended. "My mother is crazy and my father is an ex-drunk. I think I got the drunk part."

"It's possible," Phil equivocated.

Haley couldn't meet his eyes. "Do you think I need to tell any of that to the new parents?"

Phil drew in a long, pensive breath, held it, and let it out slowly. He patted her hand. "Maybe fifteen or twenty years from now, if they have cause to ask."

Haley fixed him with a serious eye. "Really, truly?"

"It is a dilemma, Haley, but that's my best answer. However, if you were drinking during your pregnancy, at all,

I'd have a different answer. Then your baby would be at risk of fetal alcohol syndrome, which is very serious. You would need to disclose that upfront."

Haley exhaled with relief. "No, I stopped after that eggnog fiasco the night I got pregnant. And I got morning sickness pretty quick so I figured I might be pregnant and knew not to drink or drug at all. I changed a *lot* of habits then." She smiled at Phil. "Thank God."

Phil's face brightened. "You are sunshine when you smile like that." He savored a bite of cookie. "Is that all that's on your mind?"

She drank some tea before asking, "How do you know if you're an alcoholic?"

"Well, I can tell you how I knew, and I can steer you to a few pages in one of Gwen's books that will help you answer that question."

"How did you know you were one?"

"A few things happened. I picked up a drink one New Year's Eve, blacked out, and came to the next morning in Buffalo in some woman's bed."

"Let me guess. She wasn't your date."

Phil grimaced. "Nor was she my wife, who was frantically calling the police and the hospitals around Rochester, hunting for my body, hoping I was still alive so she could kill me herself."

"You loved Edie, didn't you, Phil?"

"More than myself. More than alcohol. And I'm so blessed that she took me back after a month in rehab. But that incident made me see clearly what had happened over and over again. As soon as I picked up the first drink, I had no control. Our first step in the AA program says we admitted we were powerless over alcohol and our lives had become unmanageable. Based on the evidence, I knew I was an alcoholic."

Haley looked him in the eye. "I took a cup of spiked eggnog and ended up pregnant. And it wasn't the first time

I'd had a drink without intending to and went on to drink more without wanting to."

"Did you know it was spiked?"

Haley rolled her eyes. "I knew I was at a party with no parent supervision, but I told myself it couldn't possibly hurt. Yes, I knew. And I knew I'd left my pills back in the dorm a week earlier. But I felt awkward and I knew a drink would help me relax." She puffed out her frustration. "I barely remember the rest of the night." She rested her hand on her belly. "But there was no way to explain away the pregnancy."

"Your young man has stood by you?"

Haley pursed her mouth. "I pushed him away until last week. I didn't want him to know, because I was afraid he'd quit school. And because I was ashamed."

"Haley." Phil tested his voice to be sure it was kind. "That must have hurt him terribly."

"Yeah." Haley swallowed and licked her lips.

"Are you in agreement about the adoption?"

She nodded. "But it's really hard." She choked on a sob.

Phil let her cry for a bit before telling her, "You know, Haley, one of the things I like best about the AA program is it gives us a way to clean up all that wreckage and lead a better life. I had thirty years of wreckage to clean up by the time I woke up in Buffalo with Susie Q. And I've had thirty years to enjoy sobriety, twenty-five of them with Edie. It turns out that, although our disease is progressive, so is our recovery. Not a bad deal."

Haley sat up straighter and challenged, "Even if you're young?"

"You don't have to wait thirty years to get sober. I sponsor a young man of thirty-one who's been sober—I mean continuous sobriety—for fifteen years."

"Whoa. That's cool."

"And it's a lot of hard work," Phil added. "Sweetheart, you

can check us out any time and join us any time. You might want to try a couple of meetings while you're in Tompkins Falls."

"You really think that would be okay? Even if I don't know for sure?"

Phil looked into her doubt-filled, brown eyes and smiled warmly. "It would be more than okay." He shrugged. "And think about talking to Gwen, if you haven't already."

"Maybe I will."

"Ahoy!" Rick's shout made them laugh. "The Green Lizard has come ashore."

Phil and Haley locked eyes. "Green Lizard?" they chorused.

"He must be joking," Phil quipped. "No one would name a canoe the Green Lizard."

"My father might."

"If your cheerful hello is any clue," Peter said, "things at the Forrester house are way better than yesterday."

Gwen's mouth stretched in a grin and her insides did a happy dance. "Everyone's full of energy and good cheer. Rick and Haley have a new batch of cookies for you. Can you come for supper?"

"Best offer I've had since you offered furniture from the attic for my guest bedroom. In fact, I thought I'd come by soon and take a look. That is, if the offer still stands."

"Of course it does. Come now. Rick will lend a hand with the hauling if you find some pieces you like."

"I've been thinking, though"—his voice grew serious—"we need to make this a business transaction."

"Oh." Gwen started. "Okay, if you want. How about you pay me a dollar for each item you take?"

"I was thinking of pricing things as though for a garage sale or even an estate sale."

"That would take so much work right now. I'll save that

step for the actual garage sale, and maybe you can help me do the research, when the time comes. How does that sound?"

"I appreciate that, and I accept your terms. One dollar each. And you have veto power if I unearth some treasure you didn't realize was up there under the rafters."

"If you insist."

"I do."

Gwen did a quick check to make sure she was alone. "You drive a hard bargain, Officer Shaughnessy," she said in a sexy voice.

"You ain't seen nothin' yet, ma'am."

At that moment, the timer for the last batch of cookies buzzed and Haley materialized with Rick on her heels.

"Hold that thought," Gwen told Peter.

"That's a lot of roof." Peter gawked at the peaks and rafters above the main section of Gwen's old house, before heading to the left, through stacks of file boxes. "Must cost a bundle to keep it in repair."

"I'm sure." Rick waded into the hodge-podge of appliances, unlabeled boxes, and old lamps that lounged in armchairs. "Haley said Gwen put a lot into the place before she moved back, after her parents and her husband died. New roof, insulation, and windows. She made the lakeside porch into an all-weather oasis. And that kitchen. You've seen how functional that is."

"Best room in the house. It's no mystery why everyone congregates there. The mystery is why she wants to live out here, so isolated, especially when the place requires so much upkeep."

"She loves it," Rick said with a shrug. "It makes her feel connected to her family, even though they're gone. And the property is primo. Great view of the lake, her own launch ramp, her own beach. I'm sure she'd get a couple million for it if she wanted to sell."

"Even with that killer road?"

Rick snorted. "If it were me, I'd have re-engineered that road before I tore apart the kitchen." He came to a halt and put his hands on his hips. "What am I trying to find?"

"Furniture for a second bedroom for my sister, Bree." Peter came to a wall and checked around him. "Everything over here is clothing racks," he said dismissively. "She likes antiques, I think, but she's not a girly girl, so nothing too fussy."

"Well, I've got some old dressers and bedframes over here," Rick called. "Might do the job for you."

"Hold up your hand." Peter spied a hand waving in front of a cobweb-covered window. He found a direct route. "Bonanza," he agreed.

After examining four old dressers, he settled on a tall cherry chest with smooth-running drawers and a bedside chest that matched. "These are great. But I can't let Gwen give them to me for a buck each."

Rick shrugged. "She offered. Unless she decides she wants them, I wouldn't argue."

"Maybe. So, what's our plan, partner? Clean them off first or haul them down to the garage?"

"I say haul. Any old rags up here are probably vintage clothing that someone would be happy to buy."

"And I was just going to clean off that window with this." He held up a gray coat with a flannel lining.

"No way, man, that's a waxed cotton hunting jacket. That would bring a lot at a garage sale."

"How do you even know that?"

"My grandfather in Watervliet used to hunt fowl and small game to feed the family. I remember when he found a coat like that at an estate sale, he grabbed it up for a song, said it was worth a lot. It kept him dry and warm out there in the field. That's all I know. I was just a little guy then. He died not long after."

"So what happened to the coat?"

"My grandmother probably sold it at a garage sale for way more than a song." Rick shrugged. "Did you need a bedframe? This metal one is newer, but the hardwood next to it is also in good shape." The metal frame was adjustable and sturdy. "Could work for a twin or double mattress."

Peter crouched down and rubbed dust off the hardwood frame. It was a match for the dressers, but it was made for a queen-size bed. He might want it for his own queen-size bed. In fact, he might want to swap out his furniture to Bree's room and claim the cherry pieces for himself. That wasn't in the spirit of Gwen's offer. He hedged, "Let's find the headboards first."

In the end they found a pretty, carved oak headboard for a twin bed. It would go well with the dresser and chair he had in his bedroom now, and he would just need a twin mattress to finish Bree's room.

The cherry headboard was queen-size with carved pineapples at each corner.

"Wow," Rick declared. "That's for you and Gwen."

Gwen padded down the stairs, fresh from her late-afternoon shower. She always stopped at the end of the workday, sluiced away any lingering frustration or anxiety, and turned over her clients to her God for another day.

The house was cool and quiet. Haley had yelled to her, just before her shower, that she and Rick were heading out for a walk. No bangs or bumps sounded overhead, so she assumed Peter had finished with his furniture hunt.

Good smells drew her to the kitchen. She cracked opened the oven door and spied a pan of bubbling eggplant parmesan. Phil had sent them home with two beautiful eggplants from his garden and "Edie's secret recipe." Gwen salivated as she inhaled the aroma of cheesy vegetables and herbs.

Cookies sat on cooling racks, although they were already cold to the touch. She sampled one while she packaged them, half-dozen at a time.

Out in the garage, Peter grabbed a towel and wiped the worst of the grime from his hands. He tapped on the glass of the kitchen door and grinned at Gwen.

"I want you to pass judgment on our find," he told her. "Rick and I brought these down for your approval." He swept his arm over the chests of drawers and headboards.

She stepped down to the garage. A happy sigh escaped her as she passed between the old dressers. "It's the furniture from my dad's bedroom," she told Peter with a note of awe in her voice. "And my old headboard from when I was a child. It's all cleaned up and beautiful." Her eyes sparkled with joy.

"Just like you," he said.

She blushed.

"For someone who's been dealing with drunks and druggies all day, you're amazingly serene."

Gwen's head jerked as if she'd been slapped. Eyes focused on the tall cherry chest, she told him in a frosty tone, "I love my work, Peter. I help a lot of people get their recovery on track and get their lives back. It can be frustrating and tedious, but it's worthwhile." She shifted her gaze to his face, narrowed her eyes and defied him to counter her. "I make a difference."

He shifted on his feet, settled back on his heels, and told her evenly, "It's just that I worry about you having your office way out here. Have you thought about getting an office in one of the professional buildings, where there's security and safety in numbers?"

Her answer was terse. "Not really, no."

He forced a lighter tone. "It must be hard for some of your clients to navigate your road in winter."

She shrugged. "I have it plowed."

He kept quiet.

"But you're right. A few cancel on stormy days, and some stop for the winter months."

She gave him a tight smile. "Which is not the best thing for their recovery." She folded her arms across her chest. "It's something to think about."

He nodded, hands in his pockets. He watched her steadily until the left side of her mouth twitched with a little smile. He said gently, "Did we just have our first fight?"

"Yeah, I think that's what just happened here." She sucked in a big breath and blew it out as a laugh.

He withdrew his hands from his pockets and examined himself, from T-shirt to sneakers. "I'd suggest we kiss and make up, but I'm all grimy and sweaty."

"No bugs or leaves." She pointed to his hair with a smile.

He grinned at that. "Speaking of the canoe, Rick said you took it out on the water and it's seaworthy. Or lake worthy."

"It handled great. No leaks. We should go for a paddle one day soon."

"Let's. I'm not working Friday night. Maybe we could head out early Saturday morning."

"I can probably do that."

He fondled a pineapple on the queen headboard. "But, listen I started to ask you if you're okay with me taking these pieces."

"Of course."

He pressed, "It's a lot, and it's really beautiful."

With a playful scowl, she demanded, "You're correct, and you owe me"—she pointed to each item and counted— "five bucks, mister."

He gave her a sexy grin as he dragged his wallet out of his back pocket. He opened the bill compartment, riffled through and extracted a five-dollar bill, then held it out with two fingers. He licked his lips as she slid the bill past the vee of her black knit top and tucked it in her bra.

Her voice was sultry and her eyelashes fluttered when she asked him, "The cherry's for your bedroom, right?"

Peter's mouth dropped open. "The . . ." He recovered with a laugh. "The cherry pieces, yes. And I'll put the oak headboard and my old stuff into the second bedroom. Then I just need a mattress for the twin bed."

"And finally Bree can come to Tompkins Falls and meet everyone?" Gwen asked brightly.

He plucked the sweaty T-shirt away from his chest. "Well, probably none of that will happen until I get cleaned up and eat something."

She stepped back and offered, "If you want, there's a shower down the hall on the left, across from my office. Help yourself to whatever. Grab a few cookies on the way."

"Salvation," he said and bounded up the steps.

Gwen called after him, "After your shower, we'll have supper, whether the kids are back or not. I have a seven o'clock meeting tonight."

"Thought you were done for the day." Peter reappeared in the doorway, cookies in hand.

"Uh . . ."

Haley and Rick burst through the outside door. The oven timer buzzed.

Rick told them. "Supper's ready. You're staying, right, Peter?"

"And that's what's new with Baby Forrester Walker." Gwen picked up her half-full mug and waited for a reaction from Deirdre.

"I'm glad for Haley and Rick. And you're okay with having someone adopt the baby?"

"I am." Gwen's mouth curved in a smile. "Peaceful and grateful."

"Yes, I can see," Deirdre said, "and it looks good on you."

Gwen started to say something but hesitated. She checked the clock by the front door of the Bagel Depot. Half past eight already.

"What time do they close?"

"Nine o'clock. What were you going to say?"

"Peter and I had our first fight today."

Deirdre sat back and drummed her fingers on her empty mug. "Do tell."

Gwen recounted the exchange in detail. "What do you think?" she asked her sponsor.

"I think you gave him priceless Stickley antiques for five bucks and agreed to move your entire practice closer to town, while he got away with calling your clients 'drunks and druggies.'"

"Deirdre—"

"You asked. That's what I heard."

"Not helpful. That's the most negative spin anyone could give to what happened. And you and I use the words 'drunks and druggies' all the time."

"Okay."

"And it's not Stickley," Gwen huffed.

Deirdre chin rose. "Does he know you're at a meeting tonight?"

"He knows," Gwen snapped.

"Does he know it's an AA meeting?" Deirdre insisted.

"He—maybe not."

"Why not?"

"We got interrupted." Her eyes shifted as she recalled the scene.

"And there wasn't another moment when you could have clarified?"

"It didn't seem worth it to create an issue. We were all enjoying dinner, laughing, talking about things we all love— the canoe, the walks through the woods, Phil's vegetable garden. And then it was six-thirty, and I blasted out to my car."

"Peter didn't walk you out?"

"He helped Rick clean up the kitchen for Haley who made the eggplant parmesan for us."

"Sounds homey and fun." Deirdre's eyebrows were knit with frustration.

"It was. We enjoyed it."

"Gwen, you need to put a stop to his jabs."

"I'm pretty sure I did that," Gwen asserted.

"But you're bending over backwards to accommodate him instead—"

"I disagree."

"—instead of telling him you're a sober drunk so he can see for himself what that means and decide for himself if he wants a relationship with you."

Gwen's mouth was tight, and her temples throbbed.

"Bottom line," Deirdre insisted, her voice loud, "the way you're playing this game is dishonest."

"I'm not playing a game," Gwen snapped.

"The hell you're not," Deirdre yelled.

Heads turned toward them.

The young man at the register stood.

Gwen's eyes flashed.

Deirdre calmed her own breathing. She held up a hand to appease the other customers and nodded to the young man. "Sorry," she called. "Honey," she pleaded with Gwen, "this is a ticking time bomb, and you can't ignore it unless you're prepared to lose this relationship."

Gwen snatched her purse and stood. "Thank you." She walked out of the restaurant and made it to her car before she cried.

Gwen took in a lungful of crisp morning air and let her paddle rest for a moment while Peter propelled them away from the cobblestone boat ramp. Closing her eyes, she reveled in the feel of the canoe gliding effortlessly in the still water.

Behind her, Peter laughed. "Hey there, partner. It works better when you put the paddle in the water."

Gwen's answering laugh rang out. "You don't miss a thing, Officer."

"No, ma'am, I'm a highly trained investigator."

She tightened and released her shoulders before dipping her paddle in the sparkling, blue water. "Where shall we go first?" she called back.

He jumped on it. "I want to see the gumdrops up close. How about some figure eights around a few of them?"

"Gum—oh, you mean the little islands. Cool idea," Gwen agreed.

"How many are there, anyway?"

She chuckled. "You know, anytime I tried counting, I got so caught up in their beauty, I lost track, so I gave that up years ago."

"That's how it should be, and maybe that's why no one else knows the answer. Let's head to the left and around the closest one. We'll make a loop behind it and then decide what comes next."

She nodded and settled her butt more comfortably against the seat.

"I like that view, you know."

Gwen laughed. "Is that why you picked the stern?"

"That, and I'm a control freak."

"You are not," she chided.

They paddled quietly for a few minutes and came within thirty feet of the first island. "I'd forgotten, they're even more beautiful when you're close enough to see the textures of the different evergreens."

"Do you know all the kinds?" Peter asked.

"Most of them. The hemlocks are the soft, lacy ones along the shoreline. They're my favorite."

"You have a lot of hemlock in your woods."

"Yes, and behind the hemlocks on the shore are several kinds of fir and spruce and other pines."

"From my place, the islands appear as one shade of shimmering dark green."

"The shimmering is probably the hemlocks. The underside of their needles is silvery."

"From here, it appears each island rises straight up from the lake bottom with no good places to land. Do people find ways to explore them?

"Not much. There's one tiny island with a beach my parents knew about. We tried as kids to find others, but even when you find a low spot, it's almost impossible to haul a canoe ashore. Unless you think to bring a rope to tie it, somebody's going to get wet."

"Like getting wet would ever stop you," he disparaged.

She turned her head to explain. "But having to swim fifty yards to retrieve the canoe you didn't properly secure is not so fun. This is the best way to enjoy the islands—looping around, threading through."

They paddled without talking. Peter steered them expertly. Gwen felt her soul fill with joy.

Suddenly, Peter shifted on his seat, and the canoe pitched side-to-side. "What's that huge bird on top of the tallest tree, a few islands over?" he asked.

When he pointed with his paddle, Gwen got a shower. She yelped.

"Sorry. Not intentional. Do you see him?"

She shaded her eyes. "Yes, it's an eagle. See the white head?"

"No kidding? I've never seen one. He's just sitting there, surveying his kingdom."

"It's a perfect day to do this." Gwen grinned back at him.

His smile flashed white in the morning sun, and he mapped a serpentine path with his hand. "Let's weave among the next three islands." He switched his paddle to the left side of the canoe and dug in.

"You're a good pilot," Gwen praised. "I can't believe it's been fifteen years since you sat in a canoe."

"It's like riding a bike, I guess. You never forget. How long has it been for you?"

"Probably fifteen years since this canoe was in the water, but Jeb and I had a canoe. I don't know what happened to it." She shrugged. "We got it out on the water quite a bit when we were first married. His work made it harder each year." She paused. *That wasn't the reason, Gwen.* She puzzled for a moment. *No matter.* "So I'd take it out alone sometimes, especially in the evenings. It's a good way to relax after a stressful day. I should do that again, now that we know the old Green Lizard is seaworthy."

"Who's idea was 'Green Lizard'?"

"My brother Bill. I think he was twelve. We should have Haley paint over it and draw some flowers."

"Good idea. But seriously, Gwen, you know I'd rather you didn't go out on the water alone."

"He said sternly from the stern," Gwen quipped.

"I mean it, Gwen."

"I know, and it's smart to be careful, you're right. You and I should paddle together sometimes."

Peter apparently wasn't ready to let the safety issue drop. "Do you know what I said to Sam about you that first night after Haley broke in?"

"What?"

"We left your road for the highway and he asked what I thought of you."

"And you said . . ."

"Something like, 'She's made of steel or she's out of her mind.'"

Gwen turned from the waist to see him.

"You're our scout, remember." He motioned for her to turn back.

She gave him the eye before complying. "What did you mean by that?"

"I was baffled why a beautiful woman would live alone in such an isolated place."

"Until Haley broke in, there had been no trouble of any kind at the Forrester homestead."

"I am really, really surprised. Why do you think you never had trouble way out there?"

"Having that corkscrew road is a deterrent by itself, I think. And it's a tight neighborhood. My next door neighbors—Phil on the town side and the Petermans on the other—walk the paths every day watching for anything out of the ordinary, and when the leaves are off the trees in winter, we can see each others' homes. We all have security systems. Everyone takes security seriously."

"Good, I'm glad to hear that."

"It must feel very different from living in a city the size of Syracuse," she speculated. "Do you like the change?"

"Very much. From the first, even when I interviewed, it felt like I was meant to live here."

"Like fate?" she asked.

"Like God's got a plan. And I see what you mean. Already I've lost track of how many islands we've seen." He rested his paddle for a moment.

"Did you grow up Catholic?" Gwen asked.

"Yes. You?"

"Episcopalian, mostly. Mom and Dad wanted us to know about the Bible and go to church, but they also wanted us to know about other religions. We sometimes attended services with friends of theirs who were Jewish or Baptist or Quaker. I remember going to a Seder dinner one year at the Jewish family's home."

"Your folks were pretty open-minded."

Gwen set down her paddle. "Yes, and I'm glad for it." She twisted to face him. "Do you still practice Catholicism?"

"I always meant to." He hesitated. "Cynthia—my wife, my ex—didn't have any religious practice, so I was on my own with that. I just fell away gradually. But I still have faith. I don't think I could do what I do without believing in goodness and truth. How about you?"

"I'm not a churchgoer, but I pray all the time, and I feel very close to God."

"I can hear in your voice how much prayer and God mean to you." To keep them on a straight course, he drew the water hard with his paddle and feathered each stroke at the end.

Gwen smiled at him, faced forward, and picked up her paddle. "Yes, they do. That's one of the reasons I love living on the lake. It's very spiritual, always changing, like life. Being so close to the islands, there is spectacular beauty. Like our eagle up there. I tune into those moments, and they help me stay positive throughout the day."

"So being out on the water, the way we are, is not just about exercise?"

"And it's not just about enjoying the moment." She glanced back. "It's about getting to know you better." Suddenly she switched her paddle to the other side and used it as a brake. "Trouble on the right."

They had drifted close to a rocky outcropping. While Gwen braked, Peter swept his paddle in a wide arc. The canoe moved forward on a safer path.

"Nice job," she cheered.

"We're a good team."

"And we are deep in the heart of these islands," she observed. "I'm not sure I've ever been here."

"That happens when you go where the spirit moves," Peter said.

"I like it."

"So, what do you think?" he asked her, his tone intimate. "Were you and I fated to meet?"

"I think it's part of God's plan for my life," she answered with a nod, her voice quiet and serious. "What do you think?"

Peter tapped the surface of the water with his paddle. "I think it's more than coincidence that Haley broke into your house just as Sam and I were coming on duty." He dug in his paddle again. "The call from your security company came in a few seconds before we left on patrol, and we shouldn't have gotten the call at all. I checked on it later, and a call like that, outside the city limits, would normally have gone to the Sheriff's department. No one knows why it worked out the way it did."

Gwen turned back to face him. "Really?" She grinned. "Your eyes are sparkling."

Peter's head jerked up. "He's flying!"

Together, they watched the eagle lift from the tallest tree and soar with flat wings in a wide arc. "Where's he going?" Peter asked.

"I don't know, but I do believe he'll be back."

Chapter 8

A black-clad hostess with a cheerful smile seated Gwen and Justin at a table on the porch of the canal-side restaurant. She handed them menus, told them their waiter's name, and left them in peace. They collapsed in their chairs, barely half an hour after their meeting with the adoption attorney in Rochester. Haley and Rick had begged for twenty minutes to stroll by themselves along the canal path.

"We will be four eventually," Justin said when the waiter arrived. "Right now we're dying for iced tea—unsweetened?" He looked to Gwen for confirmation and she nodded.

"Water, too, please," she added. "And sweet potato fries for two, while we peruse the menu."

"Outstanding," Justin agreed. "Unsalted, please."

"Yes, sir." The waiter left with a bow.

Gwen set aside the menu and massaged her temples with her fingers. "I can't think, let alone make a decision."

Justin's answering chuckle gave her courage to ask, "How do you think it went?"

"Very well."

"Elaborate, please."

"I'm impressed that the legal firm independently verified the Hahns's financial standing and home environment. Thanks to Haley and Rick's thorough preparation, their attorney Melinda knows exactly what's important to them. She'll now use her expertise to negotiate with the Hahns's attorney for the best possible agreement."

"I was so proud of Rick when he pointed out that the most important agreement has already been reached." Gwen smiled into Justin's eyes. "The Hahns *will* adopt Baby Forrester Walker and provide a loving, safe environment with the advantages they value." She ticked them off on her fingers. "Education, engagement in physical activity and sports, support for creativity, and access to nature." She teared up. "And then Haley said anything else would be a bonus. I wanted to cry, I was so proud of her."

"At times I thought you and I could have stayed home." Justin smiled directed Gwen's attention down the canal path.

Haley, wearing the tailored red dress they'd found at Eastview Mall, stood on the path with Rick behind her, his tie askew, hands on her shoulders. A boy of three or four touched Haley's belly, under the watchful eye of his very-pregnant mom. The boy giggled and turned around to touch his mom's belly. The mothers laughed and chatted. As they strolled on, Rick's hand rested protectively on Haley's back.

"They're really okay with this," Gwen said, hoping it was true.

"Will Haley stay with you for long?"

"I'd like that, but it's up to her. We haven't had that conversation. Thank you," she said as the waiter presented them with a platter of crisp, hot fries and refilled their water glasses. Gwen reached for a sizzling fry and blew on it. She asked Justin, "What comes next with the attorneys? Am I involved after this? Yum, have some of these."

Justin reached for the longest fry. "As I understand it, the Hahns's attorney will come to Tompkins Falls with them to meet face-to-face with Rick and Haley's attorney—probably next week. They'll negotiate the final agreement, using Rick and Haley's input, and Melinda will call to explain the results and any next steps. After that, neither of us is involved, but Haley and Rick sign various documents, like the birth certificate, when the parents take the child into their custody."

"What did you think of Melinda?"

"Very competent attorney. And compassionate. I hope she never loses that quality."

"Will we meet the Hahns when they're here?"

"Most definitely. They'll stay two nights at the Manse. I've proposed taking the Hahns, you, Rick, and Haley to the Manse for dinner after the Hahns meet with both attorneys."

Gwen frowned as she reached for another fry.

"What? You don't think that's a good idea?"

"Have the Hahns agreed?"

"Melinda is waiting for the go-ahead from us. I told her I'd pose it to you first."

"Let me eat lunch first," she hedged.

"Fair enough." Justin signaled the waiter for two more menus and iced teas. "I will check in with Gianessa, if you'll excuse me."

Haley and Rick passed Justin on their way into the restaurant and spotted Gwen on the porch.

Gwen appraised their faces. Haley's forehead was smooth, and her mouth curved with a gentle smile. Rick had a worry wrinkle in his forehead and tension in his jaw and cheeks.

"Good walk?" Gwen asked.

Rick answered, "Man, I needed that."

Haley nodded.

"Are you both okay with what transpired in the attorney's office?"

Haley opened her eyes wide. "Yes. She gets what we want, and I trust her to represent us with the Hahns's attorney. Rick?"

Rick nodded. "I'm especially hoping they'll make a contribution to Haley's education. Mine is pretty well covered by research monies and scholarships."

"I agree, it would be a big help for Haley to have tuition support," Gwen said. "I want both of you to understand, though, that I'll help Haley in any way she needs, including but not limited to college expenses."

"But—" Haley started to say. Rick and Gwen both gave her stern looks. She sat back. "Thank you," she said. Her lower lip quivered.

"First things first," Gwen said with a smile. "Right now, let's eat."

"Where's Justin gone?"

"He's checking in with Gianessa."

"It was nice of him to come with us today," Haley said, "and to set up the contact with Melinda in the first place."

Rick cleared his throat. "He's gone out of his way for us. How can we repay him?"

"There is no need," Gwen said simply. "Justin is doing this out of generosity and out of gratitude. As a middle-aged man expecting his first children, twins, he's very touched by your situation, and he's—" she wobbled her hand "—repaying me." She smiled at Rick and then at Haley. "Let's leave it at that, shall we?"

Rick narrowed his eyes and slowly exhaled. His cheeks relaxed. He shifted his jaw back and forth and reached for his iced tea. "Thank you, Gwen."

"Don't mention it. I am starved."

"News flash." Haley giggled.

Rick grinned.

"This from Haley who's had at least a dozen fries since she sat down." Gwen reached for her menu.

Gwen's Monday morning bike ride brought her to the town end of the park as Peter finished lacing his running shoes. She walked her bike to his bench.

Startled, he greeted her, "Hey, beautiful."

His big hug took her breath away. She pressed her cheek to his five o'clock shadow and told him, "I love these public displays of affection."

"What? When did I ever hug you in public?"

"I remember kissing at the end of the willow path not long ago."

"You liked those kisses, huh?"

"Uh-huh." Her insides danced at the memory.

His eyes sparkled. "How about I run alongside your bike as far as the parking lot?"

"Let's do it."

Once underway they both adjusted their speeds and found their rhythm. "Thanks for leaving that message. I'm glad things went well with the lawyer. I was on the phone with Bree for a long time last evening."

"How's she doing?"

"Not well. She's trying to hold down two jobs, but her lifestyle works against it. Would you be upset if she came to live with me?"

"Of course not. I have Haley, after all. How does Bree feel about moving here?"

"She likes Tompkins Falls, but there's something she's not saying about living with me."

"Any idea what?"

"Other than I'm a son of a gun with a bad temper?"

"Are you?" Gwen was surprised to hear him say it.

"Siblings can bring out the worst in each other, you know?"

Gwen groaned in sympathy. "Bill and I—Haley's dad— are at each other's throats when we're in the same room."

"Now *that* is out of character." He moved behind her to let a runner pass.

"For you, too, I think."

"Anyway, I hope she'll come and meet some young people who'll help her think about the future and change her habits. Sara, my dance partner at the chief's dinner, would be a good influence, and I think they're about the same age."

"You really love your sister, don't you?"

"She's the most important person in my life, and I feel responsible for her and protective of her. I want the best for her."

"That goes a long way, Peter." Gwen smiled over at him. "In the end it's what wins."

"God, I hope you're right. Sometimes when I'm with her I think I'll be the world's worst parent. Helping out with Haley and Rick has given me a totally different perspective on parenting. There may be hope for me yet."

Gwen took the plunge. "Did you and your wife plan to have kids?"

"No, I was game, but she said she didn't want any. I respected her wishes." He laughed hollowly. "But after she filed for divorce, the next time I saw her, which was only a month later, she was five months pregnant. Not by me."

"I'm sorry, Peter."

"Thanks, but it helped me get over losing her. Until I saw her pregnant I'd been broken-hearted. After that, I was just pissed. I had been seeing a police trauma counselor about the shooting, and he told me that all the negative energy could either destroy me or, if I turned it around, could push me through my physical therapy."

"Good way to think about it." She gave him a warm smile and reached out a hand. "I'm glad you got away from old business after you healed. Glad you came to Tompkins Falls."

"Same here. What are you doing today?"

"I have clients from ten until four. Otherwise, I haven't given it a moment's thought."

"Want to take the canoe out?"

"I would love to, but I'm meeting a woman friend at seven-thirty. Come for supper?"

"Got a better idea. I'll come by at five, and we can have burgers at Ralphs."

"You are a wicked man, Peter Shaughnessy. Ralphs is my downfall."

"The fries?" he teased. "The milk shakes?"

"You're killing me, Peter."

They had reached the parking lot at the one-mile point on the willow path. Peter said, "I'll stop teasing if you'll accept the invitation."

"Done."

The attorneys locked in their meeting with the Hahns for Wednesday in Tompkins Falls. After a round of phone calls that had Justin chuckling about "the insanity of pending parenthood," the Hahns agreed to his dinner proposal. However, Laura Hahn insisted on a private dinner with just Gwen, while Helmud would join the men and Haley at the Manse Grille.

Justin added, "Gwen, honestly, I don't know why she wants to speak with you and only you, but if you're willing, let's go with it."

"Anything for the cause," she agreed.

She was a little apprehensive about her private session with Laura Hahn, but she was much more concerned about how she, Haley, and Rick would occupy themselves Wednesday afternoon while they waited for Melinda to phone with the results of the big meeting. Haley and Rick, she knew, were sweating the details.

Baking cookies was getting old, and there was no need to fix dinner. Gwen would prefer to get them all exercising, but what could all three of them do that wouldn't exhaust Haley?

The answer confronted her when she arrived home with her bicycle Wednesday morning. There in the center of the garage floor was the mound of grit, bugs, and leaves deposited by the canoe when she and Peter had hauled it down from the rafters. Nearby, an empty bottle of Murphy's and old rags from the furniture cleanup, lay wherever they'd been tossed—in pails, on boxes, and hanging from tools. All around her was abundant evidence that she habitually neglected her garage until the first snowfall, when it was time to park the Range Rover under cover.

"Hey, gang," she said over breakfast. "I could use your help this afternoon to straighten out that garage."

Rick smirked.

"Oh, did you notice it's a mess?"

He laughed. "Primo project, Gwen, and we'll be glad to help. Haley, if you'd rather not get down and dirty, maybe you could keep us in iced tea and sustenance."

"I'm on it."

Gwen squinted at them. "What am I missing?"

Haley giggled.

"We were going to offer to do it today to keep ourselves from going crazy," Rick confessed. "We figured we'd be plenty busy and still be close to your phone. Having you supervise will make it a lot easier."

"You guys," Gwen said. "You're the best.

When Melinda's call came at three that afternoon, the garage was ship-shape. Rick, fresh from the shower, was foraging in the refrigerator for a snack. Haley was napping on the lakeside porch and Gwen was in her bedroom rummaging through her closet for the right thing to wear to dinner with Laura Hahn. *Competent but non-threatening. Why are all my clothes some shade of neutral?*

Rick snatched up the receiver and shouted for them to join him in the kitchen.

"Melinda, it's Rick. We'll all get on speaker in a second. Gwen and Haley are racing from the far corners of the house."

"Hi, Rick," Melinda said with laugh. "It's all good, no need to worry."

Rick squeezed his eyes shut and swallowed hard.

Seeing his anguish, Gwen took the phone from his hands, moved it to the island, and punched the speaker button.

Haley circled Rick's waist with her arm and drew him to the island.

As she settled on a stool, Haley giggled at Gwen. "What are you wearing?"

Gwen looked sheepishly at her flowered T-shirt and plaid shorts. "Sorry, I was trying on clothes, and I grabbed whatever was handy."

"I heard that," Melinda teased. She gave them a moment, cleared her throat, and said, "Are we all ready?"

"Go ahead, Melinda," Rick said.

"Well, as I said to Rick, it's all good. The papers are signed, and the Hahns, whom I like very much, will assume custody of your child as soon as humanly possible after the birth. Gwen will contact them by phone after the delivery. And I'm confident they will provide a wonderful home." She paused. "Do you need a moment to catch your breath and pass a box of tissues?"

Rick and Haley held hands and let the tears fall.

"Let's give them a few moments," Gwen said.

"I understand. Listen, there is more good news coming right up for Haley and Rick. Gwen, maybe you can take notes. And you know you can call me any time to clarify anything in the agreement."

"You'll be sending us the agreement?"

"Absolutely. I'll overnight it when we've finished, after I've had a chance to document our discussion and clarify any points of confusion. How's everyone doing?"

Rick squeezed Haley's shoulder while she blew her nose. "Ready?" he asked her, and she nodded.

"We're good, Melinda."

"To set the stage," she said, "I need you to understand that some private adoptions involve significant payment to the mother, although the state places limits. First, as is often the case, the adopting parents have agreed to cover all medical expenses related to Haley's prenatal care and the birth of the child. Second, it was decided there was a conflict of interest for the Hahns to cover my fees, so that was off the table. Far more important, however, the Hahns considered the impact of the pregnancy on Haley's education and her living situation. They're awarding Haley the monetary equivalent of two years' tuition, room, and board at the state university rate."

Haley gasped and glanced at Rick.

"Thank you, Melinda," Rick said. He followed with a fist pump and a relaxed smile.

"Haley," Melinda continued, "it's important for you to understand that money is a lump sum and does not need to be used at your current school; technically it does not need to be used for your education."

"Of course I'll use it for school," Haley said.

Gwen patted Haley's hand.

"Now, Rick," Melinda continued, "this is interesting, and it came directly from the Hahns, nothing we asked for."

"What?" Rick looked from Haley to Gwen and back.

"They were impressed that you weren't asking for help with your education, but they are concerned—don't laugh, folks—with the vehicle you are using to drive back and forth from the Albany area to support Haley through the birth of the child. They're awarding you the monetary equivalent of a new-model, compact car. While they aren't stipulating it be used that way, they were very concerned about your safety and your continued presence."

"How did they even know about my car?" Rick was baffled.

Gwen caught his eye and mouthed, "Justin?"

"The guy doesn't miss a thing, does he?"

Melinda's brisk tone signaled she was ready to wrap up. "That's basically the agreement, surrounded by a lot of legalese. But there is one more thing that will make you chuckle."

"What's that, Melinda?" Gwen asked.

"This did not come from the Hahns, but I was asked to convey—without revealing the identity of the sender—that a gift certificate is on its way to Haley that she can use at

Eastview Mall to rebuild her wardrobe after she delivers. Haley, I wish we'd thought of it ourselves. I'm sure losing all your things from your mother's house has been very difficult."

"Wow. All that's left to replace are my art supplies that Ursula trashed."

Gwen spoke up. "Let me do that with you, Haley."

"Thank you." Haley's eyes widened. "So that's everything," she choked out. She buried her face in her arms on the island. Her shoulders shook with sobs.

Rick massaged her back. "Melinda, thank you."

"Just doing my job," she replied. "You were both very clear about what would make your lives easier through this hard time. Gwen, watch for the documents to arrive tomorrow."

"I will."

"Now give yourselves some time before meeting the Hahns for dinner tonight. Again, I like them very much, and I believe you will, too. In my estimation, they will be stellar parents for this baby."

After the call, Gwen laid claim to the porch while Haley and Rick chatted in the kitchen. She touched base with Justin and Gianessa to fill them in on the results. Gianessa denied any knowledge of the gift certificate.

"Nervous about dining with Laura, Gwen?" Justin asked.

"Yes, but I'm doing it anyway."

"I'll send waves of calm your way the whole time," Gianessa promised.

"That will help."

"And call me if you need to. I'll just be here listening to the rain the weatherman promises."

"Love you both," Gwen said and rang off.

When Peter heard the results of the negotiation, he concluded, "I'm glad to know they're thoughtful, caring people."

"And generous."

"Are you still worried about the dinner with Laura Hahn tonight?"

"I'm taking out all my anxiety on what to wear."

"Wear the silver gown," he advised.

She laughed from her belly. "That dress is exclusively for you, Peter Shaughnessy." The words were out before she realized she'd said them.

"Now, I'm glad to hear that," he told her, his voice husky, "because I am over the moon for you, Gwen Forrester."

Justin arrived with the Hahns a few minutes before seven. Rick rushed out through the garage to greet them on the turnaround. Haley was close on his heels. Gwen left the door open and hung back in the kitchen. She listened to the tone of the conversation and smiled as it moved from stilted to easy-going. Rick laughed suddenly, and Gwen's face relaxed in a smile.

Just as she reached for her purse, Haley offered Justin a two-minute tour of the immaculate garage. *What is up with that?*

Justin roared with laughter and said, "This spotless space can't be a garage."

To Gwen's further confusion, someone rang the front door bell. *That's what guests do on a formal occasion, Gwen.* She hustled to answer their ring but stopped when she saw the clutter in her entryway.

"Coming," she promised. In desperation, she threw open the closet door and tossed in orphan sneakers, piles of magazines, and a bent golf club. She closed the closet door, straightened her navy, silk dress, and smoothed her hair.

When she opened the front door, a pair of porcelain blue eyes, bright with anticipation and longing, tugged at her heart. Helmud Hahn pressed her hand, bowed his head, and said, "Lovely to meet you, Dr. Forrester." The effect was charmingly Old World.

"Gwen, please." She admired his self-assured posture and beautifully chiseled face.

"Gwen, my wife and I honor the pain this must cause you and your niece and her young man."

Gwen swallowed. "Thank you for saying that, Helmud." She forced a cheerful smile. "It's a pleasure to meet you at last. Syd and Danny think the world of you and your wife, Laura."

"You know our friends?" Helmud's face broke open in a smile.

"We met at the Cushman wedding in July, Justin's marriage to my friend Gianessa."

"I see. Laura and Danny bump elbows all the time through their work, and he's my tennis partner. We plan to stay in touch, even after Laura stops working."

"So many wonderful changes ahead for you," Gwen said.

His curt, "We are beyond ready, Gwen," made her jump. He turned back to the walk and reached out a hand to someone. "Gwen, meet my wife, Laura." He motioned her forward.

Laura walked stiffly up the porch steps and welcomed her husband's strong arm around her shoulders. She was a brunette beauty with a smile that was frozen in place. Her brown eyes were dark with worry.

Laura is afraid, and it has to do with me. Huh?

"Sweetheart," Helmud encouraged, "meet Gwen Forrester, Haley's aunt."

Gwen extended her hand and cocked her head. "Laura, I'm so happy for you and for all of us. We've been on pins and needles, and I'm so relieved now that the agreement is signed. We appreciate your generosity."

"Yes, we have been on pins and needles, too, haven't we, Laura?" Helmud said. He rewarded Gwen with a smile. "It's such a relief to have everything decided and formalized."

Laura cleared her throat. "I thought we'd have our own dinner, Gwen," she stated, as if the plans had not already been made. "How does a salad sound to you?"

"Perfect. If you don't have a place in mind, I'll drive us to a favorite spot in Canandaigua. I can drop you at the Manse after."

"Yes." She turned to her husband and took refuge in his arms.

Why is she is terrified? Pretending she'd forgotten her wrap, Gwen excused herself and stepped away to give them privacy. Then, blue silk shawl in hand, she slipped past the Hahns onto the front porch and down to the walk, where she breathed in the serenity carried on the lake breeze. *God, how can I help Laura?* Laughter floated to her from the turnaround. She hurried around the corner to join Justin and the others.

Haley and Rick chatted with Justin beside the Hahns's silver SUV. Justin's bonhomie dominated the mood. Even so, Rick's laugh was as stiff as his body. Haley spotted Gwen and managed a shaky smile.

"What do you think of them?" Gwen asked quietly.

Haley and Rick exchanged glances. Haley told her, "Laura is really scared. You've got to check her out for us."

Gwen hugged her. "We'll have a long talk, don't worry."

"Helmud's really funny," Rick added, "and he's wicked smart."

Gwen turned to Justin for his reaction.

"Good people." He nodded.

The click of Laura's heels on the walk announced the Hahns's approach. Gwen gave everyone a warm smile and said, "My stomach is ready for a good meal. Anyone else?"

"Do you need to lock your front door, Gwen?" Justin asked.

"Ohmigod, how could I forget? I don't even know where the key is. I'll go back through the house."

Justin raised his voice for the Hahns's benefit, while Gwen dashed inside. "Laura, I understand Gwen will drive you in her car and drop you at the Manse afterward. I suppose you women will pick at salads, while we wolf down steaks."

Haley countered, "I'm going to have a salad, too. The Grille does have salads, right, Justin?"

"The Manse Grille has a menu for every appetite. If the grilled shrimp salad is on the specials tonight, you must get it. Rick, maybe you can help Haley into the back seat?"

Helmud stood resolutely by his wife until Gwen emerged from the house. He kissed Laura's cheek and held up his hand to the women in farewell. "Gwen, pleasure to meet you. Take good care of her." His eyes bored into hers.

Gwen saluted.

Laura's lips trembled, but she nodded to Gwen and walked beside her to the Range Rover.

Gwen nudged the wine list closer to Laura, who fidgeted with the silverware. "They have a good selection of local wines, Laura. The server will answer any questions or make a suggestion if you want."

"Oh. Nice. What do you like?"

"As your designated driver, I'm having the mango iced tea, but don't let that influence you."

"Okay." Laura's voice was barely audible.

Gwen gave a silent prayer that a glass or two of something would help. Reminding herself this private dinner was Laura's idea, and it wouldn't do any good to take control, she sat back in her chair and opened the big menu in front of her.

The waiter was a regular who introduced himself to Laura as "Ben" and greeted Gwen by name. "Evening, Dr. Forrester." He told the specials and asked, "What can I get you ladies to start?"

Laura answered, "My husband and I had a lovely Riesling last night at the Manse. I don't recall the vineyard, but the label had a heron or some bird like that."

Ben nodded. "Good selection, ma'am."

"Iced tea for me, Ben," Gwen said. "And a plate of your stuffed mushrooms for us to share while we decide."

"Very good."

Laura's eyes roamed over the menu as if she were unable to make sense of it. Gwen had already decided on the harvest salad, made with local goat cheese and fresh vegetables and berries from a nearby farm. Just as she opened her mouth to offer a suggestion, Ben returned with their drinks and a sizzling plate of *hors d'oeuvres*.

To Gwen's relief, as soon as Laura took one bite of a stuffed mushroom, her eyes closed and pleasure washed over her face. The creases in her forehead vanished, and her mouth curved. "Heaven," she mumbled around the succulent crab, spices, and mushroom. "I'm going to like this place."

Gwen chuckled. "I'm glad. Everything is good here." Gwen told her about the farm-to-table ingredients in the salads. "And the trout special sounds amazing. Everything's from nearby, so it's going to be fresh and delicious."

Laura decided on the Lake Erie trout, potato-turnip mashup, and fresh garden vegetables. "I didn't realize how hungry I am," she said as she reached for another crab-stuffed mushroom. This time, she followed each bite with a swallow of wine.

Before finishing the second glass of Riesling, Laura had divulged every detail of the room that would be their son's. Then, in an abrupt change of subject, she asked about Gwen's experience renovating the Forrester home and, without waiting for an answer or stopping for a breath, told her, "Our house in Pound Ridge had everything we wanted except a decent kitchen. We pushed out the back wall to create a big family space plus an up-to-date kitchen, and we added a bluestone terrace beyond the new family room. It's become Helmud's and my favorite hangout after work. We really hope we'll have some Indian Summer, so we can take the baby out there."

"It sounds wonderful. I'm thinking you won't miss your job."

Laura waved it away. "There are so many ways I can use my skills and creativity as a mom." Her voice caught. She covered her mouth as tears fell from her gentle brown eyes. "I can't believe this is really happening." She pleaded with Gwen, "Please, please, don't change your mind about the baby." Laura buried her face in a fistful of tissues.

"Of course not, Laura. I am thrilled to have everything agreed and formalized. Legally decided," she added for emphasis.

Laura's shoulders shook with silent sobs.

Gwen slipped from her chair and knelt at Laura's side. "Laura, this is your baby—yours and Helmud's." She touched her hand to her own belly. "I'll have my own." *God, let it be true.*

Laura suddenly turned accusing eyes on Gwen. "I just can't imagine how you can let go of this child." Laura's eyebrows pinched together, her tone harsh with judgment. "It's inconceivable to me."

Gwen gasped and struggled to put her professional face in place. Then stopped. *No, I'm not here as a therapist. I'm here as a woman, and this is a deeply personal conversation. No mask.*

A movement caught her eye, and she nodded to Ben as he set down their meals. The distraction gave her a moment to pray. *Help me do this with dignity and grace.*

"Laura, knowing how long you and Helmud have tried to have a child, I can see why you question my decision. As Haley's aunt, I know she is a long way from being able to parent this baby, and Rick's education is too important to sacrifice. I gave a lot of thought to stepping in as the baby's mother, but my head knew it was absolutely the wrong thing, and—"

"But your heart, Gwen." Laura forced her fist against the table. Her growl was that of a mama bear protecting its child. "What did your heart want?"

Gwen's heart raced at the attack. Tears slipped from her eyes, and her voice shook when she answered, "When

I finally had the courage to listen to my heart, I knew that what I wanted, first and foremost, was a good man to be my life partner." She heard the ring of truth in her own words, and her voice grew stronger. "I sincerely hope children will come into that marriage—our own children or ones that he brings to the union or both." She sat back on her heels. "All in good time for me, but your time is now, Laura. This little boy is meant to be your baby. I am convinced of that." She squeezed Laura's hand.

Laura's fist relaxed.

Thank God. I couldn't take any more.

Gwen slipped back into her chair and took a big swallow of iced tea. A phrase rang in her head, one she heard around the rooms of AA. *Be true to yourself.* For the first time since Haley's arrival and Peter's appearance in her life, she knew in her gut, her heart, and her soul that she was on the right path.

Ben came unbidden to the table, topped off Gwen's drink, set a mango iced tea by Laura's plate, and moved smoothly to his next table.

Gwen studied the salad in front of her. She counted four different kinds of tiny lettuce, three colors of miniature tomato, and three varieties of berry. *I wish Haley could paint this colorful salad for me.* She prayed for her stomach to relax and enjoy the beautiful meal.

When Laura finished with her tissues, she spied the cold drink by her steaming plate of food. "Perfect. Did I order this?"

"Must have," Gwen said and picked up her own fork. "Let me know how you like the trout."

"What's the final verdict on Helmud?" Gwen asked Rick. They sat on her lakeside porch, with the windows open to the evening breeze off the lake.

"He's a solid guy. Like I said before, he's funny and

smart. Good head for finance. He and Justin really got into it. Way over my head. He'll be a good dad."

"I can't believe anything is way over your head," she said with a chuckle. "You're the most brilliant person I've ever met, Rick."

"I've got my own little niche. Everyone does." He smiled softly. "Like Haley's botanical art. And your psychotherapy." His eyebrows pinched together. "I don't know about Laura, though. What's up with her?"

"Laura was scared to death I'd change my mind and pull the plug on the adoption."

"You weren't going to, right, even if you legally could?" Rick asked.

"Correct."

"Will she be a good mom?"

"Yes. No doubt in my mind. Besides being totally invested in raising this baby, she's imagining how her work skills will contribute to PTA and play groups and all the community stuff she'll be involved in as a mom. And she has the nursery planned to the ultimate detail, so it will evolve as the baby grows. Do you think your son will like a fish-and-boats theme?"

"It was my dream as a kid." Rick's voice caught. "I know he'll love it."

"Still okay with giving him up for adoption?"

"Still sure it's the right thing. And I know for sure they're the right parents. They're naming him Karl Erich Hahn. Haley and I both like it. Did you know my name is not Richard, it's Eric?"

Gwen exhaled a burst of joy. "I had no idea, Rick. Did the Hahns know?"

"No, and we didn't tell them." His tears spilled over. "We just let it be a sign that this is the right thing for everyone." He reached for Gwen's hand, and they sat quietly, with the breeze playing around their faces.

"I'll be up early and spend a little time with Haley before I go back to Albany."

"You know you're welcome here anytime, Rick."

"Thanks." He stood. "You okay here alone?"

"Very much okay. Sleep well."

She waited for Rick's door to close upstairs before digging out her cell phone. Peter answered on the second ring.

"Hey, I was hoping you'd call," he said. "Hold on."

Gwen waited until he killed the volume on a football game. "It went just fine."

"You're exhausted."

"I am, and peaceful. How are you?"

"Annoyed at Syracuse for fumbling the ball."

"You always know how to lighten me up." Gwen laughed softly and rested her head against the high back of the rattan chair. "Who are they playing?"

"Boston College, but I'm all yours," he told her. She heard a click and a *swoosh*. "Just opening the door to my porch. You know, I can see your place from here."

"I'm waving from my porch."

"You're sitting in the dark?"

"I am. Haley crashed the minute they got home, and I didn't even see her."

"Rick's a good man."

"Yeah, he is. He's done really well with this whole mess, and I know it's been hard for him. Peter, thank you so much for helping him."

"No problem."

"You are going to be great dad, you know."

"You think so?" His tone was wistful.

"I do." Her eyelids drooped. "Will you take it personally if I fall asleep in the next twenty seconds?"

"I want you to spend those twenty seconds walking up the stairs to your bed."

"Excellent idea."

"Sleep well, pretty lady. I'll call you tomorrow."

Gwen awoke to rain pounding the windows. She turned off the alarm and fell back to sleep without intending to. When she jolted awake again, she heard Rick's car rattle and splash up her steep road. "Eight o'clock," she grumbled at the clock. "Guess I needed it."

After a quick shower, she dressed in soft navy sweats and thick socks, and padded downstairs. She found Haley on the porch staring through rain-streaked windows at the lake. "Morning, sweetie."

Haley jumped. "Hi, you missed Rick." She raised her cheek for Gwen's kiss.

"He and I had a good talk out here last night. He said you crashed in the car on the way home."

"I was toast. I slept, like, ten hours."

Gwen brushed a wayward strand of hair from Haley's cheek. "You okay?"

"Yes." She stood and stretched and rubbed her belly with a smile. "Sad that Rick had to leave, but happy that I can be with my little guy for at least another month, and I don't have to worry anymore about what happens after he's born." She gave her aunt an impulsive hug. "Thank you."

"I love you, sweetie." Gwen enjoyed the warm hug for a moment. "Want breakfast?" At Haley's answering nod, she headed to the kitchen.

Close on her heals, Haley advised, "That coffee's old. I'll make a new pot for us."

"Music to my ears."

"And you need to tell me all about Laura. Rick said you said she's okay, but I need to hear it from you."

While Gwen toasted oatmeal bread and fixed mushroom omelets, Haley brewed coffee and set out butter and two kinds of jam—blackberry for herself and marmalade for Gwen. She set the island for two and, once Gwen had artfully arranged the toast around each omelet, carried their plates from the counter.

"So why did Laura want to meet with you privately?" Haley broached as she slid onto her stool.

"Laura has been through hell for years trying to have a baby," Gwen said. "She is so fiercely determined to be this baby's mother"—she pointed her fork at Haley's big, round belly—"that she was not going to leave any loose ends. Meaning, she had to be convinced I was not going to rush in at the last minute and claim the baby as my own. Which I'm not. It was a tough discussion, but I respect her mama-bear instincts, and I'm convinced she'll be a great mom to your little guy."

"How did you find all that out?"

Gwen's eyebrows nearly met above her nose. "It was a strange conversation," she admitted and forced a chuckle. "She had me in tears."

"What?" Haley squawked.

"Yeah, she couldn't imagine how I, a thirty-two-year-old widow, with no children, could step aside and let the baby go to a stranger."

Haley's toast had stopped halfway to her mouth. Blackberry jam dripped on her placemat.

Gwen set down her fork and picked up her coffee mug with both hands. Elbows on the island, she told Haley, "You know, usually when I have a difficult conversation, I'm acting as a therapist and I wear my professional face and my"—she shifted a bit on the stool—"my armor. Laura stripped all that away so she could see what was in my heart. I've never had anyone do that." She took a big drink of coffee. "It showed me that, being in touch with my heart, on a deep level, is okay, even if there is pain there."

Gwen smiled into Haley's big, chocolate eyes. "I grew

from that attack, as a woman and as a therapist. And I firmly believe Laura Hahn was meant to be your baby's mom."

"Do you want to be a mother, Gwen?"

"Yes, but first I need to find a man to share my life. Then make a healthy marriage together. And then make a baby with him."

Haley used her spoon to scrape the jam from her placemat. "Good thing I grabbed the navy placemats this morning."

"We need to get serious about this beautiful breakfast, before it gets cold," Gwen said. "Maybe today we can pick the room for your art studio and, later, head to Rochester for art supplies."

"I'm in."

Chapter 9

As she slipped into the chair across from Gianessa in the café of the Bright New Day Spa in suburban Rochester, it was on Gwen's tongue to say, *Are you all right?* She knew her friend well enough to know a question like that would meet with resistance.

Instead, she asked, "How do you like all this pampering?"

Gianessa's face was pale and pinched, but she responded with a bright smile. "There's nothing like a good facial and a shoulder-and-neck massage to ease the stresses of pregnancy."

Gwen swallowed her glass of water in three gulps. Gianessa toyed with her glass. Gwen reached across the table. "Seriously, I can see you're in pain. I think we should leave and see your doctor on the way home."

Under Gwen's sharp-eyed gaze, Gianessa admitted, "There is a pain that I haven't felt before, but I don't think it's labor."

God, help us. Gwen made her voice stern. "Call your doctor right now. The no-cell-phone policy does not pertain to emergencies."

"Surely it can wait."

"Surely I will call 911, if you don't call your doctor right now."

Gianessa hesitated five seconds, fished out her phone from the pocket of her robe, and speed-dialed Dr. Bowes. After the first hello, she clutched her belly through the two-minute conversation. Tears brimmed and spilled over.

Gwen did not wait for the conversation to finish. She called for an ambulance, signaled the hostess, and arranged for their locker contents to be brought to them.

As soon as Gianessa finished with her doctor, Gwen asked her, "When is Justin's plane due to land in Rochester?"

"A few minutes after noon."

Gianessa dropped her phone on the table and covered her face with her hands. "I cannot lose these babies, Gwen."

"You won't. We are on our way to the hospital which is just twenty minutes away."

The spa owner materialized, followed by an attendant carrying clothes, purses, and sandals. Satisfied that all the customers in the café were female, Gwen loosened her robe and dressed at the table. She used Gianessa's phone to speed-dial Justin. The call went to voicemail, and she told him to meet them at the hospital.

Emergency medical personnel rushed in with a gurney and assisted Gianessa. Gwen was not allowed to ride in the ambulance, so she tore out to her car with Gianessa's things and stayed on their tail at heart-pounding speed all the way to the Clifton Springs Emergency Room.

Dr. Bowes had prepared the staff for their arrival. A nurse accompanied Gwen, who held Gianessa's hand as the gurney raced down the hallway to the surgical wing. On the way, while Gianessa moaned, "Find Justin," and pleaded, "Save my babies," the nurse calmly explained that the fibroid in the wall of Gianessa's uterus was the suspected problem. The babies were in distress but far enough along, so a Caesarean section was the most likely course of action. At five or six weeks short of full-term, their chances were very good.

"Do I have your consent, Mrs. Cushman?"

Gianessa nodded and sobbed.

The nurse looked Gwen in the eye.

"Mrs. Cushman nodded her consent for the C section."

"Is Mr. Cushman here?"

"Not yet. I am their friend, Dr. Gwen Forrester."

"We need you to stay until the husband arrives."

"Of course I will." *What aren't they saying?* Gwen breathed through her panic. *God help me.*

In the cubicle that served as a staging area, a nurse inserted a needle into a vein in Gianessa's arm, attached a tangle of tubing, and hung a plastic pouch from the IV rack. Gwen stroked Gianessa's hair and watched intently as the nurse fiddled with the tubing until the pouch dripped steadily.

An anesthesiologist introduced himself and explained, "The cocktail I'll be administering is carefully formulated for the health of the babies and your comfort, Mrs. Cushman."

"I wish you hadn't said 'cocktail,'" Gianessa said with a sorry excuse for a laugh.

"Why's that, Mrs. Cushman?"

"I'm four years clean and sober, and I'm scared to death of relapsing on Oxycotin or anything else."

"Does Dr. Bowes know this?"

"Yes."

"Then you have nothing to worry about. She will take care of you every step of the way."

"Including this step?" Gianessa asked sharply.

He rocked back on his heels. "The mix of drugs I have for you are those she specified for you, yes."

"Thank you. I'm ready now." She gave him one of her dazzling smiles, and he blushed.

Gwen kissed her forehead and said, "You and the babies will be fine. I'll be waiting right outside with Justin."

Gianessa gripped Gwen's hand like a lifeline as the anesthesiologist introduced his potent mix to her IV line.

"It's all going to be fine," Gwen soothed.

Monitors beeped. Attendants checked off items on their clipboards.

Gianessa's eyes softened and her tension ebbed as the drugs took hold. Her grip on Gwen's hand eased and let go.

"Step away, ma'am," the nurse ordered.

Gwen backed against the cubicle wall as the team rushed the gurney carrying Gianessa down the hall and through the doors into the surgical suite. With a shuddering exhale, Gwen collapsed onto a rolling stool and shook uncontrollably.

An aide arrived with juice and a blanket. "Adrenaline," she told Gwen in a cheerful voice. "It gets me the same way every time."

"It's warm," Gwen said about the blanket as she wrapped it around herself. "Thank you."

"Our ambulance guys said they couldn't shake you. That must have been some wild ride."

Gwen laughed and cried at the same time.

"Honey, you just let it all out." She rubbed Gwen's back. "I'll help you to the waiting room as soon as you're able to stand."

"Will my friend be all right?"

"Of course she will. Dr. Bowes is the best. They'll do just fine in there."

Cocooned in her blanket in the surgical waiting room, Gwen sipped sweet, hot tea and stared out at the trees. Green leaves danced in the sunshine and songbirds flitted among the branches. The moment it rang, she snatched up her cell phone. "Justin?"

"No, it's Peter. What's wrong? Where are you?"

Gwen recounted her harrowing experience. "I'm alone right now. Justin will be here soon. I hope." She checked the clock on the wall and said a prayer for all the other people before her who had anxiously consulted the same clock. "It's been twenty minutes since she went into surgery."

"What can I do? Do you want me to come there?"

"Thanks, no. I hope Justin wasn't delayed. He's flying in from New York City, and, unless he has picked up my message, he has no idea what is happening."

"What's his flight number?"

Gwen told him, and a few second later he told her, "They landed on time half an hour ago. He must be on his way to the hospital."

Gwen exhaled with audible relief. "How's *your* day going, Officer?"

"Better than yours," he said, his tone bright. "I called to tell you I'm on my way to practice with the Sneaks."

"Tony's basketball team? How cool is that?"

"I got the word as I left for work last night."

"That is such good news. I'm so glad you called."

With a loud laugh, he added, "We've got the best team name for all of the security and police teams. 'Sneaks,' like snoops and sneakers, get it?"

"I love it." Gwen grinned. "You sound like a little kid, you're so excited. What are the other team names?"

"There are the Gumshoes, the Sleuths, the Spies, the Secret Service—you get the idea. Hey, did I tell you Bree's coming Monday for a couple of days?"

"About six times," she teased. "Things are going your way, Peter."

"And we're still on for canoeing this Saturday? You pick where we're going this time."

"We are on for Saturday. I'm excited."

Justin pushed through the door to the waiting room, turned accusing eyes on Gwen and demanded, "What happened? Why is she in surgery?"

Gwen chalked up his anger to fear. She told him everything she knew. "It's been forty minutes. We should hear soon. You need to breathe, Justin. Sit with me over here by the window." She motioned him to the other armchair in her corner.

He yanked at his tie and tossed his briefcase on the floor. "Why wasn't I here? If anything happens . . ." He sat heavily.

Gwen reassured him, "Dr. Bowes gave you the okay to travel this week. As far as anyone knew, Gianessa had another 5 or 6 weeks. And you're here now."

His anger deflated, and he looked every one of his forty-six years.

Gwen scooted to the edge of her chair and reached for his hand.

Though his grip was strong, the agony in his voice tore at Gwen's heart. "Was the spa a mistake, Gwen?"

She'd wondered the same thing and had concluded, "No. It actually put us closer to Clifton Springs. And the spa is organized to serve pregnant women and others with health issues, with EMTs two doors away. They immediately got her into an ambulance with her insurance card and other ID. No question, no fuss."

"Remind me to make a donation."

"Okay." Gwen smiled.

They jumped to their feet when the door from the surgical area burst open.

"Justin," Dr. Bowes greeted him. "Your wife and babies will be very glad to see you."

"They're all right?"

"The babies were in distress, but they are fine now. We did a C-section. Boy and girl are both healthy and beautiful. Right now, we need to talk about your wife."

Justin paled and swayed.

Gwen put a steadying hand on his arm.

"As I suspected," the doctor continued, "the fibroid in the wall of her uterus that we've been watching was the culprit. She has lost a great deal of blood. We have tried to control the situation, but now I need your consent to remove the uterus."

Justin's mouth opened, but no words came out.

Gwen's stomach did a dive, and she was glad she hadn't eaten lunch.

"The consequence, of course," the doctor explained, "is that your wife will be unable to have more children. If we don't do the hysterectomy, even if we are able to control the bleeding and she eventually conceived, it would be a very, very high-risk pregnancy. Much higher risk than this one."

"I—I didn't know," Justin stammered.

"No, of course she didn't tell you the extent of our concern. But she did follow my orders carefully the past few weeks." She fixed Justin with a stern eye. "I love babies, Justin, but my advice in this case is for you and Gianessa to accept the safe course of action and cherish the two beautiful, healthy babies that you have."

"Where the safe course of action is to remove the uterus?" he clarified for himself.

Dr. Bowes nodded.

"You have my consent," he choked out.

As Dr. Bowes left them, he bowed his head and squeezed his eyes shut. A sob shook his shoulders.

Gwen reached for him, and he leaned on her. "It's the right thing to do, Justin." *Thank God I didn't have to make the decision for them.*

"She will *hate* this," he hissed.

"Probably. But she will love the babies and love you. And she will heal faster."

He nodded. "I want her well, Gwen. I want my family well."

"And they will be," she told him. She kept her arms around him until his breathing eased.

The elevator disgorged Joel and Manda, and Gwen greeted them with a tired but happy smile. "Congratulations. I just saw your new Cushman cousins. They are the most precious babies ever born."

Joel drew her into a hug. "Gwen, thank you for getting her here."

"Have you talked to Gianessa since the surgery?" Manda asked.

Gwen shook her head. "Justin was called into recovery a minute ago by a smiling nurse, and I made my exit. He'll be glad the reinforcements have arrived."

"He's all right?"

"He is. I'll let him explain."

Joel picked up on her cautionary tone. He narrowed his eyes.

Gwen kissed his cheek and confided, "It will be all right, but he had to make a hard decision, and he's shaky. Good that you're here."

"You're heading home?" Manda asked, her gaze shifting uneasily from Gwen to Joel.

"Yes, sweetie." She hugged Manda tight and kissed her temple. "I need to check on another very pregnant person. But, first, is there any way I can help you two?"

Joel nodded. "Please let Phil know the good news. And can you swing by their new house? The movers should be finishing now, and they expected Justin before this." He fished a key out of his pocket. "Front door. Check all the sliders to be sure it's locked up tight. I'll keep calling the groundskeeper until I get him."

"And can you call Gianessa's sponsor Carol, too, and Sara?" Manda added.

"I'll do that. Give Gianessa my love."

Her first call, though, as she exited the hospital, was to Haley who screamed with joy and relief at the news.

"And I was jealous of you two, thinking you were still at the spa."

"I wish. Listen, sweetie, I have some errands to take care of, but I needed to know you're okay."

"Of course I'm okay. No worries."

"I'll be home as soon as I can. Let's have a girls-only night. How does that sound?"

"Cool. I'll pick out videos from your stash and find us some food."

"That's my Haley."

"Gwen, it's Gianessa," the sleepy voice told her at eleven the next morning.

"Hi, girlfriend." Gwen abandoned the salad she'd been fixing for lunch and perched at the island. "How are you feeling one day after delivery?"

"Exhausted. I wanted to thank you for getting me to the hospital in time. Dr. Bowes just yelled at me and said I nearly died."

"Why would she yell at you like that?" *What is she thinking?*

"Because I was being difficult. The drugs are making me feel like Superwoman, and I wanted to take my babies home today."

"Don't even think about it," Gwen scolded. "Your priorities are to heal and get off the drugs. Justin has nannies and nurses lined up to do the baby care, so you can just enjoy the twins while you're recuperating."

"She said I lost a lot of blood. I keep falling asleep in the middle of conversations."

"So I shouldn't panic if you suddenly drop the phone?"

"Right. Justin and I called Pop and Ariella this morning with the news, and they're thrilled—boy and girl twins, just like them. I want them here, but they can't come for a while. Their restaurant in Milan is catching on. Justin says we can visit them again when I'm well."

She is so drugged.

"I told your sponsor, Carol, the good news," Gwen said. "She's thrilled you're okay and that the babies are healthy."

"Aw, thanks."

"And Sara shrieked so loud, you probably heard her in Clifton Springs."

"I did," Gianessa joked.

Gwen burst out laughing. "Now I know you're going to be okay. You've got your sense of humor working already."

"Gwen, can I ask you something in confidence?"

"Of course. Anything."

"Since I can't have more babies, I think it's time I gave some thought to my career. I'm wondering where Manda is with her planning for the holistic rehab center, and I want your take on how Justin will feel about my working."

"I think once you're home and healing, that's a good time for you to ask Manda and to have a long talk with Justin."

"Yes, but what do you think?"

"I know Manda is working hard on her business plan, which she needs to complete for graduation in May."

"And what would Justin say about my jumping into that project?"

"What do *you* think?" Gwen turned the question back to her.

"I think, like me, he'd be torn between having me shine in my work and having me home with our babies."

Gwen smiled to herself and nodded. *Drugged or not, that sounds exactly right.*

"Gwen?"

"I agree completely," Gwen said quickly, "but I want to caution you to go slow and make your physical recovery the priority for the next few months or even more. Think of all the guidance you gave Joel as his physical therapist last winter. You continually cautioned him not to overdo because that would set him back, right?"

"I see. And it was almost six months before he could stand for his wedding vows."

"Exactly. You'll need someone to put the brakes on for you, and Justin will be very protective. That's why I think it's important that the two of you talk about it. Openly. Together."

"Mmm."

"You're falling asleep, aren't you?"

Gianessa's musical laugh floated across the connection. "Come visit me tomorrow," she said.

"I'll try." Gwen listened to the silence for a few seconds before saying. "Sleep well, see you soon."

"Oh," Gianessa said. "I almost forgot. We're really calling them Jack and Jill."

"You are seriously fit, woman." Peter commented as they came ashore at the end of a long, hard paddle. They had set out from Gwen's as soon as the morning fog lifted, on a diagonal course to Cady's Point. By land, it was the full width of Chestnut Lake and eight miles south of the city limits of Tompkins Falls.

Gwen hopped out of the canoe with a smile. She hauled the bow onto the beach and favored him with sparkling brown eyes. When he sat admiring her for another ten seconds, she put her fists on her hips with a laugh. "You're going to sit there all morning?"

"Can't blame a guy for admiring the view." He stowed his paddle under the crossbars.

Gwen straddled the bow to steady the canoe while he stepped along the center seam and climbed out. Together, they hauled the boat out of the water, rolled it over, and tucked it into the scrub at the edge of the sand.

He caught her hand and embraced her. "You said you were bringing me here to learn about a legend. I want to know what you mean."

"Come on, I'll show you."

"No." He shook his head slowly. "I'm not letting you go until you explain."

"I'm not sure I can." Gwen's forehead puckered. "You kind of have to experience it."

"Okay, then tell me what it's about."

"It's about healing."

"Healing." Peter narrowed his eyes. "As in recovering from illness?"

"Exactly." Gwen's smile radiated her own wellness—white teeth, rosy cheeks, bright eyes. "Physical healing, emotional healing, spiritual healing. Yes."

"Sometimes I don't get you." He held her tighter.

She ran her hands over his shoulders and lifted her mouth for a kiss. The loud motor of a passing boat and wolf whistles from its occupants interrupted their necking.

Gwen's cheeks flamed.

"Ignore them."

"I'm trying." She cleared her throat and squared her shoulder. "Back to our mission. If we explore Cady's Point, I think you'll tune into what I mean, probably in the next fifteen minutes. If not, we'll do something different."

"I'm thinking I'm going to win this bet." He touched his forehead to hers and smiled. "Do I get to pick the something different we do instead?"

She laughed and nodded. "But you need to know the legacy of Cady's Point, which is important in the history of Tompkins Falls and Chestnut Lake. Ready?"

He cocked his head. "Timer's running on your fifteen minutes."

She grinned as she motioned him to lead. "Just walk straight ahead until we reach the path."

"Straight through all this brush?" he squawked.

"Go boldly forth, my hero."

Peter pushed through buffalo berry and sumac, and they entered a thick, tranquil forest of evergreens and hardwoods. In another minute they reached a winding path, where he paused.

"What are you hearing?" Gwen asked.

"Birdcalls. I smell lingering wood smoke, and I feel some presence." He turned to Gwen with a question in his eyes. "What is it?"

"Come with me." She tugged his hand and led him along a narrow, sunlit path to a broad clearing with a car-sized, flattop boulder. They climbed onto its smooth, hard, sun-warmed surface. Gwen sat cross-legged. Peter leaned back on his elbows and stretched out his legs.

"When we first talked about coming here," he recalled, "you said this was sacred ground for the Native Americans."

"It was. This boulder is in the center of a tract of lakeshore, about one square mile, that was said to be a place of healing and ceremony for a Native American tribe that lived here before the European settlers came. The square mile, and many surrounding acres, came into the possession of my friend Lorraine's family more than a hundred years ago. They eventually named it Cady's Point."

"As in Elizabeth Cady Stanton?"

"Spelled the same, but that's all. Cady Stanton may have been a distant relative, but Lorraine never found a connection. Believe me, she tried. Lorraine's grandmother, as you've guessed, was a Cady, and that's where the name Cady's Point came from.

"Because it was pretty far from town and didn't have a commanding view of the lake, the family never developed it. Still, it was the target of an Indian Land Claim decades ago."

"A lot of land in the Syracuse area was disputed, I remember."

"All through the Finger Lakes, too. No one knows the details, but Lorraine's grandparents settled the Cady's Point land claim sometime in the seventies or eighties, with an army of lawyers, it is said, for a huge sum of money. Her parents sold off the surrounding acres, which were developed as building lots with large private homes. Bottom line, Lorraine inherited this square mile of once-sacred land, with a clean title. As kids we played out here—swimming, biking, climbing trees, exploring the lakeshore by foot and by boat. Then as I grew up, I became aware of the healing energy in this place. Knowing how it affected me made me curious about the many ways people heal."

"What do you mean? Like the mind-body connection?"

"Exactly, and you know how that worked, in your own case. You talked about using your anger at your ex-wife to power through your physical therapy. Energy like that can destroy you or help you heal. That awareness led me to become a psychologist, rather than a physician like my dad."

Gwen's brow furrowed. Some dark memory nagged at her, taunting her about a time in her own life when she'd used fury to propel herself forward. She couldn't get a grip on it, though, and didn't care to at the moment. She shook it off in favor of a bright smile.

Peter missed the brief period of her unease. His eyes were closed. "Right now," he said, "I can feel the sunlight warming my muscles, almost like a massage after a workout. You know, if this stuff works for everyone, Lorraine could have opened a high-end spa here."

"Lorraine keeps her toys to herself. She bulldozed another clearing and built a magnificent home that I'll show you. She planned to live there with her husband."

"But she doesn't live here now," Peter guessed. "No one does."

"You're right. Lorraine did marry and live in the house for a few years. Then she decided it was jinxed."

"Why's that?"

"Come on."

Gwen hopped off the rock and led him down yet another path, this one dappled with sunlight that filtered through the leaves high above them. At the end of the path, they passed through two giant oaks into a large clearing. In its center was a sprawling, glass-and-stone showplace.

Peter whistled. "Wonderful. Except . . ."

"What?" Gwen waited.

"Well, for one thing, the grounds are nothing but scruffy lawn, mowed, but riddled with crabgrass. Let's look around."

He set out to circle the contemporary mansion. "You're sure no one's home?"

"Deserted," she affirmed from a few paces behind him.

After examining every side and peering in a few windows, he stopped where they'd started. "Spectacular home, but if I owned this land, I'd want to build where I could see the lake, somewhere on the cove where we landed. That would be amazing. And I wouldn't just hack a big circle, like this, in the middle of the woods. And I'd want landscaping."

"I agree. Do you notice any other differences between the other clearing and here?"

"There's none of that peaceful mojo." He massaged the back of his neck with one hand. "Even with the sunshine, the hairs on the back of my neck are bristling. They have been since we left the path."

He crossed his arms over his chest. "You said she lived here for a while and left because it was jinxed? What went on here? It's almost as creepy as the drug-infested neighborhood I used to patrol."

When the story was not forthcoming, he followed her line of sight. She was fixated on the front door, and her eyes brimmed with tears. He came close beside her and touched her hand. "She's your friend, and it's a painful story, isn't it?"

"Thank you for sensing that." Gwen reached one arm around his waist and held tight.

"You didn't realize I'm a perceptive guy?" His chuckle lightened the mood.

"I knew." She lifted her face for a kiss. "It always comes out when you talk about your sister. And the way you are with Haley and Rick."

He wanted to sweep her off her feet, haul her back to the lush clearing, and make love in the sunlight. With gentle hands, he smoothed the wind-tangled hair from her cheeks and touched her warm, waiting lips. Her passionate kiss took him by surprise.

When it ended, she met his gaze, her eyes troubled.

Something is so off here. "Tell me the story."

"Let's go back to the clearing first," she said with a shiver. "I liked our hot rock. We can talk there."

He scanned the line of trees, searching for the start of the path, but couldn't see it. Panic tickled his gut. "How do we get out?"

Gwen led him to the two large oaks, and they passed between them onto the wide path.

As they wound through the woods for a hundred yards, he observed, "You know this land intimately."

She nodded.

When they emerged into the clearing with the boulder, he smiled with relief. There it was again—the calming presence. It enveloped the place and everyone that entered into it. *If they're open to it*, he amended, wondering about Lorraine and her husband.

Gwen joined him on the big rock and reached out her hand. He slid behind her and massaged her shoulders until she moaned with pleasure. "You have magic hands." She leaned back in his arms.

"Now tell me the story. What happened in the house that Lorraine built?"

"Do you remember meeting Joel Cushman at the chief's party?"

She sighed when he kissed her temple. "Yes, I remember."

"Joel and Lorraine were engaged, once, five or so years ago. In anticipation of their marriage, she built that house."

"Why do I think she didn't tell him about it or involve him in its design or placement?"

"Good instincts. That was typical of their relationship. Lorraine knew best, and Joel was expected to go along."

Peter exhaled a laugh. "Joel doesn't strike me as someone who operates that way."

"Correct. He broke the engagement. Lorraine was furious and embarrassed. She married, on the rebound, a smoking-hot professor from Tompkins College, and she had two beautiful baby boys with him."

"And they lived in that house in the clearing?" he asked, his tone skeptical.

Gwen nodded. "The truth was, he was a degenerate sot who disgraced himself, defiled their marriage, and put the college in jeopardy. She divorced him, took the two boys to live in England, and—"

"England? Why?"

"She has a couple of college friends who have estates in the Thames River Valley, not far from London. She bought her own little estate in their enclave, and she lives there with the boys. Travels a lot. Lives a life of leisure."

"Like the rich and famous?"

"Rich, yes. But she keeps a very low profile."

"What happened to the husband?"

"He got the house in the divorce settlement and trashed it."

She shivered, and he guessed she had omitted something. He tightened his arms around her.

She relaxed against him. "He was subsequently ousted from Tompkins College and, I think, blackballed at every other college in the region, if not the state. Anyway, Lorraine bought the house back from him for the equivalent of his legal fees, and then he disappeared."

"As in, somebody killed him?"

Gwen snorted. "No, but a few people wanted to. He slunk away and, I guess, found another rock somewhere."

"To crawl under," Peter added.

"By the way, your outgoing Chief Barker was very active in that investigation, and Joel feels indebted to him for what he did. Hence the festive party in his honor when he retired."

"Say that again. Why would Joel be grateful?"

Gwen hesitated. "His wife Manda was impacted by some of the husband's dirty dealings. I'd like to leave it at that. Okay?"

"Geez. Tompkins Falls is sounding like Peyton Place."

She snuggled closer, and he wrapped her tight. "I think every town and city has a story like that."

"Why didn't Lorraine sell the house? There must be a dozen wealthy New Yorkers who fall in love with the area every time they come, and who want a vacation home on the lake."

"Actually, Joel tried to buy it from her. He wanted to bulldoze the house and build Manda's dream."

"After whatever happened, Manda actually wants to live on that site?"

"No, she wants to create a holistic wellness center that taps the healing energy of Cady's Point, closer to where we're sitting."

"Hm." He sat quietly, his face raised to the midday sun. "It makes sense. I really can feel that soothing energy. That's why I said that earlier about building a high-end spa."

"Manda is definitely tuned into the healing force. I'm not sure Lorraine ever was, to tell you the truth. When I said she's self-absorbed, I wasn't being unkind. It's a fact."

"Okay, but isn't it likely Manda's project will jinx the place, too, just like Lorraine's house did?"

"I think her house was jinxed because she didn't acknowledge the healing force and because the husband she chose was beyond healing."

"He was a real bastard, wasn't he?"

"Yes, he was." Gwen wiggled away and turned to him with a bright smile. "My theory is the healing force is in the land, not in the tribe or the owner. Manda's holistic center will work because she has profound respect for the force, just as the Native Americans did. Lorraine, on the other hand, was oblivious."

"Which I can believe, just from where she chose to build the house."

"Exactly."

His eyes narrowed.

"What?"

"A rich woman builds a beautiful house like that, and then everyone else just wants to trash it or bulldoze it. What's up with that?"

"Lorraine lives by her own rules," Gwen answered with a grim smile. "People tolerate it up to a point and then they rebel."

He cocked his head. "Are you and she still friends?"

"Yes, we are. One of my core beliefs is you don't abandon your friends."

"You're very different from her."

"I'm fortunate that my life followed a different path, one that took into account other people's beliefs and concerns."

"Joel seems more like you than Lorraine," Peter observed.

"Yes. Manda, too. You, too."

"Thank you. If we hadn't gotten such a late start and I weren't so hungry, I'd have passionate sex with you, right here on our hot rock."

She winked. "This rock is hard, mister. I'd have to be on top."

He laughed. "We should have brought a picnic."

"Next time."

"Can we make it back across the lake before we starve to death?"

"One way to find out," Gwen answered and scrambled off their rock.

Peter stayed where he was for a moment, as a nagging doubt played in his head. "Did you mean that," he asked her, "about her husband being beyond healing?"

Gwen brushed the dust off her shorts and plucked a few twigs from her shirt. "Some people get lost in their pain and rage, and they can't find the way to heal."

Just like I couldn't find the way out of the creepy clearing back there, even though it was clearly marked by those big oak trees? He shook off the rogue thought, jumped down from the boulder, and followed Gwen back to the canoe.

Just before the Tuesday night women's AA meeting, Gwen told her sponsee, Manda, "You'll do a great job leading the beginners' group. You don't need me in there with you. A few very experienced women are there, so you'll have support. Do your best, and we'll talk after. Okay?"

"Wish me luck."

"Luck." Gwen hugged her and gave her a little push toward the front room.

The beginners' meeting focused on the first step of AA and encouraged newcomers to ask questions and to get help with their sobriety.

Manda smiled at everyone as she strode into the room. She took her place at an old school desk between two windows and opened the Big Book to a favorite passage. She would use the words to begin her share about how she realized she was an alcoholic who needed the help of others to get sober.

A dozen women stood talking inside the circle of chairs when Manda announced, "If someone will close the door, we'll get started." Within seconds, everyone was seated and quiet.

"Hi, I'm Manda, and I'm an alcoholic."

"Hi, Manda." The group chorused.

Manda read from the Big Book, closed it, and set it reverently on the desk. "I love those words. I say them out loud every morning as soon as I get up." She observed the women's faces. One seemed to be a newcomer. She cried quietly into a fistful of tissues. Manda gave her a warm smile. "I cried at every meeting when I got here."

The woman turned to her with liquid, sea-green eyes.

Manda told her, "The amazing thing is, you don't ever have to feel this bad again." She continued, "I've been sober a year and a half, and my whole life has changed since I put the drink down." She felt herself tear up. "It was rough for a while, but the women in this room, and in other meeting rooms, helped me. I didn't have to drink, no matter what. I learned how to handle whatever life brought my way. One huge difference between today and a year and a half ago is that I don't try to handle everything on my own anymore. I have a sponsor to advise me about using the AA principles and steps in my life. I have a mentor at work and at school. I talk everything over with my husband." She laughed at herself. "I still can't believe I'm married. Some of you remember, when I came into AA, I was 'off men for life.'"

The group laughed, all except the teary-eyed newcomer. Her head was down, and she twisted a ring around and around on her pinky finger, while her right foot tapped a nervous rhythm on the carpet.

Manda told more of her story for a few minutes, then softened her voice. "Since this is a beginners' meeting, we encourage newcomers to ask for help about anything that threatens their sobriety or to ask questions about the AA program."

The group followed Manda's lead and sat quietly for a moment to give the newcomer a chance to speak up.

The girl licked her lips. "I guess that's me, right?"

Manda gave her a big smile. "Welcome. Can you tell us your first name?"

"I'm Bree, and I'm an alcoholic/addict."

"Hi, Bree," the group chorused.

"Hi. I'm pretty new and I don't know what to do about something. I apologize if it's not about alcohol exactly, but I really need some help because it's about staying sober and being honest."

Manda had frozen when she heard the newcomer's name. It was an unusual name, and it was the name of Peter's sister, who'd be this woman's age. The same Peter who'd "forbidden" his sister to be an alcoholic. And this woman was tall and strong like Peter and had dark curly hair and eyes the color of green sea glass.

Manda realized people were waiting for her to say something. Her gaze skimmed over the group with panicked eyes.

One of the women, Carol, who'd been sober a while, calmly advised, "Bree, why not give us the short version? If it's not really a topic for a meeting, I'm sure one or two of us will talk with you after the meeting."

Manda exhaled in relief and nodded her thanks to Carol.

Bree gave a nervous laugh. "Okay." She licked her lips. "So I'm staying with my brother for a few days, and I didn't tell him I was coming to a meeting because he hates alcoholics. But I needed a meeting, so I told him I was going for a walk and to find a cup of coffee, and I came here. He lives past the marina up on the bluff by the park, so it wasn't too far.

"Anyway, the thing is he wants me to come live with him, and I-I want to do that and to go on in school, but I have to go to meetings and I don't know how to make that work. I wish he understood about the disease. I didn't choose to be an alcoholic. I just am one, like our father was. And these meetings are the support I need to stay clean and sober. But Peter doesn't get that. I don't know if I should move here and live with him and sneak around so I can go to meetings?" Bree's voice broke. "That doesn't feel like the right thing."

Her tears spilled over. She took the tissue someone offered, dabbed at her eyes and continued, "But if I stay in Syracuse where all my old friends are, I don't think I can stay sober. They're on me all the time about partying with them, even though I've told them I'm not drinking or using anymore." She reached for another tissue. "I'm so scared I can't think straight."

"Bree," Carol said, "that's definitely a topic for a beginners' meeting like this. I think everyone here has suggestions. What comes to my mind is 'be true to yourself.' What I'm thinking is that the highest priority for any newcomer is her own sobriety.

"Someone told me when I was new that my sobriety came first . . . at any cost. If I had to change people, places and things by giving up old friends and habits, then that's what I had to do. If particular family members did not support my program, then maybe I should avoid them for a while, too."

Bree rolled her eyes.

Carol continued with a knowing smile. "And if both those things were true I'd better get myself to a meeting and cry about it and ask for help."

Bree laughed from her belly, and everyone joined her.

Carol nodded to Manda.

Manda stepped back into her role as leader of the meeting. "Carol pointed out several tools—asking for help; putting your sobriety first; being true to yourself; changing people, places, and things. Those are important for every newcomer. Who'd like to speak next?"

The group continued the discussion, and Manda tried to stay focused so she could move the discussion along. Still, half her mind was on the fact that Peter's sister was a self-admitted alcoholic and his attitude was a problem for her. Should she tell Gwen? But Gwen was constantly reminding her to protect everyone's anonymity. She shouldn't tell anyone else who was in attendance at this meeting. But she really needed to talk to her sponsor, or someone, about this. Maybe she'd grab Carol afterward and ask her advice.

After the close of the meeting, though, Carol was with a group of three women gathered around Bree. Manda returned to the main meeting room and kept an eye on the door to the beginners' room, while she talked with friends. Finally, Carol came out with Bree, and the two of them walked together toward the parking lot. Manda wouldn't have the opportunity to talk with Carol tonight, but at least Bree wouldn't be walking home alone in the dark.

"So, chickie"—Gwen's voice sounded behind her—"how did your meeting go?"

"Good. Thanks, really good."

"See, you didn't need your old Mother Hen Gwen," Gwen teased.

"You were right. The women with more time were able to step in and keep us on track."

Gwen cocked her head. "Why, what happened?"

"Oh, someone new wasn't sure if her question was okay for a beginners' meeting," Manda said breezily. "That's all."

"That's all," Gwen repeated, her voice rich with skepticism.

"Yeah."

Gwen stood quietly. Wait Time was one of Gwen's most effective therapy tools.

Manda felt the pressure. Her eyes darted around the room. "Yikes, there's a newcomer standing by herself. Let me see if I can help her."

She dashed across the room, leaving Gwen with her mouth open.

From his post at the bedroom window, Peter saw a strange car stop outside 14 Lakeside Terrace. A newer-model sedan, possibly a Malibu, white or ivory. A woman was driving, but he couldn't see her face clearly. The car sat with the motor running and the lights on.

Peter shifted his weight to his left foot and crossed his arms. After a few seconds, he tapped his right foot.

Finally, Bree got out of the passenger side. An interior light came on and showed him the driver's face. It was a woman he'd seen a few times, but he couldn't think where. Maybe around town hall or the library. Redhead, no-nonsense, friendly. She was probably okay, but she was about twenty years older than Bree. Where had Bree met her?

Bree glanced at the window, waved to him, and headed for the front door. The sedan circled the cul-de-sac and headed downhill.

He heard Bree's key in the door.

"You didn't have to wait up," she called, her voice defensive.

A laugh escaped him. "Bree, it's not even nine o'clock. And I'm working tonight, not going to bed like normal people." He decided to play it light as he stepped into the living room. "So did you have fun?"

"Yeah, I went for a walk and stopped for a coffee and met some nice women." She shrugged. "Carol gave me a ride home. I'm going to turn in now."

"Wait, aren't you hungry?"

Bree shrugged. "Not really. When do you go to work?"

"Ten-thirty. I'll be home around seven-thirty in the morning—eight, if I go for a run. I'll try not to wake you."

"No problem. Have a good shift."

He opened his mouth to thank her, but she'd already closed the door to the guest bedroom. He heard the shower come on.

He retreated to his bedroom, plugged his headphones into the TV, and adjusted the volume on the Big East game. Syracuse was ahead by six points.

Chapter 10

"You sound like a little kid, you're so excited." Gwen felt warm all over at Peter's answering laugh. He'd called to tell her about winning their second game last evening. "You're a big asset to the Sneaks."

"You know, honey, it's great being part of the team. These guys do the kind of work I do, security and police work, and we all love the sport and are good at it. I finally feel like part of the community. Plus, I haven't laughed this much in a long time."

Honey. Jeb called her *Darlin'*, and she always wondered if he was being cute or didn't think she was worth the ending *g*. *Honey* was so solid, so traditional. Her stomach did a happy dance.

"I know it's one more thing to fill up my schedule, but we can still find time to be together, right? Are you okay with this?"

"With you being on the team?" She had tuned out longer than she realized, and he must have noticed the silence. "Are you kidding? It's great."

"You know, someday I want to be shooting baskets with my kids."

"You will." She reached for the phone cord, and sighed at the empty air around the cordless landline. She'd loved, as a teenager, tangling her fingers in the cord while she talked with her boyfriend.

"Did it go okay with Bree when she visited?"

"I loved having her, but we didn't do much together.

"What does she like to do for fun?"

"Come to think of it, we used to take a basketball to the junky old court down the street and slam it around. She was pretty good."

"Hey, next time she comes, take her to Overlook Park and shoot a few," Gwen urged.

"Great idea. Listen, I've got to go. I'm glad I caught you before your day got started. I figured, if it was too rainy and windy for me to run this morning, it was probably too lousy for you to be out on your bike."

"You were right. Sleep well, Peter."

"Bye, honey."

The word felt like a caress, and Gwen tingled. She held the phone against her heart for a moment. A smile curved her mouth as she imagined three little Shaughnessys bouncing the ball on the court at Overlook, the smallest child straining to throw it in the basket, Peter scooping her up to shorten the distance so she could make the shot.

"Sweetie, you don't usually take anything for pain." Haley shrugged. "Why today?"

"I almost forgot, Deirdre called to apologize and said she'd appreciate a call back. That's word for word. What's that about?"

"Thanks, I'll take care of it." She jotted a note on the phone pad. "Haley, tell me about your pain."

Haley set down the bottle of Tylenol and leaned her full weight on her arms for a moment. "My back is so sore. I don't know what I did."

"You didn't fall or lift something or move something heavy?" Alarms sounded in Gwen's head.

"No. I walked in the rain while you slept in, just over to Phil's, but he wasn't there. And halfway back it just started hurting."

"And that was how long ago?" Gwen swallowed and reached for her cell phone. She surveyed the salad ingredients on the counter and sent up a silent prayer that Haley had told her before they ate a big lunch, not after.

"Well, for sure, it was before you got up. You were making breakfast when I got back, remember? You ordered me to take a hot shower." She jabbed her finger in Gwen's direction and laughed. "Now I know why they call you Mother Hen Gwen."

Four hours. "Phil sometimes rides to the Early Risers meeting at the Bagel Depot," Gwen said casually, as she searched her organizer for the set of questions Dr. Bowes had given all the labor coaches. "He stays to talk over coffee and breakfast." She ran her finger down the list. "Is your pain all the time, Haley?"

"It's funny. It goes away and then it comes back again."

"Is it getting stronger or more frequent?"

"Both." She turned to Gwen, her eyes wide. "Uh-oh."

"The doctor said your labor could start with back pain," Gwen reminded her.

"Ohmigod." Haley sucked in a breath. "This is scary."

"And you're doing really well, sweetie. Let's call Dr. Bowes." Gwen scrolled to the obstetrics hotline number for Dr. Bowes' clinic and pressed the number. She gave the receptionist Haley's name and due date, told her Haley's status, and held out the phone for Haley. "I'll bring your bag down just in case."

While Haley answered questions, Gwen flew up the stairs, grabbed Haley's duffle, double-checked the contents, zipped it shut, raced into her bedroom for the Louise Penny novel she'd just started and raced back downstairs.

Haley was already on the phone with Rick. "Gwen's back, and we're leaving right now." She placed a shaking hand on her belly. "I love you, too, Rick. Drive safe."

Gwen put on a big smile. "Ready?"

Haley nodded once, her mouth a grim line.

"Are you okay to walk out to the car?"

"If you walk with me."

Gwen slung the duffle over her shoulder and reached an arm around Haley's waist. "Let's do it."

After a white-knuckle drive to the hospital, Haley was grateful for a wheelchair ride to the obstetrics area. Her water broke on the way down the hall. Gwen helped her out of her clothes, once they had some privacy.

Dr. Bowes brief exam determined that Haley was nearly ready for the delivery room. "Need drugs, Haley?"

Haley shook her head. "Just courage and Gwen."

The doctor smiled. "We're with you, Haley. I'll be along soon. They won't let me miss it." She winked. "Gwen and I are just going to talk for a minute right now."

While the nurses prepared Haley, Dr. Bowes asked, "Has Rick been notified?"

"He's on his way."

"And the adopting parents?"

"Our agreement is they'll be called immediately after the baby is delivered."

"And you'll handle that phone call?"

"I will, yes. She's a few days early. Any reason for concern?"

"None. She's here, she's doing well, and we'll do our job."

Three hours later, a healthy baby boy announced his arrival with lusty squalls.

Haley watched every move as the team cleaned him and bundled him in a receiving blanket. She welcomed him into her arms and kissed him all over. He quieted as she whispered little words to him, until a nurse came for him.

"He'll be right down the hall," she told Haley. "The team will help you wash up and settle in your room. Then you and the baby can spend some time together, if you want."

"Definitely." Her eyes closed with exhaustion. "Gwen?"

"I'm right here." Gwen smoothed the hair from Haley's sweaty forehead.

Haley's breathing quieted. "He's strong and healthy, isn't he?"

"He is. You did a great job."

"Thank you." She looked Gwen in the eye. "For everything."

"Gwen," the nurse said firmly, "we'll see you in Haley's room in about twenty minutes. "Someone will come for you in the obstetrics waiting room."

Gwen's forehead creased as a headache descended. On her way to the waiting room, she rummaged in her purse and shook out two Tylenol. She left word on the Hahns's answering machine and gave the good news to Justin and Gianessa. *Wish they were home.*

A quiet spot by a window gave her the opportunity to pray for courage to help Haley and Rick through the tough part—letting go of their beautiful little boy. Her chest tightened at the enormity of it. *Take care of yourself, too,* a voice whispered. She saw that the cloudy sky was giving way to patches of blue to the west. A shaft of sunlight blazed a path across the parking lot, over the lawn, and into the woods, where yellow and orange leaves danced in the wind. Peace filled her heart.

The ding of the elevator got her attention. She put on a welcoming smile for Rick, as he got off, his hair in disarray and his forehead creased with worry.

"Haley's okay?"

"She did great. It was a quick delivery. I'm so grateful for that."

Gwen's touch on his forearm made him jump. "You're wound tight, Rick. Try to let go of some of that before you see her and the baby."

Eyes closed, he nodded his understanding. "The baby's okay?"

"He's got a great set of lungs," she told him with a chuckle.

A smile tugged at one corner of his mouth. "Did you tell Helmud and Laura?"

"I left a message. They're probably both at work."

"Think they'll come tonight?"

"I'm betting they'll wait until morning. Rick, I don't want Haley to be alone here tonight."

"I plan to stay here with her and the baby," Rick insisted.

"Thank you. If the Hahns show up, call me on my cell right away."

"Absolutely."

A nurse summoned them, and Gwen suggested Rick go ahead. "I'll be there in a few minutes."

She walked out into the sunshine, slipped on her sunglasses, and found a bench out of the wind.

"Hey," Peter answered on the first ring. "What's up?"

"Haley and Rick's baby has arrived, and Rick is spending a little time with mother and son right now."

"Wow," he crowed. "Mom and baby are okay?"

"Yes."

"Are you okay? Your voice is shaky."

"I have a screaming headache that is slowly improving."

"What can I do?"

"Rick will stay the night here at the hospital with Haley, and I don't think the Hahns will make it until tomorrow. Tonight, I want to leave Haley and Rick alone with their baby. I'm hoping you and I can get something to eat in an hour or so."

"It happens that I am in the middle of making one of my famous meatloaves. Why not come to my place, and we'll have a meal together and relax?"

"That is so perfect." A wash of sun warmed her muscles. "I've never been to your place."

"That's because it's been messy with half unpacked boxes and a backlog of laundry."

Gwen laughed, and the tension rolled off her shoulders. "Is it still a mess? We could use my kitchen."

"Nope. The boxes were emptied and out of here before Bree's visit, and I just finished the last load of laundry."

"Cool." His happiness and energy were elixirs. "We'll kick back together, just the two of us."

"It's open," Peter called. He set the steaming loaf pan on the stovetop and pinched the potatoes. Gwen inhaled the aromas of good, home cooking, and her mouth watered. She leaned one hip against the island and watched him work, her eyes roaming over his wide shoulders and slender hips, admiring his deft, sure movements.

"Food is right out of the oven," he said. "Salad just needs to be tossed." He turned.

One black curl fell onto his forehead. His green eyes swept over her. "That is a hungry look."

She rushed into his arms, offering her mouth, and pressing her breasts against his chest. His kiss seared her lips. He drew her hips hard against him and anchored her there with one leg. She reached with cool hands under his navy Henley, and he yanked it over his head and flung it behind him.

While she unfastened his jeans, he undid the buttons of her flannel shirt. "You're sure?"

"So sure."

He kicked out of his jeans and boxers, eased the shirt off her shoulders, and freed her breasts from the lacy bra.

Eyes dark with desire, he carried her to the bedroom and laid her on her back on his bed. She offered her breasts and gasped with pleasure as he sucked one, then the other. When he eased back to unbutton her jeans, she stroked his erection. "Is this for me?"

"All for you. Why don't you wiggle out of these"—he tugged on the belt loop of her jeans—"while I suit up for us?"

She laughed with delight and obliged him by stripping off her jeans and her lace bikini. She rolled onto her side to drop her clothes to the floor, and Peter lifted her hips and moved in between her legs. "Do you like it from behind?" he asked as his hard shaft rubbed against her crotch.

"I'll like anything with you." She braced her arms against the beautiful, old cherry headboard with the pineapples.

Strong hands cupped her breasts and fingers teased and squeezed her nipples. When she cried out with pleasure, he slipped one hand down her abdomen, parted her wet lips, and teased her with a gentle finger. "You're trembling," he whispered. "What do you need?"

"Please," she urged him.

"Tell me what you want, Gwen."

"You. Inside me."

He eased back and slowly entered her. "Like this?"

"All of you," she begged. She squeezed him with her pelvic muscles. "Deep inside me."

He held her hips tight and drove into her. She cried out as waves of pleasure swept over her, and he plunged again. Her breath caught in her throat and she mewed and panted as he drove again and again until he came inside her.

She shuddered as he pulled out of her, lay beside her, and drew her back against him.

"Wow," she said on an exhale.

"I knew we'd be good together," he murmured while his hands fondled her breasts.

"I didn't know we'd be that good."

He laughed from his belly, and she lifted his hand to her mouth to kiss each of those talented fingers.

"Headache gone?" he asked.

"It's back, but I'm sure it's from hunger."

"Food hunger?"

She shifted onto her back. "Food hunger." Her eyes sparkled as she studied his chiseled features, his eyelids heavy with satisfaction. She tangled her fingers in his black curls and kissed his mouth. "And later, Officer Shaughnessy, I want you for dessert."

He teased one nipple with his thumb. "You can have me all night long."

She stretched one arm over her head. "You're not working later?"

He shook his head and raised himself onto one elbow. His gaze made a lingering, head-to-toe sweep.

"And that's mostly why I didn't come here right away when Ursula threw me out," Haley said.

She and Gwen sat side-by-side on the sofa in front of Gwen's fireplace, sipping hot cider. Flames leapt and danced around the logs. Rick had left that morning for classes at RPI, and the baby was already snuggled into his boat-themed nursery in Pound Ridge. Haley was home with Gwen, struggling with an onslaught of hormones and emotions.

"I don't think I understand."

"I was so ashamed."

"Of being pregnant?"

"Well, that too. But mostly of my drinking and what it led to. I drank out of control and drugs came after. And to get drugs my friends and I went to places we shouldn't have gone, and one of them did things she shouldn't have done. I was afraid to tell you all that. You're so perfect, and I was so ashamed."

"Haley, I am so far from perfect." Gwen exhaled a moan. "And I'm sorry I gave the impression of being anything other than approachable. Sweetie, I would want to be the first person you thought of who could help you."

"I know that now. But then, I was too ashamed to think straight." She blew a rude noise with her lips. "My brain was a mess last fall, I swear. Do you know I don't even remember packing to go home with Rick for Christmas? We were halfway to Ursula's, when I checked my purse and didn't see my birth control pills. I took off my seat belt so I could ransack my duffle in the backseat. And there were no pills. So, Rick's yelling at me about riding without a seatbelt, we're on the Northway in heavy traffic and I didn't dare ask him to turn around and go back to campus." She rubbed her forehead. "The rest is history." She shook her head. "He so didn't deserve that."

Gwen waited a beat and asked casually, "I wonder if you were in a blackout when you packed?"

"I've heard that word, but I don't know what it means. What's a blackout?"

"Alcohol and drugs can cause brief periods of amnesia when we appear to be functioning, but the brain is not recording it, and we're under the influence the whole time. The memory of what we did during those periods never comes back. That period of alcohol-induced amnesia is called a blackout."

Haley focused intently on the flames. "So. Yes. I packed in a blackout. And I had blackouts other times, too. Like, I don't remember how I got back to the dorm the first time I got so drunk. Or the times we did drugs. I was just so relieved to wake up in my own bed, I didn't want to think about it." She shuddered.

"Blackouts are a symptom of alcoholism," Gwen said. "And they're dangerous. When people drive drunk in a blackout or people get into a bar fight in a blackout, they can kill, in a blackout, and never remember doing it." She shifted to see Haley's face. "I—Gwen Forrester, your paragon of virtue—called my husband a selfish prick, in a really loud voice, in a room full of his colleagues, and his partners delayed making him a partner for six months because of that. They told him to 'get the little woman under control or find another firm.' When he told me that the next day, I had no recall."

Haley stared at her aunt, her eyes wide with disbelief. "You really did that?"

"I could tell it was the truth, by how upset he was and by how the rest of them treated me after that. It was a wake-up call about my disease." Gwen looked sideways at Haley. "When you talk about being ashamed, I get it."

"That is so totally not you."

Gwen caressed Haley's cheeks. "And doing drugs and forgetting your pills and doing acrobatics in a moving vehicle on the Northway while your boyfriend has a heart attack are not how the Haley Forrester I know and love behaves. But I can understand it, because alcohol made me into the worst version of myself."

"That's exactly what it did to me."

Gwen stroked Haley's beautiful, tear-stained cheekbones with her thumbs. "Alcoholism is a shameful, dangerous disease. We do stupid, unconscionable things when we drink. AA has given me, and a lot of other people, a way to stay sober, one day at a time. And, even better, a way to clean up the wreck we've made of our lives."

"Phil said that, too. And more, that I don't remember right now."

"I'm glad you've talked with him." She planted a kiss on Haley's forehead and sat back with a loving smile.

"How do you ever make it right?" Haley squinted with doubt. "I don't even know where to start, especially with Rick."

"I did my amends with a sponsor for guidance. It was hard work, but it paid off." She smiled with sparkling eyes. "When the time comes, Rick will tell you what he needs from you to make things right."

"Do you think I'm an alcoholic?" Haley's voice was panicked.

"That's something only you can decide, Haley. Around the program, we say no one can tell you you're an alcoholic, except you. Maybe you could come to a meeting with me and listen to how other women decided they were alcoholic."

Haley's voice was barely audible when she asked, "Could I? Come sometime to a meeting with you?"

"Sure. We could go to the women's meeting in Clifton Springs on Friday. There are some meetings that meet every day, like Early Risers first thing in the morning, and Happy Hour right after work."

Haley laughed. "I can't believe they named an AA meeting Happy Hour."

Tony's right hip slammed against the hard floor. "What the—" He sat up and directed a murderous glare at his opponents, scrutinizing each face to identify the guilty party.

"Not like you to be clumsy, bro," Sam said and gave him a hand up.

"Clumsy, my ass. That was a foul." Tony limped off his anger and massaged his hurt pride.

Sam fell into step. "Quite a few unnecessary falls the past two games, you notice? Werner. Johnson. Now you. What do you think is up with that?" He already knew what was up. Or thought he did.

He'd had his eye on Peter since Werner had broken his anonymity and, along with it, Johnson's and Tony's too. Sam knew about Peter's attitude toward drunks. Apparently, it extended to sober drunks—guys in recovery, like his brother and two teammates.

What he'd done to trip Tony was nothing a ref would catch, especially since it was against a guy's own team. But, as the players had repositioned themselves on the rebound, Sam had seen Peter plant a foot wider than he needed to, right where it would throw a fellow player. Not in a way that would cause injury. Just a sneaky, deliberate nuisance. And it was the same move he'd used last game for Johnson and Werner.

"Yeah, now that you mention it. Keep a watch on us and see what we're doing wrong."

"Think I already know," Sam said.

Tony drilled him with a look. The buzzer sounded.

"We'll talk after," Sam told him.

The Sneaks celebrated their 60-50 victory with burgers at Ralphs and traded a few friendly insults with the losing team across the dining room. Because Sam and Peter were on duty at eleven and Tony had an early morning carpentry gig before his shift at the college, the Sneaks wrapped up by nine o'clock.

"What do you think's the problem?" Tony demanded as the brothers walked to Sam's car.

Sam's gaze swept the parking lot. He waved goodbye to Werner and waited for his door to slam shut. "Pretty sure it's our newest recruit," he told Tony.

"Your partner?" Tony shouted in disbelief.

"Real sorry I got him on the team." Sam's mouth was a grim line as he stashed his bag on the rear seat.

"You can't be serious." Tony's face contorted with disbelief.

To give his brother time to calm down, Sam walked slowly around to the driver's door and paused. *I know I'm right about this.*

As soon as he rolled forward out of the parking space, Tony was on him. "You'd better make sense in the next ten minutes, little brother. I don't need your workplace issues showing up on the court—especially not during season play." He jabbed his finger at Sam. "I should boot both of you from the team."

Sam didn't point out that would leave the Sneaks with three players. He eased the Cruze onto the highway and headed toward Tony's apartment on the west side of Tompkins Falls. "My partner has a thing about drunks," Sam began with a calm he did not feel. "His father was one. Do you remember when Werner gave away your anonymity a couple weeks ago?"

"Not really," Tony huffed.

"We were at Ralphs," Sam reminded him, "and Werner said something like 'Bunch of drunks' and clapped you and Johnson on the shoulder."

"Yeah, I remember now," Tony said. "We were sitting together on one side of the booth. Johnson came back with something about sober drunks being the best teammates."

"And you pontificated about AA for way too long." Sam laughed to break the mood.

"And your point? What's that got to do with all the falls lately?"

"That's when the so-called 'clumsiness' started, the very next game. I just happened to see Peter's face after Werner took that fall that knocked the wind out of him. I didn't like what I saw."

"Which was?"

"A smug smile. And he was closest to Werner, but he didn't reach out a hand to help him up."

"No, you're right," Tony remembered. "I helped him up. I wondered why Peter didn't."

"Probably no one would have suspected a teammate of tripping, but I know my partner and I know how he is about drunks. He always gets out of booking the drunk drivers."

"Why? Is he afraid it's catching?" Tony's laugh was caustic. "Or worried he'll take a swing at one of them? I can't believe your police captain is letting him get away with it."

"I'm thinking it's time to let the captain know about it."

"Why haven't you?"

"Everybody hates paperwork so much, we're glad to have Peter do it instead of us."

"It's not right," Tony contended. He glanced at the passing scenery—two car dealers closed up for the night.

"No, we shouldn't let him get away with it." Sam forced out a breath. *I'll talk to the captain tomorrow.* He checked his speed and eased up on the gas.

"So, what, you've been watching him on the court? And you've seen him interfere with Werner, Johnson and now me?"

"Exactly."

"And that's how we're falling all of a sudden? You're saying it's deliberate?"

"Appears to be."

"Ask him." Tony spat the words. "Tonight."

"I will." Sam shook his head and muttered, "I fucking hate this."

They drove in silence for another mile.

"I just thought of something," Tony said.

Sam glanced over and read worry on his brother's usually carefree face.

"How's he treating Gwen? She's sober in AA. I know her. She wouldn't let him get away with crap like that."

"He must know." Sam tapped his thumbs on the steering wheel.

"Or not," Tony said.

Sam exhaled, "Shit."

"They're pretty serious?"

"Yeah, they are. I think they're sleeping together now."

"What can we do? Gwen's my friend. I don't want to see her get hurt."

"Not much we can do. She's nuts to keep it from him." Sam steered into the apartment complex and idled at the door to Tony's building.

"But you'll confront him tonight about the tripping?" Tony persisted.

"Yes. And I'll talk to the captain about the DWIs. Can you say something to Gwen?"

"I don't know, man." Tony hesitated with his hand on the door handle. "Let me sleep on it." He swung out of the car, retrieved his bag from the backseat, and waved. "Thanks for the ride, bro. I'll catch you at the Bagel Depot in the morning."

The station was quiet at two-thirty in the morning. "Time for a basketball break?" Peter asked.

Richards grunted. "I'll hold the fort. But Pinelli's on edge. He needs a workout."

Sam's head snapped up. *Guess it's obvious something's eating me.* "Yeah, I'm in. Let's see if the kids are around tonight."

Shouts greeted Sam and Peter as they filed through the side door. On the court behind the building, three young teens dribbled and laid up a few shots, accompanied by loud, good-natured ribbing.

Sam called to them, with a smile on his face. "You guys are lucky no one lives in this neighborhood. They'd have you arrested for disturbing the peace."

"Like you'd ever lock us up," the tallest, Stretch, shot back, his mocha face alive with good humor. He poked at the ball Peter carried under his arm and dislodged it. "Let's see what you got, Shaughnessy."

Peter grinned, retrieved the ball, and put a hook shot through the net.

The scrimmage revved up with Sam and Peter making sure each of the boys had their share of success.

"Stretch, you playing for North High this year?" Peter asked as they cooled down.

"Yeah. Practice starts way early."

"Well, that's good, right?"

Stretch scowled. "How's that good?"

"It means your coach is already keeping you on track with your fitness. He'll be watching you on your schoolwork, too, all season."

"Yeah, I see that." The young man brightened.

Sam flashed a smile at Peter. "My partner's right. You've got a good coach, Stretch. See you guys tomorrow night?"

"Probably." Stretch tucked his ball under his arm and followed his friends.

The teenage joshing and laughter faded away as the boys turned a corner. Sam bounced the ball a few times. *You can do this. You've had plenty of practice confronting Tony. You know how tough love works.* "Talk to you a minute, partner?" He tucked the ball under his arm.

"Sure. What's on your mind?"

Sam's gaze was neutral, his tone earnest. "I watched you trip three of our own players in the past two Sneaks games. Are you aware of that?"

"You're crazy." Peter flushed.

Sam continued, "Werner first. When he had the wind knocked out of him last week, you had a smug smile on your face, and you didn't bother to help him up, even though you were standing next to him. You tripped Johnson later the same game."

"This is nuts. What did I supposedly do to Johnson?"

"You brought your right foot down at the edge of his path," he said and pointed to the side of his own foot. "Not enough to injure him, just enough to throw him off." He pretended to trip but righted himself and faced Peter.

The muscles in Peter's face twitched.

"Then you did it again to him in the first ten minutes last night, and you got my brother the same way after the half."

"No. I. Didn't." Peter glared. "Why are you accusing me this way?"

"I'm putting two and two together, friend." He bounced the ball twice. "And I don't like the way it's adding up." He bounced the ball again two times and tossed it to Peter.

"I have no idea what you're talking about." Peter slammed the ball down and caught it with one hand on the way up.

"Maybe you don't," Sam allowed, "but I know what I'm seeing. I see you weasel out of dealing with DWIs week after week. And I watched your face when we were at Ralphs two weeks ago when Werner outed himself and Johnson and my brother, as being in AA. You looked like you smelled road kill." He paused and saw a flicker of recognition in Peter's eyes. *And maybe a little self-doubt.*

"And the very next game, I saw that self-satisfied smile on your face, like I said, when Werner went down, and I watched you trip Johnson. Same thing twice last night—Johnson and then Tony, like I said. Those are the facts, as I see them."

Peter snarled and leaned closer. "And I say you're making it up. I don't know why. We've always been good partners. I don't know why you'd trash me this way."

Sam lifted his chin and kept his voice even. "It's not trashing, partner. It's confronting you with the facts. If you really aren't aware of all this, then smarten up. Take the next three DWIs. Watch where you plant your feet on the court. And make sure you give a hand to a teammate who needs one." He held Peter's gaze a moment longer. "This thing you have against drunks is poison. I need you to take a look at it, if we're going to stay partners."

Peter stood in silence, his jaw set, his eyes snapping.

Sam walked off the court and reentered the station house. Alone.

Peter fired the ball at the backboard. The board vibrated while the ball sailed into the chain-link fence and died on the court.

Get it together, Shaughnessy. It was mid-shift, and he couldn't afford to spin out of control.

His chest heaved, and the rasping in his throat reminded him of those painful days after Cynthia's betrayal, when he wasn't yet fully recovered and couldn't slam around the court to work off anger. All he could do then was shoot baskets in a disciplined workout, and he'd found that calmed him better than any rampage ever had.

Do it.

Peter dribbled, pivoted, and lofted the ball through the net. Again, he dribbled, feinted, took a stand and shot. And again. When he was nine for ten, he dribbled to the gate, tucked the ball under his left arm, and stopped with his hand on the latch.

Sam's not a liar, and he doesn't have it in for me. That was all Peter knew for sure. He swung the gate open and shifted the ball under his right arm. *What if what Sam said is true?*

Chapter 11

"We've got morale problems," Tony groused to Sam at the Bagel Depot a week later. "You notice?"

Two weeks had gone by since Sam's confrontation, and Peter had cleaned up his act with his teammates.

"Maybe." Sam chewed his bagel sandwich. "What I see is you being cold to Peter, Peter being cold to Werner and Johnson, and them being cold right back. We're winning, but nobody's having fun." He stared with work-weary eyes above the rim of his coffee mug. "Is that what you mean?"

"You think I'm being cold?'

Sam nodded.

"So if I get my mojo back, maybe everyone else will, too?"

"Worth a try," Sam said with a shrug.

"What about you? You look like hell, little brother."

"My partner's still not pulling his weight with the DWIs."

"Didn't you talk with the captain?"

"No, I was waiting to see if he'd get it together. I hoped if he got the message about the team, he'd realize it's the same problem with the job. Guess not, so it's time to put a bug in the captain's ear."

"It's time." Tony nodded and punched his brother in the arm. "You've got the data, right?" At Sam's nod, he advised, "Tell the man what you know, and let him take it from there."

"Yeah," Sam said reluctantly. "I hate this."

"Shaughnessy, you're a good officer." The captain's tone was clipped. He studied Peter's face as he continued, "But you're not pulling your weight in one important area."

He held up his hand to stave off interruptions. "We both know there are differences between a large city and a small city environment, but it may not be clear to you that in Tompkins Falls every officer handles all types of violations." He leveled his gaze at Peter. "Including DWIs."

Peter flinched.

"I can see from the record," the captain continued, with a glance at a printout on his desktop, "that you and Officer Pinelli bring in several DWIs every week, which is to be expected on the night shift. Why is it that, over the past four months, I see your name on two DWI bookings and Officer Pinelli's name on every other?"

Peter's gaze swept the room as if the answer lay outside himself.

The captain rose, then walked around his desk to stand two feet in front of Peter. He had the advantage in height and bulk. "I have no evidence that you're letting drunks off the hook, which would be grounds for dismissal."

"No, sir." Peter's heart raced, and his eyes flashed.

"I've spoken to your partner about this, and he is of the opinion you have a low tolerance for drunk drivers and a disdain for them as human beings. Perhaps not every DWI is an alcoholic, Shaughnessy, but this police force recognizes alcoholism as a disease.

"The drunk driver's actions are contemptible and punishable by law, no question, but an alcoholic is a sick individual in need of training and treatment. Booking him on a DWI charge may be the first step toward his recovery. If you'd ever attended a meeting of Alcoholics Anonymous you would have heard that in at least one member's story at that meeting. It's that common."

Peter's cheeks burned, and his fists clenched and unclenched at his side.

"I won't write this up as a reprimand at this time, if you are willing to do the following." He paused.

"Yes, sir." Peter cleared his throat.

"You will attend the AA meeting here in town this Friday evening, before your shift. Your presence, from start to finish, will be noted and reported to me. And I need to see your name, legitimately, on two-thirds of the DWI bookings for your squad over the next three months. Any questions?"

Peter swallowed, croaked, and found his voice. "One, sir. How do I find the location and time of the AA meeting?"

The captain grimaced. "At the back of City Hall, two doors down from the station, you'll see a door with a triangle inside a circle, labeled Central Office. I believe they're open daily from nine in the morning until four in the afternoon. Walk in, introduce yourself, tell them what you need and they'll see to it." He folded his arms over his barrel chest.

"Thank you, sir."

The captain fixed Peter with a stern eye. "I'd prefer not to lose you, Shaughnessy."

"Yes, sir," Peter said with a start. "I mean, no, sir."

"That will be all."

Peter did a smart about-face and exited. He charged down the hall with tight fists and hot exhalations. A secretary coming on duty stepped to the side and flattened her back against the wall.

At three o'clock Peter parked behind City Hall and locked the Jeep. He spotted the triangle in a circle and walked casually to the door. With cautious look around, he entered and removed his sunglasses. To his surprise, calm settled around him.

A tall man with a gentle smile, perched on the edge of a desk, waved and said, "Be right with you, sir." The man's attention was on the woman sitting at the next desk, with a phone in her hand. He offered advice, which the woman added to what she had already communicated to the person at the other end of the connection. When she hung up and turned, Peter saw her face.

It was Carol, the woman who had driven Bree back to Peter's when she'd visited a few weeks ago. Startled, she gave him a big smile. "How's your sister?" she asked cheerfully.

Peter glared at her, and her smile changed to a puzzled frown.

The man stepped closer to Peter and rose to his full height. "How can I help you today, sir?" he asked, his tone all business.

"I need the place and time for an AA meeting this Friday evening in Tompkins Falls."

"That would be seven at the Presbyterian Church. Isn't that right?" He glanced at Carol.

She nodded once, her eyes warily on Peter.

The man added, "Feel free to take a meeting list, sir."

"That's all I needed." Peter stepped back and walked out of the tranquility of the office into harsh sunlight.

When he saw a man wearing a navy CUSE sweatshirt enter the meeting room for the Friday night AA group, Joel's hand jumped and coffee sloshed over the rim of his mug. As the man's angry green gaze swept closer to him, he said a silent prayer, put on a welcoming smile, and moved forward to greet him. Lifting his mug to the new arrival, he said, "Peter, glad you could join us tonight." He held out his hand and added "Joel Cushman," in case the officer had forgotten his name.

Peter edged closer. "You always come here?" He didn't offer his hand.

"Every Friday unless I'm out of town. How about some coffee?"

"Sure."

"Help yourself. The mugs go through the dishwasher, so they're clean."

Peter chose a mug from the tray, lifted the nearest pot

and poured. He replaced the pot, and his gaze lifted. Tony, Werner, and Johnson stared at him from across the crowded church hall. Peter glared back.

"I can introduce you to them," Joel offered when he saw the stare-down.

"I already know them. They're my teammates."

Needing to get off his feet, Joel spotted a row with two empty chairs on the end, halfway back from the podium. "The Sneaks?" he said as he led Peter toward the chairs. "I heard you're having a winning season."

"Yeah, thanks."

Joel motioned for Peter to go ahead of him to the second chair. *Got him trapped.* "I was glad to meet your partner, Sam Pinelli, at the dinner for Chief Barker. I knew Tony had a brother on the force. Seems like a good guy."

"He is. Real solid. Look, are you in this thing?" Peter demanded.

"Do you mean, am I a recovering alcoholic?"

Peter grunted.

"Yes, I've been sober coming up on fifteen years. Chief Barker threw me in jail when I was a badass teenager, after my family was killed, and I was fortunate that the people in my life gave me a lot of tough love. I'd be dead without that and without AA."

Peter's forehead creased with a frown. "You're my age, and you've been sober fourteen years?"

Joel nodded without comment and sipped coffee.

"Does your wife know?"

Joel's coffee sloshed over the rim again. *Do not laugh.* He held the mug out so the drips landed on the carpet instead of his chinos. "Yes, Manda knows." He refrained from adding that his wife was also "in this thing."

A gavel cracked at the front of the hall, and fifty people took seats in the rows of chairs. As the room settled, Joel confided to Peter, "That's my sponsor, Phil, speaking tonight.

He's Gwen's neighbor on the lake. He and I take meetings into the prison down county."

Peter's cheeks filled and he blew out disbelief.

Joel gave him a sideways glance, which Peter acknowledged with a raised eyebrow. *Got his attention.*

If he hadn't mentioned taking meetings into a prison and told him Phil was Gwen's neighbor, Joel doubted Peter would have paid attention to the old guy with the gravelly voice at the podium. Phil was eighty. He'd been sober thirty years. He told the group he "finally threw in the towel" when he woke up in a strange woman's bed while his wife was home calling hospitals, hunting for his body. "Mrs. Philips didn't raise her little boy to cheat on his wife," Phil said. "That was a flashing neon sign that I couldn't ignore. Booze had stopped working for me a couple years before that, but I had kept on doing the same damn thing, thinking I could find my way back to happy, carefree drinking." Phil shook his head and peered out at the audience.

He spotted Joel and looked hard at Peter with a fleeting scowl, probably wondering who he was. "I got into rehab, and they directed me to AA. We lived in Rochester, where I worked for Kodak. Edie had grown up on Chestnut Lake, so, when I retired some years later, we moved to the old house on the lakeshore. I have a closed Big Book meeting there on Wednesdays. Now that Edie's gone, I sponsor men in this program, take meetings into jails and prisons and generally provide an ear or a chair on the porch for anyone who's sincere about their sobriety and having a hard time of it.

"I'm eighty and I still need to be useful," he told them. "These twelve steps show me how to be of maximum service every day, and seeing a newcomer grab onto the hope in these rooms and the tools of our AA program brings me joy.

"After we break for the seventh tradition, the meeting is yours. Someone come up with a topic or a question for us."

Empty baskets appeared at various points around the

room, and the place buzzed with conversation. "What's the seventh tradition?" Peter asked Joel.

"We support ourselves. People put a dollar or two in the basket to help pay the rent and buy the coffee. You don't need to put in anything. Care to share your thoughts about what you've heard and seen so far?"

Peter examined the contents of his mug and swirled the cold coffee. "I was wondering what my life would have been like if my father had gotten sober. I don't remember hearing my father laugh or talk about being useful or about joy. Everything at our house was grim and tense and negative. I like what he said about being useful and being of service. My whole life I wanted to serve and protect."

"And now you do that for our city, Tompkins Falls," Joel said. "Thank you for your service."

Peter seemed antsy, but he listened to the thirty minutes of discussion that followed. The meeting concluded with everyone standing and saying the Serenity Prayer.

"Any thoughts or questions?" Joel asked Peter casually as they strolled toward the door.

"How did you meet that old guy Phil?"

Joel's face came alive with a grin. "Walk out with me and I'll tell you."

They shouldered through groups engaged in noisy conversation, and stepped into the quiet of the church parking lot. "When I moved back to Tompkins Falls a while back," Joel said, "I didn't know many people at meetings. Phil got in my face one day and said, 'You gonna join us or sit back there with a smug smile on your face every meeting?' So I took that suggestion and a few others, reluctantly at first. He's made a better man of me."

Peter glanced back toward the church.

"Did you forget something?"

"No, but I think I was supposed to check in with someone. The captain didn't tell me who."

"That was me," Joel said with an easy smile. "Glad you came tonight, Peter. I live downstairs from you, you know. Manda and I moved in a couple of weeks ago. If you ever want to talk, I'm there most evenings after six. Manda and I would be glad to have you join us for supper." He gave Peter a friendly wave and walked toward his Passat.

Gwen kept her arm around Haley's shoulders as they breezed into the women's meeting at Clifton Springs the same Friday evening. "Good, Manda's here ahead of us," she noted. She pointed out a vivacious brunette talking with two other women at the coffee pot. Gwen lifted a hand to get Manda's attention. Manda separated from the group and came toward them.

"Manda, meet Haley," Gwen announced. "I'll let you two discover what you have in common, and I'll save seats for you both," she promised.

Haley watched her disappear into the crowd. With a gulp, she turned doubtful eyes on the pretty woman with the sparkling, deep-blue eyes, who said, "Hi, Haley, I'm Manda. Welcome."

"Hi, Manda. This is my first time at a meeting."

"I hope you'll hear something you need. I've been sober about a year and a half now, and my life's way better sober."

"Um, Gwen, my aunt, said I should talk to you." Haley blurted out, "I'm not sure if I'm an alcoholic, but I know I can't drink without awful things happening." She giggled nervously and surveyed the meeting room. "I'm surprised there are so many girls around my age here." She saw women of all ages, colors, shapes, and sizes.

"We're the lucky ones, I think," Manda told her with an easy smile, "getting sober while we've got our whole lives ahead of us."

"Did drinking get really bad for you?" Haley asked shyly.

"Humiliating and dangerous," Manda said simply. "How about you?"

"Well," Haley lowered her gaze, "I got pregnant and really messed things up with my boyfriend. I don't know if I can ever forgive myself for hurting him the way I did."

Manda placed a gentle, manicured hand on Haley's arm. "I am so grateful the twelve steps have given me a way to make things right with the people I hurt. If you're an alcoholic, and if you stay with the program and work through the steps with a sponsor, I know it can help you that way, too."

"Really?" She probed Manda's eyes and saw the strength of her conviction. "Whew."

"We've got about one minute before the meeting starts. Haley, would you be at all interested in coming with me and my friend Sara this Saturday? Sara's not in the program, but we like to go to thrift shops around the Finger Lakes and have lunch someplace. It's just a fun chick thing, and we always find something we can wear for, like, a dollar." She grinned.

"Sara the hairdresser at the Manse Spa?"

"Yes, do you know her?"

"Yes, count me in."

Deirdre Calhoun was not in her usual spot at Lynnie's Chestnut Lake Café Saturday morning. She sat by the door in the back room of the Bagel Depot, planning to snag Joel after the Early Risers meeting. She had been two rows behind Joel and Peter at the Friday meeting and wanted to know what had motivated Peter to show up.

She put the question to Joel over coffee and bagels after the meeting, but Joel just shrugged. Joel, she knew, was too cagey, and too faithful to the AA principle of anonymity, to disclose that the man had been Gwen's Peter or to discuss his motivations. "Where was Gwen Friday night?" he asked her. "I usually see her at that meeting."

"As if you don't know," Deirdre countered. "She and Manda were at the women's meeting in Clifton Springs."

"Oh, that's right."

"You don't fool me."

Joel turned his gray-green gaze on her. "What do you think would have happened if Gwen had been with you Friday night?"

Deirdre sat back. "That's the real question, isn't it?"

"When Manda and I sat with them at Chief Barker's fête, I had the impression Peter didn't realize Gwen's in recovery herself. Either that or he's incredibly insensitive."

"Well, Friday night was the first I'd laid eyes on the man. I only know what Gwen has told me," Deirdre said.

"What made you think he's Gwen's Peter?"

"I was going on appearance and name. You just filled in the rest. Thank you."

"You beat me at my own game." He grinned. "Tell me, Deirdre. Is there any reason for me to worry about my friend Gwen?"

"I'm plenty worried," Deirdre answered, her mouth set in a grim line. "She insists he knows she's in recovery. I tell her, until she has that discussion with him, upfront, it's a ticking time bomb."

"Think he'll tell her he went a meeting?" Joel asked.

"That would depend on why he was there in the first place." Deirdre's eyes crinkled at the corner and she batted her eyelashes. "What do you think?"

Joel tapped his bagel on the plate and set it down. "I think they're both keeping secrets, and they might need their friends. Soon." He pushed back from the table. "Good to see you, Deirdre." He walked out without a backward glance.

"Are you graduating soon, Haley?" Manda asked her.

"I'm a junior, so a year from next May." Haley watched out the window as they sped toward their thrift shop destination. The fall foliage was just past peak. Leaves flew from the trees. Red, orange, plum, and russet, all different leaf formations and patterns of veins. She wished she could reach out the window and grab them as they fell, catch them, and paint them in her new studio at Gwen's.

"What college?" Sara wanted to know.

"Uh, University at Albany. I'm really lucky they have online classes and directed studies or I'd be losing a whole year."

"What's your major?"

"Botany and art." *I don't want to be a tagalong. I want to make friends.* She screwed up her courage. "I have an online business, creating botanical prints and posters. Oh, and cards, too."

"Another entrepreneur, Sara," Manda said.

"Really? Do you have a business, Sara?"

"I am creating one. Have created one. Have designed one that's going to open in June." She laughed at herself. "Why is that so hard for me to say?"

"It's funny, I'm like that, too," Haley said. "My boyfriend can talk about my business easier than I can. Tell me what you're planning." Haley enthusiasm brought out smiles in Manda and Sara.

"It's a specialty shop, a boutique that features accessories for working women who want to turn a basic wardrobe into dozens of variations. I'll have scarves, hats, jewelry, clip-ons, shawls, belts, faux flowers, hair ornaments, you name it. All good quality, but affordable."

"I think it's brilliant," Manda said.

"Thank you, Manda." Sara told Haley, "Manda is one of my cheerleaders, and she has given me solid feedback about my business plan. I couldn't have made it this far without her."

"It's a smart idea," Haley said, "especially to focus on working women. When I walk through the mall, I see shops with a lot of cheap stuff and young teens shopping there. And the bling in the high-end department stores gets pricey."

Haley added, her voice tentative, "Rick, my boyfriend, wants me to try using their new, 3D printer at RPI to make flower accessories, especially pins and earrings. The ones I see in gift shops are kind of boring, all one color. I think I can do better."

"Haley, you should talk to the graphics arts people at RIT, where I'm getting my degree," Sara said. "Who knows? If you're successful, maybe we can sell your flower accessories in my shop. Did I tell you, it's opening in June in Canandaigua?"

"Is that close to Tompkins Falls?" Haley asked.

"Next city to the west, on Route 20," Manda answered. "We're driving east on Route 20, so you won't see it today. Sara, do you think you and Sam will get married before or after you open the store?"

"Oh, wow, I don't know. I hope he proposes at Thanksgiving. I love him more all the time."

"When did you start dating?" Haley asked.

"Last spring after I gave Reliable Randy the heave-ho. At first I was really self-conscious that I'm a whole year older than Sam. But he's very mature, and being on the police force, he's seen a lot more of the dark side than I have."

"Isn't he Peter's partner?"

"Yes," Sara said in surprise. "That's right, you know Peter because he and Gwen are hot and heavy."

"He is so handsome. Peter, I mean."

"Sam is, too," Manda added quickly.

"I think Gwen and Peter are meant for each other," Haley stated. "You should see, just the way they work together, even when they talk at dinner, you can tell how in synch they are with each other."

"They'll probably be married before Sam and me," Sara said with a laugh.

"They don't get much privacy with me at Gwen's. I am so glad they're getting away for the whole day today, canoeing down the lake to see the foliage."

The farther south they paddled, the denser the trees grew on the steep hillside and the more brilliant the colors, as late-afternoon sun intensified the reds and golds.

"Sad to think this may all be gone after the storm," Peter remarked.

Gwen's paddle faltered, smacked the water, and splashed her. "What storm?"

"Tonight. They're saying rain starting around sundown, damaging winds, lightning, and thunder."

"When did you hear this?" How far had they come? With Peter's strong arms in the stern and a light wind behind them, they were farther south than she'd ever paddled along the eastern shore—maybe ten miles from the house.

"I heard the report on the way to your place. Large, fast-moving storm, tracking farther north than expected, will do a clean sweep of the Finger Lakes."

Fear and anger surged, and she made herself pause. *That's unfair. He doesn't know the lakes.*

With false calm, Gwen set her paddle across the gunwales and searched the shore. She saw no roads anywhere on the steep, rocky hillside. Only a few tiny fishing cabins were visible, tucked into coves, all of them boarded up for the season. From this point south, the lakeshore was progressively steeper and less inhabited.

If they headed for the south end, they'd find the only hamlet closed up tight. By tradition, last weekend was when the few stores and cottages celebrated the end of their season, with a bang, and then shuttered their buildings until May.

"Getting tired?"

"We need to turn around."

"We'll be back before dark. It's beautiful here. So quiet."

Gwen said sternly, "No, we won't make it back before the storm if we don't head back now. We'll have a headwind all the way back. I wish I'd known about the storm and paid attention to how far we'd come."

"Are you—"

Gwen whipped around to glare at him.

"You're serious. It's serious." He dug his paddle in deep and brought the canoe to a stop.

Gwen swung her paddle in a wide arc to turn the boat quickly. The light headwind chilled her wet T-shirt. She rummaged behind her for her plaid wool shirt but wished she'd also brought her jacket. She buttoned up with shaking fingers.

"We'll paddle hard and watch the sky," Peter said with maddening calm.

They gazed to the west, just as charcoal clouds swallowed the sun.

Panic grabbed Gwen by the throat. She braced her hands on the gunwales to steady her shakes and get her breathing under control. *God, help me get it together.* They would need every reserve of strength—Peter's and her own.

She dug in her paddle and matched Peter's rhythm. The repetition of their strokes steadied her. "Together we can do this," she asserted with more courage than she felt.

"How well do you know this stretch of shore?" he asked, his voice calm. "If we have to, is there someplace we can put out until the storm blows over?"

"Not this far south. If we can make it three or four miles I'll begin to recognize places."

"How far are we from your place?"

Too far. "At least ten miles."

They'd gone no more than half a mile when a cold wind quartered from the northwest and raised a few whitecaps out beyond the midpoint of the lake. Above the wind, Gwen heard their breathing, the fall of droplets as their paddles rose in unison, and the swish as both paddles sliced in for the next push forward.

"I'm sorry I got us into this," Peter said.

"You didn't know how fast the lake can change. I didn't know about the storm, but I should have. It's a done deal. Let's just go as far as we can and, if the storm closes in, find a reasonable landing spot and hope we find shelter nearby."

"Agreed."

Half a mile farther the wind was enough louder that she heard only her paddle and her breathing. A backward glance showed her Peter stroking hard, in unison with her. He nodded.

The wind picked up speed. Gwen's breathing grew labored. A wave gushed over the gunwale behind her. And another. *Keep going.*

The pitch of the hillside changed subtly. She rested for a few seconds and squinted at the shoreline, seeking a welcoming cove or a low spot where they could land. *Nothing yet.* She dug in hard for another mile, but she wished she could hear Peter so they could work in synch. As it was, she made his job harder. Whether she paddled too fast or too slow, he had to correct their course.

With the looming storm, the sky darkened as if it were twilight. She turned back to Peter and saw his head low, his shoulders straining. She dug her paddle in and prayed. Every stroke mattered.

About half a mile farther, waves assaulted the canoe. Gwen's lungs labored, and her shoulders burned. The eerie light gave her shivers, but it was bright enough for her to see a stream and a thin waterfall that sliced through the hillside and plunged into the waters of a rocky bay.

Nine Mile Bay. The hillside from this point north was still steep, but rough tracks cut through the tree cover. Four-wheel-drive vehicles had access to a few remote houses much of the year. *We'll find shelter.*

"Soon," she yelled above the wind.

A flash of lightning on the western shore shot fear through her body. A sob escaped her.

"I'll maneuver as close to shore as I dare," Peter shouted. "You pick a spot."

Gwen focused on every ledge, outcropping, and patch of ground. "Up ahead twenty yards," she yelled and dug in her paddle. "See those bushes with the path going up?" She pointed with her right hand, and the wind grabbed at her paddle. She gripped it with both hands. *No mistakes.*

Lightning flashed up and down the western hills, and thunder cracked and roared. They fought the waves and wind for ten yards. Three waves in succession breached the canoe and propelled it dangerously close to shore.

With no warning, a submerged rock ripped open the bow, and the next wave rolled the canoe on its side.

Gwen's stomach churned as the next wave sucked her out of the boat. *Use your head!* She grabbed for the gunwale and held tight to her paddle.

Drenched and shivering, she found a foothold on the stony lakebed as she wrestled the waves for possession of the canoe.

"Peter!" she shouted. "Where are you?"

"I'm okay."

Peter had retrieved his paddle. He squeezed her shoulder as he crossed behind her. "Are you hurt?"

She shook her head.

His fingers found the damage where the sharp point of a ledge had sliced into the bow's canvas, along the gunwale for about six inches, just ahead of where Gwen had been kneeling.

The ledge itself was a smooth shelf about eight inches under the water. If they could get over or around it they would have foothold to the start of the path Gwen had spotted.

"We'll slide over this, rather than go around." Peter shouted in her ear, over the roar of the wind.

"You pull, I'll push," Gwen said. Thunder drowned

out her words, but her accompanying arm motion communicated her plan.

"Good team," he encouraged and raised his thumb.

Peter slid backward across the ledge and took a wave full in his face. He shook the water out of his eyes and reached out for the boat. The next three waves lifted it, and they floated it across in three easy moves.

At Peter's nod, Gwen let go of the stern and slithered across, like a seal.

Another round of lightning and thunder warned them to get out of the water quickly, with no time to regroup.

After they trudged through the angry waves for ten yards, with the crippled canoe between them, they dragged it to the shore and shoved it onto its side to empty it as much as possible. A footpath wound upwards through wind-whipped shrubs. "Let's climb toward that stand of evergreens," Peter called back. "I'll keep an eye out for a place to secure this, and you watch for a cabin."

At first, the path was well worn and still dry. They carried the sixty-pound boat between them, with the wind eddying around their bodies, vying for possession of the canoe.

Gwen lost her grip once and fell to her knees.

Peter stopped, looked back at her, and encouraged, "We're almost to the evergreens, and I see a clearing we can use. Worst case, we can flip the canoe and shelter under it. Can you make it another twenty feet?"

Gwen licked her lips and hauled herself up. Lightning approached the shore. She grabbed the gunwale, lifted the canoe, and signaled for him to move ahead.

By the time they had tucked the injured canoe into the clearing, a wall of water had advanced halfway across the lake. Peter wrapped his arm around her shaking shoulders. "Did you see any sign of shelter?"

Lightning lit the hillside and flashed on a plate glass window fifty feet above. "There!" she yelled.

Peter grabbed her hand. "Let's go."

Rain turned the path to mud and lashed their backs. Finally, they clambered up the half dozen steps to the deep front porch of a log house. Gwen peered in the front windows while Peter hammered the front door.

"No one home. Just try it," Gwen urged.

When he turned the knob, the wind flung the door open. Peter pulled Gwen inside with him, forced the door shut, and dead-bolted it.

Outside, the storm howled and rattled the door. Rain lashed the windows and drummed on the roof. Peter tried a light switch. "No power."

His breathing eased, but Gwen coughed and struggled to catch her breath.

He helped her to the sofa, grabbed a blanket from the back, and wrapped it around her shoulders. "Sit still," he ordered. Lightning illuminated the room and showed him a lantern on a low table. He struck a match and lit the lantern, then adjusted the wick until it gave off a warm glow that transformed their refuge into someone's cozy living room.

"You learned that in Boy Scouts?" Gwen rasped. She gave him a weak smile.

"Camping trip with the guys." Peter chuckled. "Glad I paid attention."

She shivered as she held out her hands to the warmth of the lantern.

Another lightning flash showed them a woodstove in the corner on a brick platform. "You know how to work that?" Peter asked.

Gwen nodded and took the hand he offered. When she opened the door of the firebox, she laughed in disbelief and sank down, cross-legged, on the braided rug. "Thank you, God." Small logs, kindling and wadded newspaper had been laid, ready for a match. She reached for the box of matches on the hearth. "Whoever lives here is probably just away for the weekend."

He squatted beside her and together they watched the flames catch the kindling and lick the logs. He tucked the blanket around her shoulders. "I'll bring more wood."

Gwen nodded, her face lit by the flames.

An iron caddy held split logs, large and small, stacked high. He carried half a dozen the same size as those already burning and set them beside the stove. He followed with half a dozen larger ones. Gwen never moved, but her body trembled with cold. He handed her two small logs and a larger one and watched her feed them to the flames. Her hands steadied as she worked.

He squatted beside her and put an arm along her shoulder. "Let's get you into a hot shower, and I'll use the stove to make us cocoa and marshmallows or whatever I can find." He helped her to her feet.

In the compact, immaculate bathroom, Gwen peeled off her sodden T-shirt and bra and dropped them in a pile beside the shower enclosure. Too late, she sized up the towel situation. A man-sized bath towel hung from a hook on the back of the door. *Oh well.* She'd get warm first and worry about it after.

She struggled with the button at the waistband of her jeans, but her icy fingers could not undo the button or grasp the zipper pull. She stopped a moment, got the shower going, and let the hot water warm her hands. Undressing took no time with working hands. She kicked her panties and jeans and soggy socks on top of her other clothes.

Warm water streamed through her hair, down her face and her breasts and belly, warmed her thighs and knees and feet. She turned slowly, reveling in the soothing, body-temperature cascade. Steam opened her breathing passages. Her cough ceased and her throat relaxed. Energy surged as she lathered her body all over with spice-scented soap.

Peter knocked at the bathroom door. "Got enough towels in there?"

"None."

"I'll leave them right outside."

"Hey," she said, her voice playful.

"Hey what?" He opened the door a crack.

"Suppose I use up all the hot water?"

The door swung open, and Peter stuck his head in. With his eyebrows set in a V, he growled, "You better not."

She grinned as steam escaped into the hallway and the glass shower door lost its layer of fog. Peter drank in the sight of her naked body, and she liked the sexy smile that lit up his face. "Join me while it's still hot?"

He peeled off his polo shirt, kicked off his sneakers, and tugged off his jeans and boxers. Carefully. Gwen let out a quiet "Whoa" at the muscled, male anatomy a few feet away.

Peter slipped in beside her and drew her against him. "Some women go a long way for privacy."

She locked her hands behind his neck. "I couldn't let the opportunity pass us by. Get warm first."

"Woman, I have never been so hot. Are you sure you're up for this?"

"I've got my second wind."

He lifted her, and she wrapped her legs around his hips, then hummed with anticipation as he backed her to the wall of the enclosure. He sucked one breast while he fondled the other with his fingers.

Gwen's fingers raked through his wet hair and tugged at the curls. "Don't make me wait," she urged.

He eased back enough to drive inside her, and she moaned with total satisfaction. "That's right where I want you."

When she lifted her arms, her back arched, and he pinned her hands above her head. She struggled a moment before giving into his mastery. Through eyes wild with passion, she saw in his face the heat and hunger that burned in her.

He drove into her again and again.

On the verge of passing out, she gasped, "I can't, Peter."

He released her hands, and she circled his neck with her arms. He eased back, and she loosened her legs and collapsed against him.

She awoke beside him on a nest of chair cushions next to the wood stove. A pile of damp towels lay nearby. He had found warm, wool blankets to cover them.

"Are you all right?" he asked, his voice filled with concern.

Startled, she raised up on one elbow.

"Did I faint?"

"You collapsed in my arms. You had me worried."

She flopped on her back and stretched her arms overhead with a chuckle. "You blew me away."

"Couldn't take it, huh?"

"I have never felt so ravaged and loved and pleasured."

"It did get a little intense. Maybe because we could have died out there in the storm."

"But we didn't," she said quickly. "We're okay." She rolled into him.

This time their lovemaking was tender and unhurried. Gwen straddled him and rode him until, with a growl, Peter rolled her under him and drove her to her peak. She held him tight inside her and shuddered when they climaxed together.

He lay beside her, trailing his fingers over her breasts.

Gwen dreamed she heard a car door slam. When she rolled to her left side, a wall of muscle lay in her path.

"Morning," Peter whispered. "I think our host just came home."

Gwen scrambled to sit up. "Where are our clothes?" she said in a panic.

"In the drier. Power came back on during the night. I'll fetch them. Stay put."

Soon after he left her, Gwen heard a footfall outside

and saw a man's head at the window. He ducked out of sight when he saw her.

"Peter," she squeaked, her heart hammering.

Peter returned fully dressed and handed over her clothes. "He took off down toward the water, probably checking on damage from the storm. Get dressed right here. I'm going out to meet him."

Remembering the muddy path from the night before, Peter exited the kitchen into the driveway and followed the path the owner had taken that wound through the copse of evergreens. He caught up with their unwitting host where he squatted by the canoe.

The man appeared to be in his sixties, clean-shaven, fit, and neatly dressed. His back was to Peter, but he gave a nod as Peter snapped a broken branch in his path.

"Did my ledge take you by surprise?" he asked. His fingers explored the rip in the canvas.

"Yes, sir."

"Might be able to repair the canvas, but your backbone and ribs in the front are unstable." Hand on the tip of the bow, he jiggled the boat. "It's not going to get you home."

"I see what you mean, sir."

The man turned and held out his hand. "None of this 'sir' stuff. Name's Foster."

"Peter Shaughnessy." Peter took the outstretched hand and admired the man's strong grip.

"Either of you hurt?"

"My friend's pretty shaken up, but nothing worse. We sure were glad to find shelter here. We owe you, Foster."

"The roads were so bad, I stayed in Clifton Springs until this morning."

"When did it stop? We were comatose."

"Around two in the morning. Is the power still off?"

"It came on during the night. We used your drier for our clothes and the towels."

"How about some eggs and toast before I drive you back wherever you came from? I'm famished," Foster said.

"Gwen makes a mean omelet, Foster."

They hauled the damaged canoe uphill and left it in the driveway. While Foster fastened a rack to the roof of the truck, Peter enlisted Gwen to fix them breakfast.

The aroma of fresh coffee greeted him.

"He had the coffee maker already set up, too, like the woodstove," Gwen told Peter. "I just pressed the button. I figured this morning would go better for everyone with hot coffee."

"Good thinking. He'll take us back to your place after we eat." Peter gave her a warm hug, followed by a sheepish look. "I volunteered you to make omelets and toast."

"I'm on it." She met his kiss and waved him back outside to load the canoe.

He and Foster helped themselves to the two chairs at the kitchen table. Gwen served them and ate her meal with her back resting against the counter.

"I used to have a dock over that ledge," Foster said. "It broke up in a storm just like last night's, probably ten or fifteen years ago now. I found planks all over the hillside for a year." He took another bite and rumbled his approval. "Someone helped themselves to the posts the next summer. I never bothered to rebuild. I don't need it with the kayak."

"So last night was unusual?" Peter asked.

"We get storms all the time, but last night was something special. Same thing where you live, Gwen?"

"I have my parents old home which is protected some by the little round islands in the northeast corner of the lake."

"The gumdrops," Foster said.

"Hah. I thought I was the only one that called them gumdrops," Peter chortled.

"No, to me they've always looked like spearmint gumdrops," Foster said.

Gwen and Peter exchanged a smile.

"Best omelet I've ever had, Gwen," Foster told her when they finished. "Are you folks ready to head out?"

"I'd like to do the dishes first and clean up the bathroom and living room," Gwen offered.

"Appreciate it," Foster agreed. "Peter, how about coming down to the shore with me to check for damage." He stood and stretched. "Or bodies."

When Gwen's eyes opened wide, he relented. "Kidding."

Chapter 12

Gwen sat between Foster and Peter in the cab of the truck as they bounced up his road to the highway.

"This road is as challenging as yours, Gwen," Peter said.

"Hard to maintain them, don't you find?" Foster asked her.

"I've slipped from proactive to reactive. It would be easier if I had a schedule of things that needed repair around the property. I'm actually wondering if the ash trees will still be standing when we get home. I meant to call the Extension about Emerald Ash Borer—"

"Gwen, did you call Haley to see if she's all right?" Peter's voice was anxious.

"I couldn't. My phone was a casualty in the storm."

Foster slipped his phone to her. "Your daughter?" he asked.

"My niece is staying with me. She had a baby a few weeks ago, and she was probably scared to death last night."

Haley answered on the first ring, and Gwen explained that they'd be home shortly. Haley agreed to help them offload the canoe. "We never lost power, but it was a wild night," she told Gwen.

"I'm glad you're okay, sweetie. Please give Phil a call and make sure he's all right."

"I did. He's fine."

"Love you." Gwen handed back the phone. "Thanks, Foster."

They rolled along the highway in silence for six miles. Peter kept his arm along the back of the seat behind Gwen, and Foster appeared to be deep in thought. Suddenly he asked, "Gwen, don't I see you at Clifton Springs now and then on a Friday evening?"

Gwen started. "Yes. I knew your voice was familiar."

"I stay out in the hallway, because it's a women's meeting. I was a counselor there for thirty-two years. I still see a few clients and try to support them after meetings."

A smile washed over Gwen's face. "That's right, you were there when I started my practice."

"Ten years ago?"

"Nine. I've been sober eight years now."

Peter's body stiffened.

"I remember you before you made the decision—shaking and scared, probably just like you were in the storm last night."

"I was a mess. I couldn't do it anymore."

"If I recall correctly, you had a hard time for a few years."

"My husband died and both my parents died. But I didn't have to drink."

"Still use a sponsor?" Foster asked.

"I do. She's famous for tough love."

"I don't know about you, Gwen, but the sober life still feels like a miracle to me, even after thirty-one years in the program."

"Maybe I'll see you sometime at Clifton Springs. My Tuesday night group takes in treatment meetings during December and March, and a few of us go to the Friday women's meeting, once or twice a month. My road is that yellow sign up on the left. Beware, the turns are very tight."

Foster navigated her private road slowly, and Gwen kept an eye on the canoe as they bounced down the hillside.

Peter sprang from the truck the moment they stopped, and Haley rushed out to meet them. He undid the straps and directed Haley to help.

With her hand on the passenger door, Gwen said, "Foster, I'd like to bring you a couple weeks' worth of groceries, to repay you for the unauthorized use of your home."

"I wouldn't say no, Gwen. You know where I live.

Monday and Thursday mornings are the best times to catch me there, before ten."

"I'll be there Thursday. Thanks for everything."

After he backed the truck around, Foster said out the window, "Sorry about your canoe."

"There are worse things," Gwen said and waved cheerily as the battered truck rumbled up the drive. *There's a connection I want to keep.*

Silence behind her made her turn around.

Peter stood tight-lipped, halfway to his Jeep, glowering.

Haley fidgeted beside the canoe, her forehead puckered, as she glanced from Gwen to Peter and back again.

Gwen's chin came up, and she instinctively folded her arms across her chest. "Thank you for offloading the canoe," she said, her voice neutral though her heart hammered.

Peter grunted. "Thank Haley."

"It wobbles in front." Haley sounded flustered. "What happened?"

Gwen walked over to Haley and gave her a warm hug. "We were caught in the storm and collided with a ledge. We ended up at Foster's, and he was kind enough to give us a ride home. Right now I need to talk to Peter for a minute, and you and I can catch up after, okay? Thanks for your help, sweetie."

Haley shrugged. With another puzzled glance at Peter, she stepped into the garage and up to the kitchen. Slowly, she closed the door.

Gwen faced Peter's anger, stood still, and let him make the next move. She didn't have long to wait.

Peter demanded, "When you take meetings into Clifton, are you there to drum up business?"

Gwen jerked her head as though he'd slapped her face. Her voice shook when she replied, "I never 'drum up business' at AA meetings. We're there only to stay sober and help others stay sober."

Peter shifted his weight. "So why do you go?" His tone was nasty.

"To stay sober and help others."

Silence.

"Treatment meetings are especially important to newcomers in a drug and alcohol rehab program," she explained. "The women we see are usually desperate, and some are looking for a long-term solution."

"You're an alcoholic?" he said derisively.

Gwen's mouth was dry. "You know I am."

Peter studied the ground. He nodded. "I guess I do now."

Gwen felt cold inside. She remembered Deirdre's words, cautioning her to get her alcoholism out in the open for discussion. "Peter—"

He strode to his Jeep.

"I never kept that a secret," she defended.

He laughed with scorn and wrenched the door open.

Gwen raised her voice. "You knew my life was—is—all about recovery."

Peter turned back to confront her, "It was about *other* people's recovery, the way I heard it."

"And mine."

"It's interesting that detail never came into the conversation. You know how I feel about drunks."

Gwen felt heat in her cheeks. "Which is basically why, once I knew that, I didn't bring it up in conversation. Why try to talk about something we disagree about?"

Peter threw up his hands. "I think it's called honesty."

"I never lied to you."

Peter's laugh was hollow. "No, you just didn't tell me. You quietly—silently—betrayed me."

There's that word again—betrayed. "That's bullshit. Maybe your wife betrayed you, but I didn't."

Peter's face flushed an angry red. "You fucking led me on."

Gwen yelled, "Peter!"

He slammed the door, ground the ignition, and peeled out. Gravel sprayed behind him and pelted, first the canoe, and then Gwen. When a sharp, flying stone hit her left wrist, it hurt almost as much as her heart.

Sobbing, she fled into the house, ran cold water on the welt, and splashed some on her face.

"Gwen?"

Gwen turned to Haley and held up her hands to fend her off. "Later, sweetie. I have to do something first." She phoned Deirdre on the landline, arranged to meet her in the park, grabbed her keys and purse, and tore out to her car.

Late the next morning, Gwen squatted by the bow of the battered canoe and, with her finger, traced the jagged rip in the canvas.

"How bad is the damage?" Haley asked.

Startled, Gwen tumbled on her backside and laughed at herself. "I didn't hear you come outside."

"Sorry, I didn't mean to scare you."

"To answer your question, I hope it's repairable. Unlike my heart," she added under her breath. She rose to her feet, but lurched to the left, with a hissing intake of breath, as her hip protested.

"You feeling okay?"

Gwen had no desire to discuss her painful muscle aches and bruises, or the details of Saturday's stormy adventure and wild sex. "Nothing a good canoe ride won't fix. Want to take it along the shore for a bit? I want to see if there's more damage than the tear in the canvas, before I ask around for someone to repair it."

"It looks wrecked, but we can try it."

Gwen grabbed the front crossbar. Haley walked around the canoe, gave Gwen a nod, and lifted the stern.

They struggled with the canoe, down the grassy path to the cobblestone boat landing.

To distract herself from the strain on her sore shoulders and hips, Gwen told Haley, "Your dad and grandpa made this boat launch when your dad was twelve. We were old enough by then to go canoeing without our parents, but it was too much for Bill and me to carry sixty pounds overhead through the woods to the area where the beach is now. We didn't have the big lawn leading to the beach, back in those days. My dad proposed the boat launch, and your dad, for some reason known only to him, insisted we use genuine cobblestones."

"You're telling me they cleared this path and leveled the shore and hauled stones by themselves?"

Gwen thought back. "Not by themselves, no. Someone local—I can't think who it was—did the clearing and hauled in the cobbles. The guy worked side by side with them to prep the site. Talk about sore. Mom made my dad and your dad quit after the site prep. She got tired of hearing them groan their way through breakfast and dinner. Anyway, there were at least two truckloads of cobbles brought in. Some big guy joined the first guy, and they spread and leveled the stones. The whole project took a week, and probably cost more than the garage."

Haley's voice was wistful. "It's so cool that you did stuff like that. And you all ate breakfast together every morning?"

"Yes." Gwen's heart contracted with happiness. She flashed a smile back at Haley. "Every day. And dinner, too, unless Dad was at the hospital delivering a baby. Thanks for the memory."

Haley flashed a smile. They eased the Green Lizard down the ramp and let it float. Haley stepped aboard and walked down the center seam to the bow. "The floor feels broken up here," she said.

"I restocked the life belts. Grab one and put it on."

Properly belted, Haley perched on the rush seat and readied her paddle. Gwen shoved off and hopped aboard.

"Let's head toward Phil's," Gwen decided. "There are plenty of places along the way to put out if we take on water."

Which we're already doing. She made mental notes of the leaks along the center seam.

"It's beautiful out here," Haley enthused. "I'm so glad I got to do this. I didn't dare when I was pregnant."

Blue jays screeched from the islands, making Gwen's forehead throb with a headache. Just as Phil's beach came into view, they encountered chop, which caused the canoe to bounce some.

"Hey, Phil's on his porch." Haley gave him a cheery wave, and he saluted with his mug.

Gwen lifted her gaze and added her own wave. By then, though, the canoe was lower in the water, and the bottom held a good two inches.

"Is the rip in the canvas letting in water?" she asked.

"No, but the whole front seam is." She looked behind her and saw the water between her and Gwen. "Ohmigod, we're sinking." She squealed. "What do I do?"

"Paddle as hard and fast as you can." Gwen angled the canoe toward shore. "It's shallow here, don't worry, and we're closing in on the beach."

They muscled the sinking ship another twenty feet toward Phil's sandy shore. Haley said, "Phil's freaked. He's waving his arms and pointing to his phone."

Gwen's throat was too hoarse from yesterday's ordeal to shout. "Haley, tell him we're okay."

Haley yelled as loud as she could, rested her paddle for a second, and waved her arms in a baseball 'Safe' gesture. "He's cool. He's coming down to the shore to meet us."

"Paddle. Don't let him put one foot in the water. Please."

They made it a few yards further before the gunwales

dropped to the level of the lake. Gwen slid off her seat and stood on the rocky lakebed in thigh-high water.

She reached a hand toward Haley. "Better climb out before it sinks under you."

Haley followed orders and called to Phil, "Gwen says to keep your feet dry. We'll tell you the story if you'll make us hot cocoa."

Gwen heard Phil's hearty laugh. She sputtered, "I never said that about hot cocoa."

Haley teased her. "But you'd drink some, wouldn't you?"

"It sounds really good."

She and Haley dragged the canoe to the beach and used their combined power to tip it. Water gushed onto the sand. The Green Lizard looked more like a beached whale.

"Two hot chocolates for two beautiful women wrapped in beach towels," Phil said as he set the tray on the ottoman by his fieldstone fireplace. Yellow flames leapt and logs crackled. Edie's old enamel mugs added calming blues and greens to the cozy scene.

"Sure you don't want sweaters and socks?"

"I'm good," Haley assured him.

Phil was less worried about Haley than Gwen, who looked bereft as she huddled on the loveseat, two feet from the grate, arms wrapped around herself.

Haley exchanged a worried frown with him. "Want me to check the drier, Phil?" she queried.

He nixed the idea with a dismissive wave. "Get a hot drink in you first." He settled into his favorite chair. "I made a phone call to Joel, and he'll be here in half an hour to take you both home. I don't want you walking on the path in those waterlogged sneakers—either one of you."

Haley opened her mouth.

"Planning to argue, young lady?" Phil asked with a cautionary tone.

"Nope. Good plan. Thank you." That rated a smile from Gwen.

"Drink your cocoa, Dr. Forrester."

Gwen reached for the last mug on the tray.

"That's better." Phil lifted his mug to his lips and took a noisy slurp. "Edie's secret recipe," he told them. "Nothing like it."

"There's vanilla in this," Gwen said with delight. "I love vanilla."

"Gwen doubles the vanilla in every cookie recipe," Haley told Phil.

"That must be why I like the Forrester cookies so much." He stretched out his legs toward the fire. "I wish you'd make me some molasses raisin some time. But skip the vanilla."

With a warm smile, Gwen told him, "The ingredients just flew onto my shopping list."

"When are you going to tell me what happened to the canoe?" Phil prompted.

Gwen's face crumpled, and she stared into her half-empty mug.

"She and Peter paddled down the eastern shore Saturday and got caught in the storm," Haley answered. "They crashed and spent the night in a cabin somewhere. Some guy brought them home in the morning, with the canoe strapped to the roof of his truck."

"Do you know Foster Mendel from Clifton Springs?" Gwen asked Phil.

"Sure. He's a legend over there. Been sober forever, helped a lot of people."

Gwen nodded, her gaze on the flames that licked the logs.

After a silence punctuated by noisy slurps, Haley said boldly, "Then Peter and Gwen had a shouting match and they broke up."

Gwen set her mug on the hearth with a clang and burst into tears.

Haley turned doubtful eyes to Phil, and he assured her, "I think Gwen needs to cry. In fact, I'm pretty impressed she's held out this long. Losing a boyfriend and a canoe in a single weekend is not to be suffered in silence."

Gwen wailed and stomped one bare foot on the brick hearth. "Ow."

"Haley, why don't you check on the drier now?" Phil suggested. "I'll see to Gwen."

Haley mouthed her thanks and tugged her towel tight around her as she left them.

Phil picked up a box of tissues from the coffee table and deposited it on the ottoman, then sat on the loveseat next to Gwen.

When the flood of tears abated, Gwen plucked six tissues from the box and asked Phil, "You really think it's beyond repair?"

"The canoe? No question, Gwennie."

Gwen dried her face and blew her nose with four of the tissues. She used the fifth to blot any remaining moisture. "I thought so. I don't know which hurts more."

"What do you mean?"

"Losing Peter or losing the canoe."

"It's not a contest."

"I guess."

"I don't believe I've ever seen you have a meltdown, my friend."

"I don't much." She smiled wryly. "I keep that professional face in place most of the time."

Phil squeezed her shoulder. "Sometimes it's good to let your friends in."

"Yeah. Thanks."

Gwen bundled up her damp tissues with the remaining dry one and laid the little package on the tray. She and Phil sat side-by-side, watching the flames.

When Haley returned, fully dressed, shoes in hand, she told Gwen, "Your turn."

Phil pressed down on Gwen's shoulder to keep her seated a moment longer. "Will I see you both here at my Big Book meeting this Wednesday?"

Gwen frowned. "Your meeting is closed, Phil. Alcoholics only."

Haley told them, her voice shaky. "I've decided I am an alcoholic."

Gwen glanced at her niece, cut to Phil, and back to Haley. "Absolutely, Haley and I can walk over together."

"In dry shoes and socks, please," Phil said with a chuckle. "And clothing."

"Speaking of which," Haley added, "I'll take you up on that offer for socks, Phil. These are dry, but it's going to be killer to walk on gravel in one thin pair."

"Two pair of thick socks coming up. Gwen, is that Joel's car I hear on the driveway? Get yourself decent before he thinks I've had an orgy in here."

"You saw it coming, didn't you?" Gwen asked Joel over salads at Lynnie's Chestnut Lake Café. He had driven the women home so Gwen could fetch dry shoes. Haley begged off lunch with them to spend time in her studio. Gwen agreed to lunch if she could treat Joel.

"Manda and I were both very concerned. First, about Peter's attitude toward his sister's drinking and, well . . ."

"*And well* what?"

Joel studied the mound of unwanted green peppers at the side of his bowl. "I should have remembered Lynnie's salads come with peppers."

Gwen sat back with a huff. "Phil knows more about Haley's alcoholism than I do. You and Manda are talking about my affairs behind my back. Clue me in, good buddy. *And well* what?"

Joel's face flamed. "Your friends have been concerned for a while. Peter has made some enemies on the basketball team. You probably know his teammates Werner and Johnson, who are in the program, as well as Tony. Peter's been less than cordial to them since he found out they're in recovery, and it prompted Tony and Sam to be concerned about you. They concluded you hadn't told Peter you're one, and he hadn't picked up on it himself."

Gwen plunked her elbows on the table and buried her face in her hands with a groan. "I screwed this up so bad. What is wrong with me?"

"That is the right question," Joel said sharply. "It takes two to make a mess this epic. I'm sorry if that sounds callous."

"It sounds like tough love, which is what I need right now."

"Is Deirdre helping?"

Gwen poked at the last two pieces of chicken in her bowl. "More or less. She's got some issues of her own right now, and it's messing up our communication."

Joel signaled for the check.

"Mine, remember?" Gwen pointed out.

"You have no idea how much I hate having a woman pick up the check for me." Joel glared at her.

"Force yourself." Gwen snapped.

Joel burst out with a laugh. "When you put it that way . . ."

Lynnie appeared, and Joel gestured to Gwen. "The lady insists on picking up the tab."

Gwen fished a credit card out of her purse and placed it on the bill. Lynnie made a hasty retreat.

"And finish that full disclosure you started a few minutes ago." Gwen said as she pushed her salad bowl away.

"What full disclosure?"

She slapped her hand hard on the table. "The one that started with *and well*."

"I need you to simmer down first." Joel said.

Gwen huffed, and her cheeks flamed. She licked her lips. "Sorry."

"Manda wasn't sure if she could confide in you or not about seeing Peter's sister at an AA meeting."

"What?"

Joel held up his hands to placate. "She's not sure where anonymity begins and ends. And since Manda and I have no secrets, she and I talked it over after she chaired a beginners' meeting. The sister—"

"Bree. Her name is Bree," Gwen said grudgingly. "I know that much."

Joel smiled easily. "Bree has been struggling to stay sober. She'd like to live with Peter, but she doesn't dare talk about recovery with him or let on that she's in the program."

"Why not?"

Joel nailed her with a look. "Seriously, Gwen?"

"What?"

"You didn't disclose your alcoholism to him. You can understand, better than I, why his sister is keeping her alcoholism from him."

"I—no, I don't think I understand much of anything right now."

"I suppose you're wondering why I didn't tell you Manda and I knew Bree was already in the program?" Deirdre said at the Bagel Depot as she and Gwen debriefed after the Tuesday women's meeting. Bree had been in attendance at the meeting and greeted Manda with squeals and hugs, as if they were old friends.

Gwen's cheeks flamed. "You knew, too? Why the secrecy?"

"It's all about anonymity."

"Spare me."

Deirdre held up her hands in a signal for calm. "Manda chaired a beginners' meeting. Bree was there, in tears, in a quandary. She needed to go to meetings while she was at her brother's but knew he would have a fit if she told him about it. She didn't like sneaking around, because it felt dishonest. She got some good advice at the meeting, and obviously she's here again."

"You knew all this and didn't tell me?"

"Gwen, not everything is about you."

"I can't believe you said that. Don't you think I'd want to know?"

"Manda needed to talk after that meeting, and I guess you had been on her case about breaking someone's anonymity, unintentionally. She didn't dare tell you about Bree, because she was sure she'd blurt out Bree's identity to you."

"Oh." Gwen covered her face with her hands.

"You see now?"

"Yeah. Thanks for being there for her."

"I'm always there for her, you know that. And she had never before come to me that way."

"So why didn't you tell me after?" Gwen searched Deirdre's face.

"As I remember, you and I had just had that blow-up about keeping your sobriety from Peter. Honestly, Manda's situation—and Bree's—just faded out of my consciousness. There was no intent to exclude you from anything."

Gwen sipped her decaf and examined her fingernails. They had been chipped, split, and bruised in the storm. *I need a manicure.*

Deirdre sat back. Gwen took the last sip and frowned at the empty mug in her hands. Deirdre prompted, "What are you thinking?"

"Just afraid Peter will turn on Bree the way he did on me."

"She's scared."

"That would be a disaster. They mean so much to each other, and this could drive them apart. I feel helpless about it."

"Or," Deirdre said, "it could be a turning point for Peter. What is it we hear at meetings? The day will come that we have to choose between losing what's most important to us or giving up our obsession."

"And Peter has said Bree is the most important person in his life. What would you say is his obsession?" Gwen asked Deirdre.

"From what you've told me, Peter is consumed with anger about his father the drunk, to the extent he's excluding people he loves from his life. Is that obsession? You decide."

"So . . ." Gwen sat up straight. "What? Pray for them both?"

"Yes, and practice what we know from Al-Anon. Detach with love. It's not in your power to avert a crisis."

Gwen shuddered as she shouldered her purse and reached for her jacket.

"I'll bet you wish I'd never broken into your house."

Gwen hadn't heard Haley come onto the porch. With all her niece had to deal with, her own tear-streaked face made her ashamed. She softened her lips into a smile. Haley's eyes brightened as Gwen reached out for a hug. "No. Way. Your aunt is just having a pity party."

Haley rushed into the hug. "I'm so sorry about you and Peter. I really, really thought you were perfect together. I wanted so bad for things to work out."

Gwen squeezed her tight. "Me too, sweetie."

"What's his problem anyway? Is his manhood threatened by how much money you have? Didn't you tell him it's just inherited?"

"No. He doesn't know I have a bundle of money. He knows I have a big old house that's a money pit." Gwen chuckled. "He's pretty cool about money."

"So why did he break up with you? Or don't you want to say?"

"Let's walk, and I'll tell you what I think is going on. It might sound a little familiar to you."

Haley grabbed their jackets while Gwen locked the kitchen door. Haley led them on the shoreline path. Clumps of dry, brown leaves clung to the oaks, and a fickle breeze off the lake set them rattling and shaking.

Gwen's smile was wistful as she recalled walking here with Peter when all the trees still blazed with color.

"So, what's up with Peter?" Haley said from a few paces ahead of her.

"Peter's dad was a drunk. He was mean and unreliable, and the whole family suffered. Peter never let go of the anger he has toward his father, and he thinks all drunks are scum. And when he realized I'm an alcoholic, that was it for him. In his experience, alcoholics are unreliable and untrustworthy and make terrible parents. So he ended our relationship."

"He can't really think you . . ." Haley stopped and turned to Gwen.

"Yes. That's what he thinks. And I can't fault him for wanting to marry someone reliable and trustworthy who'll be a great mom for his children."

Haley glared.

Gwen's gaze was steady.

Haley sputtered. "Can't he see that you're responsible and financially stable and-and all those things his father never was?"

"Apparently he can't see the difference between a sober alcoholic in recovery and a hopeless drunk."

Haley shook her head in disbelief. "Why the hell not?"

"Darned if I know."

"Isn't that going to hurt him on the job when he's dealing with drunks and drug addicts?"

"You have a very good point, Haley." Gwen cocked her head. "I hadn't thought of that. Let's sit a minute." Debris had piled up on both sides of the path. Gwen spotted a fallen log by the water's edge and motioned Haley to follow. She stepped carefully over big branches and tossed aside any loose ones in her way. They sat side-by-side on the log, arms touching.

"I never get tired of gazing at our lake," Gwen told her.

"I love it here, too. Thanks for letting me stay here with you for now."

"Stay as long as you like, as long as it helps. It's good for me to have you here."

"Thanks for saying that. Gwen?"

"What, sweetie?"

"When you said Peter's story might sound familiar to me, were you talking about his sister? Did she get pregnant or something?"

"I don't really know what trouble she got into. I was really thinking about your parents. Your dad's an alcoholic, and your mom's abusive in her own way."

"So, do you think I'm hanging onto stuff, like Peter?"

"Yes, and that concerns me. Peter's fixated on his dad, and you have said several times you're afraid you're just like your mother."

Haley leaned forward with her hands on her knees. "Yeah. But I really do want to have children someday. And I'm smart and talented, and I want to have a good career. Probably the career before starting a family."

Gwen rubbed her back. "Well, that tells me you're not much like your mother."

"But she's all I know about being a mother. It's, like, burned into my brain that a mother's job is to put down her child, to squash her hopes and dreams, to tell her she's fat and ugly and whatever." Haley's voice got louder with every phrase.

She jumped from the log. Her foot snagged on a half-buried limb and she pitched toward the water.

Gwen tried to stop her fall but couldn't grab her in time.

Haley twisted as she crashed through the tangle of branches. Although she managed to keep her body on dry land, her left arm plunged into the cold water, and her cheek bled where she'd scraped it on a broken branch.

Gwen's heart pounded as she reached for her. "Anything broken?" she asked with false calm.

Haley shook her head.

Gwen took a wide stance with one foot in the water and reached her hands around Haley's waist. She hauled her up and helped her back to their log.

Haley's face crumpled with pain.

"Tell me where you hurt," Gwen ordered.

Haley shook her head. "I'm okay, except I could have broken my left wrist." She sobbed. "I need it to do my art. I have to be able to do my art. I hate Ursula so much, and I was just being stupid about that."

Gwen circled Haley's shoulders with a gentle arm. "You're going to be just fine, Haley, but all that bitterness toward your mom needs to come out. I know working through the twelve steps with a sponsor can help you, and you may want to consider seeing a therapist for a while."

"Maybe. Rick wants me to see a therapist. I want to try the AA route first. I think you and Phil will tell me if I need more. It would be really great not to put myself down anymore. Or blame things on my mother. That's not very grown up, is it?"

"You're very wise, my Haley. Carrying around the past is not the way to live a happy life. Look what the bitterness is doing to Peter."

Chapter 13

Peter arose the next afternoon to find Bree making a pot of coffee. "Hey, sunshine, thanks for doing that."

"Sure. Did you sleep okay?"

"Just okay. Last night was busy—three DWIs and a fire downtown that left a couple of stores vulnerable to looting. All that ran through my dreams all night."

"I hate when that happens. I'm sleeping, but my mind's not resting."

"Exactly." He shook his head. "I hate dealing with DWIs. These two last night were ridiculous."

Bree tensed.

Peter was oblivious of her discomfort. "The first one— the guy—was only about twenty, not even old enough to drink legally. He'd stolen a car and gone joy riding with his girl. They skidded off the road into a field and rolled over. The girl was hurt pretty bad—no seatbelt—but the guy walked away without a scratch—belligerent son of a gun, no concern for his girlfriend. I'm glad Sam offered to book him. I wanted to pop the guy."

"Does your temper get in the way on the job sometimes?"

"Why did you say that?" Peter glared at her.

"It's obvious," Bree muttered to herself as she retreated to the kitchen. "Want eggs?" she asked brightly.

"Yeah," he said grudgingly, "thanks."

Bree fixed an omelet with vegetables and cheese and presented it to him with a cheerful, "*Voila.*"

"Hey, something new. Since when are you making omelets?"

"I've been practicing. It's not perfect, but I'm working on it."

"It's good," Peter said with his mouth full.

"Weren't you dating someone that made the best omelets you ever tasted?" Bree ventured.

He nodded, swallowed, and reached for his coffee. "Gwen. We broke up."

"Blond? Pretty? How come you broke up?"

"She lied to me, and I won't tolerate that. You know what happened with Cynthia." His voice got louder with each statement. "I won't stand for deception in a relationship. I'm searching for a wife, not a traitor."

Bree backed away from his mounting anger. In the kitchen, she filled the frying pan with sudsy water.

"Gwen lied about being a drunk," he ranted.

Bree concentrated on scrubbing the pan.

"You know how I feel about drunks. The woman we arrested last night, the other DWI, was my age." He was shouting now, loud enough for neighbors to hear. "She was driving her sloshed boyfriend home from a party. Her blood alcohol level was over the legal limit, too, so we brought them both in. Sam took care of the man; I got stuck with her. She got all flirty and clingy with me and I finally shoved her in a cell."

He drained his coffee and walked into the kitchen to fill his mug from the pot, which stood on the counter, a few feet from the sink, where Bree worked on the frying pan.

Bree shied away from him, her heart pounding.

He held the pot of hot liquid in one hand and asked her, "You don't drink anymore, right?"

Bree gripped the edge of the counter, shook her head, and inhaled slowly through her fear while he poured the coffee. When he set the pot back in the coffeemaker, she swallowed hard.

"What is up with you?" he demanded. "You're acting like you're afraid of something."

"I am," Bree told him and drew herself up to her full height. "When you get angry like this, it's always about drunks.

You turn into a different person, somebody I don't want to be around. I'm afraid to be in the same room with you."

"Bree—" He reached for her.

She backed out of the room, looked wildly for her purse, and snatched it from the table by the front door. Peter grabbed her arm.

"You can't go out there. It's pouring and about forty degrees."

"Let. Go." She glared at him. When his muscles eased the slightest bit, she snapped her arm out of his grip and rushed out of the apartment, slamming the door behind her. As she pounded down the stairs, a door opened into the first-floor apartment. She stared into a pair of gray-green eyes. "I'm very sorry we disturbed you, sir."

"Do you need help, Bree?" he asked, his voice filled with concern.

How does he know my name? She squeezed her eyes shut against tears and shook her head. "No, thanks," she said and slipped out into the downpour. She made it only halfway down Lakeside Terrace before taking shelter on one of the porches, where she huddled, shivering and sobbing.

Manda found her there a few minutes later. "Here," she ordered and pressed a towel into Bree's hands. "Dry off as much as you can and then put this on." She held up a hooded, lined, rain jacket and tossed it onto a nearby porch chair for Bree. "Either you come back to Joel's and my place, or I will get the car and drive us somewhere for a hot chocolate. Those are your two choices."

"I'm not going back."

"Then stay here while I get my car." She gave Bree a quick hug before dashing to the parking spaces behind the buildings.

Bree buried her face in the towel for a few seconds and then wrapped it tightly around her. Even in the warmth of the borrowed rain jacket, she shivered as they drove past the marina.

The sign at the road read 'Lynnie's Chestnut Lake Café.' Manda turned in to the parking lot and stopped the car. "Bree, what happened today with your brother that made you run out into the rain?"

"I just couldn't take his anger anymore. He used to be like that before Dad died. Dad would beat one of us, and Peter would go wild. Then Peter got big enough so he was stronger than Dad, and the beatings stopped. But he was so angry all the time. And then Dad died, and he calmed down. He got really serious about school and he was on the basketball team. And one day he told Mom he was going to be a cop. I remember she hugged him and cried and told him she was so proud of him. We were both really proud of him." She clasped her hands. "I can't stop shaking."

"Here." Manda chose a pair of gloves from the console between them. "These might help. We'll go inside in a minute." She took the key out of the ignition. "We heard Peter yelling upstairs. I've never heard him yell. He's usually upbeat and helpful. Joel was really worried when you ran down the stairs."

"I'm sorry."

"I know. That's not the point. We were worried about you, so I came after you. I don't know if Joel will say something to Peter or not. Joel's recovering from a horrible accident, so he can't afford to get in any kind of fight."

"God, this is awful. Peter hates drunks, and he had to book a couple of DWIs last night, and he was telling me about them and he got all hot and bothered about it. He started yelling, like he used to. I've been trying to get up the nerve to tell him I'm an alcoholic in recovery, and I was afraid he'd turn that anger on me." A shudder shook Bree's whole body. "I love my brother and I'm afraid for him. And for me. I don't know what to do."

"Put both hands around the mug," Manda ordered as she handed Bree a steaming mug of hot chocolate. They had chosen a booth away from the few customers. "I'm getting us something to eat."

Bree thanked her. In less than a minute, she was calmer and warmer. She took a big swallow of sweet, milky, hot chocolate and directed a smile at Manda who stood talking with the owner near the cash register. The café was deserted at three o'clock.

"How do you like that hot cocoa?" Lynnie lifted her voice to Bree.

"It's seriously great, ma'am," Bree called back.

"Don't you 'ma'am' me, honey," Lynnie said with a merry laugh. "And I want you to eat every bite of the sandwich I just fixed for you."

Manda brought two plates to the table and set down a sandwich for Bree and a salad for herself. "Eat."

"Thank you." As she lifted the sandwich to her mouth with both hands, Bree said, "I'm going to take the next bus back to Syracuse."

"Do you know when it leaves?" If Manda was surprised, she didn't show it.

Bree's shook her head. Manda used her smartphone to find the answer.

"There's one at four-fifteen."

"I can make it," Bree said with a glance at the clock, "if we don't take too long here."

"If you want, I'll drive you back for your stuff and take you to the bus station."

"Thanks." Bree's green eyes shone with tears.

"What are your AA meetings like in Syracuse?" Manda asked.

"Not as good as here, but I've only tried the ones in walking distance. I need to explore more. There must be meetings with young people, and some of those meetings must be on a bus route.

"And you can get rides, once you find a meeting you like. People really want to help out newcomers by giving rides and sharing about how they stay sober. All it takes is the courage to ask for help."

Bree's forehead wrinkled with doubt.

"That's been my experience, anyway."

They ate in silence. When Bree picked up the second half of her sandwich, she stared at it from all sides and set it back on the plate.

"You can take the rest with you," Manda pointed out. "That would save worrying about what's in the refrigerator for supper."

"You're right. That would be smart." She picked up another tortilla chip and crunched it.

"Do you cook for yourself?"

"Yeah, I'm pretty good. Nothing special. I like the way Lynnie puts lettuce and onion and tomato in her sandwiches. I should do that more."

"Veggies are good for you."

"I'll ask for a box," Bree offered as she pushed back from the table. "Do you want one, too?"

Manda gave the rest of her salad to Bree. When Bree protested, Manda told her, "You can buy me a hot chocolate next time you're in Tompkins Falls."

Back at Lakeside Terrace, there was no sign of Peter. "Maybe he's at basketball practice." Bree shrugged. "I'm just glad he's not here."

They made short work of clearing Bree's things out of the apartment. "You should leave him a note so the police aren't dragging the river for your body."

"Yeah, I guess." Bree took the paper Manda held out and wrote, "Heading back to Syracuse. Please go to an Al-Anon meeting before you call me again." She placed the meeting information Carol had given her on the countertop with her note.

"Let's go." Swallowing hard against her tears, Bree

grabbed her duffle and the bag of food and followed Manda out to the car.

The early-afternoon rant that had caused Bree to blast out of the apartment made Peter curse himself. *Shaughnessy, you need to clean up your act around your sister*. A shower had calmed him, but Bree did not return.

He had tried calling her, but her cell phone played a tune from her bedroom. She'd left the phone in her hoodie, which was on her bed.

Annoyed with himself for driving her out in the rain without a jacket, he had run down the stairs, gym bag in hand, already late for practice, and swung into the Jeep. He was still fuming when he arrived at the gym.

"Whoa, buddy," Sam cautioned. "Simmer down. This is practice, not the Coliseum."

"What are you talking about?" Peter snapped.

"We're not fighting life-and-death battles here. Check your anger at the door. Whatever's going on with you has no place on the court. We're here to work on our skills and our teamwork."

"Sorry, you're right, partner." He exhaled his frustration. "Give me a minute to change." Finding the locker room empty, he collapsed on a bench and folded his hands. He had meant to pray, but he just stared at the row of lockers and made a mental list of all the dents and scrapes he saw there.

Sam found him on the bench a few minutes later, still not dressed for practice. "Want to talk?"

Peter shook his head and changed into his gym shorts and T-shirt. "Let's do it." He preceded Sam to the court, reached out for the ball Werner threw him and joined the warm-up.

They played for two hours, and Peter made more baskets than he'd ever made in practice. Still, it made no difference to his teammates. Tony was cold. Johnson was hostile. Sam and Werner included him in plays, but the buoyant mood of early season was missing.

"We need to mix it up a little, Tony," Werner offered as they cooled down. "Relying on just the five of us is risky. What if one of us got the flu or something? We don't even have a sub we can count on."

"We lost Peterman when his kid got sick," Tony said. "And Oscar had too much going on at work to be reliable. Who else can we get? Anyone know a good player or two?"

Peter shook his head. Sam bounced the ball. Werner shrugged.

"Aren't we a merry band tonight?" Johnson groused.

Sam shot him a look. "Having a couple more players is a good idea, I think. Tony, why don't we each try to find someone this week and see who we come up with?"

"Yeah, I like it," Tony agreed. "It's almost five o'clock. Let's work the ball another half hour." He shoved it at Peter. "Lead us off, Shaughnessy."

Peter broke, dribbled to midcourt, dodged Johnson's block, and passed to Tony. Tony laid it up and moved out of the way for Werner to take the rebound.

Everyone but Johnson scored more than they missed. Tony clapped Johnson on the shoulder as they cooled down. "I need you back on your game next week."

"It's his fault," Johnson said defensively and jerked his head toward Peter. "I keep thinking he's going to trip me, and I can't concentrate on the shot."

"It's no one's fault but yours," Tony countered. "You're not shooting baskets outside of practice, are you?"

"So now you're taking his side?" Johnson yelled. "We used to be a team before he showed up."

"We used to be in second-to-last place before he showed up."

"And we've dropped in the standings every week since a month ago."

"Time out," Tony snapped. "Personal issues have no place on this team," he said directly to Johnson. "We've all agreed to that rule." He directed his gaze to Peter. "We play together, right?"

"We play together," Peter agreed.

Johnson puffed out his chest and jabbed a finger in Peter's direction. "Well, maybe I don't want to play on a team with him."

Peter stiffened. Sam glanced left and right, bounced the ball once, then held it still.

Peter shifted on his feet. "Let me make it easy for you and the team," he said, his voice quiet. "I quit."

Tony reached out, but Peter brushed past him into the locker room, where he threw on his jacket, grabbed his clothes in one hand and his duffle in the other, and exited into the hallway.

Tony and Sam intercepted him at the double doors to the parking lot. "I need you on the team, Shaughnessy," Tony said, his voice tight.

"Well, thanks, but the team doesn't want me on the team."

Sam gave him a warning. "Peter, if you leave now, you're screwing me, Tony, Werner, the Sneaks, and the league. You sure that's what you want to do, partner?"

"I screwed up. I'm done trying to fix it. The team's better off without me."

"Peter!" Tony yelled, but their star player pushed through the door and disappeared into the dark.

Back in his parking space behind 14 Lakeside Terrace, Peter turned off the engine and placed his hands on the steering wheel. One glance at the crucifix dangling from the rear view mirror told him he'd made his biggest mistake yet as a newcomer to Tompkins Falls. Tony was right. He'd screwed them all, just because that punk-drunk Johnson had gotten to him.

He dragged his things into the apartment, stuffed the duffle into the closet, and headed to the shower. Clean and dressed, his next priority was to square things with Bree. Maybe they could talk over a good meal. They had time to hash things out before he had to leave for work. "Bree," he called, "want to go out for supper?"

His voice echoed. He spied a note on the counter. "Heading back to Syracuse," he read aloud.

He walked to Bree's bedroom. He wanted her here. But there was no duffle bag, no iPod, no hoodie on the bed. Just the furniture from his old room and the bed from Gwen's attic, neatly made.

Bree had left the blinds open to the view of the lake.

Peter stood at the window, his gaze on Gwen's house, with its cheerful lights burning.

He closed the blinds.

The next morning, in the half-light after his shift, Peter laced up his running shoes, pulled on a weatherproof anorak and set out on the willow path. The lakeshore was deserted—not even a duck looking for a handout. He'd short-changed his warm-up, so it was not a surprise when a cramp stopped him after a mile and a half.

He bent over and kneaded his calf, then limped until the cramp eased. With his hands in the kangaroo pocket of the anorak, he walked the remaining distance. Although he searched his memory going back to high school, he couldn't think of a time he had felt so lonely. *And it's my own fault.*

He'd driven Bree away. He'd quit the team over a stupid comment by a stupid teammate. And before all that, he'd completely dismissed Gwen from his life, without even trying to understand why she'd kept her alcoholism from him.

At the time, her deception had felt as underhanded and treacherous as Cynthia's betrayal. He had warred with himself ever since, trying to convince himself he'd overreacted. But even now, he was sure in his heart that he had no business being married to a drunk who would neglect his children and make his life hell. Didn't that describe any drunk, including Gwen?

He knew Gwen was reckless sometimes—living by herself in that isolated spot, canoeing alone, going out on the lake without checking the weather forecast. But she wasn't drinking, he was pretty sure of that. Bottom line, he couldn't rely on her as a wife and mother, could he?

Too risky.

He should be looking for someone who had no problem with alcohol. Someone who wanted a family and a solid marriage. Someone . . . someone like Gwen, only sober.

Too confusing.

A noise drew his attention. He half hoped it was Gwen on her bike, but the sound came from the parking lot, a car door closing.

Joel Cushman stood beside a shiny sedan and did a few stretches before walking onto the willow path. He took a few steps toward Peter and stopped.

"Morning, Joel," Peter greeted him.

Joel held up his hand in a friendly greeting. "Not the best weather for a morning run," he commented. He had his collar up, but, like Peter, his head was bare to the elements.

"I often run after my shift. What brings you here?"

Joel stuffed his hands in his pockets and waited for Peter to reach him. "Walk with you a minute?" Joel asked.

"Sure." Peter shrugged and moved to one side of the path. Joel fell into step next to him, and Peter adjusted to Joel's pace.

"I just talked with Tony after the Early Risers meeting," Joel told him. "He's really upset about you quitting the team. He and Sam are both concerned about you. I am, too, after that shouting match you had with Bree yesterday afternoon."

Peter flinched but made no comment.

"I took a chance you might be running this morning."

"And as you can see I'm walking instead," Peter said with a hollow laugh. "I was in too much of a hurry to do a proper warm-up, got a cramp before I made it to the end."

Joel snorted. "Anytime I get impulsive like that, it bites me. It didn't used to matter, but when I turned thirty, shortcuts that used to work didn't work anymore."

"Tell me about your accident," Peter said. "I heard you were in a coma for a while."

"Yeah, it was bad. Tony and I took a drive in his truck one afternoon, when the weather was supposed to be above freezing all day. I wanted to check out Cady's Point with Manda's business plan in mind. Tony is a good friend who's also a good sounding board for things like that. On our way home, we had just turned onto the highway when our truck hit black ice. We spun around a couple of times before sliding off the road. Came to rest in a stand of pines. The point of impact was where I sat. Fractured my skull, reinjured my right leg, and assorted other damage. If not for Tony, I'd be dead."

"What did he do?"

"Got on the phone and didn't quit until the rescue squad got me out of there and a helicopter took me to Rochester to the trauma center. I couldn't ask for a better friend."

"Were you married to Manda then?"

"Not yet. I was about to propose to her. It happened a couple weeks before Christmas. Manda was coming up on nine months sober then; she wouldn't mind my telling you that. Normally, someone that new in sobriety doesn't get too involved romantically, but the two of us knew we were soul mates and I didn't want to wait any longer to ask her to marry me."

"Your injury must have been a rough time for her."

"It was. But the program—AA, I mean—rallied around her. People found her a place to stay near the hospital, made sure she ate meals and had someone to talk to. She found meetings at the hospital and went every day. Gwen drove up every day the first week and every weekend after that, took Manda to stay with her on the lake when Manda needed a break. Manda never felt like drinking, but it was hell not knowing if I'd recover." He paused for a breath.

"My Uncle Justin was my only living relative, and he was unreachable in the beginning, so Manda was carrying the whole responsibility." He added with a smile, "By some fluke, the hospital thought she was already my fiancée. Otherwise she would have been turned away, like everyone else, and not allowed to see me. No one takes credit for that misinformation, but I have my suspicions."

"You think Tony did it?"

"He'll never admit it. Manda and I are just grateful for it, even though it placed a heavy burden on Manda." He stopped walking and turned to face Peter. "The program helped her through it. We got engaged while I was still in the hospital. Then I did six months of grueling physical therapy with her at my side. And it paid off. We were married in the rose garden at the Manse last summer, and I was able to stand through the ceremony."

"Happy ending, but I'm sorry you had to go through all that, both of you."

"Life happens. You just deal with it."

"Yeah, I guess."

"I need to turn back now. I'm glad I caught you."

"Geez, you're soaked."

"All for a good cause," he said and walked slowly back the way they'd come.

Peter watched him for a minute, noticed how he favored his right leg. *Manda got through all that and didn't drink?* He couldn't wrap his head around it.

"Are you mad at me?" Manda squinted at Gwen. They walked along the lakeshore with their hands in their pockets. A chilly wind blew from the southwest and hurled waves across the granite breakwater at the entrance to the marina.

"No, sweetie, just puzzled about why you didn't ever talk to me about Bree being at meetings."

"I'm sorry."

"I'm not looking for an apology, honest. I just feel very bad that you didn't think I could be helpful to you or to Bree." She waited, hoping Manda would come forward with her thoughts.

When the silence stretched on, Gwen screwed up her courage and said, "Lately quite a few of my friends have kept things from me and discussed my life behind my back. They say they've been concerned, but until Peter and I broke up, no one spoke to me directly. Well, except Deirdre. And Joel, come to think of it."

"When did he do that?"

"At the chief's dinner."

"Oh yeah, you two talked while the rest of us danced."

"Were you concerned that long ago?"

"Hell, yes. Peter made those bizarre statements about forbidding Bree to drink. I didn't see that working out well."

I wish my vision had been that clear. Gwen pulled her collar closer around her neck and struggled to fasten an awkward, little button. "Tell me why?"

"Obviously, you and Peter lived on two different planets where alcoholism was concerned. Recovery is central to your life. But his dad's untreated alcoholism warped his childhood."

Gwen met her gaze and gave a sheepish smile. "It was that clear, huh?" She kicked a stone out of her way. It skipped across the soggy brown grass and rolled down the slope toward the water.

"Think you'll get back together?"

"No." Gwen laughed dryly. "Like you said, it didn't end well the first time."

"I am so, so relieved to hear you say that. But I know you want to find the right man and start a family."

"Think I'm capable of finding the right man?" Gwen asked.

"Of course, if you want to. I'm not sure you really want to." Gwen raised her eyebrows in surprise, and Manda said,

"Remember when I first got sober I was off men for life? It was hard for Joel to break through."

"I remember. And, to be honest, in my heart, I really believed Peter was the one, and I still love him." She kicked at another stone on the path, but it did not budge out of her way. "Ouch. I really, really need to move on. I don't know where to look next."

"Joel probably knows someone," Manda ventured.

"Joel probably knows better than me the kind of man I should be dating."

"Are you being sarcastic?" Manda asked.

"I am serious. I think it's time I let my friends help me find out what's best for me."

"And find out who's right for you."

Indian Summer played a visit to the Finger Lakes the following week. Temperatures rose into the low seventies, and abundant sunshine made it feel like eighty. Gwen's phone rang at two o'clock on Tuesday. She listened with a straight face and offered sympathy when her remaining client canceled.

Yippee! Free to play outdoors, and she knew exactly whom she wanted to play with. She pressed Gianessa's number on her new phone and crossed her fingers.

"Hey, Gwen." Gianessa laughed. "Why aren't you out in the sunshine?"

"That's where I'm headed. Are you and the twins free? Want to stroll in the park?"

"We are free and loving the sunshine on our new little deck. Come on over. We have heaters set up, but they're not even turned on."

"I'm on my way. Need anything? Sunscreen? Toys? Iced tea?"

"I could kill for an iced Americano from Lynnie's."

"Coming up."

"And one of her caramel brownies."

Gwen chuckled. "Just one?"

"Just one. The twins have their bottles, and Justin is being a martyr, fasting from chocolate until Christmas." She laughed from her belly. "I have no idea why. He's lean and fit and healthy as a horse." She added in a cooing voice, "Babies, Auntie Gwen is coming to play with us."

Gwen thought she heard a rattle in the background. *Nonsense. They're too young for rattles.* Still, her heart leapt. "I can't wait to see Jack and Jill and how they've grown."

"Better hurry," Gianessa said, "they could grow another inch before you get here." She broke the connection.

Lynnie had recovered from the lunchtime rush when Gwen breezed through the door of the Chestnut Lake Café.

"What can I get for you, Gwen?"

"How about half of a turkey panini with provolone and tomato and spinach?"

"Mustard and mayo?"

"Just mustard. And I'll need one large iced Americano, one large unsweetened iced tea, and two of your magnificent caramel brownies."

Lynnie narrowed her eyes. "I can't even guess who you're meeting."

"I'm hanging out on Justin and Gianessa's new deck with the babies."

Lynnie's face softened. "Aw."

"Yeah." Gwen's voice continued the glissando of Lynnie's sigh. "It's what life is all about."

Lynnie pointed. "It's good practice for your own little ones."

Gwen caught her breath, and her cheeks grew warm. *Can I handle motherhood? I can't even handle a relationship.*

Lynnie hummed as she assembled the panini. While it grilled in the press, she started the espresso, filled a to-go glass with iced tea, and selected the two most decadent brownies from the pastry case. Finally, she filled a tall to-go glass with ice and poured in the thick, fragrant espresso, added cold spring water and gave it a shake. "Chips?"

Gwen shook her head and handed over the total plus a generous tip. "I'll tell you all about the little ones the next time I'm in."

"Tomorrow morning too soon?" Lynnie said with an eager grin. "It's very special to have a new generation of Cushmans in Tompkins Falls."

Gwen called a greeting as she came through the Cushman's living room. "You all appear to be loving your sunshiny deck."

"Aren't they adorable under their very cool umbrella?" Gianessa flashed a smile.

The babies' little blond heads locked onto Gwen's voice. Jack lifted his hands as Gwen approached.

"It's your Auntie Gwen," Gianessa told them. She rose and did a languid stretch before taking the drinks and bag of food from Gwen.

"No one would believe you delivered twins two months ago. You look amazing." She squatted down and offered her finger for Jack to clasp.

Gianessa opened the bag for her brownie and settled back in a shady armchair with her cold drink. "I'm going to be so wired in twenty minutes," she predicted.

Gwen chuckled and swiveled to tell Jill, "Yes, Mommy will be wired." Jill giggled as Gwen poked her belly. "I didn't think babies could laugh at this age."

"They can't. It's your magic."

"Or my imagination," Gwen said. She stroked Jack's chubby cheek with her thumb before standing up.

The women watched the twins for another minute until both babies closed their eyes in sleep and their heads drifted toward each other.

"Are they always in synch like that?"

"Mostly, yes." Gianessa gave a contented sighed. "Who'd have thought we could sit out on this deck before next spring?"

Gwen shielded her eyes with her hand as she stood at the railing to view the lake. "I am passionate about this lake. I love it in every mood, and most especially when the water sparkles like this—diamonds on lapis. I only see it this way in late fall when the sky is cloudless and deep blue." She turned to Gianessa. "You and Justin have the best vantage point."

"We do. He always wanted to build a house up here in the birches." Eyes wide, she took in the beauty. A manicured lawn swept down from the new house, almost half a mile, from the birches to the lakeshore.

One of the sleeping twins made a bubbling sound. Gianessa and Gwen turned to see Jill with her mouth pursed in sleep. "This is heaven," their mother said.

"And you deserve every beautiful moment." Gwen drew her baseball cap out of her back pocket and fitted it on her head.

"Come sit. You have to have your lunch before you can eat your brownie," Gianessa ordered.

"Yes, Mom." Gwen plunked down at the table and reached for the bag. "When did they finish the deck?"

"Saturday. Justin took off work yesterday afternoon, and we hung here with the twins for a few hours. It did us all a world of good, just to relax and feel the warm breeze."

"How are you feeling?" Gwen unwrapped her sandwich and spread out the wrapper on the teak table. She picked up half the sandwich with both hands and planted her elbows. She opened her mouth wide, took the first bite, and rolled her eyes.

Gianessa laughed. "Lynnie makes the best, doesn't she?"

Gwen growled with pleasure.

"I'm healing quickly," Gianessa answered the original question, "but I tire easily. I am so grateful for our round-the-clock nannies and for the nurse who comes every morning to help me start my day."

Gwen eyed her. "But everything's okay, or not?"

"I'll be fine. I had it all planned to deliver naturally at full term and to have more babies in the years to come, but the universe had other ideas." The crease in her forehead betrayed the sadness she felt about that. "We are so fortunate to have two healthy little ones—a boy and a girl."

Gwen set down her sandwich and looked at the pink and blue bundles, side-by-side in the shade of the tan market umbrella. "Yes, you are blessed." She turned compassionate eyes on her friend. "But I'm sorry there won't be more."

"Our children can grow up together, Gwen." Gianessa cleared her throat and rallied her energy. "I believe you're ready to have your own"

"Speaking of the universe, I had it all planned that Peter would propose and we'd get pregnant right away, but we can see how that worked out."

"Unless and until he dealt with his issues, it wasn't going to work."

"I see that now. I underestimated how damaged he is by his father's alcoholism and his wife's . . ." She shook her head and gazed out at the sparkling lake. "It shocked me that he would just wash his hands of our relationship because I'm an alcoholic. And I know I need to move on. I really do want to marry a strong, honest man who'll go the distance with me."

"So," Gianessa said with a sly smile, "are you ready to start fresh with a new guy and see what happens?"

"You said that like you've got a guy in mind for me." *Let your friends help you, Gwen, remember?*

"In fact," Gianessa said, "Sunday afternoon, we had some of the new Tompkins College faculty for *hors d-oeuvres*."

"Are you really up to entertaining?" Gwen scolded.

"Full disclosure. I made a guest appearance. Justin did all the work."

"Okay, tell me about the new guy." She took another juicy bite of her sandwich.

"You and Rand Cunningham will turn heads when you walk into a room together. He's that perfect for you."

"Good looking?"

Gianessa blew out hard and shook her hand as if it needed cooling.

"And he probably has an interesting brain, if he's one of the new crop of professors at the college."

Gianessa confirmed it. "Brilliant communications professor, knows how to get the students fired up. Bit of an egotist, but I think he's teachable."

Gwen narrowed her eyes. "How young is this guy?" A slice of tomato slipped out of the sandwich and plopped on the wrapper.

"As a matter of fact, Sunday was his twenty-ninth birthday."

Gwen retrieved the tomato and popped it in her mouth. "That's only three years difference. Has he ever been married?"

"Broke up with a fiancée a couple of years ago and still hasn't found anyone he's serious about."

"And he broke it off why?"

"Said his girl decided she didn't want children after all."

Gwen tipped her head back and forth. "So far so good." Her hands dripped with mustard and tomato. She gestured at Gianessa with her chin. "You never told me you were a matchmaker."

Gianessa laughed and waved it away. "I had the opportunity to screen him, with you in mind. I liked him." She raised her eyebrows. "So, shall we have him over for homemade pizza this Saturday afternoon? It will be a very early supper, five o'clock, since I'm ready for bed by eight these days."

"You found a way to make gluten-free pizza?"

"Justin and I have perfected our crust. You won't know the difference."

Gwen wiped her hands and forearms with half a dozen napkins, gathered her mess back into the bag, and sat back with her brownie. "I'm game."

Chapter 14

Gwen arrived at the Cushmans Friday evening, fashionably late. With wet feet.

Gianessa answered the doorbell and laughed at Gwen's woebegone face.

"Squish." Gwen pointed to the puddle forming around her probably ruined loafers. "I need to fix my potholes, girlfriend."

"So I see." Gianessa handed her the kitchen towel from her shoulder. "I have very cute slippers you can wear," she said with a conspiratorial wink.

Gwen's eyes lit up. "Pink with kittens?"

"I *never* share those. These are black with gold braid, perfect with your black cashmere sweater." She lowered her voice. "And those skinny, dark-indigo jeans are going to kill the guy. Very sexy, Dr. Forrester."

While Gianessa fetched the slippers, Gwen toweled her feet and studied her date. Rand Cunningham stood with his back to her, beside Justin, at the wall of rain-lashed windows. The two were deep in conversation.

Justin gave her a surreptitious wave. She drew a chuckle from him by lifting one bare foot and waving back with the towel.

Rand continued his monologue, oblivious of Gwen and Justin's exchange. Gwen liked the rear view—longish blond hair, striped shirt, navy sweater over his shoulders, preppy chinos, a tight butt, and polished Cole Haan loafers. The look tallied with the immaculate, white Mazda MX-5 Miata in the driveway. So much for her expectation of a starving scholar with a mountain of grad school loans to pay off.

Gianessa pressed soft slippers against Gwen's arm. "What do you think?"

"I see what you mean. Very nice back view." She took the slippers. "Ooh, these are sexy." She slipped on the black velvet mules and gave Gianessa a quick hug.

"Go get him, girlfriend. I'll ask Justin to put the pizza in the oven, and we'll let you two get acquainted." She beckoned her husband with a megawatt smile and a crook of her index finger.

Rand stopped his monologue when Justin excused himself. He caught sight of Gwen and lifted his nearly empty beer glass in a gesture of welcome. "Dr. Forrester?" His smile was as white as his Miata.

"Gwen." She offered her most charming smile. "Rand, welcome to Tompkins Falls and to Tompkins College."

Bright blue eyes appraised her from head to toe. "Thank you." He raised one eyebrow. "Can I get you a drink?"

"I'm good. The pizza just went into the oven, and I can hold out until we sit down." She grinned and tested, "I love it that Justin and Gianessa cook together."

"Yes." His tone was dismissive. He gestured to the view. "Too bad the rain set in. I'm sure this is a beautiful view on a sunny afternoon."

"You know, for me, it's always a beautiful view." She moved closer to the glass and peered through the downpour to the gray lake. A stiff wind stirred up whitecaps in its path as it bullied across the surface. "Times like this I wish I were a poet or an artist who could capture that moody, gray dynamic, the wind and waves and—"

"I actually write some poetry."

"Do you? I'm a fan of Mary Oliver."

Rand shook his head. "Not my taste, I have to say."

"What do you write about?" When he didn't answer, she chuckled. "Or is that a ridiculous question? I'm a psychologist, and I don't know your field."

"No, I'm just thinking how best to respond. Do you know much about the current movements in poetry?"

"Not at all."

"Well," he said with a shrug. "Perhaps I'll do a reading one day, if you're interested."

"I'd like that."

"Are you from around here, Gwen?"

"I grew up on this lake." She pointed to the cluster of round islands. "Just south of the last island. Do you enjoy water sports?"

"I rowed crew at Groton, but that's a dozen years ago. I'm a golfer half the year and play squash and tennis indoors the other half."

Definitely comes from money. She waited a beat, expecting him to ask what sports she played, but he did not. "Tell me what you like so far about the Finger Lakes."

When he launched into a recap of the winery tours he'd taken with colleagues, she felt her head sink into her shoulders like a threatened tortoise.

Rand had catalogued his favorite wines at each of six vineyards by the time Justin announced, "Ready when you are, folks."

Gwen's neck cricked as she swiveled toward Justin. Their host stood with his hands on the back of a chair at the dining room table.

He gave her a smile of encouragement. "Gwen, if you'll sit here, we'll have Rand directly across from you. Rand, do you care for another Heineken?"

Shoot me now. Her gaze locked with Gianessa's.

"Gwen," Gianessa beckoned to her from the kitchen, "give me a hand with the, er . . ."

"Yes, coming."

Gianessa drew her close and whispered, "What's wrong?"

"I *loved* Heineken. It spells vacation in Maine to me. How will I ever kiss a man with Heineken on his breath?"

"Well, you don't have to worry about that tonight,

right?" Gianessa giggled. "Fix yourself something to drink. Unless you want to bargain with Rand for one of his beers?"

"Not funny."

"Hurry before the pizza gets cold. Justin, what are we missing?" she called.

"Just you and Gwen, sweetheart."

It took nearly an hour but, between Gianessa's charm and Justin's bonhomie, Gwen's shoulders finally relaxed. Rand eased back in his chair after he finished the last slice of their pizza.

"Delicious," Rand said. "That crust rivals any I've had in the Finger Lakes."

Justin reached across the table to give his wife's hand a squeeze. "We thank you," he said, "and we agree with you."

Gwen laughed.

"Every vegetable tasted fresh from the garden," Rand added. "What were those cheeses, Gianessa?"

Gianessa shook her finger. "The cheese is my husband's forte. What did you use, dude?"

"I can't believe you call him 'dude.'" Gwen let out a laugh.

"And he loves it," Gianessa insisted.

"I do." Justin nodded. "Mainly mozzarella and Italian fontina. Did you miss having meat, either of you?"

"Not I," Rand assured him.

Gwen shook her head. "And you made your own dressing for our salad, Gianessa?"

"Always," their hostess confirmed. "That way it's fresh, and it's free of additives."

"Those babies of yours will have only the best," Gwen predicted.

"That's the plan," Justin confirmed. "You just missed seeing them, Gwen. Nanny put them down a few minutes before you arrived."

"Before I arrived *late*," Gwen translated with a laugh.

"But you've seen them, right?" Rand asked her. It was the first time he'd looked directly into her eyes all evening.

"Yes, and I adore them." Gwen liked the answering crinkle at the corner of his eyes.

"Gwen had Jill laughing the other day, Justin."

"What?" Rand protested. "Infants can't laugh, can they?" He turned to Gianessa as the arbiter.

"Their Auntie Gwen has magic powers," Gianessa claimed.

"Does she?" Rand tipped his head as he contemplated Gwen.

"Stop, you're embarrassing me." Gwen's face flamed.

Justin intervened. "Gianessa tells me I should start up some faculty soirees, like we had in London. I want to know what you two think about that."

"Say more," Rand encouraged.

"Yes, I don't know anything about faculty soirees," Gwen lied. Justin had done intensive therapy with her last spring, and she had heard about the lively, alcohol-free soirees on his old campus.

"We used to gather once or twice a month," Justin said. "Faculty and spouses or invited friends. We'd play music, read from our work, talk about ideas and trends, drink espresso and tea, that sort of thing. Nothing formal, just a pleasant time together."

"How many would come, Justin?" Rand asked him.

Justin picked up a spoon and studied both sides of the bowl. "A couple dozen on average, though we may not get that many here at our small college. There were a few regulars, but the makeup varied each month."

"Mostly from the humanities?" Rand asked.

"No, we had a married couple from the natural sciences who never missed a soiree. In fact, she was an accomplished poet."

"Rand," Gwen said, "you could read your poetry."

Justin jumped on it. "Ah, do you write? I should have known."

"I do," Rand said with a nod.

"Do you publish?" Gianessa asked.

Rand favored her with a smile. "I don't have a book out yet, but I have placed a few poems in literary magazines.

"I'm much more active with a community of poets online. Among us we have several well-respected poetry sites that give voice to new talent.

"I actually edit one of those sites with a friend. We're always on the lookout for serious, talented students in creative writing programs."

"That's right." Gwen reached her hand across the table and rested her fingers on his hand. "I heard you're brilliant at motivating your students."

"I won't even ask you who said that." Rand blushed to the tips of his ears.

Justin held up his hands. "Couldn't have been anyone at this table, could it, Gianessa?"

The four of them laughed.

"And I think our hostess needs to call it a night." Gwen gave Gianessa's hand a squeeze.

"You saw that yawn, didn't you?"

"I've enjoyed this so much," Gwen told them.

"Yes, delightful," Justin agreed.

"Gianessa, let Gwen and me clean up for you," Rand offered.

"Nonsense," Gianessa told him.

"Careful, Rand," Justin warned, "you'll get a reputation as a perfect catch."

"I'm sincere," Rand said with a note of humility.

"I know you are," Gianessa replied, "but Justin and I have it covered."

"Mostly, our housekeeper has it covered," Justin said with a chuckle. "My job is to load the dishwasher and start it up, and Maya will do the rest, first thing in the morning."

"In that case," Rand said, "I'll say goodnight and walk Gwen to her car."

Gwen exchanged Gianessa's slippers for her wet loafers and thanked Justin for helping her on with her coat. As she preceded Rand on the curving walk to her car, she noticed the rain had stopped.

"Good people, don't you think?" Gwen tested.

Rand rested his hand on her back. "They certainly are. I was a little nervous. It's rumored Justin will be president of the college next year."

"He'll make a good one," Gwen said. *I'll bet he only agreed to the date because Justin wanted it.*

"Have you known them long?" Rand asked her.

"I only met Gianessa when she moved here last year. Justin I've known all my life, although we're years apart in age. Tompkins Falls is, in some ways, a small town. People who've lived here for generations tend to know each other, regardless of age."

"I have a lot to learn."

Gwen turned with a warm smile. "I have no doubt you'll succeed here, and I hope you'll like it."

"Thank you, Gwen. That means a lot. May I call you?"

"I'd like that."

Rand's answering smile seemed genuine. "If you had to pick—play, symphony, or jazz quartet—which would you choose?"

"I haven't seen a play in way too long. That would be my top pick, although all of the above sound good."

"I'll work on that." He gave her a quick kiss on the cheek and sauntered to his rain-washed white car.

Nice back view, but it doesn't compare to Peter. Gwen caught herself mid-thought. She allowed a pang of regret before challenging herself. *Move on, Gwen.*

"Absolutely, we can make your Facebook page." Haley pushed up the sleeves of her RPI sweatshirt and flexed her fingers. "Want to start now?"

Gwen grimaced. "This will require food. And patience."

"You get the food. I'll get my laptop."

Gwen had cookies out of the freezer and a pot of tea brewing by the time Haley got back.

"You're writing it all out in longhand first?" Haley teased.

Gwen lifted her eyes from an apparently arduous task. Her brow was furrowed, and her fingers gripped the pencil. "No, this is a list of what I want to be able to do on the Internet. Just in case you want to coach me after we finish my page."

Haley bounced onto a stool at the island. "What would you like on your page?"

"Just the basics about my therapy practice."

"So, we'll make a professional page," Haley said. "First, though, we have to set up a personal page for you."

"I don't want a personal page."

"We can make it private, no worries."

"But I don't have anything to say online. Can't we just skip the personal one?"

"Nope. It's like you need a bachelor's before you can get a Ph.D. You need a personal page before you can create a special page, like a product page or an artist page or whatever."

"Okay." Gwen reached for her mug of tea. "Do we have to use my name?"

"We'll use your nickname and make it private. Watch me."

Haley tapped the keys, dragged and tapped her finger on the trackpad, and keyed some more.

Haley announced, "*Voila!*"

Gwen's mouth dropped. "We're done? Where did you get that picture of me? That's not half bad."

"I have lots of pictures of you that I downloaded from my camera. I picked this one because it's cheerful."

"That's the day we went apple picking."

"Yes." She gave her aunt a sideways glance and saw her eyebrows raised with curiosity. "Of course, no one's going to see your picture on a private page, so it doesn't really matter." At Gwen's pout, Haley asked, "Still want it kept private?"

Gwen nodded without comment.

"Moving on to your professional page." Haley kept up a monologue as she created another page. "You should think about making your personal page about healthy living or great cookie recipes. How do you want your name to read on your new professional page?"

"Gwendolyn C. Forrester, Ph.D."

When Haley walked her through choosing a photo, Gwen surprised Haley. She selected one Haley had taken on the lakeshore. Gwen grinning, the corners of her eyes crinkled. She wore her favorite plaid wool shirt and blue jeans. All around her, sunshine ignited the colorful fall leaves. "Why this picture?"

"I suppose I should get a formal portrait done, but I'm going with the real me and letting the sunshine spell hope for a prospective client."

"Cool idea. When did we take that shot?"

Gwen hesitated and said quietly, "Right before Peter and I canoed down the lake and crashed in the storm."

Haley cringed. "Sorry for bringing it up."

"No, it was a beautiful morning."

"Think you'll ever get back together with him?" At Gwen's silence, Haley sized the photo to fit Gwen's new Facebook page. She asked questions about information to post and tags to use. "Okay, we've described your practice, given contact information, added metadata so people can discover you, and now we're done. Until you want to say something new."

"I like it. Thanks, sweetie."

"Let's take a break and then come back to your list."

"My list?"

Haley slid off her stool. "The things you want to be able to do on the Internet."

"Oh. Right." Gwen stood and stretched. "Are the cookies thawed?"

"Just." Haley arranged their cookies on a white plate and added a spring of holly from the bundle on the counter.

"When did you bring in the holly? What are you planning to do with it?"

"You'll see later. First, I want to bring you up to date about Rick and me."

Gwen started. "What's happening with Rick?"

"Rick and I talk—well, text—every day. He has taken the new environmental engineering students under his wing, at his mentor's suggestion. You can tell he likes it, and the students are excelling in their lab work. Professor Singh, his mentor, says he'll make a good teacher. It's cool hearing about the changes in him."

Haley's update brought calm and happiness to Gwen. Rick had been stressed when he arrived for the birth, and drained when he left two days later. He had spent just twelve hours with Haley and the baby, before the Hahns took the little one home with them.

"Can I invite him for Thanksgiving?" Haley asked.

"Of course. You know I'd love to see him. Christmas break, too, if he can. It's up to you."

"I'll ask him. I wonder . . ."

"What are you thinking?" Gwen prompted.

"No, it's selfish."

"I'd still like to hear it."

"I'm thinking how lucky Rick is to have a mentor. Not," she added quickly, "that I'm not grateful for all you and Gianessa are doing for me. I would be in the depths of depression without both of you supporting me."

"Thank you, sweetie. But a mentor's role is different. Professor Singh is Rick's mentor in his field, engineering, and he's guiding Rick to explore career options, like teaching, research, and whatever. That is beneficial to him as he begins his career."

"Exactly. Professor Singh wants Rick to get a taste of the corporate world, which is where the big money is, so Rick is interviewing all this month for possible internships with companies. Rick seems more interested in teaching and research, but Professor Singh keeps reminding him that, if he became a professor, he'd be preparing engineers who would go to work at twice his salary, and he needs to think about how that would feel. You know how sensitive Rick is about money."

"That's good mentoring." Gwen reached for another cookie.

"Yes, and that's why I need a mentor." Haley brushed the crumbs off her hands. "Except, I have no idea where to find one. And no idea what I want to do after college."

"So let me ask some ridiculous questions, and maybe we'll identify the next step for you."

"Cool."

"You love your photography. You love your art. You're passionate about flowers."

Haley nodded emphatically after each statement. "'Yes' to all of that. I almost forgot, I want to show you my new product line." She moved the laptop across the island and opened her business website for Gwen. "I'll give you the tour."

Haley dazzled her aunt with her new line of greeting cards. Each card featured Haley's flowers on the cover. The messages were words of encouragement and friendship. Those with sketches of emerging spring bulbs were especially for pregnant women. Those with baby's breath and pastel flowers were meant for new moms. "I'm going to try one with holly," she gestured to the bunch of holly on the counter, "for baby's first Christmas. I call the line 'In Bloom' and they're selling really well. A shop in Saratoga Springs stocks them, and the lady says she'll mention them to shopkeepers she knows in Florida. She thinks I should add shower invitations and birth-announcements."

"These are precious. And you know exactly what messages meant the most to you when you were pregnant, so they are authentic and very personal. No wonder they're selling."

"Thank you." Haley warm smile held a tinge of sadness. "Rick arranges the printing, just like with the posters and prints. He has an in with a couple of the graphic arts people at RPI, and they have contacts all over the capital district. Because everything is electronic, they can print on demand, and they ship within the United States."

"And you still make a profit?"

"I do pretty well. My online business has covered all my books and art supplies the last two years, plus my camera and the laptop and software, and I've been able to save a bunch, too. The lady in Saratoga Springs made me agree to a higher price because she says I've been selling myself short. So I upped it on the cards, and the sales are strong." She paused for breath. "And I really love doing it."

Gwen gave her shoulders a squeeze. "I can see that. So are you thinking you want to do more with the botany? Or with business? Or with art? Or . . ."

"I know I'm supposed to say botany, but—"

"What does your heart say?"

"My heart knows I'm really smart with science. But I don't know what career path I'd have in botany." She reached for the last cookie. "I'd like to talk to some people who do."

"I'll bet Justin could find a couple people for you to talk to, if you asked him."

"I never thought of that. That's a great idea." She drew her eyebrows together. "You really think it's okay for me to just ask him?"

"Absolutely."

"And maybe I could talk to somebody in graphic arts." She bounced on her stool. "Rick can give me names at RPI."

"And, you know, there's a graphic arts program at RIT."

"That's where Sara is getting her MBA in December. I wonder if RIT is as expensive as RPI."

"Something to investigate." Gwen pressed in the phone number for the Spa at the Manse.

"Maybe I could get a job and financial aid."

"Remember you have the money from the Hahns, and your aunt has a few million dollars with nothing to spend it on."

"You've got a million dollars?"

"Besides my inheritance from my folks and from Jeb, plus Jeb's life insurance, I also have—" She raised her eyebrows. "Hi, I'd like to book two haircuts with Sara."

Gwen listened and said, "Gwen Forrester and her niece Haley."

Another pause.

"Two o'clock today? We'll be there."

"Terrific," Haley said with a laugh. "That is so lucky."

"I think Sara is phasing out at the Manse. It sounded like she's not taking any appointments, but she knows us so she agreed."

"Now it's your turn." Haley folded her arms. "You heard all about Rick and me. I want to hear what you're thinking about Peter. And I need to hear about this new guy Rand—the one who inspired you to create a Facebook page."

"There's no getting out of it, is there?"

Haley gave her head a firm shake.

"Okay. I'm very sad about what happened with Peter, and especially because Deirdre and others have made me see I was partially at fault."

"How so?"

"I should have been upfront with him about being a recovering alcoholic."

"It's not like it's anything terrible," Haley defended. "And it's not like you were deceiving him."

"But to Peter it was something terrible. And he felt I was deceiving him. I tell my patients all the time, 'You don't get credit for your intentions; you get credit for what happens.' And what happened was he felt deceived and angry."

"But—"

Gwen held up her hands. "He has his own issues, but I contributed and I need to own that. There, I've said it."

Haley huffed. "Sucks."

"Yeah, but I should have seen it coming. I knew it was a big deal to him. What we had was really good, and I was focused on enjoying it, not on making sure it would last through the rough times."

"Think you'll ever get back together?"

Gwen shook her head and took a deep breath. "And that's my loss."

"So, tell me about Rand."

"Rand Cunningham is a poet and a brilliant professor." Gwen moved the laptop in front of her and keyed in the web address Rand had given her. His site popped on the screen. Gwen turned the screen so Haley could see. "Check it out. This is something he does with a buddy to get students' poetry into the public eye."

"Hm." Haley's tone was polite.

Gwen clicked around the site and gave up after a couple of unanswered, "See, isn't this cool?" She sniffed. "You don't fool me, Haley Forrester. You're not even trying to be interested."

"I just think you and Peter are perfect for each other."

"Well, Peter doesn't," Gwen snapped.

Haley jumped at Gwen's sharp tone. "I'm sorry," she apologized. "And I did ask you to tell me about Rand. Is he cute?"

"He's very handsome, very preppy." *In fact, a lot like Jeb. Uh-oh, I'd better talk to Deirdre about that.* "He's a bit full of himself," Gwen added, "but, as you can see, he has reason to be."

"And you're going out with him again?"

"Yes. This Friday night."

Haley said dutifully, "I hope you have a good time."

"I'm so sorry you and Rand had a bad time," Gianessa commiserated. "And so glad you're getting me out of the house for some girl talk. This is the first time I've ventured out socially with the twins, and I can't imagine ever doing it alone."

"Two babies are way more work than one?"

"Amen."

They had jockeyed two infant-sized strollers through the narrow front door of Lynnie's Chestnut Lake Café, moved tables and chairs to clear a path and, finally, parked themselves.

Lynnie bustled over, all excited. "If you'd come at the height of the lunch rush, I might have been too busy to see these two little angels."

Gianessa laughed her musical laugh. Gwen hadn't heard it in months.

"We knew better, Lynnie. Let me introduce my children—Jack and Jill Cushman."

Lynnie squatted in front of the strollers and peeked at the little faces in their buntings and blankets. She cooed when she told them how happy she was to make their acquaintance. "I don't even need the blue and pink blankets to know who's who," she told Gianessa.

"Jack is a big boy, built like Justin, and Jill is delicate, like me. They're both very sweet babies. I am lucky."

Lynnie rose with a satisfied smile and asked, "What can I get you two?"

"Latte for me," Gwen told her. "Cinnamon sprinkled on top."

"The same," Gianessa agreed.

"Large for both of you?"

They nodded in unison and laughed.

Alone again, Gianessa quizzed, "So you're not going to see Rand again?"

"He's a good guy." Gwen shook her head. "We're just not a fit for each other."

"I'm so sorry. I had hopes. Tell me everything."

"We started with a delicious dinner at a restaurant right in the city."

"Rochester?"

"Yes, very close to the theater. But the food could not make up for the noise all around us. It drowned out every attempt at conversation. Rand downed two bottles of beer—Corona this time—right off the bat. All through the meal, he alternately fidgeted and glared at the neighboring tables."

"Guess you didn't linger over coffee and dessert?" Gianessa said wryly.

"No, and you know that's my favorite part of the meal."

Gianessa chuckled. "Those are beautiful, Lynnie."

Lynnie set down their lattes and glanced at the sleeping babies. "You'll let me know if they wake up, right?" She hustled back to the cash register to take care of a departing customer.

After Gwen took her first sip, Gianessa prompted, "So dinner was a bust. What then?"

"We got to the theater early. We chatted—kind of stilted—as we perused the photos of the cast and their bios and the sketches of the costumes. Other couples started to arrive, and Rand and I wandered into the café. I had a latte, and Rand had a brandy."

Gianessa tapped her fingers against the glass mug. "You don't think he has a problem?"

"I think he was just regretting the whole night, even then."

"Uh-oh, was the play awful, too?"

Gwen raised both eyebrows. "It was a yawn for me. Rand groaned and sheeshed the whole time. At intermission, I suggested we go somewhere for coffee instead of staying for the rest of the play."

"Good idea," Gianessa agreed.

"Not. Rand took it personally, snagged a table in the café, and ordered another brandy. I told him if he was going to drink that, I wanted his keys. He slapped his keys on the table, slugged down the brandy and had a coughing fit." Gwen glanced at her friend with mischief in her eyes.

"I can't believe this." Gianessa's mouth dropped open.

"Wait for the best part."

"Ohmigod, what happened?" Gianessa grabbed her arm. "What did you do?"

"I didn't need to do anything for things to get really interesting."

"Tell me!" Gianessa shook Gwen's arm.

"Some cute blonde came over and helped him stop coughing. You know that trick where you raise your arms straight over your head?"

"Yeah. It's embarrassing, but it works every time."

"Exactly, and this little blonde was probably the only woman in the world who could get someone with Rand's ego to do that in a room full of dressed-up theatergoers."

"More." Gianessa clapped her hands. "Tell me more."

"Well, it worked, and Rand eyed her like she was an angel sent from heaven to save him. He. Was. Smitten."

"Ohmigod," Gianessa trilled.

Gwen nodded. "She cozied up to him and put her fingers on his pulse. I asked her if she was a nurse. No surprise, she is. And I don't know why, maybe because she looked all of twenty, I asked her if she'd just finished her degree."

"Did she?"

"She did. She's adorable." Gwen let out a laugh. "I felt like his mother or something. And I played it for all it was worth."

"What? What did you do?"

"I asked her name, and she handed me her beautiful new business card. She actually just got her masters and is a nurse practitioner. I happened to notice she had no wedding ring."

"You set them up?" Gianessa guessed.

"Exactly." Gwen had not seen her friend so animated since her wedding in July. "I told her Rand's name and what he did for a living and how *important* he is. And I suggested she check out his website—which, by the way is really impressive. Then I tucked *her* card into *his* jacket pocket."

"I can't believe you did that."

"And I told her I was driving Professor Cunningham home now, but she should call him in the morning to see if there were any ill effects from the brandy down the windpipe."

"You are too much." Gianessa wiped tears from her face.

"And then I made my exit. I didn't care if Rand followed me or not. I had the keys, and I knew where the car was parked."

"You were mad enough to leave him there?" Gianessa's eyes opened wide.

"Yes, except he blocked the car as I exited the parking garage. We had a little tiff about who was going to drive, but he wasn't about to drag me out of the driver's seat in the cultural center of Rochester."

"Ohmigod, Gwen." She reached for a napkin to blot her eyes. "I haven't laughed this hard in a year."

Gwen shrugged. "I guess, sometimes you have to go with what the universe hands you. I think Rand and the cute nurse practitioner are made for each other."

"You're a better sport than I am. And I promise I won't tell Justin any of this."

Gwen sat back and licked foam off the rim of her mug. "Why not?" Her eyes sparkled.

"He'd shoot Rand, and we need him at the college."

"You are the perfect partner for Justin as he leads the college into the future." Gwen said a silent prayer that Gianessa's return to good health promised many happy years for the Cushmans.

"Thank you for saying that. For believing it." Gianessa's gaze locked onto Gwen's. "Like you said, we go with what the universe hands us." She raised her mug. "Onward."

Gwen grinned. "Onward."

They clinked glasses.

"And just in time," Gianessa said slyly.

"What do you mean?"

"Match Number Two. Justin has someone a tad older waiting in the wings to meet you."

"Craig Marone," the musclebound thirty-something told Gwen with a firm handshake.

"I'm Gwen." She raised her glass of sparkling water to his and clinked. "Since Gianessa and Justin have everything under control in the kitchen, we can hang here for a few minutes."

"Nice to meet a woman who doesn't drink wine."

"You're not a drinker?" Gwen flashed a bright smile.

He pursed his mouth and shook his head. "Defiling the temple."

"I can tell you work out. Are you into sports?"

"Body building," he answered.

Gwen expected him to follow up with at least one sport, but that was the whole answer.

"You're very fit, Gwen." He winked. "How do you do it?"

"A variety. Until last week, I was biking every morning, twelve miles. In season I swim in the lake. This winter I'll swim at the Y in the morning, and I have a power yoga class twice a week and do a Pilates routine at home."

"What do you do for work?"

"I'm a psychologist, specializing in addictions. And you?"

He eyed the glass in her hand but didn't turn his speculative gaze into a question. "I'm the Chief Information Officer at the college," he answered. "I don't know how it is for you, but, now that my father has passed, my mother is on me all the time to give her grandchildren. Do you get pressure like that, too?"

"No, my parents are both gone. But—"

"Dinner is served," Justin said. "Come while it's hot."

The Cushmans had reprised their menu of gourmet pizza and salad, but they'd added a loaf of garlic bread for the potentially larger appetite among them. This time Justin did not ask if they missed meat. She was pretty sure Craig had expected steak at the president-to-be's house.

Conversation centered on the college, in spite of Gwen and Gianessa effort to bring it back to families and babies. Craig was apparently not interested in either, in spite of his mother's desire for a grandchild. Justin was increasingly uncomfortable, fidgeting and harrumphing.

When Gianessa pleaded a headache, Craig lost no time departing. Justin walked out with him while Gwen accompanied Gianessa down a flight of stairs to the babies' rooms.

Gianessa gave her time to coo at the sleeping twins before asking, "Do you think he's gay?"

"He's dating because his mom wants grandchildren. I think so. I wish him well, but that's not a union I'm eager to take on."

"I am so sorry, Gwen. I'm sure Justin had no idea when he suggested this."

"Not a problem. Be honest. Do you have a headache?"

"No, but I am a little tired. And I have a hunch Justin wants to talk with you about something. With our guest and me out of the picture, you two can talk as long as you want."

Gwen gave her friend a lingering hug. "Love you," she whispered. "Sleep well."

On her way upstairs, Gwen's forehead throbbed. She longed for a baby that would grow up with Gianessa and Justin's twins. She remembered the day in August, after Haley's arrival, when she'd stopped her bike on her road at dawn and watched the mother deer with her faun and the flock of chickadees. She was sure then, and she was even more sure now, that she didn't want to raise a child on her own, as a single mom.

At the moment, though, Justin waited for her in the living room, and she hurried to find out what he wanted to talk about.

Chapter 15

"I'm concerned about her." Justin had prepared coffee and sweets, and he set them on an ebony cocktail table between two chairs.

"Tell me why." Gwen reached for her mug and a shortbread cookie. While she thought Gianessa was recovering well, Justin knew his wife better than anyone.

Justin's smile was a grim line. "I was hoping you'd tell me I'm being overprotective or dramatic."

Gwen slipped off her loafers and tucked her feet under her. "Is it physical?"

Justin shook his head. "According to the doctor, no, she's well. Nor is there any sign of postpartum depression. And I know the passion and love in our marriage are strong."

"And she has plenty of help with the babies and the house," Gwen added with a smile. "You're giving her the support she needs with the hard work of raising twins."

"Yes, although she tells all of us to stop fussing," Justin chuckled. He studied his hands and spread his fingers, as if the answer might lie between them.

"She has said to me that she's sad about not being able to have more babies."

Justin's head shot up. "She said that?"

"Yes. Is it news to you or just a surprise that she told me?"

"I'm surprised that she shared it, and glad. She's been wearing a brave face about it. Fortunately, I'm not sensing any anger toward me about making the decision for the hysterectomy."

"It was the only reasonable decision. I also know she's thrilled to have a boy and a girl and all of this abundance with you."

"And I'm back to wondering why she has those worry lines in her forehead when she thinks I'm not looking."

Gwen smiled to herself as she recalled the concern Gianessa voiced at the end of their phone conversation, while Gianessa was still in the hospital.

"What?" Justin insisted. "You know something, don't you?"

She set down her mug. "Has she talked with you about her career?"

"In the past, yes, but not in a while."

"And what had she said in the past?"

"Gianessa is sensitive about becoming dependent on me, the way she became dependent on her first husband. It's not that she expects our marriage to end." Justin inhaled deeply. "I'm confident of that. But she's a smart, gifted professional, and she wants to make a strong, original contribution to her field." Justin sat forward. "That's it, isn't it, Gwen? Her career. She's worried about getting it moving again."

"Yes. She shared with me that, knowing she cannot have more children, she should now set some career goals. At the same time, being showered with abundance every day and loving all of it, plus the fact that she is just bouncing back from surgery, she may feel conflicted about taking next steps. And, mostly, she doesn't know how *you* feel about it. I had urged her to have that conversation with you."

Justin exhaled and slurped his espresso.

"How would you feel if she turned some attention to her career, Justin?"

When he sat back in his leather chair, it creaked and squeaked under him. Gwen hadn't heard that masculine sound in years.

How she had loved those quiet evenings at home before

she married. Her father reading in his leather chair, her mother in a cozy wingchair.

Maybe her dad's leather chair was still in the attic. *Rick can bring it down at Thanksgiving. Then all I need is the man.*

Justin's deep voice interrupted her musing. "I do want her to pursue her career, but I've done two things I maybe shouldn't have."

"Say more." Gwen gave him her full attention.

"I've urged her to let the nannies do all the work while she rests, goes to the spa, finds a yoga group she likes, and so on."

"You slave driver." Gwen laughed.

Justin joined in. "I never thought to draw her out about her professional goals, but I will do that now. Worse, though, I've failed to secure the property for the holistic rehab facility. You probably know all about Manda's dream."

"Yes, the holistic center that caters to those who need to make fundamental changes in their thinking, eating, exercise, and stress management, in order to deal with serious health issues."

"Exactly."

"Gianessa's credentials as a physical therapist and her gifts as a healer make her the perfect person to shape the vision for that center," Gwen said.

"Precisely. And we believe the right location for it is Cady's Point."

"I understand and agree." Gwen pushed aside the memory of her canoe trip there with Peter. "It has healing power, and it is a beautiful, serene setting for the center. Are you going to buy it from Lorraine?"

Justin hung his head. "Lorraine refused to sell it to me or to Joel. At any price. First she gave Joel the runaround when he tried to buy it as a wedding gift for Manda."

"I had heard about that. What happened when you tried to buy it?"

"I failed. Even with Gianessa's coaching, Lorraine saw right through me. Whenever I added a million to my purchase offer, she wanted two million more. When I realized she had no intention of selling to me, I walked away."

Gwen cocked her head. "Out of curiosity, what did you give Manda and Joel as a wedding gift?"

He shrugged. "Just the half of the Cushman grounds where they want to build their home in a couple of years."

"Half of these grounds, where we're sitting now?"

"Yes. I was the sole heir of the estate. Deeding half to Joel and Manda was Gianessa's suggestion. Now that I've razed the family mansion, the way is clear for them to build their home on the level spot just south of the mansion as soon as they're ready. It's perfect for their children to play, when the time comes."

Gwen leaned toward him. "It makes me very happy that you and Joel will be living together on the Cushman grounds, raising what the townspeople are calling the new generation of Cushmans."

"Are people saying that?" Justin's eyes lit up.

"Yes, and I think it's giving them hope and a sense of stability that one of the founding families of Tompkins Falls is coming back. Well two families, really, since Joel is also the last of the Tompkins line."

Justin's voice caught. "I must tell that to Gianessa." He took a swallow of coffee and cleared his throat. "And to Joel and Manda."

"There's your toast for Thanksgiving." She gave him a few moments to gather himself.

When he picked up a napkin to dab at his mouth, he also blotted his eyes. "So, I failed to secure the land Gianessa and Manda want for their facility, and their planning seems to have come to an abrupt end."

"Not so." Gwen held up her finger.

"No?" Justin's voice was an octave higher and infused with energy. "What do you know?"

"I know that Manda had to declare her masters project at St. Basil's a year ago, and she chose to focus on the holistic rehab. She has kept herself going with her research and her business plan. She actually sounded you out a few times about one aspect or another, although you may not have realized what she was doing."

"I had no clue." Justin chuckled.

"Her proposal has been accepted. She's moving into the final stages of her business plan and she'll have her masters in May. Another celebration we all can look forward to."

"Then all she needs is the venture capital—which is my job—and a place to build."

"You're putting up the capital?"

"I am. That's the deal we made last winter—over breakfast—when Joel was still in the hospital. The offer stands, as long as I approve her business plan."

"Justin." Gwen waited for him to make eye contact. "I have an idea."

"You're wearing a Cheshire Cat grin," Justin narrowed his eyes, but not before she saw a twinkle.

"As Lorraine's lifelong friend, I can buy Cady's Point from her. I'll come up with a story. I don't know"—she waved her hands—"I'm sick of maintaining the tortuous Forrester road and the antiquated house, or something. And I'll tell her she needs to let go and to move on with her life. Some combination like that. She won't suspect I'm getting it for Joel's wife and your wife. She has no idea I have a relationship with any of you." She nodded decisively.

"Except you'll need to meet her in person, and keep a straight face. Documents must be signed, and money handed over. You'll need more of a plan than that," Justin said.

"Okay, I'll start by calling her and reminding her about our nasty winters here and say I need cashmere. And I'm coming to London, the source of all cashmere, and I want to go on a shopping spree with her. Harrods is best for cashmere, isn't is?"

"Perfect. Meet her in London for your Christmas shopping, see a couple of plays with her, give her your best story and hand her a check." He strode to his desk. "How much do you think you'll need?"

Gwen shot to her feet. "Justin, stop! I don't mean for you to underwrite this transaction."

He turned in surprise. "Oh, right, she'll want to know where you got the money. What will you tell her?"

Gwen sat down again and motioned him back to his chair. "You had no way of knowing, and I don't think Lorraine knows either. I've been sitting on almost nine million dollars from a wrongful death settlement related to my husband's accident. It's time I spent some of it."

"I knew you had lost your husband." Justin's face puckered with sympathy. "I had no idea his death had brought you a windfall."

"Jeb was a skier, involved in Ski Patrol. He responded to a rescue call—two boys on a gondola lift. Their car had twisted and almost derailed in a high wind. It turned out there was something defective about the car—I don't know the details. Anyway, he climbed a tower, used the cable to get to the car, and got the boys to shimmy down a line to safety. As soon as they scrambled out of harm's way, the car fell off the cable, crashed onto the rocks below, and Jeb was killed." Gwen sucked in her breath. It had been years since she'd told the story or even thought of it.

"You're trembling." Justin's hands covered hers. "Are you all right?"

She nodded. "Jeb's parents ordered an investigation and filed suit, on my behalf and theirs. I was in such a daze I didn't even know they'd done it. They won, and we split seventeen-and-a-half million."

"Your hands are ice," Justin said.

She shook her head, unable to stop her train of thought. "The money meant nothing to me, and I've never done anything with it."

"By now you could have bought an estate in the same little enclave in the Thames Valley, where Lorraine lives surrounded by her wealthy college friends. Personally, I'm glad you stayed with us in Tompkins Falls."

"What they're doing, holed up in that valley, except when they're on a cruise or shopping in Paris or skiing in Gstaad, is an escape. An empty existence. This is where I belong—treating addicts and alcoholics right here on the shores of my favorite lake."

"My favorite as well." He squeezed her hands.

She squared her shoulders. "Lorraine has no business hanging onto Cady's Point. If I'm the only one who can pry it from her, then that's what I'll do. For Manda, for Gianessa, for all the people who will get treatment at this new holistic center and as a result, turn a corner in their lives."

"I've got an idea." Justin sat back and regarded her with a twinkle in his eyes.

"Tell me." She set down her coffee.

"The name Forrester, thanks to your grandparents and your parents and now you, has always been affiliated with health care and with care of the whole person, here in Tompkins Falls. I'd like you to give the Forrester name to the new holistic rehab center on Cady's Point."

Gwen caught her breath.

"I'm sure Gianessa and Manda will agree," he said.

Tears sprang to Gwen's eyes. "Dad and Mom would be so proud."

"And you must consider yourself one of the trustees as well."

Unable to speak, Gwen nodded.

"As for your imminent trip to London, I insist on making your travel arrangements, at my expense. And I want you to take Lorraine to a couple of plays on me. Don't tell her, of course." He grinned.

"It's brilliant." Gwen brushed her cheeks dry. "I'll pin down a date with Lorraine and polish my story about why I need to move off the old homestead and live on her land."

Justin sobered. "This will get Gianessa's career back in gear. Starting up the Forrester Center is exactly the professional role she was meant to play, and the time is right."

"Let's not say anything until I've got the land," Gwen cautioned.

"Agreed," Justin said. "I want this to succeed, and my money's on you."

Gwen had no problem convincing Lorraine to meet her in London. She hinted she had a fascinating opportunity that required Lorraine's cooperation.

"You're opening a practice someplace exotic that I *must* visit," Lorraine guessed.

"No, I hadn't thought of that."

"You're moving to London." Lorraine squealed.

"Hm. No."

"I know," Lorraine said. "You're getting married again, aren't you?"

"Maybe. But you can't tell anyone." Gwen refused to divulge anything more or to tell Lorraine her role in it until they were face to face. "How soon can we meet for shopping in London?" she asked.

Lorraine rattled off her social calendar for the next ten days, finally admitting that everything could be moved or canceled. The two of them agreed to meet, in London, the day after next, for a week of culture, fine dining, shopping, and scheming.

"Scheming?" Gwen questioned.

"Of course, dearest. Whatever it is you're up to, you'll need me to advise you. I'm a much better schemer."

Gwen laughed.

"Gwen, you haven't a devious bone in your body. You need me."

"You're so right, Lorraine. I can't wait to see you."

"Ta."

"Love you, bye."

As soon as she hung up, she was confronted with a bigger challenge.

"You're going to leave me for a whole week?" Haley wailed. "Without a car? Alone? In this big house?"

Yikes, I didn't think of that. "Yes," Gwen said. "And we have one day to plan it so you'll have fun, food, friends, and whatever your heart desires." She grabbed a pad of paper and a pencil. "Let's get busy."

Haley agreed to drive Gwen to the airport in exchange for the use of her car. And she agreed to buy her own gas. Together, they drew up menus for meals and snacks for a full week. Then they made a comprehensive grocery list and spent a few hours together at Gwen's favorite supermarket.

Haley remembered that Thursday was her trip to RIT with Sara, so she arranged to take Sara to supper that evening. Sara reciprocated by inviting Haley to go with her and Manda on a thrift-shop adventure that Saturday. "This will be fun," Haley said, "and I'll go to AA meetings. Maybe I'll take supper to Phil's house the day of his meeting. Do you think he'd like that?"

"He would love it."

"And I have work to do for my classes, too."

"Think you'll ever have time to talk with me on the phone?" Gwen teased.

"You mean, I get to hear, first-hand, what you're up to?"

"You get the exclusive story."

"Cool. Maybe some day," Haley said shyly, "you and I could take a trip together, someplace special."

"Pick a place," Gwen said with a fond smile.

Haley's eyes danced. "Those gardens in the Pacific Northwest—near Vancouver."

"Sounds good. I don't know anything about them."

"I'll do some research while you're away."

She's going to be okay.

Gwen dodged a gaggle of women shoppers as they exited Harrods onto Brompton Road. "Which way?" she asked Lorraine.

Lorraine stepped neatly to Gwen's right and blocked the way. "First, show me what you bought."

Gwen held up her single shopping bag and steeled herself as her imperious friend probed the contents with a stern face.

"It's as I thought. Casual sweaters and another pair of jeans." She tapped her designer-booted foot. "Gwen, from this moment forward, you will take your wardrobe seriously. And I am in charge."

Gwen bowed her head and studied the boot that fit Lorraine's shapely leg like a glove. In contrast to Gwen's charcoal duffle coat, black straight-leg trousers and gray cowl-neck sweater, Lorraine wore a long, brown suede skirt, a butterscotch cashmere turtleneck, and an espresso leather coat, with a signature silk-and-wool scarf tossed over one shoulder.

Gwen gave Lorraine's slender waist a squeeze. "But I like sexy jeans and cashmere sweaters. So does my future hubby."

"Completely missing my point." Lorraine waved her hands. "I don't care what you wear around the house or at the supermarket. I care about your public face. Now that you'll be living in the house I built on Cady's Point, you are representing me and all the women in my Cady lineage."

Gwen put on her professional face for a moment—the one that hid every emotion—and reconsidered her story. She might be on shaky ground with this complication. Did Lorraine plan to monitor her every move as the new owner of Cady's Point? Did she have some distant relative on the lake that cared about such things? Gwen seriously doubted it. Lorraine was probably just manipulating her into a shopping bender.

Come to think of it, I have nothing appropriate to wear as a trustee of the Forrester Center. She would be attending board meetings and receptions and fundraisers. *And I do need color in my wardrobe.*

With an admiring smile, she told Lorraine, "You're completely right. I desperately need two or three decent suits. Oh, and something colorful, like silk tops and scarves. And a smashing cocktail dress or two. You know I'm clueless about these things."

Lorraine beamed. "We'll ship everything, never fear, so you don't need to carry extra luggage."

Gwen's eyes opened wide as her lips formed the word "Everything." *Remember, the deed to Cady's Point is not yet yours.* "You are an angel, Lorraine. I bow to your style and wisdom."

"Marvelous." Lorraine took Gwen's elbow steered to their right. "Come, we'll start with Armani for suits. And Gucci has a smashing black dress with your name on it. Then—"

"Then tea at the Ritz, my treat, I insist. We have several more days to do all this, you know." *God help me.*

"Justin, I called as soon as I could. We're at the Ritz, where we're having tea. I'm in the ladies' room. It's a go, but Lorraine insists—and I agree—that both our attorneys need to be present for the closing—here in London, in two days, if at all possible."

"Oh, thank you, God. You are a miracle worker, Gwen. Let me make notes as we talk." She heard him tapping keys.

"I will somehow convince Oscar to make the trip. I may need to come with him and show him London for a few days."

Gwen rested her backside against a gilded vanity. "Please, please don't show yourself or let Oscar divulge to a single soul that you're involved in this. Or even that you're in London. Lorraine would pull the plug, we know that."

"Understood. I hear the strain in your voice. Something's wearing on you, isn't it, Gwen?"

"I feel like I'm on a runaway train." Her laugh sounded hysterical, even to her ears. "Every time I think it's settled, there's another bend in the track that throws me."

"I warned you it would be like that. She is devious. You're not used to operating out of deception. Does it bother you to deceive your lifelong friend?"

"Thank you for acknowledging that little detail," Gwen said with a dry chuckle.

"I apologize for not thinking of it until after you'd taken off for London. I half-expected you to turn around and abandon the mission."

"Well, don't blow it out of proportion. In the first place, Lorraine has lived her entire life manipulating people to her will or her whim. She would never view this with the same scruples I do."

"And what are your scruples telling you?"

"I did a lot of soul-searching about this on the flight and made my peace with it. I am simply out-maneuvering her to do the right thing. I really believe, in the depths of my soul, this rehab is important for the Finger Lakes area—for the people it will employ, for the patients who will benefit from it, for the practitioners who will work in harmony with specialists from other fields." She glanced at her scuffed walking shoes. *How can Lorraine walk all day in those boots with the three-inch heels?*

"Furthermore, in denying the land to you and Joel, Lorraine has been petty and selfish. The land means nothing to her now, except that it carries her grandmother's name. Besides, in light of the dissolution of her marriage to the degenerate she lived with in that house on Cady's Point, the whole place has bad juju for her. And most important, as her friend, I can see that she has not moved on from that experience, even though she's living an ocean away.

"And, finally, from my perspective, this transfer of ownership is important to my dear friends, Manda and Gianessa, who are willing to stake their careers on the wellness center. And it's important to you, Justin. You're putting up the capital."

"Did I hear a 'but' in that speech?" Justin asked.

Wise guy. "But." Gwen smiled at her phone. "You're correct. It's hard. Besides, at some point, Lorraine will discover the deception."

"We hope not for a while. And what will you do when she does?"

"I'll defend my actions with the self-righteous speech I just made. If she forces my hand, I will tell her I'm building a rehab with my family name on it . . . on land that will continue to carry her family name. I can play up the public honor of having the Cady name associated with it." Gwen paused for a breath. "Anyway, that's my story, so far as I've thought it through."

Justin was quiet. She heard him clicking keys. "Are you having second thoughts?" she asked him.

"Not at all. What would you think about making her a board member or something along those lines?"

"Absolutely not! She can have no involvement in this operation. That would open the door to sabotage."

"I see your point."

"I don't even want her to be a patient at our rehab. If I could think of a way to prevent that, I'd put it in the agreement as well."

"I will discuss all this with Oscar on the way over. He's an old hand at this sort of thing."

"Thank you. And thanks for letting me spew."

"I hope it has eased your mind. Tell me, does the Ritz serve those little dark chocolates with the pomegranate filling?"

"Aren't they're delicious?" Gwen let out a sensual moan. "They have them at Harrods, too. Let me know where you're staying, and I'll have a box sent to your hotel room."

"We'll rendezvous somehow, Gwen, perhaps at an AA meeting. Rest assured Oscar and I will have you covered legally, on all sides."

On the last day of the London shopping extravaganza, Gwen made a long call to her niece. Haley had handled the time alone with maturity and good humor. She'd raved about her trip on Thursday to RIT with Sara. On Wednesday, she had fixed eggplant parmesan for Phil, using Edie's recipe, then lugged it along with salad and cookies to Phil's, on the path through the woods. He'd teased her about being Little Red Riding Hood. *Must find a red shawl for Haley.*

"You're beaming like a proud parent," Lorraine said. "She's done well on her own?"

"She blows me away sometimes. I need one last gift before I'm ready to bring our shopping to an end." She told Lorraine about the red shawl, and Lorraine directed their tired feet to a nearby boutique. Gwen made her purchase, stealthily added a scarf that Lorraine had admired, and picked another for herself in a delicate, peach-and-gray print.

Over dinner, Lorraine toasted with champagne and Gwen clinked glasses—hers filled with sparkling water.

"The deal is sealed," Lorraine said. "Your flight is booked, and you have one more day in England. Why not come home with me tomorrow on the train and spend time with my boys?"

Gwen's face lit up. "I'd like nothing more."

"We'll have my driver pick them up at school as soon as we arrive. I'll catch up with friends, while you and the boys do whatever you wish. Then tea, just the two of us, and you can return to London by train tomorrow evening or first thing in the morning, before your flight."

"Tomorrow evening, I think."

Gwen already had plans to meet Justin at an AA meeting the next night, and he had found her a room at his hotel so they could travel home together. Although Oscar had flown back from London immediately after the closing, Justin had stayed on to see colleagues at the London campus of the University of Chicago, including Manda's sister, Lyssa.

"We should make this an annual event, dearest," Lorraine said, her eyes sparkling at the thought.

"Let's," Gwen agreed. *But more culture and less shopping.*

"Paris next November?"

Crystal rang as they touched glasses.

By the end of the day, Gwen and the boys had spent hours exploring one lane after another as they walked to the river and back. She had loved every minute—every adventure Chipper recounted, every tall-tale Alex spun for her, every detail about their private school and cricket matches. Their British accents had taken her by surprise, but of course they'd been raised since ages two and three in the Thames Valley.

They had pressed her for memories of their father, which she hadn't anticipated. *He was a snake and a rake and I hope you never know any of that.* She pleaded ignorance, except to say he was very handsome and very smart. That led to a contest for her to judge which of them was more handsome and which was smarter.

Now, lounging in Lorraine's library, Gwen was tired and hungry and on edge. Her gaze locked onto the sherry glass in Lorraine's hand. She watched it rise from the inlaid table, touch Lorraine's lips, and tip to dispense a sip of the finest Oloroso. Gwen could taste its mellow, fragrant bouquet on her tongue, feel the warmth in her throat. *God help me. Will the sandwiches and tea never arrive?*

"Tell me how much you're going to love your new clothes." Lorraine's mouth curved with a smile.

Gwen closed her eyes. *I can do this.* "You've made a new woman out of me. Elegant and chic. And I love the hints of color in all the silk and cashmere."

"I always knew best where your clothes were concerned, didn't I, dearest?" Lorraine rested her head against the back of her favorite wing chair and smiled up at the ornate ceiling. Thick, oak beams formed a grid overhead, with squares of embossed leather set between.

"You always did," Gwen agreed. Her gaze circled the walls of room and admired the bold flower paintings positioned between each of the floor-to-ceiling, oak bookcases. One of the smaller paintings, she was sure, was a Georgia O'Keeffe. Beneath it, on another inlaid table, a bouquet of lilies leant their heady fragrance to the room.

Gwen noted an empty, inlaid table by the door. She would send Lorraine one of Haley's boldest watercolors in a gilded frame and suggest it be displayed there.

"Thank you, Charles." Lorraine's voice interrupted Gwen's musing. Charles set down a tray of triangular tea sandwiches for them. "That will be all."

Gwen eyed the tray and gave it a turn so the egg and cress triangles were close to her. She took one and finished it in three bites.

"If it doesn't work out with your fiancé, you can always sell and move here, Gwen." Lorraine gestured beyond the windows to her property. "It's so civilized and charming in this little valley."

Gwen shook her head and sipped her tea. She set down the flowered cup and reached for another sandwich. "It is charming, but it's time I married a good man. Like Peter." She nearly choked on the name. In this entire scheme, it was the use of Peter's name as her fiancé that bothered her the most. She wished she'd thought to use Rand's name instead.

"Is something wrong, dearest?"

Gwen devoured the crustless sandwich and rallied a smile. "What do you mean?"

Lorraine sniffed. "You've told me next to nothing about this fiancé. I wondered for a whole day if he was real. And by the way, you've said nothing about the wedding. Will I be invited?"

Gwen covered her pain with a bright smile. "We'll probably elope. It's a second marriage for both of us. Perhaps we'll swing by here on the honeymoon."

Lorraine crossed her elegant legs and jiggled one foot. "I still don't understand why you wanted Cady's Point. Why doesn't he want to live in your family home?"

"He feels it's too isolated down that long drive. He has a point."

"And Cady's Point is not?"

"Apples and oranges. The road into Cady's Point is paved and patrolled. There are quite a few homes and estates now on both sides, north and south of your property. My property," she amended and raised her cup to Lorraine.

Lorraine winked in acknowledgement. "And it doesn't bother you that my home—your home—on the Point was the scene of a disastrous marriage?"

"I'm planning an exorcism," Gwen said without thinking. Lorraine snorted.

"Will you remarry, Lorraine?"

"No." She nearly spat the word. "Men are takers and deceivers. I'm done with them."

Gwen studied her friend's face, wishing there was some way she could help her. But she'd never been able to help Lorraine, except to be her friend.

"Remember when you were in grad school?" Lorraine's voice broke into her thoughts. "Where was it again?"

"Tufts, Boston."

"Yes, that's it. While you were there, we met in New York for a weekend of shopping."

"We saw some great plays, didn't we?"

"You always insisted on matinees," Lorraine scolded, "which cut into our shopping time." She selected the plumpest of the cheddar and tomato sandwiches and nibbled one corner.

"That was a smashing trip, wasn't it?" Gwen said. But her brow furrowed. *I don't remember anything but the plays.*

"Jeb never knew, did he?"

Gwen opened her mouth and closed it again. *Didn't she and Jeb share everything?*

Lorraine gave her a conspiratorial wink. With a throaty chuckle, she said, "Jeb didn't know a lot of things, did he?"

Lorraine sounded so sure. But Gwen had no recall of secrecy in her marriage. *Maybe she has someone else in mind.* "What are you thinking about?"

"I am remembering how nasty he was when you lived in Boston for six months for your clinical residency. I never understood how you were able to keep the whole thing from him."

"What 'whole thing?'"

Lorraine huffed. "That you were getting the doctoral degree and preparing to be a therapist." She waved a hand. "You kept the whole thing from him. I never understood why or how, Gwen. What did he have against your getting a doctorate and having a career?"

That's insane. Why would Jeb oppose it, and why would I go to such lengths to hide something like that? "Ohmigod," she whispered. The sudden memory was a punch in the stomach. With no thought to editing her response, she answered Lorraine. "Jeb was opposed to my having a career, even though it was important to me. So I paid for the degree myself and did most of the coursework online without ever telling him." Her head throbbed as she added, "But then I had to do my clinical residency in the greater Boston area, for a minimum of six months."

"Yes, and you somehow convinced Jeb you needed to be in Boston for half a year. Remind me how you did that, you wicked wife."

When Gwen's only response was a creased forehead, Lorraine probed, "Don't tell me you told him you were leaving him?"

"I'd forgotten all of this." Gwen nodded. "We'd been fighting a lot. I don't know why."

"I know why," Lorraine said. "He was a player, Gwen."

"Was he?" *Why doesn't that shock me? That should shock me.*

"Of course he was. He even came on to me once. I set him straight, in the name of our friendship." Lorraine's chuckle was sardonic. "He thought it was quaint."

Gwen swallowed hard. Another flash of memory threatened to send the egg and cress back up. She focused on the pattern in the Oriental carpet and breathed through the nausea.

Lorraine's forehead wrinkled with worry at the silence. "Dearest, I didn't tell you then about his come-on, because I didn't want to hurt you. Surely after all this time, it doesn't matter, does it? If, as you claim, you didn't know he was a player, whatever were the two of you fighting about?" She took another nibble of her sandwich.

"Jeb was obsessed with making partner." Gwen heard the bitterness in her own voice, and it made her shudder. "He wanted me to forego a career and serve him hand and foot. He expected me to entertain his clients, which I was glad to do. But when he ordered me to flirt with his senior partners, I was uncomfortable. And then he made it clear he expected me to sleep with them on demand." Gwen voice shook with old fury.

"Sleep with them?" Lorraine dumped the rest of the sandwich on her plate. "That's outrageous." She extended a hand. "You're shaking, Gwen."

Gwen had blocked this from consciousness since Jeb's death. The trouble had started when they were first married. Too embarrassed to talk with her parents or to seek counseling, she had drunk more and more heavily, in a futile effort to deal with it. Over several years, she had doggedly pursued her own career preparation, intending to divorce Jeb once she'd established her own practice.

When she had completed the Ph.D., she joined a group practice at Clifton Springs, in connection with the drug and alcohol rehab there. In fact, her proximity to the program had led her to question her own drinking and to get sober. As for divorcing Jeb, he'd saved her the bother, by dying.

At Gwen's continued silence, Lorraine said, "I knew there was trouble between you and Jeb, but I had no idea it was that serious. I rather thought you hadn't known the dark side of marriage. I actually envied you, Gwen."

Gwen met Lorrain's gaze. "Jeb and I were married six years, and I started seeing the dark side in year one. Jeb lived on the edge. He loved risk, and he thought he was being oh-so-discreet with his affairs." She took a long swallow of lukewarm tea. Her cup clanged when she set it in the saucer. She flattened her hand against the arm of the chair to stop its shaking.

"Once he understood I was not going to support his career in quite the way he planned, we lived essentially separate lives. I agreed, for appearance's sake, to stay married until he made partner. In exchange, he left me alone. He only got nasty about my living Boston for so long, because his partners had a fit about it."

She'd never talked about Jeb's infidelity or his demands. She hadn't even allowed herself to think about it. *Why now? Why here?*

"Gwen," Lorraine said sharply, "answer me."

"I'm sorry, what?" She had missed the question.

"I said that's absurd. It's completely unlike you to let someone walk all over you. Why did you?"

Gwen had no defense. "I'm not proud of it," she said. "I was drinking when it started. When I realized what his game was, I saw how he was made. Putting my foot down was not going to change that. I chose to focus on the degree, on establishing my practice, and on staying sober. That's what I needed, and it was all I could handle." She tested her hands and found they had steadied themselves. She licked her lips and finished the story. "Then he played hero and died."

"Well," Lorraine said with a smug smile, "you won in the end." She lifted her cup in salute. "His death netted you a few million to play with. I'm glad I could help you spend three million this week, Gwen dearest."

I need to bring this to a close. She put on a smile. "Don't forget we're meeting in Paris next November."

Lorraine laughed. "We'll take Paris by storm."

"Listen, my good friend, you know my flight is at the crack of dawn, and I desperately need an early-to-bed. Can your driver take me to the train station now?"

"What? Why, of course. I wasn't watching the time." She pressed a button on the remote at her right hand. "You always were the sensible one, Gwen."

Relieved, Gwen smoothed a few feathers, "Today has been such fun, seeing your magnificent estate, first hand, and spending time with Alex and Chipper. How they've grown!"

Lorraine puffed out her chest. "They are the loves of my life." Her smile radiated a mother's pride.

She does love them, and this life seems to work for all three of them. "I'll see myself out. Don't get up." Gwen pasted on a smile and walked on shaky legs to her friend's chair. "I want to remember you sitting, just like this, in your exquisite library."

Chapter 16

"Justin met me at a meeting in London that night. We flew back together and got into Tompkins Falls at some ungodly hour. Thanks for meeting me so early." Gwen glanced at the clock over Lynnie's head. She and Deirdre had talked almost half an hour already, and it was not quite six thirty. The breakfast regulars would arrive in a few minutes.

Deirdre sat back, mug in hand, and shook her head. "I knew there was something—some unfinished business with Jeb. Dating all those Jeb-look-alikes, you were trying to 'screw Jeb' over and over, and I thought it was that you missed him terribly." She drained her mug. "You had yourself fooled, too."

"Yes, exactly. The pieces are still falling into place for me. It wasn't just the streak of dating last summer, before Peter. I remember the same pattern right after Jeb died. I guess I was recreating the past, wanting the outcome to be different. Why didn't I see that?"

"You had no idea before your talk with Lorraine?"

Gwen examined the backs of her hands and touched her empty ring finger. "Other than some odd discomfort when I mentioned Jeb to Peter, no, I had no clue." She shook her head. "During my marriage, I kept Jeb's affairs a secret from everyone. And I never breathed a word about the way he intended to exploit me in his bid for partnership in his law firm. I didn't want to believe it was happening, that my marriage was a sham and that my husband saw me as a whore."

"Don't say that, Gwen." Deirdre shuddered.

"That's how it felt. Drinking helped me block it all out. And when I stopped drinking, I kept it blocked out by putting all my energy into my practice." She blew out her breath. "And when he died, I buried all of it with him."

Deirdre's index finger traced a crack down the side of her mug.

"How does that saying go?" Gwen said, "'We're as sick as our secrets.' And I was keeping secrets from myself, along with everyone else."

"Being honest with yourself is sometimes hardest of all."

"But when I wasn't honest with Peter . . ." Gwen shifted in her chair and flung an arm over the back. "I can't blame that on Jeb."

"No, you're right. Still, I think what happened with Peter has everything to do with the bad habits you developed during your ill-fated marriage."

"I hope you can explain that, because I have no idea how they connect."

"Think about it." Deirdre leaned toward Gwen and tapped the table. "You kept your entire doctoral degree from Jeb. That's the antithesis of healthy spousal communication. When you're accustomed to operating that way in a marriage, it's a simple matter to keep your alcoholism and recovery off the table with someone you're dating, especially when you and Peter had so much else competing for your time and attention. And you knew it was a hot button for him." Deirdre opened her hands.

"So, you're saying, I had a history of hiding the truth, and Peter's attitude made it attractive to hide a big truth from him." She wrinkled her face. "Pretty screwed up."

"You wanted to have a good time with Peter, you said it yourself. But sooner or later, if you wanted a serious relationship, you had to get honest with each other. Peter expected honesty right from the start, and he practiced it right from the start. You never got there." She folded her hands. "Hello, heartache."

"I owe him such a huge amend." Gwen squeezed her eyes shut. "What am I saying? He'll never give me the chance to make it right."

"Well," Deirdre said as she stood up and stretched, "all I know is I'm out of coffee, and I need food. What can I get you?"

"My stomach needs something." She thought of the two finger sandwiches she'd wolfed down in Lorraine's library. "It's been more hours than I can calculate with this jet lag. How about a hot breakfast?"

Deirdre wove through the jumble of empty tables to the register, where she had a murmured conversation with Lynnie. Lynnie handed two menus to Deirdre, then shot a quick smile at Gwen and smoothed down her green-and-cream striped apron.

"Thanks, Lynnie," Gwen called, "for letting us in before you officially opened today."

"Couldn't let the two of you freeze out in your car, could I?"

"I owe you big time." Gwen blew her a kiss.

Instead of running along the willow path in the frigid rain, Peter dropped by the Bagel Depot after his shift. He took his bagel egg and cheese sandwich to a table as far away from Tony and Sam as he could manage.

Halfway through his meal, though, Sam sat in the chair across from him and slapped the morning paper on the table between them. Peter started. "Something I need to read?"

Sam pointed his finger at one of the Notices.

Peter skimmed it once, frowned, read it again and sat back. "Where did she get three million dollars?"

"And what is she planning to do with Cady's Point?" Tony asked as he dragged another chair to the table.

Peter sat back. "Well, that one I might be able to answer."

Deirdre rushed off to an early meeting, leaving Gwen alone at the table with their eggy dishes. Gwen stretched her back and wiggled her shoulders. She sipped her coffee until her headache finally faded away.

"Gwen, join Manda and me for one last cup of coffee, will you?" Joel asked.

"Hey, hi." She stood and gave him a hug. "I have news for you, so, sure. Where are you sitting?"

"Here," he said with a chuckle. "If you don't mind. All the tables are filled."

Gwen noticed the energetic crowd and wondered how she had missed the influx.

"Sure," Gwen agreed. "Let me take these dishes to—"

"I've got them," Manda cut her off. "Relax."

"I've never see this place so wild on a Tuesday morning," Joel remarked as he settled in the chair across from Gwen. "Are you jet-lagged? When I saw Haley a few days ago, she said you were on a shopping spree in London."

"She's right, as far as she knows."

"What were you really doing?"

Manda slipped into her chair and asked, "Doing where? London?"

"London."

"Justin was in London for a few days, too," Manda said. "Did you run into him?"

"As a matter of fact," Gwen told them both, "Justin and I met at an AA meeting last night near Victoria Station, and Lyssa and her boyfriend Kyle were there, too."

"My sister Lyssa?" Manda gasped. "You saw her? How does she look? Is she okay? Is the guy cute?"

"He's handsome and sexy, she's sober and well, and she looks like a million dollars. What is she doing in London, anyway?"

"She's got a post-doctoral fellowship at the university Justin teaches for," Manda said. "She's making TV spots about financial literacy for women. It's a big research project. Justin planned to spend some time with her, and I'm dying to hear what he has to say. Is he back, Joel?"

"He's back." Joel wore a secretive smile. Instead of making eye contact with Gwen, though, he glanced around the room.

Tease. Does he already know about the purchase of Cady's Point?

"From everything I've seen online, Lyssa's making a name for herself," Joel said, his face a picture of innocence.

"She never let on about any of that," Gwen told them. "Actually she talked mostly to Justin, and I chatted up the boyfriend Kyle. I like him. And I promise you, Manda, I will scour my memory for details once I've had a good night's sleep. Let's go to a meeting together this week and catch up."

"You're on."

"Thanks, Lynnie," Joel said when Lynnie brought two menus and two full mugs of coffee for them. "So," he said pointedly to Gwen, "did you see Lorraine?" Joel's wink confirmed that he knew the news.

"Do we have to talk about Lorraine?" Manda groaned and sipped her coffee.

Gwen leaned across the table, cupped her mouth, and whispered to Joel, "Did you set up this chance meeting so I had the honor of breaking it to her?"

"It's in the newspaper," he whispered back. "I wanted Manda to hear it from you."

"Why are you guys whispering?" Manda set down her coffee mug hard.

Gwen smiled at Joel and scooted her chair closer to Manda. "While I was in London with Lorraine, Manda," she said, enunciating each word, "I bought Cady's Point from her, with Justin's help, so you can build your holistic rehab center right where you want it."

Manda's face drained of color, and then her cheeks flamed. "Oh. My. God," she shrilled. She leapt from her chair and grabbed Gwen in a bone-crushing hug.

Conversation ceased at Lynnie's Chestnut Lake Café.

Friday afternoon, Rick gripped his Android, tapped in the phone number, and waited a few seconds to be sure he was alone. The house was quiet except for a faint conversation upstairs. Gwen's purchases from London had arrived, and Haley and Gwen were checking them out in Gwen's bedroom. A bubbling laugh—Haley's—made him smile.

He pressed 'send.' After two rings, a familiar voice answered, "Hello?"

"Yeah, uh, Peter, this is Rick Walker, Haley's friend from RPI." Rick held his breath.

A moment of silence, then a friendly, "Hey, Rick, what's up?"

Rick exhaled in relief. "Just in town for Thanksgiving, ate way too much pumpkin pie yesterday and wondered if you wanted to shoot some baskets?"

"Sure, come to my place and we'll walk over to the park."

Rick's face split in a grin. "Great, where's your place?"

"I'm renting that apartment Justin Cushman showed me the day you and I shot baskets. Great place. I owe you." Peter's voice had energy now.

Rick searched his memory. That was the day Justin met him on the way back to the car and told him he and his wife knew someone who might adopt the baby. He couldn't remember anything about an apartment that Justin showed Peter, but the street name popped into his head. "Lakeside Terrace, right next to the park?"

"Right."

"On my way, man." Rick pumped his fist in the air. *One shot to get them back together.*

Peter set the phone down and reached for a mug. With steaming coffee in hand, he stepped onto the gingerbread-embellished porch off his living room.

He never tired of the view. This afternoon Chestnut Lake was steel gray and still, not a breeze ruffling its metallic surface. Without his permission, his eyes focused on Gwen's property across the lake. He saw a car crawl away from the garage and disappear into the half-mile of woods between the house and the road.

With a noisy slurp, he speculated about Rick's agenda. The last thing he wanted was to talk about Gwen. He would *not* be pressured into meeting with her. But he'd like to know how Haley and Rick and their baby were doing. Haley was one special young woman, a lot like Bree.

Peter laughed, and a puff of vapor rose into the frigid air. *Maybe Rick just needs to get away from the women and do some guy stuff.* That suited him. He hadn't shot baskets since he quit the team a month ago. *Stupid ass move.*

When Tony had come to the table at the Bagel Depot last Tuesday, Peter half-hoped they'd talk about him coming back to the team, but the conversation had been all about Cady's Point and speculation about Gwen intention for the land.

One short, cold minute on the porch in his thick navy CUSE sweatshirt was enough. Back inside, he closed and locked the porch door, placed his coffee mug in the sink and began the hunt for his basketball gear.

After ransacking the guest room with no luck, he turned to the entryway. He tore apart the hall closet and found his sneakers buried under his duffle bag, behind his hanging clothes. He remembered stuffing them there the night he'd walked off the court.

He hauled the bag to the laundry area off the guest bathroom, flipped up the lid of the washer, unzipped the duffle and pinched his nose shut with two fingers. He upended the duffle so the contents spilled into the tub. Shorts, sweat-stained T-shirts, wrinkled towels, three pungent pairs of socks. Still holding his nose, he splashed in detergent and bleach and slammed the lid shut. He dialed the temperature to hot and the cycle to extra soak. He stood a moment listening to the water gurgle into the tub. He'd wear sweats and the sneakers to go with Rick to the park.

I wish the rest of my problems could be fixed that easy.

As soon as he let go of his nose, the smell was on him again. How had he not noticed the reeking duffle bag in all the times he'd used that closet? He flung the duffle out the porch door and left it to air. If he was lucky, the stink might be gone by spring.

He slammed the door shut and twisted the deadbolt. *God, Shaughnessy, you really lost it last month.*

"How is the baby?" Peter asked. They'd exhausted small talk about sports on the walk to the court. Rick hadn't said a word about Gwen, so Peter relaxed, pretty sure Rick wasn't here on a mission to get them back together. Fleeting disappointment followed that thought, but he pushed it away.

"Thanks for asking." Rick bounced the ball a few times and tossed it to Peter. "He's getting tall. We just got new pictures from the Hahns. His hair is coming in blond like mine, and he'll have Haley's dark brown eyes. He's healthy, and things are going well for them as a family."

Peter spun the ball on one finger. "You know, I'm glad you and Haley followed through with the adoption. I was worried both of you would drop out of college, and that would have been a crime."

"Yeah. I still think it was the right decision, even though I've second-guessed myself a lot. Thanks for helping me think it through last summer."

Peter shrugged it off. "How's Haley?

"The pregnancy set her back some, but she'll be all right."

"Will she go back to Albany in the spring?"

"She's been to campus to register for spring, but all her spring courses are online, like the ones she's taking now. She'll stay with Gwen at least until summer. It's good for both of them right now."

Peter flinched at the mention of Gwen's name. He put the discussion back on Haley. "So, Haley's doing okay? She doesn't feel like she's destroyed her life or anything, does she?"

"Definitely not. She had a rough time, and she handled it well and grew up a lot. She learned from it." Rick took a deep breath all the way to his toes. "For one thing, she knows not to drink ever again."

Peter heard the change in Rick's tone. There was an agenda. He headed it off. "Let's shoot some."

He drove toward the basket, laid up a clean shot, and stepped out of the way. "Show me what you've got."

Rick caught the rebound and pounded down the court. Past the imaginary foul line, he turned, and fired the ball. It whispered through the net.

"Someone's been practicing," Peter said.

He grabbed the ball. Rick moved in to block his shot. Peter sidestepped, dribbled, and missed a simple lay-up.

They worked up a sweat, and Peter felt better than he had in weeks. But he was winded and too proud to admit it. The kid, on the other hand, was as fresh as he'd been at the start. "Let's see you put in six in a row." He stood off to one side and bent forward with his hands braced on his knees.

To his surprise, Rick did not head for the base of the backboard and pace off the distance to the foul line. Instead, he settled into his stance exactly where Peter would have, bounced the ball three times and put one through the net. "Good start." Peter put his hands together.

Rick grinned as he retrieved the ball. He returned to the foul line, bounced the ball twice, and sank another. He missed the third but put in the next three.

"You're killing me, Rick. What are you doing, playing every night?"

Rick gave him a knuckle bump as they changed places. "I'm mentoring a few of the freshmen. We play a quick game at noon. 'Bonding,' Professor Singh calls it. And if no one else shows up, I shoot foul shots by myself for the half hour."

"Keep it up, bro."

Rick smiled at the praise. "Your turn."

Peter swallowed his anxiety. After retrieving the ball he did a warm-up lap. When he settled at the foul line and hoisted the ball, it danced around the rim and dropped through the net. The success kept him going. After he made four out of six, they took up the game again.

Winded after ten fast-paced minutes, they cooled down with a few friendly shots from under the rim.

"I notice you don't pace off the foul line anymore," Peter said.

"Yeah, that disappeared when I realized I had no control over anything." Rick chuckled.

"That's a big change for a guy like you."

"Had to happen." Rick shrugged. "Being a control freak is just a waste of energy if you don't have any control. Know what I mean?"

Peter knew the right answer was to grin and agree, but the kid had just shot an arrow into his Achilles heel. He had no control over Bree, over Gwen, over the past, maybe over anything. He passed the ball to Rick. "School's going well?"

He listened with half an ear while Rick rattled on about his courses and his research. "I could graduate next

December, but I'll probably roll right into a masters program for another year and a half."

"You can afford it?" Peter asked.

"I'd get a research assistantship and live cheap, like I do now, probably intern at a couple of companies so I have a good basis for choosing a job."

"Weren't you thinking about a Ph.D.?"

"I'm still considering it. Either way I'd need the masters. I have time to decide."

"How does Haley feel about it?"

"About . . ."

Peter stood up straight and tucked the ball under his arm. "I guess I'm asking about her plans. They got derailed by this pregnancy, and I want to know if she's getting back on her feet."

"She's changed, just like I have. I mean she's still planning to get her undergraduate degree in botany, but she's turning more to her art. It makes her happy. She has a studio set up at Gwen's.

"Haley and I were a lot alike at the beginning of college. We focused on one option that we believed would get us through and land a halfway decent job. I was lucky to have a mentor at RPI who pushed me to try different options. Gwen has encouraged Haley to get out and talk to people about their jobs and what they recommend for someone with her talents and interests. I'm mostly standing on the sidelines encouraging her."

"She didn't get much from her folks," Peter mumbled.

"No, and they stopped paying her tuition. I guess it's okay to tell you the Hahns awarded her money for tuition. Gwen has picked up everything else. Haley's still trying to figure out the next right thing for her, but I know she's going to be okay."

"She's got a lot going for her."

"She does. She's wicked smart. Not logical like an engineer, but put her around plants and she's on top of thousands of details. She knows everything about flowers, fruits, and vegetables. And she's a very talented graphic artist.

"Gwen's the one that helped her deal with this pregnancy, not Haley's mother or her father. Haley's dad is an alcoholic, too, just like Gwen and probably Haley, too."

Peter didn't want to hear him talk about Haley as an alcoholic. She was nineteen and had gotten pregnant one night when she'd had too much to drink. Big deal. He slammed the ball into the pavement. Rick jumped. The ball bounced high above their heads. Peter caught it in one hand.

Rick kept talking. "Haley's dad has cleaned up his act now, but he was a terrible father when Haley was a child. And Haley's mother is in her own, sick world. Haley is lucky to have Gwen in her life. They're like mother and daughter."

Peter held on to the ball. *What's the agenda: Gwen the saint or Haley the teenage alcoholic?* He turned to confront Rick. "Why the fuck are you calling Haley an alcoholic? I thought you said she doesn't drink and the one night when she drank all the eggnog and got pregnant was almost a fluke."

Rick rose to his full height, so his gray eyes were even with Peter's. With a calm voice, he replied, "Haley says, based on her experience that night and a few other times before that, she can't drink safely. Why would I question that?"

Peter's jaw clenched with anger. When Rick didn't back down, he lowered his gaze to the cracks in the surface of the basketball court. He bounced the ball twice and then captured it under his arm. "So, what, Haley's going to AA now?"

"Yeah, she really likes the meetings in Tompkins Falls. She's been working on the twelve steps with another young woman. She feels better about herself. I like seeing the changes in her since summer. She's confident, and she laughs a lot more." He laughed softly. "To be honest, I'm falling in love with her all over again."

Peter hoped that was the end of the AA talk. "You going to get married?"

"We both want to finish school before we make another major commitment. That's at least a couple of years out. I still help with her business, and we're planning a kayaking trip in the Adirondacks next summer."

"Sounds good, man. I wish you well." Peter figured the next topic would be him getting back together with Gwen.

"Thanks. What about you? What are you planning for the new year?"

Peter snorted. "I don't know." He glanced at the cloud cover and felt himself tear up. "Regroup, I guess."

Rick nodded but didn't comment.

Peter shivered and gestured toward Lakeside Terrace. "I probably need a hot shower and some supper before my shift tonight. Listen, I'm glad you called. It was good to be back on the court. I gave up the team, and this is the first I've shot baskets in a while."

Rick blinked with concern.

Peter had said more than he intended. "Listen, say hi to Haley for me."

"Sure." Rick opened his hands as if he'd given up. "Good to see you, Peter." He walked off the court and held the gate open for Peter, but closed it when he saw that Peter was not behind him.

Peter listened for the rattle of Rick's old car. Instead, a black hybrid rolled silently down Lakeside Terrace. When it turned right onto the highway, he walked to the imaginary foul line and fired toward the net. The ball bounced from one side of the rim to the other and flopped to the court.

Gwen had just started down the stairs when she heard the kitchen door shut. She walked quietly down the remaining steps.

"Where did you go?" Haley's voice carried up to her.

"Just out," Rick hedged. "I picked up some of that bread you like." The loaf smacked on the counter.

"You're all sweaty."

"I shot a few baskets."

"Did you see Peter?"

"Yeah, as a matter of fact."

"How's he doing? Did he ask about Gwen?"

"He asked about you and the baby, and he wanted me to say hi."

"So . . . what did you guys talk about?"

Gwen hung back in the doorway to the kitchen.

"Besides you?" Rick grinned and kissed Haley. When he tried to hug her, she pushed him away playfully and held her nose.

"I need a shower, I know. We talked about guy stuff. Mainly we shot baskets. Did you know he quit the team?"

"No," Gwen gasped. "The team meant everything to him."

"Uh . . ." Rick turned toward her, his eyes narrow with guilt. "Sorry, Gwen, I shouldn't have called him, I know. But I like Peter, and I wanted to know how he is and to shoot some baskets, if he was around."

"I don't mind you calling Peter and shooting baskets with him, but from that guilty look on your face, I'm thinking you were trying to get me and Peter back together."

Rick hung his head. Haley slid off her stool and stood beside him with her arm around his waist. "We both love you, Gwen."

"And I love you both, too." Anger boiled in her chest. "But do not—Do Not—"

"I own this, Gwen." Rick's cheeks flamed. "If you want me to leave . . ."

"No," Haley shouted.

"Haley," Rick cautioned her. He came over to Gwen and said quietly, "I was wrong, and I apologize. I think you and Peter are right for each other, and I wanted to give it a shot."

Gwen relented and asked, "How is he, really?"

"He's a mess. When I asked him his plans for the new year, he had tears in his eyes and said he was probably just going to regroup. I think he's really hurting. He didn't say why he quit the team, but it can't be good."

"No, I'm sure it's not."

"So, I'm praying for him."

Gwen glanced at him and averted her eyes when she saw the depth of his concern. "I think that's all we can do," she agreed.

"So, it's okay if I stay? I won't interfere again, I promise."

Gwen hugged him. "Go get that shower. If you need some exercise later, I want you to help me bring down Dad's old leather chair from the attic."

"You got it." He pounded up the stairs.

Gwen raised her eyebrows at Haley.

"I knew nothing about it until right now." She picked up a recipe card from the island. "So, is this the old English recipe we're making for supper?"

Gwen busied herself filling the teakettle. Haley watched in silence, except to flick the edge of the recipe card with one finger.

"The recipe is nothing special," Gwen answered as she smacked the kettle down on the stove. "Lorraine and I ate in a pub one night, and I loved the stew, so I pumped them about the ingredients. Turns out they use lamb, whole cloves and bay leaf. Plus the usual."

"What's the usual? If you don't mind my asking."

Gwen chose fresh produce from of the refrigerator and tossed it on the counter next to the stove. "Root vegetables—potatoes, carrots, parsnips. And, he didn't say, but they added kale or spinach or something, so I got a bag of chopped kale, too." She surveyed the ingredients and returned for the package of lamb.

"Sounds healthy."

"And delicious." Gwen crossed the room and stretched for the Dutch oven on a high shelf in the pantry.

"Can I help?"

"Want to be the chef, and I'll coach?"

"No, I want you be the chef, and I'll chop and fetch and stir."

"Sounds great." Gwen managed a laugh.

"You're still mad, aren't you?" Haley probed.

"I'm upset at what Rick said. That Peter quit the team. It's a really bad sign. I'm scared for him."

For three days after his workout with Rick, Peter debated moving back to Syracuse. He had always felt like he belonged in Syracuse. He'd been trying his best for six months to fit in here, but he was stymied.

Somehow, he'd scored the perfect bachelor pad in Tompkins Falls, but now he had no one to share it with. He'd thrown away his relationship with Gwen because he hated drunks. He'd screwed up with the team because he hated drunks. And he'd driven Bree away with his bitterness about how much he hated drunks. Sam was right about it being a poison.

I'll give Hank a call and sound him out. Peter glanced at the clock. It was already ten o'clock, too close to his shift. *Tomorrow. He'll give me the straight story about possibly rejoining the force*.

He stretched his arms overhead and laughed in surprise. It had been nearly twenty years since he'd done that in his own house, regardless of where he lived. In his childhood home, the rooms had been just seven feet high, and the day came—long before he reached his full height—that he could touch the ceiling. He'd never measured, but the ceilings in the Lakeside Terrace apartment looked more like nine or ten feet. *Room to grow*. He frowned at the rogue thought. *Yeah, like anyone can grow after they hit adulthood*.

Another thought intruded. *I still think about drunks the way I did when I lived there, too, back in the old neighborhood*. Not everyone thought the same way. Joel Cushman was a sober drunk, and he was one of the most respected people in Tompkins Falls. With good reason. *Even I respect Joel.* He reflected for a moment. Not all drunks were the same.

Muffled chimes called to him from the coffee table. He found his phone under his sweatshirt and squinted at the caller ID window. It was a Syracuse number, and the exchange was the same as his old precinct. "Hello?"

Someone said in a shaky voice, "It's Bree, Peter. Please help me."

"Where are you, Bree?" She sounded panicky and desperate.

"In jail."

"Where exactly?"

"In South Onondaga."

Peter pressed his eyes shut. That was his old, drug-infested work beat.

"I wasn't drinking, I promise," Bree babbled into the silence, "but I was with them and Fiona was drunk and ran a red light and hit a—"

"Are you hurt?" he barked. They could sort the rest out later.

"No. The others were taken to the hospital, and there was a ton of property damage. Peter, I can't do this anymore. I can't do it by myself. Peter, please come."

"What's the charge, and what's your bail?"

"Um." She coughed a few times. "He said Protective Custody, and it's . . ." She paused as if she were asking someone for the answer. "Five hundred."

"Who brought you in?"

"He says he knows you. His name is Hank."

"Is he right there?"

"He's across the room. Did you want to talk to him?"

"When I get there, if he's around." Peter walked with the phone into his bedroom and peered out the window.

"Do you have to work tonight?" Bree asked.

"They'll understand." *If they don't, I'm fired.*

Snow had been falling about an inch an hour, but the sheen on the glass of the streetlamp told him ice had mixed in. "It may take a couple of hours, because the roads are bad."

"Oh god, I'm sorry, Peter. Please be careful. And . . ."

"What, honey?"

"I love you, Peter."

"I love you, too, Bree. I'm on my way."

"They were in this precinct trying to score some heroin," Hank told Peter. "It's cheap and it's sold everywhere on these streets. Honestly, if they'd gone on to do the drugs tonight, it would have ended much worse than her friend slamming into a minibus full of kids coming back from a basketball game. If Bree were my sister, I'd get her out of this city, away from this shit. The crowd she's running with . . ." Hank shook his head. "She says she doesn't even want to hang with them, but she's going along for the ride."

"We tried having her stay with me, and I blew it. I got all fired up about the DWIs we're bringing in, and I guess I scared her with how angry I got."

"I've seen you do that," Hank said, and put a strong hand on Peter's shoulder. "Not very often, but enough to know it's all about your dad." Hank paused. "Maybe you need some counseling. A lot of adult children of alcoholics do. Sounds like it's causing a problem with Bree and, I'm thinking, maybe on the job, too. Is it?"

Peter nodded in defeat. "I wanted to ask you about coming back here."

Hank stepped back and shook his head. "You know I want you back on the force. Everyone would say the same. But you get so emotionally involved with the kids on these streets, that you take risks. That's how you got shot. Buddy, you almost died that night. I was there. I know."

"Maybe I could study for detective or—"

"No," Hank stopped him. "You'd be great, but it's not possible right now. The way things are, they'd have you right here on the street again. You probably remember I had just made detective when I was put on temporary assignment here. That was two years ago, and they still need me here. This is top priority right now, and you and I are highly qualified for it."

Peter's eyes shifted to the scene down the hall—jacked up teens in handcuffs shuffling through the door to lockup. He thought of the late-night, pickup basketball games in Tompkins Falls with Stretch and his buddies. *I'm doing more good in Tompkins Falls.*

"Sometimes," Hank said, his gruff voice suddenly wistful, "I dream about moving to a smaller city, like you did, with my wife and her parents. Torie and I want to start a family, and she's scared to death I'm going to take a bullet some night."

Peter searched his friend's brown eyes. He suggested, "Think about coming to Tompkins Falls." *But I have to clean up my act, so they don't think any buddy of mine is a loser.*

Commotion by the desk caught Hank's attention. "Gotta go, pal. My advice? Get Bree someplace safe, away from her so-called friends, and get her some treatment. Maybe there's a rehab that also has help for families, for you." As he walked away, he called back over his shoulder, "Keep in touch, Peter. I mean it."

Chapter 17

As Peter trudged up the stairs ahead of Bree, he encountered an empty bottle of cheap gin. He set it upright at the far edge of the step and glanced back at his sister.

"Yeah, I saw it," Bree muttered.

They neared the landing for Bree's floor, and Peter tuned into the sounds from the neighboring apartments. In one unit, a woman slurred her words and a man mocked her in a loud voice. In another unit, a television broadcast the grunts and jeers of a wrestling match. Toward the end of the hall, a baby cried fretfully, with no accompanying sounds of cosseting or comforting.

His stomach clenched. *She needs people who encourage her to finish school and make a career.* He steeled himself not to get into it yet; this stinking hallway was not the place for that discussion.

When she reached the landing, Bree brushed by him. She fumbled with her key, tried, and failed to open her front door.

"Take your time," he said.

She glanced back at him, her forehead wrinkled with worry.

He identified the smell then—marijuana. A glance at the third-floor landing showed a film of smoke hanging by the door of the unit directly above Bree's.

He kept his voice light when he asked, "Anything beside pot go on up there?"

She nodded and turned back to her task. Her hands shook so badly the keys rattled. Finally, she lowered her head in defeat and handed him the key ring.

Peter opened her door and waved for her to go in first. "Let's get you warm and fed," he told her. He closed the door behind them and shot the deadbolt home, then shrugged out of his coat.

Bree hung up their coats without a word. She sniffled, and Peter wondered if she were crying, but she had turned her back to him.

He nudged the thermostat up to seventy degrees before saying, "Bree, I worry about you living here. Does it bother you?"

She didn't answer, but when she set her boots on a plastic mat, and he saw tears on her cheeks. He reached for her, but she shied away and moved into the kitchen.

"I love you, Bree, and I hate that you're in the middle of people using booze and drugs."

"I know. Me, too." Her voice quavered. She opened the refrigerator, and he couldn't see her face behind the door.

Peter blew out his frustration and examined the humble living room. The hand-me-down furniture was in good repair, and the bare wood floor was clean. He recognized a rocking chair from their house growing up and a marble-top table he'd crashed into one night when his father had backhanded him for no reason. His hand went unconsciously to the spot behind his right temple where he'd had a goose egg for a week when he was eight. A few years later, he'd grown bigger than his father, and there were no more encounters with furniture. Then his father died of liver failure, and the rest of them—their mother, Bree, and him—got on with things, peacefully.

The blue slipcover on Bree's sofa was neat and spotless. "I'll sleep on the sofa tonight," he offered. He hoped it wasn't the sofa from home that his father had peed on.

"Thanks. There's an extra pillow and stuff."

He moved one foot into the kitchen. "Can we talk?"

Bree closed the refrigerator without having taken anything out. She raised her eyes to the ceiling—or maybe to heaven. Peter wondered if she believed in God. He did. Mostly. Not that he prayed much, and rarely about anything personal.

"I think if I eat first, I'll stop shaking. Okay if I make us tuna sandwiches?"

"Sure. Thanks, honey." He had never before called her honey. He didn't know why he said it now, but the effect was dramatic.

Bree turned and reached for him. "I need you to help me," she choked out. "I need—"

He closed the distance and drew her to him. "I'm here, Bree," he rasped. "We'll figure this out."

She sobbed, great heaving sobs while he held her and rocked her. *God if she's not praying to you, I am for her*. He felt a few tears on his own cheeks, and his chest ached.

In time, her breathing quieted. "Are you going to yell?" she asked in a meek voice.

"Probably. I'm that upset. But I'm going to help you. Give me a chance."

She nodded against his chest and tightened her arms around his waist.

He stroked her back and told her again, his voice strong this time, "We'll figure this out."

Finally, she drew in a deep cleansing breath and let it out. When she snuffled her nose, he said, "Go find some tissues. I'll make the sandwiches."

"Thanks."

Before she slipped away from him, he cradled her face with his hands and planted a kiss on her forehead. She gave him a little smile but made no comment.

Once the bathroom door closed behind her, Peter heard her blow her nose a few times, and then the shower started up.

In her compact kitchen, he filled the teakettle and set it on high. He found multi-grain bread in the freezer. A blue flowered cover disguised an old toaster. Next to it was a teapot under a matching cozy.

Cans of tuna stood three high in a free-standing shelving unit, with a few other groceries—taped-shut boxes of cereal and crackers, cans of fruits and vegetables, three twelve-packs of bottled water, open boxes of tea, a jar of peanut butter and a sticky container of honey on a chipped saucer. No ants or roaches. The place was immaculate.

He opened the refrigerator in search of mayonnaise and lettuce. The expiration date on the mayonnaise was next spring, and the lettuce and tomatoes were fresh. In a drawer next to the stove, he found a cheap, manual can opener and set to work.

As he had for years at home, he assembled two sandwiches apiece, cut them on the diagonal, and plated them on Bree's chipped, aqua Fiesta ware. He grabbed two glasses from the cupboard, with the intention of filling them with tap water, but stopped. With a backward glance at the shelves, he wondered if Bree always used bottled water. He set the glasses aside and got down two mugs for tea.

The teakettle whistled. As he finished filling the pot, the doorbell rang.

"Damn." Thanks to the whistling teakettle, someone knew Bree was home.

He eyed the door, his mouth set in a grim line. Bree opened the bathroom door a crack.

They made eye contact, and she shook her head. She wore a towel wrapped around her curves, and her hair was swathed in another. One black curl escaped the towel, and a rivulet of water tracked down her cheek onto her jaw. *God, she's a beautiful young woman.* He'd do anything to protect her.

His took a step toward the door.

Bree's loud whisper implored him. "No!" With a determined face, she rushed the door.

The doorbell rang again, and a deep male voice called in a seductive tone, "Bree, baby, come on up and have some with me. We'll have a good time, baby, you and me."

Bree had beaten her brother to the door, and she turned to face him, her back braced against the hard metal. Her bare shoulder covered the deadbolt.

Peter's fists bunched as he came within an inch of her. His jaw was rigid. "Step aside, Bree."

"No," she hissed.

Peter worked his hand behind her waist onto the doorknob.

"Don't open it," Bree ordered through clenched teeth.

Their gazes locked.

"He'll go away." She placed her shaking hands on his chest and tried to push him back, but he stood like a rock wall.

She whispered. "He's high, and there's already someone with him upstairs. I could hear high-heeled shoes above me when I was in the bathroom. He'll leave, Peter."

The man's voice wheedled. "You'll be sorry, baby. I'll make you sorry next time."

"I'll kill him!" Peter hissed, and his eyes flashed with fury.

"Please, Peter, let it go," Bree begged. "I can't take any more tonight."

The man's hard-soled shoes clip-clopped up the stairs. Peter's hand relaxed on the doorknob.

When the door above them shut, Bree's head dropped back, and she gave a shaky exhale. "Help me get out of this nightmare, Peter."

"You need to be gone from here."

"Yes."

"We can drive tonight through the storm. We'll be all right, Bree."

"No, not tonight. You slid all the way from the police station, and I could hear ice pellets on the bathroom window just now. We need to stay here tonight, and we'll go in the morning."

He squeezed her arms. "Dry your hair while I set the table."

Bree texted through their meal, claiming that her friends were worried about her arrest.

Peter stayed quiet and ate his two sandwiches.

Her texts shortened. Finally, she turned off her phone.

"Thank you," Peter told her.

Bree propped her elbows on the table and rubbed her forehead with her fingertips. "I need new friends who don't drink and drug. I met some girls my age in AA, and I want to keep going to meetings so I can get my life together with their help."

"Bree, you're not an alcoholic," Peter retorted.

"I am," she snapped.

His fist hit the table, and he cringed at his own display of temper. *Keep it together. Let her talk.* "I'm sorry, Bree. Please tell me what you mean."

She drew in a deep breath and sat tall. "You know, Peter when I go to an AA meeting and I say I'm an alcoholic, no one says 'No you're not,' or 'You're too young,' or 'I forbid you to be one.'"

He winced. He had really believed that was the right way to handle it. Bree had always looked up to him and tried to follow his lead.

Bree continued. "They say 'Hi, Bree.' They say, 'Come along with us, we have a solution.' And they're living good, useful, sober lives, like I want to. Peter, I need that. If I move in with you, I *have* to go to AA, and I'm done sneaking behind your back to do it."

"Don't tell me, when you've gone out at night at my place, you've been going to AA meetings?"

"I just told you." Her mouth was set in defiance.

"How—when—why didn't you tell me?"

She threw up her hands and mouthed, "Hello."

He scooted his chair closer to the table and leaned toward her. "Honey, please tell me. When did all this start?"

"In middle school. What matters is, it got really bad last winter. That's when I couldn't control my drinking anymore and started doing drugs, too, trying to control it." Bree held herself tall and still. "I called Dad's old friend Paddy O'Donnell. Paddy's been sober a long time, and he took me to some AA meetings and introduced me to some women who were really nice. But I didn't meet anyone my age, and I thought it wasn't for me."

Peter's mouth was rigid as she talked, and his eyes flashed.

Bree took a steadying breath and continued, "My friends kept pushing me to party, and I didn't know how to say no. They were the only friends I had. And you've seen this building. I don't want to hang around here, alone, after work. That asshole upstairs won't give me any peace." Tears spilled over. "I just can't make it work for myself here."

"Answer me this, Bree," Peter shouted, "what drugs are going on upstairs besides pot?"

"Why? Are you going to arrest them?" Bree snapped. She covered her face and shook her head. "I'm sorry. You yell and I turn into a smart-mouthed teenager. Please try not to yell."

Peter's anger deflated. He sat back and studied the gutsy young woman across the table. His heart went out to her, and he hated that he had made it harder for her, through his own ignorance. He tapped her arm. "I'm sorry, too. This whole thing has blown me away. I'm not going to arrest anyone. I just want to know more about what you're using and how much and why and where it's taken you."

When she didn't answer right away, he glanced at the marble top table. "I can't believe, after all Dad's shit, you'd let this happen to you."

Bree uncovered her face and followed the direction of his gaze. She rested her hands on the edge of the table. Her voice carried the full force of her frustration. "I hated Dad, too, you know. I didn't *choose* to be an alcoholic. I didn't *let myself* be one. It's a disease and it's inherited. You're lucky, Peter, you could have been one, too."

His head swiveled toward her, and he gave it right back to her, "That's a cop-out."

"No." Her hands slapped the table. "It's reality. I have the same fucking disease Dad did, and I don't want it to destroy me, too. I need help. That's why I called Paddy O'Donnell, and he knew what I was talking about because he's got the same disease. But he's sober, and has been for a long, long time."

Peter studied the faded blue tablecloth. *That name, Paddy O'Donnell. How do I know that name?*

"Peter, he tried so hard to help Dad, but Dad couldn't ever stay sober. I can't stay sober by myself, but with AA I think I can." She said it with hope in her voice. "And I want to try. I really want to get out of here and live with you, Peter, but I need you to support my recovery."

When he turned his face to his sister, it was weighed down with pain and guilt. "Why didn't you tell me all this before?"

"When I was at your place I didn't dare tell you I was sneaking off to a meeting, because I was afraid you'd throw me out."

"I never—" He stopped. *What would I have done?* He thought back to the white car that discharged Bree at his place one night during her first visit. His eyes shifted to the twelve-packs of water on the pantry shelves. He belatedly registered the fact there was no wine or beer in her refrigerator, no bottles of booze under the sink or in the cupboard.

His dry laugh was directed at himself. "So when that woman drove you home, you hadn't been listening to Irish music over a pint at the pub?"

"No, I'd been to a beginners' AA meeting. And the last time I stayed with you, I went to two more meetings. Peter, there are young people in AA in Tompkins Falls. College kids and—" She snapped her mouth shut.

"And?"

She sat back. "I can't tell you people's names and stuff. It's anonymous."

He cocked his head. "Which means I would know some of the people you saw at the meetings?"

Bree averted her gaze.

"Like Tony Pinelli and Gwen, maybe?"

Bree nodded.

Peter balled his fists, galled that the people he'd turned his back on were the ones helping Bree, when he'd been too high and mighty to help her himself. *God, I've been so wrong.*

Bree waited for his fists to relax before speaking. "Peter, they're really great to me. They know how hard it is, and they're always wanting to help or to say something kind or encourage me."

Peter picked at something stuck on the tablecloth, jam maybe. "And it never occurred to you I might want to help you too?"

She scowled at him. "Whenever I tried to talk to you about my drinking, you yelled at me. Remember, you 'forbid' me to be an alcoholic. What were you thinking?"

He flashed on a scene at the chief's dinner-dance: Sam sitting across the table from him, goading, "You forbid her? How'd that work for you?" And he'd stupidly answered that Bree hadn't bothered him with any more drunken escapades after that. His stomach clenched, and he sucked down air to keep from upchucking the tuna sandwich.

"So it wasn't that you stopped drinking and drugging after I ordered you to stop? It's that you stopped talking to me about it?"

"Yeah," Bree confirmed, her face filled with misery and regret. "Whenever I brought it to up, you just kept talking about Dad and how much you hated him and how much he screwed up our lives. I wish you'd just forget about Dad and get real about how awful this is for me. I wish you'd learn what alcoholism and addiction are really about and help me get well."

He met her eyes, expecting to see reproach. Instead he saw a scared young woman, her forehead knit with worry, her mouth trembling, her hands flat on the table to keep them from shaking.

Frightened by her pain, Peter twisted in his chair and saw again the neat, spare living room, so much like their home growing up. "Paddy O'Donnell"—he remembered now—"was the baker that used to bring us loaves of bread, even after Dad died. And a pound of butter sometimes?" He glanced at his sister.

Bree nodded. Her shaking lessened, and her voice had strength when she said, "He told me he beat his wife one night, so bad it almost killed her."

Peter hung his head as he thought of his parents' fights.

"After that," Bree went on, "she left, with their four kids, to live with her sister in Oswego. That was his bottom. He was my age now when that happened."

Peter's head jerked back to her. "Paddy was twenty-six when he beat his wife nearly to death?" His heart raced.

Bree nodded. "He found AA, and they helped him get sober. He never drank again."

This time, when Peter glanced at the living room furniture, the years fell away. He saw the gentle, young man who came by with loaves warm from the oven and a smile for them all. "He must have been just a few years sober when he started coming by. I remember, he'd leave the loaves on the kitchen table, stop in the living room to ask how the homework was going, then head upstairs and roust Dad out of bed."

Or try to. When Daniel Shaughnessy was well enough to get up, the two men talked out on the back porch; when he wasn't, they talked in the bedroom. "Paddy was so sincere. He came back again and again, but Dad never got it." Peter asked Bree, "Did she ever come back? Paddy's wife?"

Bree shook her head. "He sees two of his kids. One of the others is in jail. And the oldest died last year from a heroin overdose." Irony twisted her smile. "It's funny; that kid died a couple days before I called Paddy. His name was Danny, like our dad."

The reality made Peter's head spin. *Danny O'Donnell. Daniel Shaughnessy. Both dead from the disease Bree has, but Paddy has it, too, and he's alive and okay.* He sucked air deep into his lungs and whooshed it out again.

Bree's eyes brightened. "Paddy told me he had the strongest feeling, when Danny died, that someone would call him, only him, for help. So he didn't drink, even though the pain was killing him. He carried his phone on him all the time and kept it turned on. I got him when he was sliding loaves in the oven, and he dropped the board and the loaves on the floor, and he talked to me."

"So you called him a year ago? You've been struggling all this time? And I just made it worse." It wasn't a question this time. His voice was thick with pain and self-censure.

Bree nodded. "I think it's cool Paddy could help me, even though he couldn't help his son Danny or our dad. I owe it to Paddy to make this work for me. And maybe someday I can help someone else. I owe him that."

Peter's face relaxed and he gave a hollow laugh, "We owe him a few loaves of bread, too, don't we?"

Bree reached across the table to touch his hand. Her gaze probed his. "Does that mean you're starting to get it?"

He nodded. Shame caught in his throat and made it hard to get the words out. "I'll do anything that will help you get well. You mean more to me than anyone or anything. Tell me what I can do."

Hope lit her eyes. "I need you to be my big brother. Help me get into a rehab and figure out how to get my life on the right track—school and work and friends and finances. Help me get out of this mess." She gestured above them. Her voice broke. "I want to be someone you're proud of. Someone I'm proud of." Tears spilled down cheeks and dropped off her nose. "I need AA. And I need you with me, helping me to get through this really bad time." She choked. "Please, Peter."

Peter's chair clattered to the floor as he shoved back from the table. He gathered her into a tight hug. "We'll do this together, Bree. It will be okay," he told her, his voice muffled by her hair. "God, forgive me."

Peter's chest convulsed with a sob, and he cried the tears he'd held back for the thirteen years he'd lived with his drunk of a father. "We'll be okay," he promised.

"Pinelli, you seem confused," Joel teased. He took another bite of bagel and surveyed the noisy dining room of the Bagel Depot. At every fourth table, he spotted someone from the Early Risers meeting. *Smart business move, hosting the meeting in the back room.*

"Confused? Try blown away." Tony pocketed his phone. "That call I just took? That was Peter Shaughnessy asking about a rehab for his sister."

"Holy…" *Who convinced him and how?* "What happened?"

"All I know is she called him from jail last night. Protective Custody."

"From Syracuse? That must have been a hell of a drive."

"I give him points for finally trying to help his sister."

"It took some courage to call you," Joel pointed out.

Tony grunted and reached for his mug.

"Bro, what's up?" Sam asked them. "Join you?"

"Just the man we want to see," Tony said. "Set your food down, and I'll pull over a chair for you."

Joel made room on the tabletop for Sam's meal. He set Sam's empty tray on the window ledge with a stack of others.

"That's a dry everything bagel, isn't it?" Sam pointed an accusing finger at Joel's plate.

At Joel's answering smile, Sam snorted, "You a martyr or something?" He sat on the chair Tony had scrounged for him and picked up his breakfast sandwich special.

"Your partner," Tony informed him as he settled back in place, "is putting his sister in rehab."

"So that's where he went," Sam mumbled around a mouthful of food.

"Ma says don't talk with your mouth full. What do you know?"

"He called in right before shift." Sam paused for a noisy slurp of coffee. "Said he had a family emergency. I figured it was something with Bree."

Brows furrowed, the three ate without speaking, until Joel asked, "Which rehab?" He brushed seeds and crumbs from his elegant, manicured hands and whisked them up with his napkin.

"I told him Clifton Springs was the best, as far as I was concerned. Gave him a few phone numbers."

"That's a one-eighty turnaround for Peter," Joel said.

The brothers nodded and chewed in silence.

"Think he'll come back to the team?" Sam asked after he'd swallowed the last bite.

"You want him back?" Tony's face scrunched with indecision.

"Hell, yes," Sam told him. "Don't you?"

The brothers made eye contact, and a silent debate flashed back and forth.

Joel sat back and took a sip of black coffee.

Tony dropped a charred edge of crust onto his plate and pushed the plate aside. "Yeah, I want him," he said. "Let's work on that, soon as he's back."

The enticing aroma of hazelnut coffee drew Bree to the kitchen. Sunlight poured through a tiny, high window. Peter stood on the blue throw rug that she'd placed over scarred linoleum. He poked at the contents of a skillet, his back to her.

"Thanks for coffee. What are you making?"

"Good morning." He gave her a smile. "Some scrambled eggs with tomato and cheese. Can you fix some toast for us?"

Bree opened the freezer and selected a loaf of cinnamon raisin. "This okay?"

Peter glanced over. "That's one of Paddy's?" he asked when he spied the name on the wrapper. He made a mental note of the address.

"Yeah, I went to the bakery last week and stocked up." She separated four frozen slices and uncovered the toaster.

"Listen," Peter said, "I made a couple of phone calls."

"Who's up at this hour?" she quipped.

"It's eight o'clock, Sleeping Beauty. Tony Pinelli's already been to a meeting. He told me there's one every morning at the bagel place downtown."

"In Tompkins Falls? Cool." She shrugged. "Maybe the bagel place needs a waitress."

"Maybe." He savored her good mood.

They stood at the counter to eat their eggs and toast and coffee. Peter filled a dishpan with sudsy water and made short work of the dishes. He scrubbed the frying pan while Bree nibbled her toast. The second she picked up the last piece, he reached for her plate.

"In a hurry?" she teased.

He glanced at the clock over the sink. "Yes." He handed her a plate to dry.

"How come you called Tony?"

When Bree finished drying the old plate, she kissed her index finger and relayed the kiss to the chip on the rim of the plate. Peter's throat tightened. *Mom used to do that with the china cups and saucers her mother gave her.*

He cleared his throat. "I figured Tony would know about rehabs. He says Clifton Springs is one of the best. So I called them, and they want us there this morning at ten."

Bree's hand froze halfway to the cupboard.

Peter took the plate from her and put it on its shelf. "What do you think, Bree?"

"I think that's really scary," Bree told him in a shaky voice, "and I want to do it." She licked her lips. "I'm still under your insurance, right?"

"Right. That will pay about half."

Her eyes searched the far corner of the kitchen. *Looking for money? For courage?*

"I've got the rest covered," he told her.

She gave him a wary frown. "How?"

"You know I rented an apartment instead of buying a house." He shifted on his feet. "I still have the down payment I saved."

"But Peter—"

"But Bree, you need a rehab. So we're going to rehab this morning. Let's get ready. It's over an hour from here."

She walked to the window and stretched on her toes to see the main street. "Looks like everything's melted and is just slush now. I'll bet the highway is okay."

"It is. I called the highway department. Clifton Springs said you'll need a week's worth of clothes, just casual stuff. I put in a load of laundry a while ago, and the drier will be done in a few minutes."

"You're taking care of me." Bree brushed away a few tears.

"Just doing what I can to make it a little easier. Why don't you finish putting the dishes away and get your duffle started while I go down for the drier load? We'll be out of here in twenty minutes."

While Maya finished clearing away the dishes, Joel watched the faces around his uncle's breakfast table. Manda showed no emotion, but her breathing was shallow. He touched her hand, and she interlaced her fingers with his and gave him a nervous smile. Gwen fidgeted with her coffee mug. Gianessa's eyes were downcast, and she wore a Mona Lisa smile. *What's she thinking?*

Justin puffed out his chest and pushed his chair back a few inches. With his deep voice, he told them, "This is a day we've worked toward for nearly a year. Everything is now in place for us to design, build and open the Forrester Center for Holistic Recovery in the coming year." He gave each of them a measured smile, which they returned.

"Oscar could not join us this morning, but he sees no issues with the necessary building permits. He has already met with the Cady's Point Neighborhood Association, and they are on board with the new center, provided we take responsibility for all the necessary improvements to the road, and we keep vehicle noise to a minimum. Which we will."

"Good work," Joel commended him, "especially considering that you, Oscar, and Gwen have only been back a few weeks."

"Oscar is focused," Justin said. "And well paid." He turned a proud smile on Manda. "Manda's business plan is outstanding. While her masters program will make her jump through hoops until graduation, as far as I'm concerned, it is solid enough and far enough along for us to proceed. Gianessa will draft an operations plan with Joel's support, and we'll initiate the processes for whatever certifications and endorsements we need."

Joel raised his coffee cup to Gianessa. "You and I will be a good team," he told her. Gianessa met his gaze only briefly.

"And while we search for the architect," Justin said, with a dramatic pause, "we will bulldoze the house that Lorraine built."

"Hear, hear," Joel seconded. He put his arm around Manda's shoulders, and she leaned against him. "A new beginning for Cady's Point."

"We'll break ground for the new center in April," Justin continued, "with the donors and trustees in attendance. Between now and then, Gwen and I will be out selling the concept." He winked in Gwen's direction. "In our spare time."

Gwen laughed. "I even have the wardrobe for it. But seriously, Joel, thank you for lining up the public relations firm. Having a professional package will give me some much-needed confidence and will make our message clear, coherent, and compelling."

"Well said." Justin nodded to each of them in turn, to indicate he had finished his formal remarks.

"Why so quiet?" Joel asked Gianessa.

"I am speechless." Gianessa flashed a smile. "Thrilled. Challenged. And very grateful that we're all in this together. I do have two babies to take care of, and I am still recuperating, but my doctor has given me the go-ahead to work on this." She lifted her face to her husband for a kiss.

"Gwen," Joel said, "I hear you've kept a building lot on Cady's Point for yourself. Where exactly?"

"On the cove," she told him. "It's half an acre at the southern edge of the property. There's a thick stand of trees that screen it from the new center, so it's close to neighbors, but private."

"I love the spot," Manda said enthusiastically. "Gwen and I went there yesterday. She has enough room for a yard for kids to play, and half of her waterfront is beach. Plus a rock ledge that's great for exploring."

"Does this mean you'll be selling the Forrester family home?" Joel said.

"I think so. Probably within the year. I'm having the road worked on after Christmas, weather permitting. I'm used to the twists and turns and steep pitches, but it's a nightmare for others, especially in winter. I don't think anyone would buy the property unless that's fixed. Otherwise, the place is in excellent condition. All I need to do," she added with a laugh, "is clean out the attic, the basement, and everything in between."

"It would serve an extended family, three or four generations under the same roof," Joel pointed out. "You'll have some interested buyers when you decide to go ahead."

"That's a lovely way to think of it, Joel, thank you."

"Searching for an architect for your new home?"

"Right now, I'm searching for a husband," she replied with a lift of her eyebrows.

"Maybe I can help with that," Joel said. *I already know who you want, Gwen. Do you?*

Peter left the Clifton Springs rehab with his head bowed and his hands stuffed in the pockets of his parka as snow dusted the sidewalk and swirled around his feet. It was only three o'clock, and he had nowhere to be until his shift that night at eleven.

A smile tugged at his mouth. Two weeks into her rehab, and today Bree's eyes had a little sparkle. He hadn't seen that since she was a kid.

She'd hugged him when he'd first arrived and they'd talked a few minutes, but they'd been separated after that. He'd gone to a lecture about The Family Disease. Funny, he'd thought that meant the alcoholic inherited the gene that made someone an alcoholic. But, he saw now, it was more than that.

Even though he didn't become an alcoholic like Bree, he was damaged by their father's disease. His own hot temper, for one thing, and all the trouble with the team and with his job. That all stemmed from his attitude toward drunks. *Sam called it a poison, and he's right.*

He stopped on the walk to breathe in the cold air, and the sulphur smell from the stream tickled his nose. *What did the brochure say?* A mineral spring had given Clifton Springs its name and its reputation. There had been a sanatorium here at one time, where people came to rest and be cured from chronic illness, like tuberculosis. And it had helped a lot of people, especially back in the days of the TB epidemic.

Cady's Point had healing properties like that.

Now that Gwen had bought Cady's Point, Manda could build the rehab she wanted there, an impressive undertaking for a young woman, younger than his sister. His eyes opened wide. *And Manda is one of the young people Bree sees at AA meetings in Tompkins Falls.*

Joel, Manda, Tony, Gwen—all were getting well from the disease his sister had. And his father had the same disease, but he'd never gotten well. *Let me be one of the people getting well.*

He thought about the Al-Anon meeting he'd been to in Tompkins Falls. It was good, but it didn't feel like what he needed. Hank had said something about counseling for children from alcoholic families. If that's what he needed, he'd do it.

He scuffed snow ahead of him as he walked half the length of the sidewalk, then stepped down to the parking lot. After brushing off the Jeep, he started it up, but sat for a moment, debating what to do next. When he reached the main road, to his surprise, the Jeep turned right and headed to the Thruway, eastbound, toward Syracuse.

At the jingle of the bell, Paddy glanced up with a smile for his customer.

Peter stood just inside the door of O'Donnell's Bakery, overwhelmed by the aroma of warm bread and the sight of floured dough on a slab by the oven. It smelled like his mother's kitchen on her day off. His throat tightened.

Paddy wiped flour off his hands and stepped to the counter. "Ye'll be lookin' like yer Da with yer Ma's eyes, young Peter."

Fifteen years later, and he knows right away who I am. Peter put on a smile and reached out his hand. "I'd forgotten you still had the brogue, Paddy."

Paddy clasped Peter's hand, gave it a good shake, and let go. "What can I do for ye today, lad?"

Peter swallowed his nervousness and directed his attention to the fresh loaves on a rack behind the counter.

Caraway-seeded rye, rounds of Italian, pumpernickel rolls, whole-wheat loaves. A whiff of cinnamon made him smile. "Two of the raisin," he decided.

"Sliced?"

"Yes, please."

Peter poured himself a cup of coffee and left two dollars in the Mason jar, while the baker selected the two best loaves, started up the slicer, and ran the loaves through.

Paddy slipped each of the warm loaves into a paper sleeve, put them on the counter, and rang up the sale. He took the crisp ten-dollar bill Peter held out, and counted out change. "Will that be all for ye today, son?"

Still not sure what to say, Peter pocketed the change and shifted one of the loaves so the two touched each other. "Paddy, I'm sorry for the loss of your son." As soon as he said it, his own shame at the way he'd mishandled Bree's recovery made him lower his eyes. "And I'm forever in your debt for saving my sister," he blurted out, his eyes on the tie at the front of Paddy's apron.

Paddy waited. Peter looked up and saw compassion burning in the baker's eyes. "Yer sister's a bright lass, and she'll do well if she can keep away from the drink. There's nothin' like AA for that."

Peter nodded. "She's in rehab for another two weeks, and then I'll bring her to live with me for a while. There are plenty of meetings in Tompkins Falls, and she can even walk to a few. There are sober, young people who'll help her and hang with her."

"Ay, I didn't like her situation in the old neighborhood. She'll be better off if she's away. But, mind, that's if she's among her own kind."

"I understand. Paddy, what else can I do for her?"

"Ye can get yerself squared away, young Peter."

"How do you mean?" Peter stood tall and squared his shoulders.

"She's told me about yer anger at yer da. And about yer breakup with the woman, the one who's workin' a recovery program herself."

Peter's cheeks flushed.

"As Daniel Shaughnessy's only son, you had a hard go of it, but ye can't be carrying around that anger, lad. It's destroyin' what's dear to ye, isn't it?" Paddy's face was hard as he said it, but his eyes burned with caring.

Peter opened his mouth, closed it again and exhaled in surrender. "It's true. They say it's a family disease."

"Ay, 'tis. And don't ye be underestimatin' it. It'll destroy ye, even without the drink."

Peter remembered what Bree had told him, that Paddy had destroyed his own marriage and never been able to repair it, that he had tried to get his son sober but lost him to a heroin overdose. And through all of that, in spite of his terrible losses, Paddy had devoted his life to helping others get sober and clean up their lives. *How did Paddy keep his focus?*

"Paddy, I think I need more help than Al-Anon," he said. "I want to be like you, to keep my focus on serving and protecting, not always reliving the past with my dad. I don't know how."

A white eyebrow lifted. "And why do ye think I have what ye want?"

"Because you didn't give up when you couldn't save your marriage. Or save my father. Or save your son. You kept trying, and you saved others."

"I helped others who wanted to be saved," Paddy corrected gently.

"That's how I want to live my life, not being angry all the time, but being of service whenever I can. I want to change. I'll do what you tell me, Paddy."

The baker leaned on his hands on the counter. "There's plenty of good counselors around." His bright, blue gaze bore into Peter's. "Find one ye can trust, and work with him." He nodded sharply. "That's what I'm tellin' ye. Get right with yerself, and you'll know how to do the rest."

Peter's shoulders sagged, and his head bowed. "I will." His voice croaked with panic at the prospect.

Paddy stood, unwavering. "Ye might start by askin' at yer sister's rehab for a good man who'll talk with ye."

Peter's head jerked up. "I know someone," he realized. "Gwen and I met him. He works there sometimes." *What's his name, the man who owned the cabin where Gwen and I found shelter in the storm?* "Foster." *First name? Last name? No matter, they'll know him at Clifton Springs.*

"Ye get onto him, this Foster," Paddy urged. "Today if ye can"

"Yes. I will. Today." The tension left Peter's body.

"Then it's happy ye'll be, young Peter." Paddy reached out his hand, and the two men shook with firm grips. "Ye come back for more bread any time ye need it, son."

"I'll bring Bree with me next time."

Paddy's eyes twinkled. "See that ye do."

Chapter 18

Twice a week Peter drove down East Lake Road, six miles past Gwen's, to the turnoff for Foster's cabin. For an hour on Monday afternoons and again on Thursday afternoons, he and Foster split wood and talked, carried wood and talked, stacked wood and talked, or just talked over coffee in front of the woodstove.

If this was therapy, it suited Peter. The first week they talked about basketball and about being on a team and dealing with difficult personalities. The next week they talked about work, about privacy and about handling gossip. In week three Foster challenged him on his priorities and how to keep his priorities straight. Then they turned their attention to relationships.

Back at the station, over the course of the month, Sam watched his partner change. Peter handled his share of drunk drivers, and he booked them with firmness and fairness. No snide remarks, no unnecessary jostling, no grumbling, no sulking at his desk. Twice, Sam heard him talk up the drunk driver program and AA.

One night Peter brought in a dozen brownies, and the squad devoured them with thanks and laughter. A few days later, Peter fetched a dozen cookies from his car for the teens that came around for basketball at two thirty in the morning. The three kids responded—not with thank you—but with orders for three different kinds of cookies.

Peter obliged with a dozen peanut butter cookies a few nights later. Then he challenged the boys to make the next batch.

Stretch obliged with some slice-and-bake sugar cookies that were half-burned. Peter quietly scraped the burned edges of his cookie and held it up for all to see. Then he took a bite and grinned at Stretch. "Good job, my man." Jeers turned to appreciative arm punches.

"I'm gonna make some that don't need no scrapin'," JD said.

That night, after they ushered the boys off the court, Sam chuckled.

"What?" Peter grinned.

"You."

"You got a problem with me, partner?" His voice was lighthearted.

"Not any more."

At his next therapy session—a frigid day with snow falling an inch an hour—he and Foster drew their chairs close to the stove and held their coffee mugs with both hands.

"How's Gwen?" Foster asked him.

"I don't know." Peter glanced over.

Foster nodded without comment.

Peter stretched his neck in both directions before he added, "We broke up right after you dropped us off at her house."

"I would not have predicted that, given how close you were when I arrived here that morning." Foster sat back and crossed his legs.

Peter opened his mouth, closed it and stared at the stove a while longer. The silence stretched on. Logs popped and settled in the stove.

Foster disappeared into the kitchen, came back with the coffee pot, topped off both their mugs, returned the pot to the kitchen, and resumed his seat by the stove.

Peter sipped coffee and stared at the stove.

"Why did you break up?" Foster asked.

"She's an alcoholic." Peter waited for a response like *Well, so am I.* or *Why is that a problem?*

When no retort came his way, he continued, "She'd kept it from me, even though she knew how I felt about drunks."

Again, Foster offered no response.

"I felt betrayed when I found out." Peter's voice had an angry edge.

Foster uncrossed his legs and leaned forward. "It's too bad. I thought you two had something good."

"I thought so, too," Peter said. His eyes darkened with regret.

"Maybe we're both right—that you two had something special there. And in that case, maybe it wasn't a matter of betrayal. Maybe it was a terrible misunderstanding between two people who had a problem dealing with a difficult truth."

"What truth do you mean?"

"Gwen's alcoholism, combined with your attitude toward alcoholics."

Peter flinched. "You're saying it's my fault?"

"No. It always takes two." Foster's gaze was focused on the stove.

Peter huffed and settled back in his chair.

"I'm just speculating here, that Gwen was pretty open about not drinking when you went out together?"

"Yeah."

"And about her work as a therapist, with alcoholics and addicts?"

Peter nodded. "Yes, she talked about that." He tipped his head. "Defended it."

"But, even so, you didn't add it up that she's an alcoholic—in recovery—herself."

Peter didn't move, but a muscle by his left eye twitched.

Foster continued, "And maybe, when Gwen realized how strong your feelings were about drunks, she avoided that topic with you." He sat quietly. "Does any of that have the ring of truth?"

"I guess." Peter cleared his throat. "That could be what was happening."

"In that case, Peter, I don't see it as betrayal. I'm more likely to call it failure on Gwen's part to be completely upfront with you. And maybe denial, on your part." He took a noisy slurp of coffee. "But what do I know? I wasn't there."

Peter drank a mouthful of the strong brew. "Cynthia betrayed me," he insisted.

"Your ex-wife Cynthia?"

"Yes. While I was in the hospital and in therapy, after I was shot, she found another man, got pregnant, divorced me, and married him."

"Now that sounds like betrayal to me. And I'd say you're well rid of Cynthia. However, Cynthia and Gwen are two different people, in two different situations. Do you want Cynthia to dictate your relationship with Gwen?"

Peter drew himself up straight, his body rigid. He made no answer, but he had a determined scowl on his face.

The two men sat quietly while the logs in the stove hissed and popped and shifted. Foster sipped at his coffee. Peter drained his mug.

"I wonder if you'd do something before our next session?" Foster proposed.

"Sure." Peter met Foster's steady gaze.

"Knowing what you know now—about the disease of alcoholism, about rehabs and therapy—Gwen's world, in short. Knowing that, write down all the different ways you can interpret what went wrong between the two of you."

"You sound pretty sure that the problem on my side was denial?"

Foster's eyebrows came together in thought. "Yes, I guess I am." He turned his sharp blue gaze on Peter. "Tell me what you think denial means."

"When something's staring you in the face and you

don't see it." He shrugged. "Don't want to, are afraid to, can't afford to, whatever."

"Yes, exactly." A warm smile crossed the counselor's face.

Peter stood up and cleared his throat. "I'll wrestle that around. See you Thursday."

Foster stood and shook his hand. "Careful on the roads, son."

Bree burst into the apartment at two in the afternoon. "I got the job, Peter!" She stopped her headlong rush to the kitchen.

Her brother was on the porch, standing in the cold, again, without a jacket, bare hands on the railing. His gaze was fixed across the lake. *Gwen's house.* Belatedly, he straightened up, ran his hands over his face and came inside. "Hi, honey. What did you say?"

"I got the job, Peter."

"That's great, Bree. I'm proud of you."

She shifted nervously from one foot to the other and hedged, "It's just serving and cleaning up at the Bagel Depot, but it's . . ."

"What?" Peter smiled. "Come on, we're trying for open communication. The counselors at Clifton drilled that into us, right?"

She lowered her gaze to the hardwood floor. "Yeah. So, I was saying it's a good way for me to be around AA people in the morning."

"That's right, they've got that meeting in the back room first thing. Tony goes, and sometimes my partner Sam meets him after for a bagel."

"Yeah. And I won't make a lot of money, but I can pay for some food while I'm living here."

"No, thank you, but you can put together a budget for personal expenses and fees to get back in school to finish your bachelor's degree."

"School really matters to you, doesn't it?"

"Believe it. I'll make us sandwiches," he offered, "and I'll tell you why."

"You're on."

They shared a sandwich, Bree's favorite, ham and cheese with lettuce, tomato, onion, and avocado. Peter told stories about his worst college classes, and Bree added a few of her own. "You know, I think you'd be a good cop, if you wanted that," he told her.

Bree snorted. "Me? The screw-up?"

"Sometimes people who've had brushes with the law turn out to be good cops."

She squirmed. "I don't see myself doing what you do—here or in Syracuse—but I like businesses that serve the public."

"Like the Bagel Depot?"

"Yeah and that café across from the park, Lynnie's. In a city like this, they don't just serve food. They're places where people meet and do business and pass on the news." She propped her elbows on the table. "Sometimes late morning and mid-afternoon, people come in to read and study, and that's very cool. I like being part of all that."

"Would you ever want to run a place like that?"

"Maybe." She grinned. "I sure wouldn't want to be a cook."

"Why? Too much pressure?"

"No, I'm a lousy cook. You know that."

"You made a great omelet last night. Almost as good as Gwen's. That's a talent."

"Speaking of Gwen . . ."

Peter pushed back from the table. Plates clattered as he cleared the table.

"Now, wait a minute," she said. "If I had to be open and finish what I was going to say back there, so do you. You brought up Gwen. What about her?"

Peter set the dishes on the counter. "I misjudged her, that's all."

He ran the plates under hot water before placing them in the dishwasher.

Bree stole up beside him. "So, what are you going to do about it?"

"It's too late."

"Around the program"—she raised her eyebrows—"they say it's never too late to make amends. Maybe it won't fix things, but you'll feel better about yourself."

Peter opened his mouth and closed it in a grimace. "Maybe you're right."

"You're changing, big brother." Bree punched his arm. "Way cool."

"Hey, I'm not the only one. You're doing good, Bree. Keep it up."

Bree gave him an impulsive hug, and he held her close. "Love you, honey," he told her.

"I love you, too. I want you to be happy."

Peter made a sound in his chest that might have been a sob.

Waitresses bustled among the tables on the lakeside porch. Holiday shoppers in high spirits stashed bags under chairs and around their feet. Outside, sunshine bounced off fresh snow and sparkled on the dark-blue water of Skaneateles Lake.

To fill the time before their hot drinks arrived, Haley, Manda, Bree, and Sara shared their finds from the morning's visit to a favorite consignment shop.

Bree gushed about her almost-new, midnight-blue jeans that were long enough for her six-foot height. Haley held up a dark brown cashmere turtleneck, stroked it, and passed it around. Manda showed off a pair of ice-blue ballet flats. Sara waved a peacock-blue flower before she fastened it in her blond hair.

"Do you guys do this every month?" Bree asked them.

"About every month, right, Sara?"

"Pretty much," Sara answered. "Manda and I started the tradition a couple of years ago."

"When we were poor," Manda said, "and needed decent clothes for work."

The waitress came with their drinks and took their orders. Shopping bags disappeared under the table.

"Ladies," Sara said and dinged her glass mug. All eyes turned to her. Sara told them, "You all know how upset I was when Sam didn't propose at Thanksgiving."

Manda's eyes opened wide. Haley and Bree looked at each other with excitement.

"Last night he explained that the ring he got, with his sister's help, was all wrong. Then he tried again with Tony's help, but that ring was all wrong, too. And after all that apologizing, he asked me to marry him and said I needed to come with him to pick out a ring we both liked."

Smiles bloomed around the table.

"It was not the most romantic proposal, but I'm really happy to be marrying Sam Pinelli. I love him and he's a good man and he'll be a great father." She held up her whip-topped espresso drink. "To love."

Two hot chocolates and one tea joined the toast.

"Big wedding, small wedding?" Manda asked. "And when's the date?"

"Summer. Details to follow. My parents said it's up to me, whether I go for broke or make it small and elegant. Whatever I want."

"You're thinking small and elegant, aren't you?" Manda guessed.

"That's what I'd really like. A couple years ago, I wouldn't have said that, but, Manda, your wedding and Gianessa's wedding had about two dozen invited guests, followed by a bigger reception. Everyone had so much fun. Sam's a little worried because he has a big family, but we're thinking we can invite the whole gang to a feast in his parents' backyard after the honeymoon. It will be a blast to kick back and have all the little kids with us."

"To happiness," Manda said as she raised her mug.

Haley, Bree, and Sara joined in.

As Bree set down her mug, she said, "Now if I could make Peter happy."

"Gwen, too," Manda said.

Haley told them, "Gwen said the other day that she is still in love with Peter, and that's making it hard for her to date anyone else." She raised her eyebrows at Bree.

"And Peter thinks I don't notice that every morning before he goes to bed, and every afternoon when he gets up, he goes out on the porch so he can see across the lake to Gwen's house. Even if it's snowing or sleeting. What does that tell you?"

"And Sam told me Peter looked daggers at him last week when he tried to fix him up with somebody's sister," Sara said.

"So what do we do about it?" Manda asked them. "Are they just being stubborn?"

"No, it's not just stubborn," Haley said, with caution in her voice. "I saw the fight when they broke up. Gwen was devastated, and Peter looked like his world had come to an end. They are both really hurting."

Bree agreed. "Peter's really torn up about this. He needs a wife he can depend on and a family of his own. Part of him is scared to marry an alcoholic, but he knows he wants Gwen."

"Gwen works her AA program really hard," Manda said, "no matter what's going on in her life."

"I know," Bree said. "I've seen how the women admire her. And my brother is finally learning about staying sober one day at a time. But, you know something else, he's not sure she needs him enough."

"What do you mean?" Manda asked.

"Every time he sees her in the news about Cady's Point, he says, 'She looks good like that. She's better off.'"

"What does he mean, 'She looks good like that?'" Haley asked.

"Those gorgeous clothes she brought back from London?" Manda guessed. "It's not the wardrobe you see on your average police officer's wife."

"Now, that's just stupid." Sara smacked her fist on the table. "Gwen's focusing so much on Manda's project at Cady's Point because she doesn't have Peter in her life. We all know she's more comfortable wearing blue jeans, right?"

"Totally," Manda said.

"Absolutely," Haley agreed. "And she wants children. Soon. But first she wants a husband and a solid marriage."

"Maybe we can get them in the same room so they *have* to talk to each other," Haley said tentatively. All eyes turned to her.

Manda grinned. "I think I know how." She waved them closer.

"Manda, wait up."

"Hey, Peter, good to see you," Manda said with a cheery smile. "Hi, Bree."

Bree winked and headed toward the coffee pot.

"Listen, Joel told me he's out of town this weekend," Peter said with concern in his voice.

Manda glanced nervously at the coffee pot. *Do not blurt out that Joel's not out of town.* In fact, he was staying in his suite at the Manse to clear the way for Peter and Gwen to have 14 Lakeside Terrace to themselves. "Yeah, uh, he's been out of town a lot lately. I sure am glad you and Bree live in our building."

"That's what I wanted to tell you," Peter said. "Anytime you feel uncomfortable about anything, give us a call. I know I work most nights, but—"

"But you're not working this weekend, right?"

"How did you know that?"

Oops. "Oh, I guess Sara said something. You know we're having a sleepover at Sara's after the meeting. Sara's engaged to your partner, Sam, and he must have said something about you being off this weekend." *Shut up, he's getting more and more suspicious.* "Gotta go."

She rushed to join Bree at the coffee pot. "I blew it."

"No, you didn't. See?" Bree gestured toward her brother. His gaze was on Gwen as she and Haley swept into the meeting room.

"Gwen looks like the wind got the best of her."

"It's brutal out there tonight." They watched Gwen unbutton her coat and loosen the big scarf around her neck.

"Good, she's wearing jeans and a peachy, soft sweater."

"See how hungry Peter is when he looks at her?" Bree said with a satisfied smile.

"Oh no, who's that man? He's going to ruin everything."

"Gwen, a word?" Foster gripped her elbow as soon as she got her coat off.

"Sure, Foster." Gwen turned to Haley. "Sweetie, I see Bree and Manda. Why don't you join them, and I'll catch up with you later?"

"Actually," Haley told her. "I'm going back to Sara's with them for an overnight. Didn't I tell you?" She patted her backpack and sauntered away.

Gwen stood with her mouth open.

Foster's hand on her arm urged her out to the hallway. "Let's chat a minute," he said and led her to a bench away from foot traffic.

Gwen dumped her coat and folded the scarf on top. "What's up?" She fluffed out her hair and smoothed it into place.

"None of my business, but I see your friend Peter here, and I wondered . . ."

"Here?" She croaked.

"If you don't want to see him . . ."

"I do." Gwen pressed Foster's arm. "I do want to see him. I just never thought I'd see him at a meeting." She searched Foster's face. "You just met Peter the one time. How did you know it was him?"

"He's been driving Bree to this meeting," Foster told her, "and a few of us men talk out here in the hall while the women meet inside." He added quietly, "I understand he's working hard on his own recovery as well."

Did he just wink? "I won't ask how you know that," she said with a chuckle. "God, I'm shaking."

Foster stood up. "It's cold here in the hall. I'll bring you something hot to drink while you get back your composure."

"Thank you." She drew the silk scarf around her shoulders, the oversized peach-and-gray she'd found in London. A few latecomers stomped snow off their boots and hustled into the meeting room. The hallway grew quiet. Gwen closed her eyes for a quick meditation.

Finally, he sat beside her, and she felt the warmth of his body. "It's hot," he said.

Not Foster's voice. "Peter. Why, how?"

"Foster said you needed tea with sugar. He didn't explain."

Gwen's cheeks flamed. Her gaze probed his green eyes, and they mirrored her own wariness. "We've been set up." She smiled as she accepted the tea. She sipped some and set it on the bench to cool.

"Joint effort." He laughed softly. "My first clue was Sam telling me I was off the schedule this weekend, overdue for a few days off. Then Bree decided to do a sleepover at Sara's."

"Haley must be in on it, too. She's riding back with Manda."

"And Joel's even out of town. Gwen, if you wanted to talk . . ."

"I do," she said. "Peter, I was so wrong not to tell you I'm in recovery myself."

"I should have known from everything you said."

"But I should have told you. I wasn't upfront about that." She shook her head. "And I haven't been honest about the problems in my marriage. It's—" She waved her hands in circles, at a loss to explain. "I didn't know how much I was hiding, even from myself." Tears sprang to her eyes.

He searched her face. "We have a lot to talk about. Bree's in recovery, and I'm getting help, too."

"I love you," Gwen whispered. "Peter, I—"

He caressed her cheekbones, touched a tear as it spilled from her eye. "I need you, Gwen. Nothing makes sense without you."

She lifted her face, and he crushed her mouth with a kiss.

A young woman giggled as she slipped past them to the restroom.

"Let's leave," he said. "I'll follow you to your house."

Gale-force winds flung snowflakes at the Range Rover's headlights and animated the thin snow cover into sinister, white snakes that writhed in her path. To calm her anxiety, Gwen switched on the radio to a classical station. When a gust buffeted the Range Rover over the centerline, she tightened her grip on the steering wheel and checked the rearview mirror. Peter's headlights were still in view.

She caught herself wishing she'd worn sexy underwear and the perfume she and Lorraine had picked out in London. *God, don't let me go right to sex tonight. We have so much we need to talk over.*

When the country road curved, the squall slammed from a new direction. *Thank God the roads aren't icy.* She glanced in the rearview mirror. There was no sign of Peter's Jeep. She slowed, until his headlights came into view, and kept her speed to the posted limit. At the stop sign for East Lake Road, she waited for a few cars, then made her left turn. Peter would have to wait for another break in traffic. A mile later, she signaled for her road and slowed for the sharp right turn.

As she plunged down the hill, the wind hurled a dead branch across the hood of the Range Rover. She shivered. Down on the flat, middle section, a massive limb lay in her path. *One of the big old oaks,* she judged from its bulk and twisted form.

She shifted into 'park' and got out to haul the downed limb off the road. Wind tore at her hair and blinded her. She paused to tie the scarf around her head and tuck the ends into the collar of her turtleneck. It was just a few seconds without gloves, but her fingers turned to ice.

As she tugged at the stubborn limb, she wished they'd agreed to go to Peter's instead. *We could still do that.* She paced back to her car, planning to wait there, and switched on the four-way flashers.

After a minute with no sign of Peter's headlights, she returned to the limb. She tried to lift it, but it was too heavy for her. With a growl, she tried again to tug it, but the more she dragged, the deeper it dug into the gravel. She howled in frustration.

An answering crack from the woods drew her full attention. Two of the largest ashes plummeted toward the road, one ramming the other from behind, like forty-foot dominoes.

Propelled by some unseen hand, Gwen stumbled down the road toward her house while, behind her, wood splintered and limbs snapped and thudded. Lights flared behind her. *Peter. He's driving into it.*

Heart pounding, she turned halfway around and danced to keep her footing. "Peter." She waved her arms and screamed to stop him from colliding or being buried, although he could not have heard her over the roar of the wind. Her momentum carried her a few more yards until she tripped over another fallen branch. She reached out with her right hand to break the fall, enough to keep from slamming her head into a rock.

She lay on her back and cradled her damaged wrist to her side. *Dad, help me.* Above her on the road, metal crunched and glass smashed. With her heart in her throat, she pictured the Jeep colliding with the fallen tree. "Peter!" she sobbed. *God, protect him.*

As its last act of destruction, the second of the rampaging ash trees sheared a heavy limb off an old oak. Gravity deposited it on Gwen's outstretched foot and spread its branches over her legs. She screamed with pain.

She was sure her foot was both stuck and injured. She lay on the cold ground, unsure how to help herself. Branches skittered across the road, flung by the howling wind. *God, help me, help us.*

Rather than freeze to death on her own road, she propped herself up on her good elbow and surveyed the pile of debris blocking the road above her. Below her, the house was a quarter mile away, but the road was clear.

Breathing heavily, she scanned the tangle of branches for Peter's headlights. A faint glow shone through the pile. *Maybe he stopped in time.* "Peter?" she yelled.

"Gwen," he bellowed, "are you all right?"

Oh, thank God. "I'm halfway down the road. Where are you?"

His high beams flashed.

"I see your lights. Are you hurt?"

"The Jeep's okay. Where's your car?"

"Under the tree." She burst into tears.

"Are you hurt?" This time, his voice came from somewhere in the woods.

Maybe he's going around. "Not really, but my foot's stuck." Her voice squeaked with panic.

"What does 'not really' hurt mean?"

"I sprained my wrist, and I can't get to where my foot is stuck."

"It's caught in the branches?"

"Under a limb."

She heard him quietly giving information to someone. "I'll alert Phil," he said.

His voice was close enough now that Gwen heard the next conversation. "Phil, it's Peter. I'm next door with Gwen, who is caught under a tree that fell on her road. Some EMTs will arrive in your driveway very soon. If we're lucky, I'll meet you all there with Gwen over my shoulder. If not, I need you to show them the path along the shore. Thanks, buddy."

Something man-sized rustled through the undergrowth on her left, and flashlight bobbed toward her. Peter emerged from the woods and squatted beside her. When he commanded, "Lie down," she did. He lifted her left hand and checked her pulse.

"Who were you talking to?"

"911. Then Phil. Lie still."

His flashlight probed the debris that covered her legs. "I can see exactly where the limb has you trapped. I'm going to clear away some of these branches so I can get closer and get a good handle on it. Then I'll try to lift it myself. If anything I do causes you pain, holler."

"Okay." She tried to sit up.

"Stay down," he said. This time he held her down with a hand on her forehead, "and lie still. You need every ounce of strength, Gwen."

"I'm really cold."

He dragged over a rock as a perch for his flashlight and tucked his parka around her torso. "Do not move."

"Okay."

"Promise."

"I promise."

He stripped aside branches as he worked methodically toward the trapped foot.

"Can you feel the ankle and the foot?" he asked.

"Believe me, I can feel them," she moaned.

"That's good, right?" he cajoled.

"You're right." She lay still and breathed through the pain. "Thank you."

As he worked, he scolded her. "I don't want to think what would have happened, if you'd been alone."

"I've thought about it," she said. "It didn't turn out good."

"I'm ready to lift. My plan is to raise it enough for you to pull your foot out. Ready?"

"Okay."

He grunted and strained to lift the limb a few inches but lost his hold before she could free her foot. She yelled in pain as the limb dropped.

Tears flooded her face. "It might be broken," she choked out.

"I'm sorry, honey." He came back to her and sat on the gravel close to her.

"Maybe we should wait."

"Definitely, we need to wait. The team will be here soon. They know someone's in danger out in this cold." He tucked the parka tighter around her shoulders and neck.

"I heard sirens while you were tearing the branches away. Maybe they're for us. Do you see anyone?"

"Lights on the path." He used the flashlight to signal their location. "Need help up here," he hollered. "They see us." Back on its perch, the flashlight illuminated Gwen's face enough that Peter could see the scrapes on her cheekbones and jaw. Blood trickled from a cut on her forehead. "Do you have pain anywhere except the ankle and wrist?"

"No." Her breathing was shallow and quick.

"Did the wrist snap?"

"No. When I fell, I put out my hand to give my head another couple seconds to dodge a big rock. I really just smacked the heel of my hand hard, and held on with my arm muscles as long as I could."

"Bet that hurt."

"Yeah. I didn't want to hit my head and lose consciousness, in case I had to phone for help."

"And did you phone for help?"

"No." *I wonder where my phone is*. "I saw your lights, and I was afraid you would be buried by the tree, and that's all I could think about." Her voice rose with panic. "And then I heard glass breaking and I thought it was the Jeep."

"Take it easy." He touched her shoulder, and she calmed. "We're going to get you out." Peter stroked her cheek. "The tree was already on the ground when I saw it."

"All that breaking glass and metal I heard—what was that?"

"Your car." He rested his hand on her hip. "I only saw it for a second when I came down the road. I was afraid you were in it, buried under the tree."

Peter swept the flashlight back toward the mound that had been the canopy of a beautiful ash tree. The light picked out something shiny in the debris. "Your rearview mirror," he told her.

She gasped. Nothing else of the Range Rover was visible. The EMTs appeared on the road now.

"Did you have any warning?" Peter asked. "Could you have backed up? We could have gone to my place."

"I thought of that, but I was so mad about the limb, I wanted to haul it out of our way. And then the trees were crashing toward me. I ran downhill for my life."

"You're saying you were out of the car when it fell?"

"Yes, I was trying to clear a big limb off the road."

"Gwen." He exhaled his frustration. "When there's a limb down on your path and the wind is blowing straight out of hell, you don't get out of your car to do battle."

She grumbled. "You're the one with the common sense. I'm the one that leaps into the fray to fix things."

"Well, getting shot taught me a few things about that," he told her. "You're lucky you're alive."

"I get that. Thanks for rescuing me."

He chuckled. "Me and two big guys who know what they're doing." He stood up to meet the rescue party.

"I'm Jimmy." The man in the lead shook Peter's hand. "And you are?"

"Peter. This is Gwen, and that's her car under the mess. Her foot is caught, as you can see. Possible fracture. I tried to lift the limb myself, but it needs two to lift and one to pull her free."

"Nice job clearing the way for us. How's this for a plan? Charlie, you grab the limb to the right of her leg, I'll grab it on the left. We lift on two. Pete, you slide your girl out on three."

Gwen screamed on 'three' and passed out.

"To guard against delayed shock," Peter read from the Emergency Room discharge papers, "keep the patient warm and comfortable. Avoid stress. Keep hydrated, preferably with sweet tea and cookies, and rest for forty-eight hours."

"You made that up," Gwen challenged with a laugh.

"Don't even think about being a difficult patient." He winked.

She lifted her mug to her mouth with her good hand. "I like my tea like my man—hot and sweet."

"For sprains," he continued in a stern voice, though the corner of his mouth twitched with a smile. "Rest. Ice. Compression." He settled against her left side and leaned back against the headboard. "Elevate the affected body parts." He kissed her left temple. "How are your affected body parts doing?"

"Thank you for all the pillows. Did you have to borrow from Bree's room?"

"She'll never know. So rest," he ordered, "and don't worry about anything."

"I do need to tell Haley."

"I called her from the hospital."

"You did?"

"And warned her not to go home until the road is cleared and told her you would be here for a week until you can manage crutches and stairs. And, by the way, Gianessa's bringing something called a knee scooter for you tomorrow."

"You guys, I am so blessed."

His mouth was a grim line.

"What?"

"You neglected to tell me your phone was not on your person the whole time you were lying out there with your foot trapped under the tree."

"Under the limb."

"Makes no difference. Suppose you'd been alone out there?"

"I know." Gwen took a big sip. "I could have been lying there injured until I died of hypothermia." She shuddered.

"Damn straight. And I will stop giving you a hard time, because it's stressing you out. We can talk about all this tomorrow. Calmly."

"Peter, I want you to know, I do have someone lined up to straighten out the road, and that work is scheduled for next month. And then—"

"That's good. And tomorrow or the next day we can line up someone to haul away the debris, including your car."

"Ugh. I need a new car."

"But," he pointed out, "they might recover your phone and purse." He patted her thigh. "You started to say something else, and I cut you off."

"What I started to say is I want to live on the cove at Cady's Point. I saved a building lot there for me."

He lifted the empty mug from her hands and set it beside him on the nightstand. "That is the perfect place for a house. Beautiful view. Private. Patrolled area. Paved, well-maintained road." He held her left hand gently.

"I want us to plan that together, Peter." His breath caught. "For us."

"I want that, too." His eyes flashed with desire. "But you need to sleep tonight." His voice was low and husky. "Tomorrow is soon enough to talk."

She tried to sit up and turn toward him but fell back against the pillow with a moan.

He lifted her wrist and checked her pulse. "Your heart is racing," he scolded. "I will take you back to the hospital if it stays that way."

"Agreed."

"Time for sleep," he ordered. "I will stay on my side of the bed." By the time he tucked the blanket around her, she was asleep. He lay beside her and stretched his arm above her head on the pillow.

"You look good there," Peter teased.

"Wearing your sister's robe, with my foot up?" Gwen teased back.

"At my breakfast table." A warm smile curved his mouth.

"What are you cooking?"

"The Shaughnessy breakfast special. Eggs scrambled with tomatoes and mushrooms. Toast and coffee."

"I smell cinnamon."

"It's cinnamon raisin bread from Paddy O'Donnell's bakery in Syracuse, the best loaf you've ever tasted. I might tell you his story later, if you're a good patient."

"Tell me now."

"First, eat. You're healing. And we need to talk about us right now." He carried the skillet to the table and dished up their eggs and vegetables, then returned for the plate of buttered toast and the coffee pot. "Need juice?"

"Nope." Gwen bit into the toast and savored the butter and spice and warm raisins. "Yum."

Peter nodded, his attention on her plate of eggs. Each time she started to talk, he pointed to her unfinished breakfast. Once the eggs were gone and only one slice of toast remained, he let her speak.

"I want to start by telling you the truth about my marriage." Her voice shook.

He peered at her over the rim of his coffee mug. "Okay."

Thank God Deirdre and I talked it through it already. Between sips of full-bodied coffee, she related how it had been for her as Jeb's wife and how she had handled it.

By the end of the telling, Peter's jaw was tight and his forehead was knit with regret. "I was a fool to think you had an ideal marriage." Peter exhaled forcefully. "I thought you didn't tell me anything because you were just too sad to talk about losing him."

"I let people think that for so many years that I started believing it myself. The whole, disgraceful truth was buried under booze and denial and half a dozen stories that were nothing but lies. Until my trip to London just before Thanksgiving. My friend Lorraine remembered more than I did, and it all came crashing back to me as we talked in her library."

Peter squared himself to the table and reached across for her good hand. "I'm sorry it was like that for you. You didn't deserve it." He caressed her fingers.

"Thank you. Ironically, his death netted me almost nine million dollars. I never spent any of it until I bought the Cady's Point property for Manda's holistic center."

"That was generous, and I think the center will be a big success and a real asset to this area."

"Justin insists we call it the Forrester Center, which is an honor for my family. My parents would be proud to have their names on a facility that will help people get their lives back on track following a health crisis." When Peter only nodded, she asked, "What do you think about it?"

"About the Forrester Center? I always thought it was a winning idea." He shifted in his chair. "But it caught me by surprise when you got involved the way you did."

"What surprised you about it?"

"The millions, for sure." He shifted again. "And going off to London like that, making a major real estate deal. That seemed out of character."

"It was out of character. And I could not have pulled it off without Justin's coaching and an attorney by my side. But I had to try. The project was stalled, and Gianessa's recovery and her career were stalled along with it. And my friend Lorraine needed to let go of the property and grow beyond the nightmare of her marriage. So, buying the land was an opportunity to help my good friends and to do something important for the community."

She took another sip. "Besides, I felt stuck, and doing something out of character, that was both responsible and useful, turned out to be a win for everyone."

"You were stuck how?"

"I had totally screwed up with you, and I knew I wasn't interested in anyone else. I knew, in my heart, I wanted to have a life partner and start a family." She lifted her eyebrows and shrugged. "I couldn't see how to go forward, and . . ."

"And now?"

"Now I'm sitting across the table from you,"—Gwen gasped as if it was hard to breathe—"and it feels like my future is in your hands."

"And how do you want your future to be?" There was a glimmer of something in his eyes. *Hope?*

"I want to be married to you," Gwen told him, her eyes wide open. "I want us to raise a few kids, live on Cady's Point, and walk through life side-by-side."

Peter's gaze shifted above her shoulder. He said, "First I need to tell you about Paddy O'Donnell, the baker." He gave a self-conscious laugh. "If he were eavesdropping right now, he'd be very happy about this conversation."

Gwen's cheeks warmed.

He gestured to the loaf of bread on the counter. "Paddy baked this bread and many loaves like it, going way back into my childhood. It's a long story." He stood up. "Why don't I make us some more toast and a fresh pot of coffee?"

"Okay, then, how is the third Saturday of February for them?" Peter asked, pencil in hand as he stood beside the calendar on his refrigerator.

Gwen squinted at the barely legible notes she'd made with her left hand during her phone conversation with Gianessa. "They're free that day." She beamed up at him.

"And you're okay with just asking Gianessa and Justin to stand up with us in front of the Justice of the Peace at City Hall? No one else in attendance?"

"I am. And you're okay with a private dinner at The Manse for close family and a few close friends?"

"Including Rick and Foster, right?" At Gwen's nod, he said, "Then, yes. As long as we can get the same menu as the chief's dinner dance last summer."

"I checked, and we can. What kind of cake?"

"Makes no difference to me, as long as you love it."

"Vanilla cake with strawberries and whipped cream?" Peter squinted.

Gwen winced. "You can say no."

"I'm thinking. Remind me what you'll be wearing." He winked.

"Okay." She laughed. "I'll wear the dress I wore to the chief's dinner dance."

"You know, that cake sounds delicious." He moved in for a kiss.

"Why is that dress so important to our wedding?"

"Because I've been fantasizing all these months about removing it from your beautiful body on our wedding night."

Also by **Katie O'Boyle** and **Soul Mate Publishing**:

Stepping Up to Love
Lakeside Porches Series Book One

Miracles happen when romance is higher-powered.

A lakeside porch in the Finger Lakes is the perfect spot for a quiet moment or a heart-to-heart with your special someone. Joel and Manda's first heart-to-heart on the breakfast porch at the Manse Inn and Spa is anything but romantic. Joel the owner of the Manse is furious with his junior accountant for using one of the spa showers. If Manda didn't have a desperate story and a spectacular body, Joel might not be feeding her breakfast and falling in love. Can Manda get sober, clean up her act, and open her heart to her rich, hunky boss? Fall in love with Joel and Manda in *Stepping Up To Love*.

Available now on Amazon: http://tinyurl.com/olr2yfg

Coming Home to Love
Lakeside Porches Series Book Two

Justin Cushman's billions can't buy him a solution for his deteriorating health. Gianessa Dupioni's broken heart won't let her look at another man until her career is back on track. When fate brings them both to a spa in the Finger Lakes and circumstances pair them in a tiny closet of a treatment room, they begin a journey of health and happiness neither believed possible. If they're to enjoy the journey, Justin will need to change his entire attitude and outlook on life, and Gianessa will need to open her heart to trust again.

Available now on Amazon: http://tinyurl.com/opnmpfg

CPSIA information can be obtained
at www.ICGtesting.com
Printed in the USA
FFOW02n0234241115
18749FF